KISS AN ANGEL

She wrapped her arms around his neck. "I want to take off your towel," she whispered.

She reached for the knot, only to have his hands press over hers. "Not so fast, sweetheart. First you've got to show me something."

Tilting back her head, she watched his eyes roam over her as she stood before him in her tiny showgirl's outfit.

"In this costume, I think I've already shown off just about everything I have."

"Maybe I want a closer look."

Other Avon Books by
Susan Elizabeth Phillips

HEAVEN, TEXAS
IT HAD TO BE YOU

SUSAN ELIZABETH PHILLIPS

KISS AN ANGEL

AVON BOOKS ◆ NEW YORK

KISS AN ANGEL is an original publication of Avon Books. This work has never before appeared in book form. This work is a novel. Any similarity to actual persons or events is purely coincidental.

AVON BOOKS
A division of
The Hearst Corporation
1350 Avenue of the Americas
New York, New York 10019

Copyright © 1996 by Susan Elizabeth Phillips
Inside cover author photo by Ron Stewart Portraiture
Published by arrangement with the author
Library of Congress Catalog Card Number: 95-94722
ISBN: 0-380-78233-2

First Avon Books Printing: February 1996

AVON TRADEMARK REG. U.S. PAT. OFF. AND IN OTHER COUNTRIES, MARCA REGISTRADA, HECHO EN U.S.A.

Printed in the U.S.A.

RA   10   9   8   7   6   5

These are my special angels, the women who have been intimately involved with my work at various times during my career. Some are writers and some are editors. The guidance and support I've received from each of them has meant so much to me. In order of their appearance in my life:

Claire Kiehl Lefkowitz
Rosanne Kohake
Maggie Lichota
Linda Barlow
Claire Zion
Jayne Ann Krentz
Meryl Sawyer
Carrie Feron

I dedicate this book to all of you remarkable women with my love and thanks.

(And to those new angels who are just beginning to flutter into my life . . . welcome!)

Acknowledgments

A number of generous people helped with the research for *Kiss An Angel*. I am especially grateful to my mother, Lou Titus, who worked so hard on the initial background material. Also, the reference librarians at Nichols Library always manage to come through for me, as does Linda Barlow. Additional thanks to Kacy Frazier, the staff at Brookfield Zoo, David Morgan, and the World Circus Museum for answering my questions.

My special appreciation goes to Jill Barnett, whose thoughtful critique of this book rescued me from craziness. And my editor, Carrie Feron, who has given me the best gift a writer can receive: the peace of mind to write.

Susan Elizabeth Phillips
c/o Avon Books
1350 Avenue of the Americas
New York, New York 10019

1

Daisy Devreaux had forgotten her bridegroom's name.

"I, Theodosia, take thee . . ."

She caught her bottom lip between her teeth. Her father had introduced them several days ago, that terrible morning the three of them had gone to get the marriage license, and she'd heard the name then. Right afterward the man had disappeared, and she hadn't seen him again until a few minutes ago when she'd walked down the staircase of her father's Central Park West duplex into the living room where this makeshift midmorning wedding ceremony was taking place.

Her father stood behind her, and Daisy could almost feel him vibrating with disapproval, but his disapproval was nothing new. He'd been disappointed with her even before she was born, and no matter how hard she'd tried, she'd never been able to get him to change his mind.

She risked a sideways peek at this bridegroom her father's money had bought for her. A studmuffin. A very scary studmuffin with his towering height, lean, whipcord build, and those eerie amber eyes. Her mother would have loved him.

When Lani Devreaux had died in a yacht fire last year, she'd been in the arms of a twenty-four-year-old rock star. Daisy had finally reached the point where she could think about her mother without pain, and she smiled to herself as she realized that the man standing at her side would have been too old for her mother. He looked to be in his mid-

1

thirties, and Lani had usually drawn the line at twenty-nine.

His hair was so dark it was nearly black, and those chiseled features might have made his face too pretty if it weren't for his strong jaw, not to mention that intimidating scowl. Men with such brutal good looks had appealed to Lani, but Daisy preferred older, more conservative types. Not for the first time since the ceremony had begun did she wish her father had picked someone less intimidating.

She tried to steady her nerves by reminding herself that she wasn't going to have to spend more than a few hours in her new husband's company. As soon as she had a chance to tell him her plan, this would all be over. Unfortunately, her plan also meant breaking the sacred marriage vows she was getting ready to take, and since she wasn't the sort of person who could take a vow lightly—especially a marriage vow—she suspected her guilty conscience had induced the memory block.

She started over again, hoping the name would poke through her mental barrier. "I, Theodosia, take thee . . ." Once again her voice trailed off.

Her bridegroom didn't even spare her a glance, let alone try to help her. He stared straight ahead, and the uncompromising lines of that hard profile made her skin prickle. He'd just spoken his own vows, so he must have mentioned his name, but the lack of inflection in his voice had escalated her emotional tailspin, and she hadn't taken it in.

"Alexander," her father spit out from behind her, and Daisy could tell by the sound of his voice that he was clenching his teeth again. For a man who had been one of the United States' foremost diplomats, he certainly didn't have much patience with her.

She dug her nails into her palms and told herself she had no choice. "I, Theodosia . . ." She gulped for air. ". . . take thee Alexander . . ." She gulped again. ". . . to be my awful wedded husband . . ."

It wasn't until she heard her stepmother, Amelia, gasp that she realized what she'd said.

The studmuffin turned his head and looked down at her.

He cocked one dark brow in a vaguely inquisitive fashion, as if he wasn't certain he'd heard her correctly. *My awful wedded husband.* Her sense of humor kicked in, and she felt the corners of her mouth quiver.

His brows slammed together and those deep-set eyes regarded her without a speck of amusement. Obviously the studmuffin didn't share her problem with inappropriate levity.

Swallowing the small bubble of hysteria that was rising inside her, she plunged on without correcting herself. At least that one part of her vows would be honest because he was certainly an awful husband for her. At that moment her mental block finally evaporated and his last name leaped into her mind. *Markov. Alexander Markov.* He was another of her father's Russians.

As a former ambassador to the Soviet Union, her father, Max Petroff, had close ties with the Russian community, both here and abroad. His passion for his ancestral homeland was even reflected in the decor of the room where they stood, with its bold blue walls, so common in that country's residential architecture; yellow-tiled stove; and multicolored kilim rug. To her left, a walnut cabinet held vases of Russian cobalt as well as crystal and porcelain pieces from the Imperial Works in St. Petersburg. The furniture was a mixture of art deco and eighteenth century that somehow worked.

Her bridegroom's large hand lifted her own much smaller one, and she felt its strength as he shoved a plain gold band on her finger.

"With this ring, I thee wed," he said in a stern, uncompromising voice.

She gazed at the simple band with momentary confusion. For as long as she could remember, she'd indulged in what her mother Lani had called a "bourgeois fantasy of love and marriage," and she'd never imagined anything like this.

". . . the power vested in me by the state of New York, I now pronounce that you are husband and wife."

She tensed as she waited for Judge Rhinsetler to invite the

bridegroom to kiss the bride. When he didn't, she knew her father had asked him not to, sparing her the embarrassment of being forced to kiss that hard, unsmiling mouth. It was exactly like her father to have remembered a detail that no one else had thought to consider. Although she wouldn't admit it for the world, she wished she were more like him, but she wasn't even able to manage the major events of her life, let alone the details.

In wasn't in her nature to wallow in self-pity, so she shook it off as her father came forward to brush his cool cheek against hers in ceremonial fashion. She found herself hoping for a word of affection, but she wasn't surprised when she didn't get it. She even managed to look unaffected as he moved away.

He drew her mysterious bridegroom toward the windows that looked down over Central Park, where they were joined by Judge Rhinsetler. The other witnesses to the ceremony were the chauffeur, who tactfully disappeared to attend to his duties, and her father's wife Amelia, with her frosted blond hair and lockjaw drawl.

"Congratulations, dear. What a beautiful couple you and Alexander make. Don't they look wonderful together, Max?" Without waiting for an answer, Amelia swept Daisy into her arms, enveloping both of them in a cloud of musky perfume.

Amelia acted as if she felt a genuine fondness for her husband's bastard daughter, and even though Daisy knew her real feelings, she gave Amelia credit for trying. It couldn't be easy to confront the living evidence of the only irresponsible thing her husband had ever done, even if he'd done it twenty-six odd years ago.

"I don't know why you insisted on wearing that dress, dear. It might be appropriate for club-hopping, but hardly for a wedding." Amelia's critical gaze passed stern judgment on Daisy's expensive metallic lace tank dress that ended in a scalloped hem a good eight inches above her knee.

"It's almost white."

"Gold isn't white, dear. And it's much too short."

"The jacket is conservative," Daisy pointed out, smoothing her hands along the sides of the boxy gold satin jacket that fell to the top of her thighs.

"That hardly makes up for the rest. Why couldn't you have gone along with tradition and worn white? Or at least chosen something more sedate."

Because this wasn't going to be a real marriage, Daisy thought, and the more she bowed to tradition, the more she remembered that she was violating something that should be sacred. She'd even removed the gardenia Amelia had fastened in her hair only to have her stepmother stick it back in just before the ceremony.

She knew Amelia didn't approve of her gold shoes either, which looked like a pair of Roman gladiator sandals with four-inch heels. They were brutally uncomfortable, but at least they couldn't be confused with the traditional white satin pumps.

"Your bridegroom doesn't look happy," Amelia whispered. "Not that I'm surprised. Try not to say anything silly to him for at least the first hour or so, will you? You really must do something about that annoying habit of talking before you think."

Daisy barely repressed a sigh. Amelia never said what she really thought, while Daisy almost always did, and her honesty antagonized her stepmother to no end. But Daisy wasn't good at dissembling. Maybe because she had seen so much of it from both her parents.

She sneaked a look at her new husband and wondered how much her father had paid him to marry her. And some irreverent part of her wanted to know how the actual transaction had taken place. Cash? Check? *Excuse me, Alexander Markov, but do you take American Express?* As she observed her bridegroom declining a mimosa from the tray being passed by Min Soon, she tried to imagine what he was thinking.

How much longer before he could hustle the little brat out of here? Alex Markov glanced at his watch. Another five minutes should do it, he decided. He watched the servant who was passing a tray of drinks stop to fawn over her. *Enjoy it, lady. It'll be a long time before it happens again.*

While Max showed the judge an antique samovar, Alex gazed at his new wife's legs, revealed for all the world to see by that harebrained excuse for a wedding dress. They were slim and shapely, which made him wonder if the rest of her body, partially concealed by her jacket, would be as enticing. But even a siren's body wasn't going to compensate him for being forced into this marriage.

He remembered his last private conversation with Daisy's father. "She's badly educated, flighty, and irresponsible," Max Petroff had announced. "Her mother was a terrible influence. I don't believe Daisy knows how to do anything useful. Granted, it's not all her fault. Lani never cut the apron strings, and she kept Daisy with her until she died. It's a miracle Daisy wasn't on board the boat that night it caught on fire. My daughter'll need a stiff hand, Alex, or she'll drive you crazy."

Nothing Alex had seen of Daisy Devreaux so far made him doubt Max's words. Her mother was Lani Devreaux, the British fashion model who'd been so famous thirty years earlier. In what could only have been an attraction of opposites, Lani and Max Petroff had had a love affair when he was just beginning to make his mark as a leading expert on foreign policy, and Daisy was the result.

Max made it clear to Alex in that stuffy way of his that he had offered to marry Lani when she had unexpectedly become pregnant, but Lani had refused to settle down. Nevertheless, Max insisted he'd always done his duty to his embarrassingly illegitimate daughter.

All the evidence pointed to the contrary, however. When Lani's career had begun to fade, she'd turned into a professional party girl and house guest. And wherever Lani went, Daisy went. At least Lani had once had a career, Alex thought, but Daisy didn't seem to have ever done anything useful with her life.

As Alex looked at his new bride more closely, he saw some resemblance to her mother. They had the same black-as-ink hair, and only indoor women could have such pale skin. Her eyes were an unusual blue, so full of color they were as purple as roadside violets. But she was much smaller than her mother—too fragile-looking for his taste—and her features weren't nearly as bold. From what he remembered of the old photographs, Lani's profile had been almost masculine, while Daisy's had a blurred quality that was especially evident in that inconsequential nose and silly, soft mouth.

According to Max, Lani had been strong on looks but short on brains, another quality the little airhead across the room had apparently inherited. She wasn't exactly a bimbo—she was too well-bred for that—but he had no trouble imagining her as a rich man's very expensive sexual trinket.

He'd always been discriminating about female companionship, and alluring as that small body was, he preferred a different sort of woman, one who had more going for her than a great set of legs. He liked intelligence in his bed partners, along with ambition, independence, and the ability to give as good as she got. He could respect a woman who cussed him out, but he had no use for sulks and pouts. This little ball of fluff was already setting his teeth on edge.

At least keeping her in line wouldn't be a problem. He gazed over at her, and one corner of his mouth lifted in a sardonic smile. *Life has a way of catching up with spoiled little rich girls. And, baby, is it ever about to catch up with you.*

Across the room, Daisy stopped in front of an antique mirror to check her appearance. She did it out of habit instead of vanity. To her mother, appearance was everything. Lani regarded smudged mascara as a worse catastrophe than nuclear holocaust.

Daisy's new haircut was chin length in the front and a little longer in the back, breezy, youthful, curling softly here and there. She'd loved it from the beginning, but she'd loved it even more that morning when Amelia had clucked over how untidy the style looked for a wedding.

Just behind her reflection, Daisy saw her bridegroom approaching. She arranged her mouth in a polite smile and told herself everything would work out fine. It had to.

"Get your things, angel face. We're leaving."

She didn't like his tone one bit, but she'd developed a talent for dealing with difficult people, and she overlooked it. "Maria's doing her Grand Marnier soufflé for our celebration brunch, but it's not ready yet, so we'll need to wait."

"Afraid not. We have a plane to catch. Your luggage is already in the car."

She needed more time. She wasn't ready to be alone with him yet. "Could we take a later flight, Alexander? I hate to disappoint Maria. She's Amelia's jewel, and she does a wonderful brunch."

Although his mouth curled in a smile, his eyes pierced straight through her. They were an unusual color, a pale amber that reminded her of something vaguely eerie. Although she couldn't quite remember what it was, she knew it made her uneasy.

"The name's Alex, and you've got one minute to get that sweet little butt of yours out the door."

Her pulse leaped with alarm, but before she could react, he turned his back on her and addressed the three other occupants of the room, his voice quiet but commanding. "I hope you'll all excuse us. We have a plane to catch."

Amelia stepped forward and gave Daisy a sly smile. "My, my. Someone's awfully eager for his wedding night. Our Daisy *is* quite a morsel, isn't she?"

Daisy abruptly lost her appetite for Maria's soufflé. "I'll change my clothes," she said.

"We don't have time for that. You're fine just the way you are."

"But . . ."

A firm hand settled in the small of her back, determinedly propelling her out into the foyer. "I'll bet this is your purse." At her nod, he picked up her small Chanel bag from the gilded console and handed it to her. Just then, her father and Amelia appeared to wave them off.

Even though she didn't plan to go any farther than the

airport, she wanted to jerk away from Alex's touch as he steered her toward the door. She turned back toward her father and hated herself for the faint thread of panic in her voice. "Maybe you could convince Alex to stay a little longer, Dad. We've hardly had a chance to visit."

"Do as he says, Theodosia. And remember—this is your last chance. If you fail at this, I'm washing my hands of you. For once in your life, let's see if you can do something right."

By now she should be used to her father humiliating her in public, but being humiliated in front of her new husband was so embarrassing she barely managed to square her shoulders. Lifting her chin, she stepped in front of Alex and walked out the door.

She refused to meet his eyes as they waited in silence for the elevator that would take them to the lobby. They moved inside. The doors shut, only to open again on the next floor and allow an elderly woman leading a tan Pekingese to enter.

Daisy immediately shrank against the elevator's rich teak paneling, but the dog spotted her. He drew his ears back, yipped furiously, and sprang. She screeched as he jumped up on her legs and tore her nylons. "Get away!"

The dog continued to claw at her. She screamed and grabbed the brass rail. Alex regarded her quizzically, then nudged the animal away with his shoe.

"Naughty Mitzi!" The woman swept her pet into her arms and gave Daisy a censorious look. "I can't think what's wrong. Mitzi loves *everybody*."

Daisy had begun to perspire. She continued to hold the brass rail in a death grip while she kept her eyes on the vicious little beast as it yipped and snapped at her until the doors opened to the lobby.

"The two of you seem to know each other," Alex said as they got off.

"I've—I've never seen that dog in my life."

"I don't believe it. That dog hated you."

"I'm not"—she gulped—"I have this *thing* about animals."

"You've got a *thing* about animals? Tell me that doesn't mean you're afraid of them."

She nodded and tried to force her heartbeat back to normal.

"Terrific," he muttered, setting off across the lobby. "That's just terrific."

The late April morning was damp and drizzly. There were no crepe paper streamers attached to the limousine that waited for them at the curb, no tin cans and JUST MARRIED signs, none of the wonderful silliness reserved for ordinary people who loved each other. She told herself to stop being such a sentimental fool. Lani had teased her for years about being hopelessly old-fashioned, but all Daisy had ever wanted was to live a conventional life. Not so unusual, she supposed, for someone who had been raised so unconventionally.

As she climbed inside, she saw that the tinted glass window separating the driver from the passengers was closed. At least she'd have the privacy she needed to tell Alex Markov her intentions before they reached the airport.

You took vows, Daisy. Sacred vows. She shook off the troublesome voice of her conscience by telling herself she didn't have a choice.

He got in next to her, and the spacious interior suddenly seemed cramped. If he wasn't so physically overpowering, she didn't think she'd be so nervous about this. Although he wasn't muscle-bound like one of those freakish-looking bodybuilders, he had the hard, sinewy physique of someone in top shape. His shoulders were broad, his hips narrow. The hands that rested on the slacks of his charcoal suit were strong and deeply tanned, with long, tapered fingers. She felt a small jolt of awareness that unsettled her.

They had barely pulled away from the curb before he began to tug at his necktie. He yanked it off, stuffed it in the pocket of his suit coat, and unfastened his collar button with an efficient flick of his wrist. She stiffened, hoping he wasn't going to take off any more. In one of her favorite erotic fantasies, she and a faceless man made passionate love in the back of a white limousine stuck in a Manhattan traffic jam while Michael Bolton sang "When a Man Loves a Woman" in the background, but there was a big difference between fantasy and reality.

The limo began to move. She took a deep breath, trying to pull herself together, and smelled the heavy scent of the gardenia in her hair. She was relieved to see that Alex had stopped taking off his clothes, but when he stretched his legs and began to study her, she shifted uneasily. No matter how hard she worked at it, she would never be as beautiful as her mother, and when people stared at her for too long, she felt like an ugly duckling. The hole in her shimmery gold nylons from her encounter with the Pekingese didn't add to her self-confidence.

She opened her purse to find a much needed cigarette. It was an awful habit, and she wasn't proud of having succumbed to it. Although Lani had always smoked, Daisy'd never had more than an occasional cigarette in the evening with a glass of wine. But in those first months after her mother's death she'd found that cigarettes relaxed her, and she'd become truly addicted. After a long drag, she decided she was calm enough to tell Mr. Markov her plan.

"Put it out, angel face."

She regarded him apologetically. "I know it's a terrible habit, and I promise I won't blow smoke at you, but I really need this right now."

He reached past her to lower her window. Without warning, her cigarette burst into flames.

She shrieked and let it go. Sparks flew everywhere. He grabbed a handkerchief from his breast pocket and somehow managed to put out all the embers.

Breathing hard, she looked down at her lap and saw tiny burn marks in her gold lace dress and on the satin jacket. "How did that happen?" she gasped.

"I guess it was faulty."

"A faulty cigarette? I've never heard of anything like that."

"You'd better let me throw away the pack in case the others are like that."

"Yes. Of course."

She quickly handed it over, and he pushed the pack into his pants pocket. Although she was shaken, he seemed perfectly relaxed. Leaning back in the corner of the seat, he crossed his arms over his chest and closed his eyes.

They needed to talk—she had to explain to him her plan for putting an end to this embarrassing marriage—but he didn't seem to be in the mood for conversation, and she was afraid she'd mess it up if she wasn't careful. This past year had been such a disaster that she'd gotten into the habit of giving herself small pep talks so that she didn't fall into the habit of considering herself totally hopeless.

She reminded herself that although her education might have been unorthodox, it had certainly been comprehensive. And despite what her father thought, she'd inherited *his* brain and not her mother's. She also had a good sense of humor and a naturally optimistic outlook on life that even the past year hadn't entirely destroyed. She spoke four foreign languages, could identify nearly any couture piece by designer, and was an expert at calming hysterical women. Unfortunately, she didn't possess even a modicum of common sense.

Why hadn't she listened when her mother's Parisian lawyer had explained there would be nothing left after Lani's debts were paid? She suspected now that it was guilt that had pushed her into her disastrous months-long spending spree following that numbing time immediately after the memorial service. For years she had wanted to escape the emotional blackmail that had pinned her to Lani's side on endless rounds of pleasure-seeking. But she hadn't wanted Lani to die. Not that.

Her eyes filled with tears. She'd loved her mother desperately, and despite Lani's selfishness, her endless demands, and her constant need to be reassured that she hadn't lost her beauty, she knew Lani had loved her, too.

The more guilt Daisy had felt about the unexpected freedom Lani's death had given her, the more money she'd spent, not only on herself but on any of Lani's old friends who were down on their luck. When her creditors' threats had grown ominous, she'd written more checks to hold them off, not knowing or caring that she didn't have enough money to cover them.

Max found out about her extravagant spending the same day a warrant was issued for her arrest. Reality crashed in, and she realized the enormity of what she'd done. She'd begged her father to lend her the money to hold off her creditors, promising to pay him back as soon as she got on her feet.

That was when he'd resorted to blackmail. It was high time she grew up, he told her, and if she wanted to stay out of jail, she was going to put an end to her extravagance and do as he said.

In crisp, uncompromising tones, he had dictated his terms. She would marry the man he chose for her as soon as he could arrange it. Furthermore, she would promise to stay married to him for six months, serving as an obedient and dutiful wife during that time. Only at the end of the six months would she be free to divorce and benefit from a trust fund he would set up for her, a trust fund *he* would control. If she was frugal, she would be able to live in relative comfort off the interest for the rest of her life.

"You're not serious!" she'd exclaimed when she had finally recovered her powers of speech. "People don't arrange marriages any more."

"I've never been more serious. If you don't agree to this marriage, you'll go to jail. And if you can't stay married for six months, you'll never see another penny from me."

Three days later, he had presented her future bridegroom without mentioning a word about his background or occupation, merely giving her an admonition: "He's going to teach you something about life. For now, that's all you need to know."

They crossed the Triborough Bridge, and she realized they'd be at La Guardia soon, which meant she couldn't wait any longer to broach the subject they needed to discuss. Out of habit, she withdrew a slim gold compact from her purse to make certain everything was as it should be. Reassured, she closed it with a snap and put it away.

"Excuse me, Mr. Markov."

He didn't respond.

She cleared her throat. "Mr. Markov? Alex? I think we need to talk."

The lids over those pale amber eyes drifted open. "About what?"

Despite her tension, she smiled. "We're total strangers who've just gotten married. I think that gives us a few things to discuss."

"If you want to pick out names for our children, angel face, I think I'll pass."

So he did have a sense of humor after all, if only a cynical one. "I mean that we should talk about how we're going to get through the next six months before we can file for divorce."

"I figure we'll just take it day by day." He paused. "Night by night."

Her skin prickled, and she told herself not to be foolish. He'd made a perfectly innocent remark, and she'd merely imagined that husky undertone of sexual innuendo. She fixed a bright smile on her face.

"I have a plan; a simple one, really."

"Oh?"

"If you'll give me a check for half of what my father is paying you to marry me—and I think you'll agree that's only fair—the two of us can go our separate ways and end this awkwardness."

An expression of amusement flickered across those granite features of his. "What awkwardness are you talking about?"

She should have known from her experiences with her mother's lovers that a man this good-looking wasn't going to be blessed with brains. "The awkwardness of finding ourselves married to a stranger."

"We'll get to know each other pretty well, I imagine." Again that husky undertone. "And I don't think the two of us going our separate ways is what Max had in mind. As I remember it, we're supposed to live together and play husband and wife.''

''That's just like my father. He's a little dictatorial when it comes to running other people's lives. The beauty of my plan is that he'll never know that we haven't been living together. As long as we don't set up housekeeping in Manhattan, where he can walk in on us, he won't have any idea what we're doing.''

''We're definitely not setting up housekeeping in Manhattan.''

He wasn't being as cooperative as she'd hoped, but she was enough of an optimist to believe he only needed a little more persuasion. ''I know my plan will work.''

''Let me get this straight. You expect me to hand over half of what Max is giving me to marry you?''

''How much is that, by the way?''

''Not nearly enough,'' he muttered.

She'd never had to haggle, and she didn't like doing it now, but she couldn't see that she had a choice. ''If you think about it, I'm sure you'll realize that's equitable. After all, if it weren't for me, you wouldn't be getting any money at all.''

''This must mean you're planning on giving me half the money in that trust fund he's promised to set up for you.''

''Oh, no, I'm not planning to do that at all.''

He gave a short bark of laughter. ''Somehow I didn't think so.''

''You misunderstand. I'll pay you back as soon as I have access to my trust. I'm only asking for a loan.''

''And I'm refusing it.''

She knew then that she'd made a mess of it. She had a bad habit of assuming other people would do what she herself would do if she were in their shoes. For example, if she were Alex Markov, she would certainly loan herself half the money just to get rid of her.

She needed to smoke. Badly. ''Could I have my cigarettes back? I'm sure that only one of them was faulty.''

He withdrew the crumpled pack from the pocket of his slacks and handed it over. She quickly lit up, shut her eyes, and drew the smoke deeply into her lungs.

She heard the sizzle, and by the time her eyes sprang open, the cigarette was already in flames. With a gasp of dismay, she dropped it. Once again, Alex swept up the butt and embers with a handkerchief.

"Maybe you could sue," he said mildly.

She pressed her hand to her throat, too stunned to speak.

He reached over and touched her breast. She felt the flick of his finger on the inner swell and jumped back, even as the sensitive flesh beaded beneath the satin. Her gaze flew upward to those unfathomable golden eyes.

"A spark," he said.

She covered her breast with her hand and felt the trembling of her heart beneath her palm. How long had it been since a hand other than her own had touched her there? Two years ago, she remembered, when she'd had her last physical exam.

She saw that they had reached the airport, and she garnered her courage. "Mr. Markov, you have to realize that we can't live together as man and wife. We're strangers. The whole idea is ridiculous, and I'm going to have to insist that you be more cooperative about this."

"Insist?" he said mildly. "I don't believe you have a right to insist on anything."

She stiffened her spine. "I'm not going to be bullied, Mr. Markov."

He sighed and shook his head, regarding her with an expression of regret that she didn't believe for a minute was sincere. "I was hoping I wouldn't have to do this, angel face, but I guess I should have figured it wouldn't be that easy with you. Maybe I'd better spell out the ground rules right now, just so you'll know what to expect. For better or worse, the two of us are married until six months from today. You can walk away any time you want to, but you'll have to do it on your own. And in case you haven't figured it out by now, this isn't going to be one of those modern, talk-things-through-so-we-can-compromise marriages like you read about in all those ladies' magazines. This is going to be an old-time relationship." If anything his voice grew softer, more gentle. "Now what that means, angel face, is that I'm in charge, and you're going to be doing what I say. If you don't, you'll suffer some pretty unpleasant consequences. The good news in all this is that after the time's up, you can do whatever you want. I won't give a damn."

A wave of panic gripped her, and she fought against succumbing to it. "I don't like being threatened. Maybe you should just come right out and tell me what these consequences are that you're holding over my head."

He settled back into the seat, and the small upward tilt of that hard mouth sent a shiver of dread down her spine.

"Aw, angel face, I'm not gonna have to. By tonight you'll have figured it out all by yourself."

2

Daisy hovered in the far corner of the smoking section at the USAir gate, taking such quick drags on her cigarette that she was getting light-headed. The plane, she had discovered, was heading for Charleston, South Carolina, one of her favorite cities, and she tried to take that as a positive sign in a chain of events that had been growing more disastrous by the minute.

First, Mr. High-and-Mighty Markov had refused to go along with her plan. Then he'd sabotaged her luggage. When the chauffeur had unloaded only one overstuffed carry-on bag from the trunk instead of the full array of suitcases she'd packed, she'd assumed there'd been a mistake, but Alex had quickly set her straight.

"We're traveling light. I had the housekeeper repack for you during the wedding ceremony."

"You had no right to do that!"

"We'll carry them on instead of checking them." He'd picked up his own much smaller bag and she'd watched with astonishment as he'd set off, leaving her to follow. She'd barely been able to hoist her cumbersome piece of luggage, and her ankles had wobbled on her too-high heels as she'd dragged it after him. Feeling miserable and self-conscious, she'd struggled toward the gate, certain everyone she passed was noting her holey nylons, scorched gold lace, and bruised gardenia.

When he'd disappeared into the rest room, she'd hurried

18

to buy a fresh pack of cigarettes, only to discover that she had nothing but a ten-dollar bill in her purse. With a sense of shock, she'd realized it was all the money she had left in the world. Her bank accounts were closed, her credit cards canceled. She'd returned the bill to her wallet and bummed a cigarette from an attractive businessman instead.

Just as she stubbed it out, Alex emerged from the rest room, and as she saw the way he was dressed, her stomach sank. The well-tailored dark suit had been replaced by a denim shirt that looked soft from many washings and a pair of jeans so faded they were nearly white. Frayed cuffs fell over scuffed brown leather cowboy boots. His shirt sleeves were rolled up to reveal strong, suntanned forearms lightly dusted with dark hair and a gold watch with a leather band. She sank her teeth into her bottom lip. Of all the things her father had done to her, she'd never imagined he'd marry her off to the Marlboro Man.

He came up to her, his own carry-on bag dangling easily from his loose grip. The fit of his jeans showed narrow hips and legs that went on forever. Lani would have been in ecstasy. "That was the final boarding call. Let's go."

"Mr. Markov—please—you don't really want to go through with this. If you'll just lend me a *third* of the money that's rightfully mine, we can put this behind us."

"I made a promise to your father, and I never go back on my word. Maybe I'm old-fashioned, but it's a matter of honor with me."

"Honor! You *sold* yourself to him! You let my father buy you! What kind of honor is that?"

"Max and I made a deal, and I'm not going to welsh. Of course, if *you* insist on walking away, I won't stop you."

"You know I can't do that! I don't have any money."

"Then let's get to it." He pulled their boarding passes from his shirt pocket and turned away.

She had no checking account, no charge cards, and her father had ordered her not to contact him. With a sinking stomach, she realized she had run out of options, and she picked up her bag.

Ahead of her, Alex reached the last row of chairs, where a teenage boy sat smoking. As her new husband passed by, the boy's cigarette went up in flames.

A little over two hours later she stood in the blazing afternoon sun in the parking lot at the Charleston airport and gazed at Alex's black pickup truck, taking in the thick layer of dust on the hood and the Florida license plates nearly obscured by dried mud.

"Just throw it in the back." Alex tossed his suitcase over the side of the truck but didn't offer to do the same with hers, just as he hadn't offered to carry it from the plane.

She set her jaw. If he thought she was going to beg him for help, he could think again. Her arms screamed in protest as she struggled to hoist the cumbersome bag over the side. She felt his eyes on her, and although she suspected that she'd eventually be grateful her father's housekeeper had managed to stuff so much into one carry-on bag, at that moment she would have given anything for Louis Vuitton's smallest tote.

She grabbed the handle in one hand and the hook at the bottom in the other. With a mighty effort, she heaved.

"Need help?" he inquired with phony innocence.

"No . . . thank . . . you." The words came out more as grunts than civilized speech.

"Are you sure?"

She had hoisted it to shoulder level, and she didn't have enough breath left to reply. Just a few more inches. She wobbled on her high heels. A few more—

With a squawk of dismay, she and the bag fell backward. She yelped as she hit the pavement, then yelped again out of pure rage. As she stared straight up into the sun, she realized the bag had cushioned her fall, which was the only reason she hadn't hurt herself. She also realized she had sprawled into an ungainly position, with her short skirt stretched tight across her upper thighs, her knees pressed together, and her feet splayed.

A pair of scuffed brown cowboy boots appeared in her

peripheral vision. As her eyes slid up along denim-clad thighs and over a broad chest to a pair of amber eyes glinting with amusement, she mustered her dignity. Bringing her ankles together, she propped herself up on her elbows. "I *meant* to do that."

His chuckle had an old, rusty sound, as if it hadn't been used in a long time. "You don't say."

"Yes, I do." With as much dignity as possible, she pushed herself the rest of the way into a sitting position. "This is what your childish behavior has led to, and I hope you're sorry."

He gave a bark of laughter. "You need a keeper, angel face, not a husband."

"Will you stop calling me that!"

"Be grateful that's all I'm calling you." He snagged the strap of her bag with three fingers of one hand and tossed it over the top as if it weighed no more than her pride. Then he hauled her to her feet, unlocked the door of the cab, and pushed her into the sweltering interior.

She didn't trust herself to speak until they had left the airport far behind and were traveling on a two-lane highway that seemed to be heading inland instead of toward Hilton Head, as she'd hoped.

Flat stretches of palmetto and scrub stretched on both sides of the road, and the blast of warm air coming through the truck's open windows whipped feathery strands of hair against her cheeks. Keeping her voice determinedly pleasant, she finally broke the silence. "Would you mind turning on the air-conditioning? I'm getting blown to bits."

"It hasn't worked for years."

Maybe she was getting numb, because his announcement didn't surprise her. More miles ticked by, and signs of civilization grew increasingly sparse. Once again, she asked the question he'd refused to answer when they'd gotten off the plane. "Will you please tell me where we're going?"

"It'll probably be easier on your nervous system if you wait to see for yourself."

"I'm not taking that as a hopeful sign."

"Let's put it this way. The place doesn't have a cocktail lounge."

The jeans, the boots, the pickup with Florida plates. Maybe he was a rancher! She knew that there were all kinds of wealthy cattle ranchers in Florida. Maybe they were taking a roundabout way south. *Please, God, let him be a rancher. And let it be like a* Dallas *rerun. A beautiful house, tacky clothes, Sue Ellen and J.R. cavorting around the swimming pool.*

"Are you a rancher?"

"Do I look like a rancher?"

"Right now you sound like a psychiatrist. You answered a question with a question."

"I wouldn't know anything about that. I never visited one."

"Of course not. You're obviously much too well-adjusted." She'd meant the remark to be sarcastic, but she didn't do sarcasm well, and it seemed to go right past him.

She gazed out the window at the hypnotically flat stretch of highway. Off to her right, she saw a dilapidated house with a scraggly tree in the front yard holding a collection of bird feeders made from gourds. The hot air blew over her.

She closed her eyes and tried to pretend that she was inhaling. Until today, she hadn't realized how addicted she was to nicotine. As soon as things settled down, she'd have to quit. She'd be in a new setting, and she'd make some rules for herself. For example, she wouldn't ever smoke in the ranch house. If she wanted a cigarette, she'd slip out onto the veranda or lie on a chaise next to the pool.

As she drifted into sleep, she once again found herself praying. *Please, God, let there be a veranda. Let there be a pool. . . .*

Sometime later, the jolting of the truck awakened her. She jerked upright, opened her eyes, and gave a choked gasp.

"Something wrong?"

"Tell me that's not what I think it is." Her finger shook as she pointed toward the moving object on the other side of the dusty windshield.

"It's pretty hard to confuse an elephant with anything else."

It *was* an elephant. A real, live elephant. The beast picked up a clump of hay in its trunk and tossed it on its back. As she gazed into the glare of the late afternoon sun, she prayed that she was still asleep and this was only a bad dream. "We're stopping here because you want to take me to the circus, right?"

"Not exactly."

"You want to go to the circus yourself?"

"No."

Her mouth was so dry it was difficult forming the words. "I know you don't like me, Mr. Markov, but please don't say you work here."

"I'm the manager."

"You manage a circus," she repeated faintly.

"That's right."

Stunned, she sagged back in the seat, but even her naturally optimistic nature couldn't find a silver lining in this dark cloud.

The sun-parched vacant lot held a red-and-blue striped big top, several smaller tents, and a variety of trucks and trailers. The largest one was painted with red and blue stars, along with the bright red legend QUEST BROTHERS CIRCUS, OWEN QUEST, OWNER. In addition to a number of shackled elephants, she saw a llama, a camel, some large animal cages, and all kinds of disreputable people, including some dirty-looking men, most of whom seemed to be missing their front teeth.

Her father had always been a snob. He loved ancient lineages and royal titles. He boasted of his own descent from one of czarist Russia's great aristocratic families. The fact that he'd given his only daughter to a man who worked for a circus was the clearest message he could have sent of his feelings for her.

"It's not exactly Ringling Brothers."

"I see that," she replied weakly.

"Quest Brothers is what's known as a mud show."

"Why is that?"

His response sounded faintly diabolical. "You'll find out soon enough."

He parked the truck in a row with several others, turned off the ignition, and got out. By the time she'd climbed down, he'd taken both their bags out of the back and set off with them.

She tottered awkwardly after him over the uneven ground, her high heels sinking into the sand. Everyone stopped what they were doing and stared at her. Her knee poked through a widening hole in her shredded nylons, the singed gold satin jacket slipped off one shoulder, and her shoe sank into something ominously soft. With a sinking heart, she looked down, only to see that she'd stepped in exactly what she'd feared.

"Mr. Markov!"

Her shriek bore an edge of hysteria, but he didn't seem to hear. Instead, he kept walking toward a row of house trailers and motor homes. She wiped the sole of her shoe in the sandy soil, filling it with grit in the process. With a strangled exclamation, she set off again.

He approached two vehicles that sat close together. The nearest one was a sleekly modern silver motor home that had a satellite dish on top. Next to it rested a battered and rust-streaked trailer that might have been green in a past life.

Let him be going to the motor home instead of that horrible trailer. Let him be—

He stopped at the ugly green trailer, opened the door, and disappeared inside. She groaned, then realized she was so numb to shock she wasn't even surprised.

He reappeared in the doorway a moment later and watched her wobbly approach. When she reached the bottom of the bent metal step, he gave her a cynical smile. "Home sweet home, angel face. Do you want me to carry you over the threshold?"

Despite his sarcasm, she chose that particular moment to remember that she'd never been carried over a threshold, and regardless of the circumstances, this *was* her wedding day.

Maybe a small bow to sentiment would help both of them salvage something positive from this terrible experience.

"Yes, please."

"You're kidding."

"You don't have to if you don't want to."

"I don't want to."

She tried to swallow her disappointment. "All right, then."

"It's a damned trailer!"

"So I see."

"I don't even think trailers have thresholds."

"If something has a door, it has a threshold. Even an igloo has a threshold."

Out of the corner of her eye, she saw that they were beginning to draw a crowd. Alex noticed, too. "Just get in here, all right."

"You're the one who offered."

"I was being sarcastic."

"I've noticed you're that way a lot. In case no one has ever pointed it out, it's an annoying habit."

"Get inside, Daisy."

Somehow a line had been drawn, and what had begun impulsively had turned into a battle of wills. She stood at the bottom of the step, her knees shaking with dread, but still trying to hold her ground. "I'd appreciate it if you'd at least honor this one tradition."

"For chrissake." He jumped down, scooped her up, and carried her inside, kicking the door behind him. As it shut, he dumped her onto her feet.

Before she could make up her mind whether she'd won or lost that particular skirmish, she became aware of her surroundings and forgot everything else. "Oh, dear."

"You're going to hurt my feelings if you tell me you don't like it."

"It's awful."

The inside was even worse than the outside. Cramped and cluttered, it smelled of mildew, old age, and stale food. A miniature kitchen sat just in front of her, its blue Formica top faded and chipped. Dirty dishes had been piled in the tiny sink, and a crusty pan sat on top of a stove, just above an oven door held shut by a piece of twine. The threadbare carpet had once been gold but now held so many ancient stains its color could only be described in terms of body functions. To the right of the kitchen, the faded plaid upholstery of a small couch was barely visible beneath stacks of books, newspapers, and remnants of male clothing. She saw a chipped refrigerator, cupboards with peeling laminate, and one unmade bed.

She whirled around looking for another. "Where are the rest of the beds?"

He regarded her evenly, then stepped around the bags he'd dropped in the center of the floor. "This is a trailer, angel face, not a suite at the Ritz. What you see is what you get."

"But—" She clamped her mouth shut. Her throat felt dry and her stomach quivered.

The bed took up most of one end of the trailer, separated from the rest only by a sagging length of wire holding a faded brown curtain that was pushed back against the wall. The bedsheets tangled with a few items of clothing, a bath towel, and something that appeared from a distance to be a heavy black belt.

"The mattress is nice and comfortable," he said.

"I'm sure the couch will be fine for me."

"Whatever."

She heard a series of metallic clinks and turned to see him unloading his pockets on the cluttered kitchen counter: change, truck keys, wallet. "I was living in another trailer until a week ago, but it was too small for two people, so I arranged for this one. Unfortunately, I haven't had time to call my interior decorator." He jerked his head. "Donnicker's in there. It's the only thing I've had time to clean up. You can try to fit your stuff into that storage closet behind you. Spec starts in an hour; stay away from the elephants."

Donnicker? Spec?

"I really don't think I can live like this," she said. "It's filthy."

"You're right about that. I guess it needs a woman's touch. There's some cleaning stuff under the sink."

He moved past her to get to the door, then paused. The next thing she knew, he had crossed back to the counter and repocketed his wallet.

She was deeply offended. "I'm not a thief."

"Of course you're not. And let's just keep it that way." His chest brushed her arm as he turned sideways to slip past her to the door. "Today we have shows at five and eight. Be at both of them."

"Stop it right now! I can't stay in this awful place, and I'm not cleaning up your filth!"

He glanced absently down at the toe of his boot, then back up at her. She gazed into those pale golden eyes and felt a quiver of dread, along with a sensation of heightened awareness that she was afraid to examine too closely.

He slowly lifted his hand, and she flinched as he clasped it gently around her throat. She felt the light abrasion of his thumb as he began rubbing the hollow just beneath her ear in something that felt very much like a caress. "Listen to me, angel face," he said softly. "We can do this easy, or we can do it rough. Either way, I'm going to win. You decide how it'll be."

Their gazes locked. In a moment that lasted forever, he wordlessly demanded that she submit to him. His eyes seemed to burn through her, dissolving her clothes, her skin, until she felt naked and open, with all her weaknesses exposed. She wanted to run away and hide, but the force of his will held her in place.

His hand moved across her throat, then brushed the boxy satin jacket down on her arms. It fell to the floor with a whisper. He touched the lacy gold strap of the dress beneath and slipped it over her shoulder. She wore no bra—the dress wouldn't allow it—and her heart began to pound.

With the tip of his finger, he drew the lace down on her breast until it caught on her nipple. Then he bent his head and put his teeth to the soft flesh he had exposed.

Her breath caught as she felt the nip. It should have been

painful, but her nerve endings registered the small bite as pleasure. She felt the brush of his hand in her hair, and then he turned away, having left his mark on her, just like a wild animal. That was when she knew what his eyes had reminded her of. A creature of prey.

The trailer door swung on its hinges. He stepped outside and gazed back at her, dropping the white gardenia he had stolen from her hair.

It burst into flames.

3

Daisy slammed the door against the burning flower and pressed her fingers to her breast. What kind of man had the power of fire under his command?

As her heart thudded under her hand, she reminded herself that this was a circus, a place of illusion. He must have picked up a few magic tricks over the years, and she wasn't going to let her imagination run wild.

She touched the small red mark on the curve of her breast, and her nipple beaded in response. Gazing at the unmade bed, she sank down on one of the chairs by the trailer's built-in kitchen table and tried to absorb the irony of what had happened.

My daughter is saving herself for marriage. Lani used to toss out the statement as dinner conversation to amuse her friends while Daisy swallowed her embarrassment and pretended to laugh right along with the rest of them. Lani had finally stopped her public announcements when Daisy had turned twenty-three for fear her friends would think she'd raised a freak.

Now that she had reached the age of twenty-six, Daisy knew she was a throwback to the Victorians, and she also understood enough about human psychology to realize that her resistance to premarital sex had its roots in rebellion. From the time she was a small child, she'd watched the revolving door on her mother's bedroom and known she could

29

never be like that. She craved respectability. Once, she'd even thought she'd found it.

His name was Noel Black, and he was a forty-year-old executive in a British publishing firm who she'd met at a house party in Scotland. He was everything she admired in a man: stable, intelligent, well-educated. It hadn't taken her long to fall in love with him.

She'd always been a woman who'd craved touch, and Noel's kisses and expert caresses had inflamed her to the point where she'd nearly lost her mind. Even so she hadn't been able to set aside her deeply entrenched principles and go to bed with him. Her refusal initially irritated him, but gradually he'd grown to understand how strongly she felt about it, and he'd proposed marriage. She'd eagerly accepted and floated through the days until the ceremony could take place.

Lani had pretended to be overjoyed, but Daisy should have known that her mother was terrified of being alone, to the point of desperation. It hadn't taken Lani long to embark on a carefully calculated plan to seduce Noel Black.

To Noel's credit, he'd managed to resist for nearly a month, but Lani always got her man, and in the end, she'd gotten him.

"I did it for you, Daisy," she'd said when it was over, and a heartbroken Daisy had discovered the truth. "I had to make you see what a hypocrite he is. My God, you'd have been miserable if you'd married him."

They had quarreled bitterly, and Daisy had packed up her possessions to leave. Lani's suicide attempt had put a stop to that.

Now she pulled the lacy strap of her wedding dress up over her shoulder and sighed. It was a deep and hurtful sound, the sort of sigh that came from the bottom of her soul because she'd lost the words to express her feelings.

For other women, sex seemed to come so easily. Why not for her? She'd promised herself she would never have sex outside of marriage, and now she was married. But, ironically, her husband was more of a stranger to her than all the men she'd refused. The fact that he was brutally attractive didn't change anything. She couldn't imagine giving herself without love.

Her eyes wandered to the bed. She rose and walked toward it. Something that looked like a piece of black rope peeked out from beneath the pair of jeans tossed carelessly onto the rumpled blue sheets. She reached down to touch the soft, worn denim, then ran her finger along the open teeth of the zipper. What would it be like to be loved by a man? To wake up every morning and see the same face staring at you over the pillow? To have a home and children? A job? What would it be like to be normal?

She set the jeans aside, then abruptly stepped back as she saw what lay beneath them. Not a piece of rope at all, but a whip.

Her heart began to pound.

We can do this easy or we can do it rough. Either way I'm going to win.

Her husband had told her there would be consequences if she disobeyed him. When she'd asked him what they were, he'd said she'd figure it out for herself by tonight. Surely he hadn't meant that he intended to beat her?

She tried to force her breathing back into its regular pattern. Men in the eighteenth century might have been able to get away with beating their wives, but times had changed. And she would call the police if he so much as laid a finger on her. She wouldn't be a victim of any man's violence, regardless of her desperate circumstances.

Surely there was a simple explanation for all this: the fire, the whip, and even that ominous-sounding threat. She was exhausted and unsettled by the shake-up in her life, and it was hard for her to think clearly.

Before she could do anything, she had to get out of her outfit. Once she'd put herself back together, she'd feel better. She dragged her bag up on the couch where she opened it and found that her dressy clothes had been removed, although what was left didn't seem much more suitable for this ragtag place. She settled on a pair of khaki slacks, a melon-colored knit poor-boy top, and sandals. The tiny bath-room proved to be much cleaner than the rest of the place, and by the time she'd repaired her hair and makeup, she felt enough like herself to go outside and explore.

The smell of animals, hay, and dust hit her nostrils as soon as she stepped down into the sandy soil. The warm breeze of late April blew across the lot, making the sides of the big top gently billow and snapping the multicolored pennants that decorated the midway. She heard the sound of a radio playing from an open window in one of the house trailers and the blare of a television quiz show coming from another. Someone was cooking on a charcoal grill, and her stomach rumbled. At the same time, she thought she caught a whiff of cigarette smoke. She followed it to the other side of her trailer and saw a fairy sprite of a girl leaning against the metal siding sneaking a smoke.

She was a delicate, fawnlike creature with straight, golden brown hair, Bambi eyes, and a soft curl of a mouth. In her early-to-middle teens, she had small breasts that poked against a faded T-shirt with a rip at the neck. She wore jeans shorts and imitation Birkenstocks that looked huge on her dainty feet.

Daisy greeted her pleasantly, but the girl's Bambi eyes stayed sullen and hostile.

"I'm Daisy."

"Is that your real name?"

"My real name is Theodosia—my mother had a flair for drama—but everybody calls me Daisy. What's your name?"

There was a long silence. "Heather."

"How pretty. Are you with the circus? Of course you are or you wouldn't be here, would you?"

"I'm one of the Brady Pepper Acrobats."

"You're a performer! That's great. I've never met a circus performer."

Heather regarded her with the perfect disdain only teen-agers seem able to master.

"Did you grow up with the circus?" As Daisy asked the question, she weighed the morality of bumming a cigarette from a youngster. "How old are you, anyway?"

"I just turned sixteen. I've been around for a while." She stuck the cigarette in the corner of her mouth where it looked vaguely obscene. Squinting against the smoke, she began tossing the rings she held into the air until she had all five of them going. Her smooth forehead puckered in concentration, giving Daisy the impression that juggling wasn't easy for her, especially as her eyes began to tear from the smoke.

"Who's Brady Pepper?"

"Crap." Heather missed a ring, then caught the other four. "He's my father."

"Is it just the two of you in the act?"

Heather looked at her as if she were crazy. "Yeah, right. Like it's going to be just me and Brady when I can't even keep five rings in the air."

Daisy wondered if Heather was this rude to everyone.

"Brady performs with my brothers, Matt and Rob. I just stand around and style."

"Style?"

"Strike poses for the audience. Don't you know anything?"

"Not about the circus."

"You must not know anything about men, either. I saw you go into Alex's trailer earlier. Do you know what Sheba says about women who get involved with Alex?"

Daisy was fairly certain she didn't want to hear. "Who's Sheba?"

"Sheba Quest. She owns the circus since her husband died. And she says any woman who tries to get too close to Alex has a death wish."

"Is that so?"

"They hate each other." She took a deep drag and coughed. When she'd recovered, she regarded Daisy with a narrow-eyed squint that was intended to annihilate, but merely looked ridiculous on a fairy sprite. "I'll bet he gets rid of you after he's fucked you a couple of times."

Daisy had been hearing the vilest obscenities since she was a child, but she still found the word disconcerting when it came from a youngster. She didn't use obscenities herself. Another quirk in her rebellion against her upbringing.

"You're so pretty. It's a shame to spoil it with that sort of language."

Heather gave her a look of worldly scorn. "Fuck off." Plucking the cigarette from her mouth, she dropped it and ground it out beneath the sole of her sandal.

Daisy gazed at the butt with longing. There had been at least three good puffs left in it.

"Alex can have any woman he wants," Heather tossed over her shoulder as she began to walk away. "You might be his girlfriend for now, but you won't be around for long."

Before Daisy could tell her she was Alex's wife, not his girlfriend, the teenager had disappeared. Even putting the best face on it, she could hardly say her first encounter with one of the circus people had gone well.

She spent the next half hour roaming the lot, watching the elephant rides from a safe distance and trying to stay out of everyone's path. She realized there was a subtle order in the way the circus was set up. The midway in front held the food and souvenir concessions along with a tent decorated with brightly painted vertical banners depicting wild animals gruesomely devouring their prey. A sign across the entrance read QUEST BROTHERS MENAGERIE. Opposite it sat a trailer with a ticket window at one end. Heavy trucks had been parked off to the side and away from the crowd, while the house trailers, RVs, and campers occupied the back.

As the crowd began gathering in front of the big top, she moved past the stands selling food, souvenirs, and cotton candy to get closer. The smells of Belgian waffles and popcorn mingled with the odors of the animals and a faint hint of mildew from the nylon big top. A man in his early thirties with thinning sandy hair and a big voice was trying to entice the onlookers into the menagerie.

"For only one dollar you'll see the most vicious Siberian tiger in captivity, along with an exotic camel, a llama the kids'll love, and a ferocious gorilla . . ."

As his spiel went on, Daisy moved around the side, passing a cook tent where some of the workers were eating. From the time of her arrival, she had noticed how noisy everything was, and now she found the source of that continuous rumble, a truck that contained two large yellow generators. Heavy cables extended out from it, some of them snaking toward the big top, others toward the concession stands and house trailers.

A woman in a robin's-egg-blue cape edged with marabou emerged from one of the campers and stopped to speak with a clown wearing a bright orange wig. Other performers began to gather under a canopy that she decided must be the performers' entrance to the big top, since it sat opposite the entrance the crowd was using. She had seen no sign of Alex, and she wondered where he was.

The elephants appeared, magnificent in their crimson-and-gold blankets with plumed headpieces. As they lumbered over to take their place, she shrank back toward one of the house trailers. Small dogs terrorized her, and if an elephant came near her, she was fairly certain she'd faint.

Several sleek horses decked out in jeweled harnesses pranced by. She nervously fumbled in her pocket for the nearly empty pack of cigarettes she'd managed to bum from one of the truck drivers and drew one out.

"Line up for spec, everybody! Let's go!"

The man, who earlier had been enticing the crowd to view the menagerie, made the announcement as he slipped into a ringmaster's bright red jacket. At the same time Alex appeared, mounted on a sleek black horse, and Daisy realized he wasn't just the circus manager but a performer as well.

Dressed in a theatrical adaptation of a Cossack's costume, he wore a silky white shirt with billowy sleeves and flowing black trousers tucked into a pair of high black leather boots that molded to his calves. A jewel-encrusted scarlet sash encircled his waist, and the fringed ends trailed down over the horse's side. It wasn't difficult to imagine him riding across the Russian steppes on his way to rape and pillage. She spotted a coiled whip hanging from his saddle, and with a sense of relief, she realized she had let her imagination run wild.

The whip lying on the bed had been nothing more than a circus prop.

As she watched him lean down from the horse to talk with the ringmaster, she remembered she had taken sacred vows that bound her to this man, and she knew she could no longer keep ducking her conscience. With unblinking honesty, she saw that agreeing to this marriage had been the most cowardly thing she had ever done. She had been too lacking in character, too unsure of her ability to care for herself, to turn her back on her father's blackmail and make her own way, even if it had meant going to jail.

Would this be the pattern for the rest of her life? Ducking responsibility and taking the easy way out? She felt ashamed remembering that she'd spoken those sacred wedding vows with no intention of keeping them, and she knew she had to make amends.

Her conscience had been whispering the solution for hours, but she'd refused to listen. Now she accepted the fact that she wasn't going to be able to live with herself unless she made an attempt to keep those vows. Just because it would be difficult didn't make it any less necessary. She had the distinct fear that if she ran away from this, there would be no hope for her.

Even as she knew what she had to do, her mind balked. How could she honor vows she'd made to a stranger?

You didn't make them to a stranger, her conscience reminded her. *You made them to God.*

At that moment Alex spotted her. Her decision was too new for her to be comfortable talking to him now, but she had no escape. She took a nervous puff on her cigarette and kept a wary eye on his fierce-looking horse as he approached. The horse was wearing exceptionally beautiful tack and trappings, including a richly embroidered crimson silk saddle cloth and a bridle set with filigreed gold medallions and elaborately mounted red stones that looked like real rubies.

He glared down at her. "Where have you been?"

"Exploring."

"There are a lot of rough people around the circus. Until

you get used to things, stay where I can keep an eye on you.''

Since she had just promised she was going to do her best to respect her vows, she swallowed her resentment toward his dictatorial manner and made herself respond pleasantly. "All right."

Her palms had begun to sweat from proximity to the horse, and she pressed herself closer against the trailer. "Is he yours?"

"Yes. Perry Lipscomb takes care of him for me. He has an equestrian act, and he hauls Misha in the trailer with his own horses."

"I see."

"Go on in and watch the show."

He flicked the reins, and she stepped back quickly, then gave a hiss of dismay as what was left of her cigarette burst into flames.

"Will you stop that!" she screeched, batting at her clothes and stomping out the burning embers that had fallen to the ground.

He looked back at her, and one corner of his mouth lifted. "Those things are going to kill you if you don't watch out." With a low chuckle, he returned to take his place in line with the other performers.

She didn't know which she found more discouraging, the fact that he'd destroyed one of her cigarettes with his theatrics or the knowledge that he seemed to have bested her in every encounter today.

She was still stewing as she took the long way around the animals and slipped in through the back entrance. She found a seat on one of the wooden bleachers. It was hard and narrow, with nowhere to rest her feet except between the fannies of the people in the next row, but she quickly forgot her discomfort as she enjoyed the excitement of the children around her.

She loved children. Although she'd never told anyone, her secret ambition had always been to teach kindergarten. Even though she couldn't imagine the dream would ever become a reality, she liked thinking about it.

The lights dimmed and a drumroll built to a crescendo as a spotlight came up on the ringmaster standing in the center ring. "Laaaadeees and gentlemen! Children of aaaaall ages! Welcome to the thrills and chills of the twenty-fifth edition of the Quest Brothers Circus!"

Music broke out, played by a band that consisted of two musicians with drums, a synthesizer, and a computer of some kind. They launched into a lively version of "I'd Like to Teach the World to Sing," and a white horse ridden by a showgirl carrying an American flag came through the back entrance. Performers holding colorful banners followed, smiling and waving to the crowd.

The Brady Pepper Acrobats appeared, three good-looking men trailed by Heather, attired in gold spangles, shiny tights, and full makeup. A rhinestone and ruby tiara with a soaring comet at its center was mounted in her hair, now softly curled. Daisy had no difficulty picking out Brady Pepper from his sons. A muscular man of medium height, he reminded her of a street tough grown older. The acrobats were followed by a group of equestrians, clowns, jugglers, and a troupe of performing dogs.

Alex came into the arena on his ferocious black horse, and he alone of all the performers didn't wave and smile. As he circled, he appeared as aloof and mysterious as his Russian heart. He acknowledged the presence of the crowd but somehow set himself apart and gave a strange kind of dignity to the garish display. The crowd cheered as the elephants ended the parade.

The show began, and as the acts progressed, Daisy was surprised by the high caliber of talent. Following a trio of Rumanian trapeze artists called the Flying Toleas, the lights dimmed and the music faded. A pinpoint of blue light came up on the ringmaster, who stood alone in the center of the darkened arena.

"You are about to see a performance presented nowhere else on earth but at Quest Brothers Circus. But first, I'm going to tell you an amazing story." His voice grew dramatically hushed, and a haunting Russian folk tune began to play in the background.

"Almost thirty years ago in the frozen wilds of Siberia, a wandering tribe of Cossack bandits stumbled upon a very young boy, wearing nothing but rags and a priceless icon hanging on a leather thong around his neck. The Cossacks took him into their community and taught him the skills they had learned from their own fathers. But only the icon he wore offered any clue as to his true identity."

The eerie strains of the Russian folk song blended with the ringmaster's hushed voice, and as the light grew brighter, the audience listened, spellbound. "Over the years a legend formed around this man, a legend his rescuers insist to this very day is true."

The music grew louder.

"They believe that he is the only direct descendent of the murdered Czar Nicholas II and his wife Alexandra." His voice grew louder. "Ladies and gentlemen, that would make the man you will see here tonight . . ." A drumroll. ". . . the *heir* to the imperial crown of Russia!"

Daisy felt a shiver of excitement, despite the fact that she didn't believe a word of the story she was hearing.

The ringmaster's voice boomed through the tent. "Quest Brothers Circus is proud to present . . . the incomparable Alexi the Cossack!"

The lights came up, the music grew fierce, and Alex charged dramatically into the arena, his black horse at full gallop. The sleeves of his white shirt billowed, and the jewels encrusting his sash blazed like bloodred droplets. The mighty horse reared. Defying gravity, Alexi raised his arms far above his head, staying mounted only by the pressure of his powerful legs.

The horse came down, and Alexi disappeared. Daisy gasped only to see him reappear, dangling gracefully from the saddle. As the mount galloped around the arena, he performed a series of skillfully executed feats that were both daring and dramatic. Finally swinging back up into the saddle, he took the bullwhip that had been hanging from the pommel and cracked it in a great arc over his head, the sound so loud that the people in front of her jumped.

Props had been set up in the dark during the ringmaster's introduction: a row of beribboned hoops topped with scarlet balloons. Circling the arena, he popped the balloons one by one, and an explosion of crimson glitter, like drops of blood, flew up into the air with each snap of the whip.

One of the showgirls lit an enormous six-pronged candelabra. He whirled the whip in a hypnotic arc over his head, then put out the flames one by one.

The audience applauded, and those in the back stood to get a better look. Alex leaped gracefully to the ground, and the horse trotted out of the tent. The lights dimmed until he was left standing alone in a bloodred spotlight. He picked up a second whip and started snapping both of them in rhythm, one arm up, one arm down, behind him, in front of him. And then he began to dance over the whips, performing the intricate movements with a deadly masculine grace that left her breathless. The dance built to a crescendo, his movements quickened, and as if by magic, the two whips became a single giant one. With a mighty twist of his arm, he cracked it above his head only to have it burst into flames.

The audience gasped, the lights went out, and the fire whip danced a mad mazurka in the dark.

When the lights came up, Alexi the Cossack had vanished.

4

"What in the hell are you doing out here?"

Daisy's eyelids sprang open, and she looked up into the same golden eyes that had plagued her nightmare. For a moment, she couldn't remember where she was, and then it all came crashing back to her: Alex, the wedding, the fire whip.

She grew aware of his hands on her shoulders, the only thing that had prevented her from falling out of his pickup when he'd opened the door. She'd come here to hide because she didn't have the courage to sleep in a trailer with only one bed and a stranger with a mysterious past who brandished whips.

She carefully extricated herself from his grasp, and in the process moved toward the center of the seat, as far away from him as she could manage. "What time is it?"

"Past midnight." He rested one hand on top of the door frame and gazed at her with those strange amber eyes that had plagued her nightmare. Instead of his Cossack's costume, he wore ancient jeans and a faded black T-shirt, but that didn't make him any less threatening.

"Angel face, you are a damn sight more trouble than you're worth."

She pretended to straighten her clothing in an effort to buy herself time. After the final performance, she'd gone to the trailer only to see the whips he'd used in his act lying on the bed, almost as if he'd left them out for further use. She'd

41

tried not to look at them as she'd stood at the window and watched the tent being taken down.

Alex had both directed the men and worked alongside them, and as she'd watched the muscles in his arms bunch as he loaded stacks of seats onto the forklift and hauled on the rigging, she'd remembered those veiled threats he'd made earlier, warnings of unpleasant consequences if she didn't do as he said. Exhausted and feeling alone, she could no longer regard the whips lying on the bed as mere performance props. They were a threat to her, and that was when she'd known she didn't have the courage to fall asleep in his trailer, not even on the couch.

"Come on, we're going to bed."

The last of the sleep-induced cobwebs vanished, and she was instantly on guard. She couldn't see anyone else around. Most of the trucks had pulled out, and the workers seemed to have gone with them. "I've decided to sleep here."

"I don't think so. In case you haven't noticed, your teeth are chattering."

He was right. It had been warm in the truck when she'd first gotten in, but the temperature had dropped since then. "I'm perfectly comfortable," she lied.

He hunched his shoulder and wiped the side of his face with the sleeve of his T-shirt. "Consider this a friendly warning. I've hardly slept in three days. First we had a nasty storm and nearly lost the top, then I've had to make two trips to New York. I'm not the easiest person to get along with under the best of circumstances, but I really turn mean when I'm sleep-deprived. Now get your sweet little butt out here."

"No."

He lifted the arm he'd been holding at his side, and she gave a hiss of alarm as she saw a coiled whip clasped in his hand. He punched it toward the trailer. *"Now!"*

She scrambled from the truck, her heart pounding. The threat of the whip was no longer abstract, and she realized it was one thing to tell herself in broad daylight that she wouldn't let him touch her, but it was quite another late at night when they were alone in the middle of a darkened field someplace in rural South Carolina.

She gasped as he took her arm and led her across the lot. As the damp weeds slapped at her sandaled feet, she knew she couldn't let herself go to her fate without a struggle.

"I'm warning you right now that if you try to hurt me in any way, I'll scream."

He yawned.

"I mean it," she said as he pulled her forward. "I want to think the best of you, but it's hard to do when you keep making all these threats."

He opened the trailer door and gave her a light slap on the rear to nudge her inside. "Could we postpone this until morning?"

Was it only her imagination or had the interior shrunk since she'd first seen it? "I don't think we can. And please don't touch me like that again."

"I'm too damned tired to attack you tonight, if that's what you're worried about."

His words failed to reassure her. "If you don't intend to attack me, why are you threatening me with that whip?"

He looked down at the coil of braided leather as if he'd forgotten it was there, which she didn't believe for a minute. How could he be so casual about it? And why was he carrying a whip this late at night if he wasn't trying to threaten her? Another thought struck her, one that sent chills through her bloodstream. She'd heard plenty of stories about men who used whips as part of their sex play. She even knew some specific examples. Was that what he had in mind?

He muttered something under his breath, closed the door, and walked over to sit on the bed. The whip uncoiled onto the floor, but the butt dangled over his knee.

She eyed it apprehensively. On one hand, she'd promised to honor her marriage vows, and he hadn't actually hurt her. But on the other hand, he certainly had frightened her. Confrontation wasn't something she was good at, but she knew she had to do it. She braced herself.

"I think we need to clear the air. I have to tell you that

I'm not going to be able to live with you intimidating me."

"Intimidating?" He inspected the butt of the whip. "What are you talking about?"

Her nervousness grew, but she forced herself to keep going. "I suppose you can't help how you are. It's probably because of the way you were raised, not that I believe for a moment that Cossack story is true." She paused. "It isn't, is it?"

He looked up at her as if she'd lost her mind.

"No, of course not," she said hastily. "When I refer to intimidation, I'm alluding to your threats and that"—she took a deep breath—"that whip."

"What about it?"

"I know a little about aberrant behavior. If you have sadistic tendencies, I'd appreciate it if you'd tell me right now instead of just hinting around."

"What are you talking about?"

"We're both adults, and there's no reason to pretend you don't understand."

"I'm afraid you're going to have to spell it out."

She couldn't believe how obtuse he was being. "I'm referring to your hints of—of—sexual perversion."

"Sexual perversion?"

As he continued to regard her blankly, she cried out in frustration. "For goodness sake! If you think you can beat me and then have sex with me, just come out and say it. Say, 'Daisy, I get my kicks from whipping women I have sex with, and you're next on my list.' At least I'd know what's going on in your head."

His eyebrows lifted. "That would make you feel better?"

She nodded.

"You're sure?"

"We have to begin communicating."

"Well, all right then." His eyes glittered. "I get my kicks whipping women I have sex with, and you're next on my list. Now I'm going to take a shower."

He disappeared into the bathroom and shut the door.

Daisy caught her bottom lip between her teeth. Somehow that hadn't gone quite as she'd planned.

Alex chuckled as the water sluiced over him. That beautiful little airhead had given him more genuine amusement in one day than he'd had in the past year. Maybe longer than that. In his experience life was a serious business. Laughter was a luxury he hadn't been able to afford when he was growing up, so he'd never developed the habit. Still, it felt good, even though he'd been forced to put up with a whole truckload of aggravation for every laugh.

He remembered her comment about sexual perversion. Even though she wasn't his type, he couldn't deny that he'd been having sexual thoughts about her. But he didn't think they were all that perverted. A man would have been hard pressed not to think about sex when he was confronted with those crushed violet eyes and that soft mouth that seemed to have been made for deep kisses.

It would have ruined the fun if he'd told her that he always carried a whip when he knew the workers had been drinking. Traveling circuses resembled the Wild West when it came to handling trouble—they took care of their own problems— and just the sight of the whip was a powerful deterrent to hot tempers and old grudges.

She didn't know that, of course, and he wasn't in any hurry to tell her. For both their sakes, he intended to keep Little Miss Rich Girl right under his thumb.

As much as he'd enjoyed their last encounter, he had the feeling his amusement was going to be short-lived. What had Max Petroff been thinking of when he'd handed over his daughter? Did he hate her so much that he had willingly submitted her to a life that was so far beyond her realm of experience? When Max had insisted on this marriage, he'd said Daisy needed a fast course in reality, but Alex had a hard time believing he had anything more than punishment in mind.

Daisy's naïveté, coupled with her rich girl's cockeyed value system, made a dangerous combination. He'd be surprised if she lasted more than a few days with him, but he'd promised he'd do his best with her, and he'd keep his word. When she decided to leave, it would be because she'd given up, not because he was kicking her out or paying her off to get rid of her. He might not like Max, but he owed him.

This was his year for paying off big debts, first with his deathbed promise to Owen Quest to take the circus out for its last season under the Quest name, and then by agreeing to marry Max's daughter. In all these years Max had never asked one thing of him as repayment for having saved Alex's life, but when he'd finally gotten around to it, he'd asked for a doozy.

Alex had tried to convince Max that he could accomplish the same objective just by letting Daisy live with him, but Max was too stodgy. Originally Max had insisted that the marriage last a year, but that had been more than even Alex's gratitude could tolerate. They had compromised on six months, a period that would end at the same time as this final Quest Brothers tour.

As Alex lathered his chest, he thought about the two men who had been such a powerful force in his life, Owen Quest and Max Petroff. Max had rescued him from an existence of physical and emotional abuse, while Owen had guided him into manhood.

On the day he'd met Max, Alex was twelve and had been traveling with his Uncle Sergey in a scruffy circus that was spending the summer playing every Atlantic coast resort from Daytona Beach to Cape Cod. He'd never forget that hot August afternoon when Max had appeared like an avenging angel to rip the bullwhip out of Sergey's fist and save Alex from another savage beating.

Now he understood the reasons for Sergey's acts of sadism, but at the time he hadn't comprehended the attraction twisted men feel for little boys and how far they'd go to deny that attraction. In an impulsive gesture of generosity, Max had paid off Sergey and taken Alex away. He'd put him in military school and provided the financial, if not the emotional, resources that let Alex survive until he could take care of himself.

But it was Owen Quest who had given Alex lessons on manhood during Alex's school vacations when he'd traveled with the circus to make money, and then later into Alex's adulthood as every few years he left the rest of his life behind and gave in to an urge to go on the road for a few months. The part of Alex's character that hadn't been shaped by his uncle's whip had been formed by Owen's long-winded lectures and generally astute observations about how screwed up the world was and how tough a man had to be in order to survive. Life was a dangerous business in Owen's view, and he didn't see much place for laughter or frivolity. A man worked hard, kept his guard up, and always held on to his pride.

Alex turned off the shower and reached for a towel. Both men had their selfish reasons for helping out a troubled kid. Max saw himself as a benefactor and enjoyed bragging about his various charitable projects—including Alex Markov—to his upper-crust friends. Owen, on the other hand, had a monstrous ego, and he relished having an impressionable audience waiting breathlessly for his dark insights on life. But regardless of their motivations, they'd been the only people in his young life who'd ever given a damn about him, and neither of them had once asked for anything in return, not until this past year.

Now Alex had a ragtag circus on his hands, along with a silly, sexy ditz of a wife, who was going to do her best to drive him crazy. He wouldn't let it happen, of course. Circumstances had made him who he was—tough and stubborn, a man who lived by his own code and no longer had any illusions left about himself. Daisy Devreaux didn't have a chance.

He wrapped the towel around his waist, picked up another to dry his hair, and opened the bathroom door.

Daisy gulped as the door swung open and he came out. Oh, Lord, he was gorgeous. With his head buried in a towel while he rubbed it dry, she could look her fill, and she saw that his body was her idea of perfect, with muscles that were well-defined but not overly pumped up. He also had something she had never seen on any of Lani's toy boys—a working man's tan. His broad chest was dusted with dark hair, and some kind of gold medal nested there, but she was too entranced with the overall vista to take in much detail.

His hips were significantly narrower than his shoulders, his stomach flat. She followed the straight arrow of hair that began just above his navel and continued down into the low-slung knot on his yellow bath towel. Heat fanned through her as she wondered what he'd look like without it.

He finished drying his hair and glanced over at her. "You can sleep with me or you can sleep on the couch. Right now I'm too tired to care which one."

"I'll sleep on the couch!" Her voice held a tiny squeak, whether from his words or the sight before her eyes, she wasn't certain.

He spoiled her view of his front by walking to the bed where he turned his back on her to coil the whips and place them in a wooden case he pulled out from beneath the bed. With the whips out of sight, she found herself able to enjoy the view of his back much more.

Once again, he turned to face her. "In exactly five seconds I'm going to drop this towel."

He waited, and as more than five seconds passed, she realized what he meant. "Oh. You want me to look away."

He laughed. "Let me get just one good night's sleep, angel face, and, I promise, you can look all you want."

Now she'd done it. She'd given him completely the wrong impression, and she had to correct it. "I'm afraid you misinterpreted."

"I sure hope not."

"But you did. I was just curious . . . not curious, exactly, but—well, yes, I guess curious. . . . That's only natural. But you shouldn't assume—"

"Daisy?"

"Yes?"

"If you say another word, I'm going to pull out one of

those whips you're so worried about and see if I can get into that perversion thing."

She snatched up a clean pair of panties and a faded University of North Carolina T-shirt she'd pulled from his drawer while he was in the shower, then flounced into the bathroom. She closed the door with a satisfying bang.

Twenty minutes later she emerged freshly showered and wearing his T-shirt. She'd decided it was preferable to the only nightwear she'd found in her suitcase, a scrap of pink silk and lace she'd bought in the days before Noel and her mother had betrayed her.

Alex was sound asleep, lying on his back with the bedsheet twisted around his naked hips. There was something impolite about staring at a person while he slept, but she couldn't turn away. Instead, she crept to the end of the bed and gazed down at him.

Asleep, he didn't seem nearly as dangerous as he did awake, and her hands itched to touch that hard, flat belly. She slid her gaze from his waist to his chest and was admiring the perfect symmetry of it when she caught sight of the gold medal hanging on a chain around his neck. As she saw what it was, she froze.

He wore a beautifully enameled Russian icon.

. . . wearing nothing but rags and a priceless icon hanging on a leather thong around his neck.

Her skin prickled. She studied the face of the Virgin Mary pressing her cheek to that of her child, and although she didn't know much about icons, she could see that this Virgin wasn't from the Italian tradition. The gold ornamentation on her black robes was purely Byzantine, as was the elaborate costume worn by the infant Jesus.

She reminded herself that just because Alex wore what was obviously a valuable icon didn't mean the cockamamie story about Cossacks was true. It was probably a family piece that he'd inherited. But she still felt uneasy as she made her way to the opposite end of the trailer.

The couch was littered with clothes from her suitcase that she hadn't put away along with a clutter of newspapers and magazines, some of which were several years old. She pushed everything aside and made up the bed with some clean sheets from the storage closet. But between the nap she'd taken and her troubled thoughts, she couldn't fall asleep, so she read an old issue of *Newsweek*. By the time she'd finished, it was nearly three. She felt as if she'd barely closed her eyes before she was rudely jarred awake.

"Up and at 'em, angel face. We've got a long day ahead."

She rolled over onto her stomach. He tugged at the sheet and she felt the brush of cold air on the backs of her bare thighs. She refused to move. As long as she didn't move, she wouldn't have to face a new day.

"Come on, Daisy."

She buried her face more deeply into her pillow.

A large warm hand settled over the fragile silk of her panties, and her eyes shot open. With a gasp, she rolled to her back, scrambling to cover herself with the sheet.

He grinned down at her. "I thought that might get you moving."

He was the devil incarnate. Only the devil would be fully dressed and shaved at this ungodly hour. She bared her teeth at him. "I'm not a morning person. Go away and don't ever touch me again."

His eyes ran over her in a leisurely fashion, making her aware of the fact that she had nothing on beneath the sheet but his old, worn T-shirt and a very small pair of panties.

"We have nearly a three-hour jump ahead of us, and we're pulling out in ten minutes. Throw some clothes on and make yourself useful." He moved away from her to the sink.

She squinted at the gray light coming in through the small, dirty windows. "It's the middle of the night."

"It's almost six." He poured a mug of coffee, and she waited for him to bring it to her. Instead, he tilted it to his own lips.

She lay back on the couch. "I didn't go to sleep until three. I'll stay in here while you drive."

"It's against the law." He set down his coffee, then bent

over to snatch up some of her clothes from the floor. He
eyed them critically. "Don't you have any jeans?"

"Of course I have jeans."

"Then put them on."

She regarded him smugly. "They're back home in my
father's guest room."

"Of course they are." He shoved the clothes he'd collected at her. "Get dressed."

She wanted to say something unforgivably rude, but she
was fairly certain he'd manhandle her if she did, so she reluctantly stumbled into the bathroom. Ten minutes later she
emerged, ridiculously dressed in turquoise silk evening trousers and a cropped navy cotton top printed with bunches of
bright red cherries. As she opened her mouth to protest his
choice of clothes, she noted that he was standing in front of
an open kitchen cupboard, looking both angry and very dangerous.

Her gaze dropped to the coiled black whip dangling from
his fist, and her heart started to pound. She didn't know what
she'd done, but she knew she was in trouble. This was it.
Showdown at the Cossack Corral.

"Did you eat my Twinkies?"

She gulped. Keeping her eyes glued to the whip, she said,
"Exactly what Twinkies are we talking about?"

"The Twinkies in the cupboard over the sink. The only
Twinkies in the trailer." His fingers convulsed around the
coils of leather.

Oh, Lord, she thought. *Flayed to death for a Twinkie.*

"Well?"

"It, uh— It won't happen again, I promise you. But they
didn't have any special marking on them, so there was no
way I could tell they were yours." Her eyes remained riveted
on the whip. "And normally I wouldn't have eaten them—
I never eat junk food—but I was hungry last night, and, well,
when you think about it, you'll have to admit I did you a
favor because they're clogging my arteries now instead of
yours."

His voice was quiet. Too quiet. In her mind she heard the

howl of a rampaging Cossack baying at a Russian moon. "Don't touch my Twinkies. Ever. If you want Twinkies, buy your own."

She bit her bottom lip. "Twinkies aren't really a very nutritious breakfast."

"Stop it!"

She took a quick backward step, her gaze flying up to meet his. "Stop what?"

He lifted the whip, thrusting it toward her. "Stop looking at this like I'm getting ready to strip the skin off your backside, for God's sake. I had to put leather dressing on it, and I was just putting it away."

She released one long breath. "You don't know how glad I am to hear that."

"If I decide to whip you, it won't be over a Twinkie."

He was doing it to her again. "Stop threatening me right this minute, or you're going to regret it."

"What are you going to do, angel face? Stab me with your eyebrow pencil?" He regarded her with some amusement, then walked over to the bed, where he pulled out the wooden case beneath it and laid the whip inside.

She drew herself up to her full five feet, four inches and glared at him dead on. "I'll have you know, Chuck Norris himself gave me pointers in karate." Unfortunately, it had been ten years ago, and she didn't remember a thing, but that was neither here nor there.

"You don't say."

"Furthermore, Arnold Schwarzenegger personally advised me on a physical fitness program." If only she'd taken just *one* of his suggestions.

"I hear you, Daisy. You're bad to the bone. Now move it."

They hardly spoke at all during the first hour of their trip. Since he hadn't given her nearly enough time to get ready, she had to do her makeup in the truck and fix her hair without her blow-dryer, which meant fastening it back from her face with a pair of art nouveau combs that looked pretty but didn't work very well. Instead of appreciating the difficulty of the task and giving her a little cooperation, he ignored her request to slow down while she applied her eyeliner, then had the nerve to complain because a teeny bit of her styling spray happened to get in his face.

He bought her breakfast in an Orangeburg, South Carolina, truck stop that was decorated with copper kettle lights and wall arrangements of shellacked bread loaves. After she'd eaten, she sneaked into the rest room and smoked one of her three remaining cigarettes. When she came out, she noticed two things. An attractive waitress was flirting with him. And he wasn't doing one thing to discourage her.

She watched him cock his head, then smile at something the waitress said. She experienced a pang of jealousy at how much more he seemed to be enjoying the waitress's company than he enjoyed hers, but she was still prepared to ignore what was happening until she remembered the promise she'd made to honor her vows. With a sense of resignation, she straightened her shoulders and made her way to the table where she gave the waitress her brightest smile.

"Thank you so much for keeping my husband company while I was gone."

The waitress, whose smiley-face name tag read KIMBERLY, seemed a bit taken aback by Daisy's friendly attitude. "It was—that's okay."

Daisy lowered her voice to a loud whisper. "Not everyone has been so nice to him since he's gotten out of prison."

Alex choked on the mouthful of coffee he'd been about to swallow.

Daisy leaned down to thump him on the back while she beamed at Kimberly's shocked face. "I don't care how much evidence the state presented. I've never for one moment believed he murdered that waitress."

This started Alex choking all over again. Kimberly quickly backed away. "I—excuse me. My next order's up."

"Run along," Daisy said gaily. "And God bless!"

Alex finally had his choking fit under control. He rose from behind the booth, his expression even more ominous than usual. Before he had a chance to say a word, she reached up and pressed a gentle finger over his lips.

"Please don't spoil this moment for me, Alex. It's the first time since our wedding ceremony that I've gotten the best of you, and I want to enjoy every precious second."

He looked like he was going to strangle her. Instead, he tossed several bills onto the table and pulled her from the restaurant.

"You're going to be grouchy about his, aren't you?" Her sandals slid in the gravel as he dragged her toward the truck with its ugly green trailer in tow. "I just knew it. You're the grouchiest man I ever met. It's not becoming, Alex; it really isn't. Whether you want to accept it or not, you're a married man, and you really shouldn't—"

"Get inside before I spank you in public."

There it was again, another of his maddening threats. Did that mean he wouldn't spank her if she did as he said or that he simply planned to spank her in private? She was still mulling over the whole unpleasant concept when he started the truck. Moments later, they were back on the highway.

To her relief, the subject of spanking didn't come up again, although, in a perverse way, she was almost sorry. If he'd physically threatened her, she could have been free of her sacred vows and at peace with her conscience.

The morning was sunny, the warm air coming in through the half-opened window not yet oppressive. She saw no reason for him to waste a perfectly lovely morning sulking, so she finally broke the silence. "Where are we going?"

"We have a date up near Greenwood."

"I guess it's too much to hope you mean the dinner and dancing kind of date."

"Afraid not."

"How long will we be there?"

"Just one night."

"I hope we won't have to get up this early tomorrow morning."

"Earlier. We have a longer jump."

"Don't tell me."

"That's the way circuses like this operate."

"Are you saying we do this every morning?"

"There are some places we'll be staying for two days, but not many."

"How long does this last?"

"The circus is booked into October."

"That's six months from now!" She envisioned an endless future of crooked eyeliner. Six months. The exact time span of their marriage.

"What are you worried about?" he replied. "You don't seriously believe you're going to stick it out that long, do you?"

"Don't you think I can?"

"It'll be a long six months," he said with far too much relish. "We'll be covering lots of miles. We have dates as far north as Jersey, as far west as Indiana."

In a truck without air-conditioning.

"This is the last season for Quest Brothers," he said, "so we're well booked."

"What do you mean, the last season?"

"The owner died in January."

"Owen Quest? The name on the side of the trucks?"

"Yes. His wife Bathsheba inherited the circus, and she's put it up for sale."

Was it her imagination, or had his mouth tightened almost imperceptibly? "Have you been with the circus for a long time?" she asked, determined to know more about him.

"Off and on."

"Were your parents circus people?"

"Which ones? My Cossack parents or the ones who abandoned me in Siberia?" He tilted his head, and she saw a gleam in his eyes.

"You weren't raised by Cossacks!"

"You must not have been listening very well last night."

"That was nothing but P. T. Barnum showmanship. I know somebody had to have taught you how to ride and use a whip, but I hardly think it was Cossacks." She paused. "Was it?"

He chuckled. "You're something else, angel face."

She wasn't going to let him derail her. "How long have you been with the circus?"

"I traveled with Quest Brothers when I was in my late teens and early twenties. Since then I've gone out for a few weeks here and there."

"What were you doing the rest of the time?"

"You know the answer to that question. I was serving time in prison for murdering that waitress."

She narrowed her eyes at him, letting him know she had his number. "Are you saying you're not a full-time circus manager?"

"Nope."

Maybe if she backed off for a bit, she'd get more personal information out of him. "Who were the Quest Brothers, anyway?"

"There was just Owen Quest. Because of the Ringling tradition, circus people think it sounds better to say a show is owned by brothers, even if it isn't. Owen owned this circus for twenty-five years, and just before he died, he asked me to take it out for its final season under his name."

"That must be a sacrifice for you." She regarded him expectantly, and when he didn't respond, she prodded him a bit more. "Leaving behind your regular life . . . your regular job . . ."

"Mmm." Ignoring her probing, he pointed to a power pole off the side of the highway. "Keep your eyes open for more of those arrows, will you?"

She noticed three red cardboard arrows, each of them imprinted with the blue letter Q, tacked to the pole and pointing off to the left. "What are they for?"

"They lead us to our next lot." He slowed as he approached an intersection and turned left. "Dobs Murray— he's our twenty-four-hour man—goes out the night before and puts them up. It's called 'arrowing the route.' "

She yawned. "I can't wait till we get there. As soon as we get in, I'm going to take a long nap."

"I'm afraid you'll have to do your sleeping at night. The

circus doesn't carry any excess baggage, and everybody works, even the kids. You have jobs to do.''

"You're expecting me to work?"

"Afraid you'll break a nail?"

"I'm not nearly as spoiled as you think."

He gave her a look that said he didn't believe it, but since she was trying to avoid another argument, she ignored his baiting. "I simply meant that I don't know anything about the circus."

"You'll learn. Bob Thorpe, the guy who usually runs the ticket window, is gone for a couple of days. You can help out until he gets back, assuming you can count well enough to make change."

"In all major currencies," she replied with a touch of defiance.

"Then you've got some housekeeping duties to attend to. You can start by cleaning up that god-awful mess in the trailer. And I wouldn't object to a hot meal tonight."

"Me, either. We'll have to look for a good restaurant."

"That's not what I had in mind. If you don't already know how to cook, I'll help you get started."

She stifled her irritation and adopted a reasonable tone. "I don't think assigning me all the domestic chores is the best way to start this marriage. We should have an equal division of labor."

"Agreed. And it's time you start taking care of your half of that equal division. There'll be other jobs, too. Once we get you a costume, I'll put you in spec."

"Spec?"

"Short for spectacle. It's the parade that starts the circus, and it's compulsory."

"You're going to put me in the show?"

"Everybody except the workingmen and the candy butchers are in spec."

"What are candy butchers?"

"The circus has a language all its own; you'll pick it up after a while. The concessionaires are called butchers because, during the nineteenth century, a man who was a meat butcher quit his job to sell concessions for the old John Robinson Show. Cotton candy is floss; the concession stands are joints. The big top is always called the top, never a tent; the only tents in a circus are the cook tent and the menagerie. The lot is divided into the backyard, where we live and keep the trailers, and the front yard, or the public area. The acts have a separate language, too. You'll get the hang of it.'' He paused. ''If you're here long enough.''

She ignored his baiting. ''What's a donnicker? I remember you used that word yesterday.''

''The toilet, angel face.''

''Oh.'' They drove on for several miles while she mulled over what he'd told her. But it was what he hadn't told her that worried her the most. ''Don't you think you should give me a little more information about yourself? Real information.''

''I can't think of a single reason why.''

''Because we're married. I'll tell you anything you want to know about me.''

''I'm not interested.''

That hurt her feelings, but once again she didn't make an issue of it. ''Whether we like it or not, we took vows yesterday. I think the question we both need to ask is, are we going to work at making something of this marriage?''

He whipped his head around, and she had never seen a man look more appalled. ''This isn't a marriage, Daisy.''

''I beg your pardon?''

''It's not a marriage, so just get that idea out of your head right now.''

''What are you talking about? Of course it's a marriage.''

''It's not. It's a . . . a circumstance.''

''A circumstance?''

''That's right.''

''I see.''

''Good.''

His stubbornness infuriated her. ''Well, since this is the only circumstance I'm involved in at the moment, I intend to work at it, whether you do or not.''

"I don't."

"Alex, we took vows. Sacred vows."

"They were meaningless, and you know it. I told you from the beginning how this was going to be. I don't respect you—I don't even like you very much—and I sure as hell don't have any intention of playing the bridegroom."

"Fine. I don't like you, either!"

"Then we understand each other."

"How could I like someone who let himself be bought? But that doesn't mean I intend to run away from my responsibilities."

"I'm glad to hear it." His gaze, slow and deliberate, slid down over her. "I'll make sure that not all of your responsibilities are unpleasant."

She could feel herself flush, and her immature reaction made her angry enough to challenge him. "If you're referring to sex, why don't you just come out and say it?"

"I'm definitely referring to sex."

"With or without your whip?" She winced as soon as the impulsive words came out of her mouth.

"Lady's choice."

His amusement was suddenly more than she could stand. She turned away and gazed out the window.

"Daisy?"

Maybe it was only wishful thinking on her part, but his voice seemed gentler. She sighed. "I don't want to talk about it."

"About sex?"

She nodded.

"We have to be realistic," he said. "We're both healthy people, and despite your various personality disorders, you're not exactly hard on the eyes."

She whirled around to give him her most withering glare, only to see one corner of his mouth tilt in something that almost certainly would have been a smile on another man. "You're not hard on the eyes, either," she said begrudgingly, "but you have a lot more personality disorders than I do."

"No, I don't."

"You certainly do."

"Like what?"

"Well, to start with—are you sure you want to hear this?"

"I wouldn't miss it for the world."

"Well, you're hardheaded, stubborn, and domineering."

"I thought you were going to say something bad."

"Those weren't compliments. And I've always found a sense of humor in a man more appealing than a lot of raw, macho sexuality."

"You'll be sure and tell me when you get to the bad part, won't you?"

She glared at him and decided not to mention the whips he kept under the bed. "You're impossible to talk to."

He adjusted the sun visor. "The point I was trying to make before you interrupted with your inventory of my personality is that neither of us is going to be able to stay celibate for the next six months."

She dropped her eyes. If only he knew that she'd stayed that way all her life.

"We'll be living in close quarters," he went on. "We're legally married, and it's only natural that we're going to get it on."

Get it on? His bluntness reminded her that none of this meant anything to him emotionally, and contrary to all logic, she'd wanted to hear something romantic. With some pique, she said, "In other words, you expect me to keep house, work for the circus, and 'get it on' with you."

He thought it over. "I guess that's about the size of it."

She turned her head and stared glumly out the window. Making a success of this "circumstance" was going to be even tougher than she'd thought.

5

As Daisy left the trailer that afternoon, she met up with a tall blond who had a chimp perched on her shoulders. She recognized her from the previous night's show as Jill, from Jill and Friends, a cute dog and chimp act. She was round-faced, with beautiful skin and hair that was a bit over-processed, something Daisy was certain she could help her with if she had the chance.

"Welcome to Quest Brothers," the woman said. "I'm Jill."

Daisy returned her friendly smile. "I'm Daisy."

"I know. Heather told me. This is Frankie."

"Hello, Frankie." Daisy nodded politely at the chimp perched on Jill's shoulders, then leaped back as he drew his lips over his teeth and screamed at her. She was already jumpy from a lack of nicotine, and the chimp's reaction further jangled her.

"Hush, Frankie." Jill patted his furry leg. "I don't know what's the matter with him. He usually likes women."

"Animals aren't too fond of me."

"You're probably afraid of them. They can always tell."

"I expect you're right. A German shepherd nipped me when I was little, and it made me leery of all animals." The German shepherd hadn't been the only one. She remembered a school visit to a London petting zoo when she was six.

She'd gone into hysterics when a goat had begun to nibble on her uniform.

A woman in baggy black shorts and an oversize T-shirt wandered up and introduced herself as Madeline. Daisy recognized her as one of the showgirls who'd ridden into the arena on an elephant. Her comfortable clothing made Daisy feel a bit overdressed. She'd wanted to look nice for her first assignment at the ticket window, so she'd selected an ivory silk blouse along with her pearl gray Donna Karan slacks instead of the discount-house jeans and T-shirts Alex had insisted on buying her before they'd pulled in today.

"Daisy is Alex's new girlfriend," Jill said.

"I heard," Madeline replied. "Lucky you. Alex is a hunk and a half."

She opened her mouth to tell the women she was Alex's wife, not his girlfriend, only to draw back as Frankie began to shriek at her.

"Quiet, Frankie." Jill handed the chimp a small apple, then regarded Daisy with the open enjoyment of someone who loved a good gossip. "This thing with you and Alex must be serious. I've never heard of him having a live-in."

"Sheba's going to have a fit when she gets back." Madeline looked as if the prospect pleased her.

Frankie stared at Daisy, making her so nervous she was having a hard time paying attention to the women. To her alarm, Jill lowered the chimp to the ground, where he clutched her leg.

Daisy took another quick step backward. "Do you have a leash for him by any chance?"

Both Jill and Madeline laughed.

"He's trained," Jill said. "He doesn't need a leash."

"Are you sure?"

"Positive. So how did you and Alex meet? Jack Daily— he's the ringmaster—said Alex didn't say anything about having a new lady friend."

"I'm a little more than a lady—are you sure about that leash?"

"Don't worry. Frankie wouldn't hurt a flea."

The chimp seemed to lose interest in her, and Daisy began to relax. "I'm not Alex's lady friend."

"I thought you were living together," Madeline said.

"We are. I'm his wife."

"His wife!" Jill let out a squeal of delight that warmed Daisy all the way to her toes. "You and Alex are married! That's wonderful."

Madeline regarded Daisy good-naturedly. "I'm going to pretend to be happy about this, even though I've been lusting after him myself for a month."

"You and half the world," Jill laughed.

"Day-zee!"

She turned to see Heather calling out to her from the far side of the yard. "Hey, Daisy!" the teenager yelled. "Alex says you're late. He's really mad at you."

Daisy was embarrassed. She didn't want these new friends to know that she and Alex weren't a love match. "He gets impatient; I guess I'd better go. It's been nice meeting both of you." With a smile, she turned away, but before she'd taken more than a few steps, something hit her between the shoulder blades.

"Ouch!" She whirled around and saw a half-eaten apple lying on the ground next to her. In the background, Frankie screamed with delight while Jill appeared embarrassed.

"Sorry," she called out. "I don't know why he's acting like this. You should be ashamed, Frankie. Daisy's our friend."

Jill's words tampered Daisy's desire to strangle the little beast. Instead, she gave both women a small wave and set off toward the office trailer. She mentally corrected herself, remembering that she was supposed to refer to this trailer as the "red wagon." Earlier, Alex had told her that's what circus offices were always called, regardless of their color.

Heather fell into step beside her. "I wanted to tell you that I shouldn't have been such a bitch yesterday. I was kind of in a bad mood."

Daisy finally felt as if she were catching a glimpse of the real person behind the ill-fitting facade. "It's all right."

"Alex is royally pissed." Daisy was surprised to hear a thread of genuine sympathy in Heather's voice. "Sheba says he's the kind of man who doesn't ever stay with one woman for long, so don't feel bad when he—you know."

"What?"

"You know. When he dumps you." She gave a wistful sigh. "It must be cool being his girlfriend even for a little while."

Daisy smiled. "I'm not his girlfriend. I'm his wife."

Heather came to a sudden stop, and her face grew ashen. "You're not!"

Daisy stopped, too, and as she saw the girl's reaction, she touched her arm in concern. "Alex and I were married yesterday morning, Heather."

She jerked away. "I don't believe you. You're lying! You're just saying that because you don't like me."

"I'm not lying."

"Alex didn't marry you. He wouldn't do that! Sheba told me he won't ever marry anybody!"

"Sometimes things change."

To Daisy's astonishment, Heather's eyes filled with tears. "You bitch! I hate you! Why didn't you tell me? I hate you for making fun of me like this!" She whirled away and ran toward the trailers.

Daisy stared after her, trying to understand the reason for Heather's hostility. Only one explanation sprang to mind. The girl must have a crush on Alex. Daisy experienced an unexpected pang of sympathy. She remembered too well what it had felt like to be a teenager with no control over the actions of the adults around her. With a sigh, she set off for the red wagon.

Despite its name, the business office was white, with a splatter of colorful stars and the Quest Brothers legend. In contrast to the cheerful exterior, the interior was dreary and cluttered. A battered steel desk sat opposite a small couch covered with stacks of paper. There were mismatched chairs, an old file cabinet, and a green gooseneck lamp with a dented shade. Alex sat behind the desk, a cellular phone in one hand, a clipboard in the other. A single glance at that stormy face told Daisy that Heather had been right about one thing. Alex was royally pissed.

He abruptly ended his conversation and stood, speaking to her in that ominously quiet voice she was growing to dread. "When I tell you to be someplace at a certain time, I want you there."

"But I'm barely half an hour late."

His voice grew even quieter. "You don't have a clue about real life, do you, Daisy? This is a job, not a hair appointment, and from now on, for every minute you're late, I'm docking five dollars from your pay."

Her face brightened. "I get paid?"

He sighed. "Of course, you get paid. That is, once you start doing some work. And don't expect to buy diamonds with the money. Circus wages are about as low as they come."

She didn't care. The idea that she would actually have some money of her own was thrilling. "Just show me what to do. And I promise, I won't be late again."

Alex took her over to the ticket window set into the side of the trailer and explained the procedure in a terse voice. It was simple, and she caught on immediately.

"I'll be checking receipts to the penny," he said, "so don't plan on borrowing any cigarette money."

"I wouldn't do that."

He didn't look convinced. "Make sure you don't leave the cash drawer unattended for even a second. This circus operates on a shoestring, and we can't afford any losses."

"Of course I won't. I'm not stupid."

She had the sinking feeling he was getting ready to argue the point, but instead he unlocked the hinged window. He stayed with her as she took care of the first few customers to make certain she had the hang of it, and when he saw that she wasn't having any trouble, he told her he was leaving.

"You're not going to the trailer are you?" she asked.

"Not until I have to get into costume. Why?"

"There are a few things I still need to do in there." She

had to get back to the trailer before he saw the mess she'd made. When she'd started to clean up, she should have left the cupboards and storage closet until last, but she'd wanted to be thorough, so she'd unloaded everything to scrub the shelves and start fresh. Now the cupboards were clean, but she hadn't had time to put anything away, and there wasn't a single surface of the trailer not covered by clothing, bedding, tools, and an alarmingly large collecting of bullwhips.

"I'm sure I can get the job finished when I'm done here," she said hastily, "so don't worry if you see some things lying around."

He nodded and left her alone.

The next few hours passed without incident. She enjoyed chatting with the people who came to buy tickets, and in several instances when the families were obviously poor, she invented wonderful reasons why they had just won free passes.

Word had spread that she was Alex's wife, and a number of the circus people made excuses to stop by the office to satisfy their curiosity. Their friendliness to a stranger warmed her. She met the men who ran the "joints," as the concessions were called, as well as a few of the clowns and several members of the Lipscomb family, who performed the equestrian act. She could tell that some of the showgirls had to work hard to hide their jealousy over the fact that she'd managed to snare Alex Markov, and she appreciated their generosity of spirit. For the first time since her arrival, she felt a sprig of hope. Maybe this would work out after all.

Perhaps the most interesting person to appear was Brady Pepper, Heather's father. He walked in wearing his costume, a white body suit cinched at the waist with a wide gold belt. Bands of gold edged the scooped neck and circled his ankles.

A showgirl named Charlene had already told her that Brady was the most attractive man in the circus next to Alex, and she found herself agreeing with them. Brady Pepper reminded her of a more rough-cut version of Sylvester Stallone, complete with muscles, a cocky walk, and a New York street accent. His tough-guy looks were appealing, although the manner in which he appraised her told her he was a dedicated womanizer. He sat down on the corner of the desk, legs splayed, a man very much at home in his body.

"So you come from circus?"

He asked the question in the aggressive, almost accusatory tone many native New Yorkers seemed to adopt for even the most mundane of inquiries, and it took her a moment to figure out what he meant.

"Me? Oh, no. My family hasn't been at all involved with the circus."

"That'll make it tough on you around here. At Quest Brothers, you don't really count unless you can trace your bloodline back at least three generations. Just ask Sheba."

"Sheba?"

"She owns the circus. Bathsheba Cardoza Quest. She used to be one of the most famous flyers in the world. Trapeze," he said, when he saw her confused expression. "Now she's training the Tolea brothers, who are flying for us. They're Rumanians. She also choreographs some of the other acts, supervises costumes, that sort of thing."

"Since it's her circus, why doesn't she manage it instead of Alex?"

"It's a man's job. The manager has to deal with drunks, knife fights, heavy equipment. Sheba doesn't like that kind of thing."

"I haven't met her yet."

"That's because she took off for a few days. She does that sometimes when the pickings aren't good enough around here."

It must have been obvious she didn't understand what he meant, because he went on to explain. "Sheba likes men. She doesn't stay with any of them for long, though. She's what you call a snob. No man counts in her book if he's not from an old circus family."

The impression she'd had of the circus owner as an elderly widow faded, and the way his mouth tightened made Daisy wonder if Sheba Quest was more to him than a boss.

"Me, my old man was a Brooklyn butcher. I hooked up

with a traveling circus the day I graduated high school, and I never looked back." He regarded her almost angrily, as if he expected her to argue with him. "My kids got circus blood though, through my wife."

"I don't believe I've met her."

"Cassie died two years ago, but we're divorced twelve years, which means I'm not exactly in mourning. She hated the circus, even though she grew up with it, so she moved to Wichita and got her real estate license, but I liked performing and stayed with it."

So she and Heather had both lost their mothers. She found herself wanting to know more. "I understand you have children."

"Heather was raised in Wichita with her mother, but Cassie had trouble handling the boys, so they started to travel with me when they were youngsters. I put together an act with them, and we've been doing it ever since. Matt and Rob are twenty and twenty-one now. They're hell-raisers, too, but what can you expect with me as their old man?"

Daisy wasn't interested in his hell-raising sons, and she ignored the unmistakable note of pride in his voice. "Then Heather's just recently come to live with you?"

"Last month, but she used to stay with me a couple of weeks every season. Still, it's not the same as having her around full-time."

His dark frown told her the situation wasn't working out as he'd planned, and she had enough difficulties with her own father to feel another pang for Heather. No wonder she was sneaking cigarettes and getting crushes on older men. While Brady Pepper was undeniably attractive, he didn't strike her as the most patient of fathers.

"I've met Heather. She seems quite sensitive."

"Too sensitive. This is a hard life, and she's too soft for it." Abruptly, he got up. "I'd better get out of here before the crowd starts leaving. Nice meeting you, Daisy."

"You, too."

As he reached the door, he once again gave her the assessing look of a man who enjoys women. "Alex is a lucky guy."

She smiled politely and wished Alex felt that way.

Only after the second show was well under way could she close the ticket window and watch Alex's act. She hoped that seeing it again would dilute the impact of last night, but his skill seemed even more impressive. Where had he learned how to do such things?

It wasn't until the show had ended that she remembered the mess she had left behind in the trailer. She hurried back and had just opened the door when Jill came up to her with a conspiratorial smile on her face. Frankie was once again perched on her shoulders, and at the sight of Daisy, he immediately began to shriek and cover his eyes.

"Hush, you stinker. Come on, Daisy, I have something to show you."

Daisy hastily closed the trailer door before her new acquaintance could see the mess inside and discover what a terrible housekeeper she was. Jill took her arm and began leading her along the line of trailers. Off to her left, she could see Jack Daily, the ringmaster, talking with Alex as the workmen began stacking the bleachers.

"Ouch!" Daisy gave a shriek as something yanked hard on a lock of her hair.

Frankie cackled.

"Naughty boy," Jill cooed, as Daisy leaped out of paw reach. "Ignore him. Once he discovers he can't get to you, he'll leave you alone."

Daisy decided not to voice her doubts about the probability of that happening.

They rounded the end trailer, and she gasped with surprise when she saw the performers, still in costume, surrounding a card table holding a rectangular sheet cake with a bride and groom in the center. Madeline, the showgirl she'd met earlier, stood nearest the cake, along with Brady Pepper and his sons, the youngest Lipscomb boy, several of the clowns, and many others she'd met earlier. Only Heather remained off to the side.

Smiling widely, Jack Daily drew Alex forward while Madeline lifted her hands like a choir director. "All right everybody. *Congratulations to you! Congratulations to you!*"

As the group sang, Daisy's eyes grew misty. These people barely knew her, but they were extending the hand of friendship. After the coldness of the wedding ceremony, the intimacy of this moment touched her. In this gathering of Alex's friends, she felt as if she were attending a real celebration, an acknowledgment that something intensely personal had happened, something that wasn't a punishment meted out by her father but a cause for happiness.

"Thank you," she whispered when the singing came to an end. She fought back tears. "Thank you all so much."

She turned to Alex, and her happiness evaporated as she saw his face, rigid with displeasure.

The crowd gradually grew silent. They took in his reaction and knew something was wrong. *Please don't do this,* she thought. *I want these people to be my friends. Please pretend to be happy.*

A few of the women looked at each other out of the corners of their eyes. The assumption that Alex was a happy bridegroom rapidly faded, and she watched several sets of eyes drop to her waistline to see if she was pregnant.

She forced herself to speak. "I don't know when I've had a nicer surprise. Do you, Alex?"

There was a long silence before he gave a terse shake of his head.

She lifted her chin and fixed a smile on her face. "The cake looks delicious. I'll bet everyone would like a piece." She gazed directly into Alex's eyes, beseeching him. "Let's cut it together."

The silence seemed to drag on forever. "My hands are dirty. You go ahead."

Cheeks burning with embarrassment, she stepped behind the card table, picked up the knife, and began cutting the cake into squares. As the silence grew more pronounced, she tried to pretend nothing was wrong. "I can't believe you put all this together so quickly. How on earth did you manage it?''

Madeline shuffled uncomfortably. ''It—uh—wasn't hard.''

''Well, I'm impressed.'' Cheeks aching with the effort of smiling, Daisy extracted the first piece, set it on a paper plate, and handed it to Alex.

He took it from her without a word.

The silence grew more deafening. Finally, Jill broke in, her eyes darting nervously between the bride and groom. ''I'm sorry it's chocolate. We did this on short notice, and the bakery was out of white cake.''

Daisy regarded her with gratitude for trying to ease the awkwardness. ''Chocolate's my favorite.''

Alex set his paper plate down on the table so abruptly the untouched piece of cake flipped off and landed icing side down. ''Excuse me. I have to get back to work. Thank you all.''

Daisy's hand trembled on the plate she was passing to Madeline. Someone snickered. Daisy lifted her head and saw that it was Heather.

The teenager shot her a triumphant smirk and ran after Alex. ''Do you need some help?''

''Sure, sweetheart.'' His voice, warm and full of affection, carried over the night air. ''We're having some trouble with the winch on the spool truck. You can help me check it out.''

Daisy blinked her eyes hard. She was an easy crier, but if she cried now, she'd never be able to face these people again. ''Let me get you some cake.'' She pushed a piece toward a man with shaggy blond hair and aging California surfer looks. She remembered he'd introduced himself as Neeco Martin, the elephant trainer, when he'd stopped by the red wagon.

He took it without a word and turned his back on her to say something to one of the clowns. Madeline stepped forward to help Daisy, apparently deciding it was best to get the whole thing over with as soon as possible. The performers picked up their cake and, one by one, drifted away.

Before long, only Jill was left. "I'm sorry, Daisy. I thought this was a good idea, but I should have known Alex wouldn't like it. He's very private."

So private he hadn't bothered to mention to any of these people that he'd gotten married.

Daisy forced another stiff smile. "Marriage is an adjustment for anybody."

Jill picked up the remains of the cake on its cardboard tray and pushed it into Daisy's hands. "Here. Why don't you take this?"

Daisy could feel the bile rise in her throat as she accepted the cake, even though she didn't ever want to see it again. "Gracious, it's getting late, and I have a million things to do before bedtime."

She fled.

For the next few hours while the big top was being packed up for its move to the next town, she dragged herself through the motions of putting everything back in the cupboards and storage closet. She was overcome with a sense of despair and so weary with exhaustion she could barely hold her head up, but she kept working.

Dirt streaked her expensive slacks, and her blouse stuck to her skin, but she didn't care. She had wanted these people to be her friends, but that would never happen now that they knew how little regard Alex had for her. And how little regard he had for their marriage. The cake ceremony had been a small sacrament, and he had treated it with contempt.

Alex entered the trailer shortly after midnight. The place still looked as bad as it had when she'd first arrived. Although she'd finally gotten everything put away, she hadn't had either the time or the energy to clean anything other than the cupboards. Dirty dishes were piled in the sink, and the same crusty pan sat on the stove.

He slammed his hands on his hips and surveyed the messy counters, the dusty table top, and the crumbling remains of their wedding cake.

"I thought you were going to get this place cleaned up. It's still filthy."

She clenched her jaw. "The cupboards are clean."

"Who cares about the cupboards? Can't you do anything right?"

She didn't think. She'd worked for hours, her marriage was a mockery, and she'd been publicly humiliated by a man who'd sworn before God to cherish her. With one sweep of her arm, she picked up the decimated wedding cake and flung it at him.

"You jerk!"

His hands automatically shot up to ward it off, but he wasn't quick enough. The cake caught him in the shoulder and erupted.

She watched the wreckage with a curious detachment. Bits of cake and icing flew everywhere. White frosting splattered his hair and eyebrows, even his eyelashes. Chocolate lumps clung to his jaw, then dropped onto the shoulder of his T-shirt. Her detachment came to an abrupt end as she watched him turn red.

He was going to kill her.

He reached up to clear his eyes at the same time that he moved toward her. She sidestepped and, taking advantage of his temporary blindness, ran out the door.

She glanced frantically around, searching for a place to hide. The big top was down, the smaller tents had disappeared, most of the trucks had pulled out. She ran across a stretch of dry weeds and shot into a narrow space between two of the vans. Her heart slammed against her ribs with sickening dread. What had she done?

She jumped as she heard a man's voice and slipped deeper into the shadows only to bump up against something solid. Without looking to see what it was, she leaned back and tried to catch her breath. How long would it take him to find her? And what would he do then?

A growling sound came from just behind her ear.

The hairs on the back of her neck stood, and an icy trickle

slithered down her spine. She whirled around. And stared into a pair of pale golden eyes.

Her body grew paralyzed. She knew what the beast was. She understood she was looking at a tiger. But she couldn't absorb the reality of it.

The animal was so close she felt its breath on her face. It bared its teeth, stiletto sharp and lethal. She smelled its scent, heard its low menacing growl grow in volume, escalating into a vicious barking roar. Her paralysis ended as the animal sprang for the iron bars that separated the two of them, and she leaped backward.

Her spine slammed up against something very solid and very human, but she couldn't tear her eyes away from the tiger. A terrible ringing sounded in her head. At that moment, the beast seemed to be the manifestation of all that was evil, and she felt as if every bit of that malevolence was directed at her. Somehow, on this feral South Carolina night she had met her destiny.

She spun around, unable to bear the force of those golden eyes any longer. As she turned into the solid warmth behind her, she knew she'd found sanctuary.

Then she felt the squish of frosting beneath her cheek. The fear, the exhaustion, the life-shattering events of the past two days overwhelmed her, and she whimpered.

His hand, surprisingly gentle, tilted up her chin. She gazed into another set of pale, golden eyes so like that tiger's that she felt as if she had journeyed from one beast to another.

"Sinjun can't hurt you, Daisy. He's in a cage."

"It doesn't matter!" Hysteria threatened her. Didn't he realize that a cage couldn't protect her from what she'd seen in the tiger's eyes?

But he didn't understand and she could never explain her fleeting sense of having come face-to-face with her own fate. She drew away from him. "I'm sorry. You're right. I'm being foolish."

"It's not the first time," he said grimly.

She gazed up at him. Even speckled with cake and frosting, he looked fiercely magnificent and utterly terrifying. Just like the tiger. She found herself fearing him in a new way, one she didn't entirely understand except to know that it had a dimension that went beyond the threat of the physical. It was more elusive than that. Somehow she feared he would damage her soul.

She had reached the limits of her endurance. There had been too many changes, too much conflict, and she had no more fight left. Her weariness reached all the way to the marrow of her bones, and she could barely find the strength to speak.

"I suppose you're going to threaten me with something terrible now."

"Don't you think you deserve it? Children throw things, not adults."

"You're right, of course." She shoved a shaky hand through her hair. "What's it going to be, Alex? Humiliation? I've already had a big dose of that tonight. How about contempt? Lots of that, too. Dislike? No, that won't work; I've gotten numb to dislike." She paused, her voice faltering. "I'm afraid you'll have to come up with something completely different."

As Alex gazed down at her, she looked so unhappy that something inside him loosened. He knew she was afraid of him—he'd made sure of it—and he still couldn't believe she'd found the nerve to throw that cake. Poor little feather head. She hadn't yet figured out that snapping those baby-cake eyes at him and going after him with those kitten claws wouldn't do her a bit of good.

He felt her shiver beneath his hands. Her claws were sheathed now, and her eyes showed only despair. Did she know she wore every one of her feelings on her face?

He wondered how many men she'd had. She probably didn't even know. Despite that open-eyed innocence, she was a natural pleasure seeker. She was also a scatterbrain, and he could well imagine her ending up in more than one playboy's bed with only the vaguest idea how she'd gotten there.

At least that was one thing she'd be good for. As he watched her, he had to fight the sudden urge to pick her up and carry her back to the trailer, where he would lay her on his bed and satisfy every one of the questions that had begun to nag at him. How would those flyaway curls feel spread out like dark ribbons against his pillow? He wanted to gaze at her naked in the rumpled sheets, see the paleness of her flesh against his darker skin, test the weight of her breasts in his hands. He wanted to smell her and feel her and touch her.

Just yesterday at the wedding ceremony, he'd told himself she wasn't the kind of woman he'd choose as a sexual companion, but that was before he'd glimpsed her round bottom peeking out from under the bottom of his T-shirt as he woke her up. That was before he'd watched her in his truck, crossing and uncrossing those sweet legs of hers, dangling that silly little sandal from her toe. She had pretty feet, small and well-shaped with a high, delicate arch and nails painted the same red as the gown on a Signorelli madonna.

He didn't like the fact that other men knew more about her sexual appetites than he did. But he also knew it was too soon. He couldn't touch her until he was sure she understood the way things were going to be between them. And by that time, there was a very good chance she would have packed up her suitcase and left.

He took her arm and steered her toward the trailer. For a moment she resisted, and then she gave in. "I'm really starting to hate you," she said dully. "You know that, don't you?"

He was surprised that her words hurt, especially since this was exactly the way he wanted it. She wasn't cut out for such a hard life, and he had no desire to torture her by drawing this out endlessly. Let her realize right now that she couldn't cut it here.

"That's probably for the best."

"Up until this very moment, I've never hated any other human being. Not even Amelia or my father, and both of them have given me plenty of cause. But you don't care how I feel about you, do you?"

"No."

"I don't think I've ever met anyone so cold."

"I'm sure you haven't." *Cold, Alex. You're so cold.* He'd heard it from women before. Good women, with kind hearts. Competent, intelligent women who'd deserved something better than a man whose emotional makeup had been deformed long before they'd met him.

When he was younger, he'd thought that a family of his own might heal that lonesome, wounded place inside him. But all he'd done in his quest for a lasting human connection was hurt those good-hearted women and prove to himself that some people's capacity to love was stolen from them before it ever had a chance to develop.

They had arrived at the trailer. He reached around her to open the door, then followed her inside. "I'm going to take a shower. I'll help you clean up when I get out."

She stopped him before he reached the bathroom door. "Couldn't you have pretended to be just a little bit happy tonight?"

"I am what I am, Daisy. I don't play games with anyone. Ever."

"They were trying to do something nice. Would it have hurt you so much to go along with it?"

How could he explain it to her so she'd understand? "You grew up soft, Daisy, but I grew up rough. Rougher than you can imagine. When you grow up like I did, you learn that you have to find something to hold on to that'll always be there for you, something that keeps you from turning into an animal. For me, it was my pride. I don't give that up. Not ever."

"You can't build your life around something like that. Pride isn't as important as a lot of other things."

"Like what?"

"Like . . ." She hesitated, as if she knew he wouldn't like whatever she was about to say. "Like caring and compassion. Like love."

He felt old and tired. "Love doesn't exist for me."

"It exists for everyone."

"Not for me. Don't try to romanticize me, Daisy. It'd only

be a waste of time. I've learned to live by my own code. I try to be honest, and I try to be fair. That's the only reason I'm overlooking your stunt with the cake. I know this is a hard adjustment for you, and I guess you're doing the best you can. But don't confuse fairness with sentiment. I'm not sentimental. All those soft emotions might work for other people, but they don't work for me."

"I don't like this," she whispered. "I don't like any of it."

As he spoke, he couldn't remember ever hearing his own voice sound so sad. "You've fallen in with the devil, sweetheart. The sooner you accept that, the better off you'll be."

He went into the bathroom, shut the door, and closed his eyes, trying to block out the play of emotions he'd just witnessed on her face. He'd seen it all: wariness, an almost childlike innocence, and a dreadful kind of hope that maybe he wasn't really as bad as he seemed.

Poor little feather head.

6

"**G**o away."

"Last warning, angel face. We're pulling out in three minutes."

She squeezed her eyes open just far enough to focus on the clock by the couch and realize it was five in the morning. She didn't go anywhere at five in the morning, so she snuggled deeper into her pillow, and moments later, she drifted back to sleep. The next thing she knew, he was picking her up.

"Stop it!" she croaked. "What are you doing?"

Without a word, he carried her outside into the chilly morning air, tossed her into the cab of the truck, and slammed the door. The chill of the vinyl upholstery against her bare legs brought her instantly awake and reminded her that she wore only his gray T-shirt and a pair of ice blue bikini underpants. He climbed in the other side, and moments later, they pulled away from the abandoned lot.

"How could you do this? It's only five o'clock! Nobody gets up this early!"

"We do. We're moving into North Carolina today."

He looked disgustingly awake. He˙ was clean-shaven, dressed in a pair of jeans and a wine red knit shirt. His eyes trickled down to her bare legs. "Next time maybe you'll get up when I tell you."

"I'm not dressed! You have to let me get my clothes. And I need makeup. My hair—I have to brush my teeth!"

79

He reached into his pocket and withdrew a flattened pack of Dentyne.

She snatched it from him, and as she took out a piece and put it in her mouth, last night's events replayed in her mind. She searched his face for some sign of remorse but saw none. She was too tired and depressed to pick another quarrel, but if she just let it go, everything would still be on his terms.

"It's going to be hard for me to fit in here after what happened last night."

"You're going to have a hard time fitting in no matter what."

"I'm your wife," she said quietly, "and you're not the only one who has pride. You publicly embarrassed me last night, and I didn't deserve it."

He said nothing, and if it hadn't been for the slight tightening at the corners of his mouth, she might have believed he hadn't heard her.

She removed the gum from her mouth and folded it in the wrapper. "Please pull off the road so I can get my things from the trailer."

"You had your chance, and you blew it."

"I wasn't awake."

"I warned you."

"You're like a robot. You don't have any human feelings at all, do you?" She tugged on the bottom of the T-shirt, which kept hitching up.

His gaze settled in her lap. "Oh, I've got human feelings. But maybe not the ones you want to hear about right now."

She busied herself trying to adjust the T-shirt. "I want my clothes."

"I woke you in plenty of time to get dressed."

"I mean it, Alex. This isn't funny. I'm practically naked."

"You don't have to tell me that."

Maybe if she'd had more sleep, she wouldn't have felt so snappish. "Am I turning you on?"

"Yep."

She hadn't expected that. She thought he'd give her one of his put-downs. Recovering from her surprise, she glared at him. "Well, that's too bad because I'm not interested. In case you haven't heard, the brain is the most important sexual organ, and my brain isn't interested in having anything to do with you."

"Your brain?"

"I do have one."

"I never said you didn't."

"Your tone inplied it. I'm not stupid, Alex. My education may have been unorthodox, but it was amazingly comprehensive."

"Your father doesn't seem to agree."

"I know. He likes telling everyone I'm badly educated because mother used to take me out of school so much. But if she was going on an interesting trip, she believed I'd benefit if I went along. Sometimes a few months would pass before she'd remember to send me back. Even then, she didn't always return me to the same school she'd taken me out of, but she still made sure I was learning."

"How did she do that?"

"She'd ask whoever she was visiting or entertaining to spend some time with me and teach me a little of what they knew."

"I thought your mother hung out with rock stars."

"I *did* learn a lot about hallucinogenics."

"I'll bet."

"But she spent time with a lot of other people, too. Princess Margaret taught me most of what I know about the history of the British royal family."

He stared at her "Are you serious?"

"Dead serious. And she wasn't the only one. I was raised around some of the most famous people in the world." Only the fact that she didn't want him to think she was bragging kept her from mentioning the rather spectacular scores she'd received on her SATs. "So I'd appreciate it if you'd stop making your little digs about my intelligence. Anytime you want to discuss Plato, I'm game."

"I've read Plato," he said, with a gratifying degree of defensiveness.

"In Greek?"

After that, they rode in silence until Daisy eventually dozed off. In her sleep, she searched for a comfortable pillow and found it on Alex's shoulder.

A stray lock of her hair flipped up in the breeze and grazed his lips. He let it play there for a while, brushing across his mouth and jaw. She smelled sweet and expensive, like wild-flowers growing in the middle of a jewelry store.

She was right about last night. He'd acted like an ass. But the whole thing had taken him by surprise, and he didn't want any kind of public celebration of something he was trying his best to minimize. If he wasn't careful, she'd get it into her head to take this marriage seriously.

He didn't think he'd ever met a woman who was so much his opposite. She'd said he was like a robot, without any human feelings at all, but she was wrong. He had feelings, all right. Just not the ones she thought were important, the ones experience had taught him he was incapable of having.

Even though he told himself to keep his eyes on the road, he couldn't resist looking down at the small, slender body snuggled so warmly against him. She'd tucked one leg under the other, displaying the soft curve of her inner thigh, and his old T-shirt had lost the battle to keep her covered. His gaze fell on the meager strip of ice blue lace that passed between her legs. As the heat gathered in his groin, he looked away, angered by his self-inflicted torture. God, she was beautiful.

She was also silly and spoiled, vain beyond belief. He'd never seen a woman who could spend so much time looking into a mirror. But despite her faults, he had to admit that she wasn't quite the selfish, self-centered socialite he'd originally thought her to be. There was a sweetness about her that was as unexpected as it was disturbing because it made her so much more vulnerable than he wanted her to be.

As Daisy came out of the truck-stop rest room where she'd managed to bum a cigarette from a female driver, she saw that Alex was flirting with another waitress. Even though he'd made it plain that he had no intention of committing himself to their marriage, the sight depressed her. As she watched him nod at something the waitress said, she realized she had a perfectly good excuse to turn her back on the vows she'd taken. Between the awful scene with the wedding cake and what he'd said afterward, he'd made himself quite clear. He had no intention of upholding his vows, so why should she?

Because she had to. Her conscience wouldn't let her escape.

She garnered her courage and, plastering a smile on her face, headed toward the orange vinyl booth. Neither the waitress nor Alex paid any attention to her as she slid into her seat. A name tag shaped like a teapot identified this particular woman as Tracy. She was overly made up but still undeniably attractive. And Alex was Mr. Charm, complete with a lazy grin and wandering eyes.

He finally pretended to notice her presence. "Back already, Sis?"

Sis!

He smiled, the glint of challenge in his eyes. "Tracy and I have been getting to know each other."

"I'm trying to talk your brother into hanging around for a while," Tracy said. "My shift ends in an hour."

Daisy knew if she didn't put a stop to this sort of thing right away, he'd think he could get away with it for the next six months. She reached over and patted the waitress's hand where she'd rested it on the edge of the table.

"You sweet, sweet girl. He's been so self-conscious around women since his medical problem was diagnosed. But I keep telling him—with the wonders of antibiotics, those pesky little sexually transmitted diseases are hardly a problem for anybody anymore."

Tracy's smile faltered. She stared at Daisy, then at Alex, and her tanned skin seemed to take on a faintly gray hue. "My boss gets mad if I talk to the customers too long. See ya." She hurried away from the table.

Alex's coffee cup clattered onto his saucer.

Daisy met his gaze dead on. "Don't mess with me, Alex. We took vows."

"I don't frigging believe this."

"You're a circumstanced man. And circumstanced men don't flirt with waitresses. Please try to remember that."

He yelled at her all the way back to the truck, throwing out words such as "immature," "grasping," and "conniving." Only after they were under way, did he finally give it a rest.

They had traveled in silence for less than a mile when she heard something that sounded very much like a chuckle, but when she looked over at him, she saw the same stern face and unsmiling mouth she'd seen from the beginning. Since she knew Alex Markov's dark Russian soul didn't possess more than a shred of a sense of humor, she decided she was mistaken.

By late afternoon, she was bleary with fatigue. Only by pressing herself to the limit had she been able to finish cleaning the trailer, shower, fix herself something to eat, and still make it to the red wagon on time to take over at the ticket window. The job would have lasted even longer if Alex hadn't cleaned up the wedding cake last night. Since she was the one who'd thrown it, his help had been unexpected.

It was Saturday, and she understood from overhearing brief snatches of conversation that the workmen were looking forward to getting their pay envelopes that night. Alex had told her that some of the workmen who handled the canvas and moved the equipment were alcoholics and drug addicts, since the circus's low wages and poor working conditions didn't attract the most stable employees. A few had been with the circus for years, simply because they didn't have anywhere else to go. Others were adventurers attracted by the romance of the circus, but they generally didn't last long.

Alex glanced up from the battered desk as she stepped into the trailer, and his mouth set in what she was beginning to believe was a perpetual scowl. "There's a discrepancy in yesterday's receipts."

She'd been exceptionally careful as she'd made change, and she was certain she hadn't made any mistakes. Coming around behind him, she gazed at the neatly printed figures. "Show me."

He pointed toward the paper lying on the desk. "I've checked the ticket numbers against the receipts, and you're short."

It took her only a moment to figure out what was wrong. "That discrepancy came from the complimentary tickets I gave out. There were only twelve or thirteen."

"Complimentary tickets?"

"The families were so poor, Alex."

"And you took it upon yourself to comp them?"

"I could hardly take their money."

"Yes, you could, Daisy. And from now on you will. In most towns the circus is sponsored by a local organization. They handle comps unless something special comes up, in which case I handle it. But you don't. Understand?"

"But—"

"Understand?"

She gave him a grudging nod.

"Good. If you think someone needs comping, you come to me, and I'll take care of it."

"All right."

He stood and frowned. "Sheba'll be back today, and she'll see that you get a costume for spec. When she's ready to fit you, I'll send someone to take over the ticket window."

"But I'm not a performer."

"This is the circus, angel face. Everybody's a performer."

Her curiosity had grown about the mysterious Sheba whose name made her husband's face cloud. "Brady said she was a famous trapeze artist."

"Sheba's the last of the Cardozas. Her family used to be to trapeze what the Wallendas are to high-wire acts."

"But she doesn't perform anymore?"

"She could. She's only thirty-nine, and she keeps herself

in top shape. But she's no longer the best, so she retired."

"She obviously takes it seriously."

"Too seriously. Stay out of her way as much as you can." He walked to the door. "Remember what I told you about the cash box. Keep your eye on it."

"I remember."

With a brusque nod, he disappeared.

She handled the ticket sales for the first performance without difficulty. Things quieted down after the show was under way, and she sat down on the trailer step to enjoy the evening breeze.

Her gaze fell on the menagerie tent, and she remembered that Sinjun, the tiger, was inside. Today, while she'd been trying to scrub the worst of the stains from the carpet, she'd thought about him, maybe because thinking about the tiger was simpler than trying to sort out her troubled feelings about Alex. She felt a disturbing urge to take another look at the ferocious animal, but only from a safe distance.

A late-model Cadillac pulled into the lot accompanied by a rooster tail of dust. An exotic-looking woman with a mane of bright auburn hair stepped out. She wore a figure-hugging chartreuse tank top tucked into a printed sarong skirt that revealed long bare legs and a pair of jeweled sandals. Big gold hoops glimmered through her tousled hair, and a set of matching bangles decorated her slender wrists.

As the woman headed toward the entrance to the big top, Daisy caught a glimpse of her face: pale skin, sharp features, full lips emphasized with crimson lipstick. She had a proprietary air about her that set her apart from a casual visitor, and Daisy decided this could only be Bathsheba Quest.

A customer approached to buy tickets to the second show. Daisy chatted with him for a few minutes and by the time he left, Sheba had disappeared. When no one was at the window, she began reading through the contents of an accordion envelope stuffed with old newspaper clippings taken from a variety of local papers.

Alex's performances with the bullwhip were mentioned in several articles dated two years ago, but not again until last month. She knew that circuses rotated their acts from one show to another, and she wondered where he'd been performing when he wasn't traveling with Quest Brothers.

As the first show ended, one of the barkers appeared, a wizened-looking old man with a large mole on his cheek. "I'm Pete. Alex told me to take over for a while. You're supposed to go back to your trailer for a costume fitting."

Daisy thanked him and made her way to the trailer. As she entered, she was startled to see Sheba Quest standing at her sink washing up the dishes from the quick snacks Alex and Daisy had grabbed that afternoon.

"You don't have to do that."

Sheba turned and shrugged. "I don't like sitting around waiting."

Daisy felt doubly chastised: first for keeping a sloppy kitchen, then for tardiness. She wouldn't add to those sins by being inhospitable. "Would you like a cup of tea? Or perhaps a soft drink."

"No." The woman picked up a dish towel and dried her hands. "I'm Sheba Quest, but I guess you already know that."

On closer inspection, Daisy saw that the circus owner wore her makeup in brighter shades than Daisy would have chosen to use herself. Not that she looked gaudy. Instead, her colorful and somewhat provocative clothing, combined with her rather flamboyant accessories, simply made it apparent that her beauty standards had been influenced by a lifetime as a performer.

"I'm Daisy Devreaux. Or rather Daisy Markov. I haven't gotten used to the change."

Some profound emotion flickered across Sheba's face, a deep revulsion combined with a hostility that was almost palpable. Instantly, Daisy knew she had found no friend in Sheba Quest.

She forced herself to remain still under Sheba's cold scrutiny. "Alex likes to eat. You hardly have anything in the refrigerator."

"I know. I'm really not very well organized." She didn't

have the courage to point out that Sheba shouldn't be snooping in her kitchen.

"He likes spaghetti and lasagna, and he loves Mexican food. But don't waste your time making him big desserts. He doesn't have much of a sweet tooth, except at breakfast."

"Thank you for telling me." Daisy felt slightly ill.

Sheba flicked her hand over the chipped counter. "This place is terrible. Alex started out with a newer trailer, but last week he got rid of it and picked up this one even though I offered to get him something better."

Daisy couldn't quite hide her dismay. Why had Alex insisted they live like this if they didn't have to? "I'm planning to fix it up," she said, although until that moment, the idea hadn't occurred to her.

"Most men want to bring their brides to someplace nice. I'm surprised Alex didn't take advantage of my offer."

"I'm sure he had his reasons."

Sheba surveyed Daisy's small figure. "You don't have any idea what you've gotten into with him, do you?"

Sheba seemed eager to prod her into a catfight, but since Daisy was fairly certain she'd come out the loser, she tilted her head toward the two costumes draped over the back of the chair. "Am I supposed to try those on?"

Sheba nodded.

Daisy picked up the top one and found that it made little more than a puddle of midnight blue spangles in her hand. "It seems awfully skimpy."

"That's the general idea. This is the circus. The audience expects to see a lot of skin."

"Does it have to be mine?"

"You're not fat. I don't see what the problem is."

"I'm not exactly a hard-body. I've never been very good about following an exercise program for more than a few minutes."

"You just have to learn some self-discipline."

"Yes, well, I've never been very good at that, either."

Sheba regarded her critically, obviously expecting Alex Markov's wife to display a little more backbone. But from having lived with her mother, Daisy knew not to engage in gamesmanship with a master player. Honesty was the only defense against experts at guile.

She went into the bathroom and removed her clothes down to her panties, but as she dressed in the scanty costume, she realized that the leg was cut so high they showed. She stripped them off and started all over.

With the costume finally in place, she looked at herself in the mirror and felt like a trollop. Two blue spangled scallops covered her breasts while a larger scallop covered her below. The body of the costume was made up of nothing more than a thin veil of tacky silver net. Sheba hadn't even included a pair of tights.

b "I don't think I can wear this," she called out through the door.

"Let's see."

She stepped out. "It's a bit too—" Her words broke off as she saw Alex standing by the sink in his Cossack costume. She wanted to run back into the bathroom, and if Sheba hadn't been standing there she would have. Why did he have to show up now when she looked like this?

"Step out so we can see you," he said.

Daisy moved forward unwillingly. Sheba walked over to stand next to him, wordlessly uniting the two of them and making Daisy the outsider.

Alex said nothing, but the way he studied her made Daisy feel as exposed as if she were entirely naked.

"Turn around." Sheba ordered.

Daisy felt like a prostitute being put on display by the madam for a favorite customer. Although the mirror in the bathroom was too small for her to observe what she looked like from the back, she had a good idea what they were seeing: two round, bare cheeks with a small scallop camouflaging the place where they met. Her skin was flushed as she once again faced them.

"We're a family show," Alex said. "I don't like it."

Sheba walked toward her and began fussing with the bodice. "I suppose you're right. She's really not big enough to fill it out properly. It's gaping.'' Daisy felt the woman's hands on her neck. "Let's see if the other one works better."

Without warning, Sheba opened the costume and pushed it down, leaving Daisy naked from the waist up. With a startled exclamation, Daisy grabbed at the puddle of spangles and net that had tangled low on her belly, but her fingers were clumsy, and it was like trying to unravel vapor. Her gaze flew to Alex.

He stood with his hips resting against the sink, ankles crossed, heels of his hands braced on the counter behind him. Daisy wordlessly pleaded with him to look away, but he didn't drop his gaze.

"God, Daisy, you're blushing like a virgin." Sheba's lips formed a thin smile. "I'm surprised anyone can spend time in bed with Alex and still remember how to blush."

The jewels flashed on his sash as he stepped forward. "That's enough, Sheba. Stop baiting her."

Sheba turned away to pick up the other costume. Alex put himself between the two women, almost as if he wanted to shield Daisy's nakedness from Sheba, which was ridiculous since he was the one she wanted to hide from.

"Let me have it." The full sleeves of his white shirt rippled as he took the red-sequined costume from Sheba, glanced at it, then handed it to Daisy. "This one looks better. See if it fits."

She snatched the costume from him and dashed into the bathroom. When she'd closed the door, she leaned against it and tried to steady her breathing, but her heart was beating and her skin burning. She'd been raised by a mother who sunbathed in the nude, and she told herself not to make such a big deal out of what had happened. But it still bothered her.

She finally managed to get into the costume, and to her relief, it had a little more to it than the other. A flame-shaped pattern of fire red sequins climbed from the crotch to the bodice, where it clung to her breasts in irregular, jagged points. The leg openings were cut nearly to the waist, giving her a giant wedgie as she eased open the door and reluctantly walked forward. At least her middle was covered.

Alex stood alone, resting his hip on the edge of the table. Daisy swallowed hard. "Where's Sheba?"

"She needed to talk to Jack. Turn around."

She bit her bottom lip and remained where she was. "The two of you were lovers, weren't you?"

"We're not now, so it doesn't have anything to do with you."

"She still appears to care about you."

"She hates my guts."

For all Alex's talk about pride, he didn't seem to have much honor, or he would never have let her father buy him, and there was something she needed to know.

"Was she married to Owen Quest when the two of you had your affair?"

"No. Now stop prying and let me see the back."

"I don't think it's prying to want to know more about you. For example, I was looking through the clipping file, and I noticed you weren't with Quest Brothers last year. Where were you?"

"What difference does it make?"

"I'd just like a little information."

"Your curiosity isn't my problem."

He was the most private person she ever met, and she would get no more out of him. "I don't like this costume. I don't like either of them. They make me look cheap."

"You'll look like a showgirl." Since she hadn't turned around as he'd asked, he walked behind her. She hated being put on display like this, and she began to move away only to feel him touch her shoulder. "Stand still." His other hand brushed her waist. "This one fits you better and won't get us closed down in the Bible Belt."

"It's too skimpy."

"Not really. The other women wear costumes this brief and they don't look nearly as good in them as you do right now."

He was standing so close that her breasts brushed against the soft fabric of his shirt as she turned to face him. A funny feeling skittered through the pit of her stomach. "Do you think I look good?"

"Are you fishing for a compliment?"

She nodded, feeling weak-kneed.

He lowered the hand that had been clasping her waist, slid it over the bottom edge of her costume, and curled his palm around her bottom. "Consider yourself complimented." His voice had a husky rasp.

Flares of heat shot through her. She drew back slightly, not because she wanted to get away, but because she wanted so very much to stay where she was.

"We really don't know each other well.

Keeping his hand in place, he dipped his head and nuzzled her neck. Her skin prickled with the whisper of his breath on her ear. "We're married. It's all right."

"We're circumstanced."

He drew back far enough for her to see the amber flecks glimmering in his eyes. "I think it's time we make our circumstance official, don't you?"

Her pulse jumped, and she couldn't have moved away from him if she'd wanted. As she gazed upward, she felt as if their surroundings had faded away until nothing was left but the two of them.

His mouth looked strangely tender for something with such hard edges. His lips parted and brushed over hers. At the same time, he pulled her close, where she felt him big and heavy against her. As his mouth settled, she experienced a moment of wonder. His lips were warm and gentle, such a contrast to the rest of him.

She parted her own because she could no more have closed herself against him than she could have flown to the moon. He drew at her bottom lip and touched the tip of her tongue with his own. The sensation sent her spiraling, and she wrapped her arms around his hips, feeling the silky material beneath her palms. She dug the heels of her hands into his buttocks.

He groaned against her mouth. "God, I want you." And then his tongue plunged inside her.

Their kiss turned into a wild animal mating. He lifted her against him and carried her backward, where he pushed her against the counter. She raised her hands to clutch at his back for balance. He stepped between her legs, and the jewels on his sash dug into the soft flesh of her inner thigh.

Her tongue caressed his. His soft groan echoed in the warm cave of her mouth. She felt his hands fumbling at the back of her neck. He moved just far enough away to peel her costume to her waist.

"You're so beautiful," he murmured, looking down at her. He lifted her breasts in his palms and brushed his thumbs over the crests, sending pleasure ricocheting through her. He began kissing her again while he teased the nipples. She clutched his arms and felt their strength through the billowy sleeves.

He abandoned her breasts and clasped the back of her thighs at the place where they met her bare bottom. It was all too much for her. The bite of the jewels into her thighs . . . the soft caress of his hands . . .

"Five minutes till spec!" A fist slammed against the door of the trailer. "Five minutes, Alex!"

She jumped like a guilty adolescent and slid away from the counter. Turning her back on him, she fumbled with her costume. She felt hot and queasy and terribly upset. How could she be so eager to give herself to a man who hardly ever said a kind word to her, a man who didn't believe in honoring vows?

She rushed toward the bathroom only to have him stop her before she got there with the soft, husky sound of his voice.

"Don't bother making up the couch tonight, angel face. You're sleeping with me."

7

While Sheba checked the cash drawer, then went through a stack of papers in the office, Daisy sold tickets to latecomers for the second show. She performed the motions mechanically, smiling automatically at the customers but so rattled by the passionate kiss she had shared with Alex that she barely heard what anyone was saying. Her body grew warm at the memory, but at the same time she felt ashamed. She should never have given herself to him with so much abandon when he regarded their marriage with so little respect.

The music for spec came to an end, and Sheba left the red wagon without speaking. Daisy closed the ticket window and was straightening the cash drawer when Heather appeared. She wore her gold-spangled costume, and her makeup looked harsh on such a young face. Five red rings dangled from her small, thin wrist like giant bracelets, and Daisy wondered if she went anywhere without them.

"Have you seen Sheba?"

"She left a few minutes ago."

Heather glanced around as if to make certain they were alone. "You got a cigarette?"

"I had my last one this morning. It's a disgusting habit, not to mention expensive, and I'm making myself quit. You'll regret it if you get hooked, Heather."

"I'm not hooked. It's just something to do." Heather began idly walking around the office, touching the desk, the top of the file cabinet, flicking through a calendar on the wall.

"Does your father know you smoke?"

"I suppose you're going to tell him."

"I didn't say that."

"Well, go ahead," she replied belligerently. "He's probably going to send me back to my Aunt Terry's anyway."

"Is that where you were staying?"

"Yeah. She's already got four kids, and the only reason she's willing to take me is because Dad pays her and she needs the money. Plus, she gets a free baby-sitter. My mom didn't used to be able to stand her." Her expression grew bitter. "He can't wait to get rid of me."

"I'm sure that's not true."

"You don't know, do you? He only likes my brothers. Sheba says it's not my fault because he doesn't know how to relate to a woman he can't have sex with, but she's just trying to make me feel better. I keep thinking if I could juggle better, he might let me stay."

Now Daisy understood why Heather always carried the rings around. She was trying to earn her father's affection with her juggling. Daisy knew all about trying to please a disapproving father, and her heart went out to this young girl with her fairy-sprite face and gutter mouth. "Have you tried to talk to him? Maybe he doesn't understand how strongly you feel about not going back to your aunt's."

She pulled on her tough-girl face. "Like he's going to care. And look who's giving advice. Everybody's talking about you. How Alex only married you because you're pregnant."

"That's not true." The cellular phone buzzed before Daisy could say more, and she went over to the desk to answer it. "Quest Brothers Circus."

"Alex Markov, please," a male voice on the other end replied.

"I'm sorry, but he's not here at the moment."

"Will you tell him Jacob Solomon called? He has my number. Oh, and Dr. Theobald is trying to get in touch with him."

"I'll let him know." As Daisy hung up the phone and wrote down the message for Alex, she wondered who these people were. There was so much about him she didn't understand and he seemed unwilling to reveal.

She realized Heather had left some time during the phone call. With a sigh, she locked up the cash drawer, turned off the lights, and left the trailer.

The workmen had already taken down the menagerie tent, and once again she found herself thinking about the tiger. She wandered over toward the place where the tent had been, feeling almost as if she had no control over her destination.

The cage sat on a small flatbed about three feet above the ground. A rim of light cast by the floodlights threw harsh shadows over the animal inside. Daisy's heart pounded as she approached, and her steps slowed. Sinjun rose and turned toward her.

She froze as she received the impact of those golden eyes. His gaze was hypnotic, both direct and unblinking. A chill slithered along her spine, and she felt herself dissolving in those golden tiger eyes.

Destiny.

The word trailed through her mind, almost as if she hadn't put it there herself, almost as if it had come from the tiger.

Destiny.

She wasn't aware that she had walked closer until she smelled the tiger's musky scent, a smell that should have been unpleasant but somehow wasn't. She came to a stop less than four feet from the iron bars and stood without moving. The seconds ticked away, growing into minutes. She lost all sense of time.

Destiny. The word rattled through her head.

The tiger was a huge male animal, with enormous paws and a bib of white beneath its throat. She began to tremble as he twisted his ears so that the oval-shaped white markings on their backs showed, and somehow she knew it wasn't a gesture of friendship. His whiskers fanned. He bared his teeth. Perspiration trickled between her breasts as an awful hissing roar erupted from his throat, a demon's sound that belonged in a horror movie.

She couldn't lower her eyes, even though she somehow knew that was what he wanted. His unblinking stare bore a challenge; *she* was to look away first. She wanted to look away—she had no desire to defy a tiger—but she was paralyzed.

The bars seemed to evaporate between them so that she no longer had any protection from him. His sharp claws could rip open her throat with one swipe of his paw. Even so, she couldn't move. She stared at him and felt as if a window into her soul had opened.

Time ticked by. Minutes. Hours. Years.

With eyes that no longer seemed to belong to her, she saw all her weaknesses and inadequacies, the fears that kept her prisoner. She saw herself floating through her life of privilege, swept along by wills stronger than her own, afraid to confront, trying to please everyone except herself. The tiger's eyes revealed everything she wanted to keep concealed.

And then he blinked.

The tiger.

Not her.

With a sense of astonishment, she watched the white markings on his ears disappear. He stretched his great body back down on the floor of the cage, where he regarded her with deadly gravity and delivered his own verdict.

You're soft and cowardly.

She saw truth in the tiger's eyes, and her moment of victory for having won their staring contest vanished, leaving her legs weak and rubbery. She lowered herself into the weeds, where she hugged her knees and sat silently watching, not quite so frightened, merely drained.

She heard the closing music from the final act and was dimly aware of the voices of the workmen as they moved around the lot, along with the noises of the concessions being packed away. She'd had so little sleep the night before that she grew drowsy. Her lids sagged but didn't close. She propped her cheek on her knee and continued to watch the tiger through half-shut eyes as he watched her in return.

They were alone in the world, two lost souls. She felt every thud of his heartbeat. His breath seemed to fill her lungs, and gradually her fear evaporated. Instead, she experienced a deep sense of peace. Her soul melded with his— they became one—and at that moment she would have been happy to be his food and sustenance because no barrier existed between them.

And then—more rapidly than she could have imagined— her peace shattered, and she was hit by such an explosion of pain, she groaned aloud. In the farthest reaches of her mind, she understood the pain was coming from the tiger and not herself, but that made it no less acute.

Sweet Jesus. She clutched her stomach and doubled over. What was happening to her? *Sweet Jesus, make it stop!* It was too much to bear.

She slumped forward. Her cheek pressed into the dirt. She knew she was going to die.

As abruptly as the pain had come, it disappeared. She gasped for air. Trembling, she pushed herself to her knees.

The tiger eyes burned with quiet rage.

Now you know how a captive feels.

Alex was furious. He stalked through the lot with Sheba Quest at his side and a whip coiled in his fist. It was Saturday night, payday for the workers, and some of them were already drunk, so he carried his bullwhip as a deterrent. At the moment, however, it wasn't the workers who were giving him difficulty.

"Nobody steals from me!" Sheba declared, "and Daisy's not going to get away with this just because she's your wife." The low, clipped tones of the circus owner's voice underscored her anger. Her red hair blazed behind her, and her eyes shot sparks.

Alex's deathbed promise to Owen had placed him in a constant struggle of wills with his widow. Sheba Quest was his employer, and she was determined to push him as far as she could, while he was equally determined to honor Owen's wishes. So far, it had been a series of compromises satisfying neither one of them, and open warfare had been inevitable.

"You don't have any proof that Daisy took the money."

Even as he spoke, he was angry with himself for trying to defend her. There was no other suspect. He wouldn't have put it past her to take *his* money—she seemed to regard that as her due—but he hadn't expected her to steal from the circus. It just showed that he was still capable of letting his sex drive interfere with his good judgment.

"Get real," she snapped. "I checked the cash drawer after she came back on duty. Face it, Alex. Your bride is a thief."

"I'm not making any accusations until I've had a chance to talk to her," he said stubbornly.

"The money's missing, isn't it? And Daisy was in charge. If she didn't steal it, why has she disappeared?"

"I'm going to find her and ask."

"I want her arrested, Alex. She stole from me, and as soon as you find her, I'm calling the police."

He stopped in midstride. "We don't ever call the police. You know that as well as anyone. If she's guilty, I'll take care of her just like I'd take care of anybody else around here who breaks the law."

"The last person you 'took care of' was that driver who was selling dope to the workers. There wasn't a whole lot left of him when you were done. Is that what you're going to do to Daisy?"

"Lay off."

"You're a real shit, you know that? You're not going to protect your dopey little bimbo from this. I want every cent back, and then I want her punished. If you don't do it to my satisfaction, I'll make sure the law does."

"I said I'd take care of it."

"See that you do."

Sheba was the toughest woman he knew, and now he looked her straight in the eye. "Daisy doesn't have anything to do with what happened between the two of us. I don't want you trying to get to me through her."

He saw a flash of the vulnerability she so rarely displayed, but it was gone as quickly as it had appeared. "I hate to deflate that ego of yours, but you seem to have an exaggerated idea of your importance to me."

She walked away, and as he watched her go, he knew she was lying.

The two of them shared a long, complicated history that went back to the summer he had just turned sixteen, when he was spending his school vacation traveling with Quest Brothers and listening to Owen's views on manhood. The Flying Cardozas had also been with the show that summer, and Alex was immediately besotted with the twenty-one-year-old queen of the center ring.

At night he fell asleep dreaming of her beauty, her grace, and her breasts. The girls he'd known until then seemed like children in comparison to the luscious and unattainable Sheba Cardoza. In addition to lusting after her, he felt a kinship with her in her drive for perfection and relentless push to be the best. In Sheba, he saw a will that matched his own.

She also had an egotistical streak, nurtured by her father, that Alex had never possessed. Sam Cardoza had raised Sheba to believe she was better than everyone else. But she also had a softer, maternal side, and although she was young, she served as a mother hen to the other members of the troupe, clucking over them when they misbehaved, filling their stomachs with her home-cooked spaghetti dinners, and counseling them on their love lives.

Even at the age of twenty-one, she liked playing the grand matriarch, and it wasn't long before she brought Alex into the clan, taking pity on the parentless sixteen-year-old who watched her with young, hot eyes. She made certain Alex ate well and badgered Owen to keep him away from the rowdier workmen, ignoring the fact that Alex had spent too many years with circuses to be sheltered now.

Alex wanted more than maternal fussing from her, but a handsome Mexican flyer named Carlos Méndez stood in his way. Like Sheba, Carlos was the last of an old circus family, and he'd been hired by Sheba's father as the new catcher.

But Sam Cardoza had more than the good of the act in mind. While Carlos Mendez's circus ancestry wasn't as impressive as the Cardozas', in Sam's eyes it was acceptable enough to make him a fitting sire for the next generation of Cardoza flyers, and Sheba pleased her father by falling in love with Carlos.

Jealousy ate at Alex. His own circus lineage was far more impressive than Méndez's, but Sheba saw him only as a scrawny teenager who had a way with horses and a talent for the bullwhip. She chattered about her plans to marry the dashing Mexican and confided that Sam had already made Carlos agree to give their children the Cardoza name.

As summer came to an end and Alex prepared to return to school, the Cardozas received word that they had been chosen to fly with Ringling the next season. Carlos strutted the lot like a cocky rooster, but he had more arrogance than brains, and on the day Alex was to leave, Sheba arrived at Carlos's trailer unexpectedly and caught him undressing one of the showgirls.

Alex would never forget that night. He came out of the top and found Sheba waiting for him. She was dry-eyed and eerily calm.

"Come."

He didn't think about disobeying her. She drew him away from the others and led him to the edge of the lot where they slipped into a small, unlit space between two of the concession wagons. His heart began to pound at her clandestine manner and the dark sense of purpose that was as forbidden as the musky smell of her perfume.

She looked deeply into his eyes. Without a word spoken between them, she opened her blouse and let it fall low on her arms. Her full breasts with their large, dark tips gleamed in a stray patch of moonlight that slivered between the wagons. She lifted his hands and put them to her.

A hundred times he had imagined something like this, but his fantasies didn't prepare him for the reality of holding her breasts and feeling those large nipples beneath his fingers.

"Kiss them," she said.

He groaned and dropped his head, overwhelmed that this magnificent woman would give him such an offering. Although he wasn't a virgin, his sexual experience was limited, and he'd never known such fierce excitement. His erection pulsated against his tight pants. At the same time, he was filled with awe and a wrenching gratitude for the gift she was giving him.

Her fingers worked his zipper. He breathed hard against her moist flesh. She reached inside his pants. He felt her touch him and lost control. With a low groan, he exploded.

He shuddered with passion and humiliation. She pressed her lips to his mouth and offered him a long, deep kiss. Then she lifted her head and, with her bare breasts still moist from his mouth, turned toward the opening at the end of the concession wagons.

That was when Alex saw Carlos standing there watching them.

The hard, triumphant glint in Sheba's eyes told Alex she'd known he was there all along, and he was gripped by a sense of betrayal so devastating he couldn't breathe. She didn't care for him at all. She'd merely used him to exact her revenge.

As she gazed at her former lover, she seemed to have forgotten Alex existed. "I'm hiring a new catcher," she said coldly. "You're fired."

"You can't fire me," the catcher sputtered. "I'm a Méndez."

"You're nothing. Even this boy is more of a man than you."

She turned away and once again sealed her lips over Alex's young mouth. Through his lust, through the haze of betrayal, he felt a chilling spark of admiration that frightened him more than his uncle's whip ever had. He understood her ruthless exhibition of pride. Like himself, Sheba would never let anyone or anything threaten who she was, no matter how dear the cost. Even as he hated her for using him as her pawn, he respected her.

Sheba spent the next sixteen years as a featured performer

for the world's great circuses, and she didn't travel with Quest Brothers again until her career had begun to fade. By that time, her father had died, and Sheba, still unmarried and childless, had become the last Cardoza.

Owen welcomed her back to Quest Brothers and built his show around her. In his infrequent telephone conversations with Alex, he revealed just enough for Alex to realize the old man had become obsessed with her.

Alex and Sheba met again two summers ago, and it was immediately apparent that the balance of power between them had shifted. At thirty-two, he had entered the prime of his manhood and had nothing left to prove, while her best years as a performer were behind her. He knew his worth and had long ago put the self-doubt of adolescence behind him. She was beautiful, restless, and for reasons he did not immediately understand, still unmarried and childless.

The fire burned hot between them, but this time she was the pursuer. He didn't want to hurt Owen, so at first he ignored her sexual aggression. It soon became apparent, however, that the circus owner was resigned to their affair, and in his peculiar way was offended when Alex continued to spurn the woman he valued above all others.

Alex eventually let her into his bed. She was lithe and supple, earthy and passionate, and he'd never enjoyed sex more. He liked her toughness, as well as the fact that she no longer had the power to hurt him. But although he cared about her, he didn't love her.

"Why haven't you gotten married?" he asked one night as he sat down at the table in her luxurious trailer, where she was preparing to feed him for the second time that day. Both of them wore bathrobes, his plain, hers an exotic paisley pattern that made the auburn lights in her hair seem even richer. "I thought you were hell-bent to have kids. I know your old man expected it."

She set a plate of lasagna in front of him, then went back to the stove to get her own. But she didn't immediately return. Instead, she stood where she was and stared down at the food she'd prepared. "I guess I wanted too much. You know as well as I do that there are some things you can't teach. The best flyers are born with natural ability, so any man I marry has to come from good family. I won't marry down, but I also want to love him. Love and lineage. It's a tough combination.''

She brought her plate over to the table. ''My father used to say it was better for the Cardozas to die out than for him to have grandchildren without good blood.'' She sat down and picked up her fork. ''Well, I have my own saying. Better for the Cardozas to die out than for me to marry some weak-hearted sonovabitch I can't respect.''

''Good for you.''

She picked up her fork to take a bite, then set it back down and began to openly study him, a teasing gleam in her eyes. ''The Markov family goes back even farther than the Cardozas. Sam told me all those years ago I shouldn't have let you go. I laughed at him because you were only a kid, but those five years between us don't mean much now, do they? We're both the last of a circus dynasty.''

Amused, he shook his head. ''And I don't have any intention of keeping the Markov dynasty going. Sorry, sweetheart, but you'll have to look somewhere else for your center-ring sperm bank.''

She laughed, picked up a dinner roll, and tried to stuff it whole into his mouth. ''Lucky I don't want you. If I did, you wouldn't have a chance.''

Their affair burned on, so lusty and pleasurable that he didn't attach significance to the increasingly possessive looks she began to throw at him or the way she gradually stopped teasing him about being her inferior. ''We're soul mates,'' she told him one night, her voice husky with emotion. ''If you'd been a woman, you would have been me.''

She was right, but something deep inside him rebelled at the comparison. He admired Sheba, but there was a ruthlessness about her that repelled him, maybe because he saw so much of it in himself. To keep her from saying more, he splayed her muscular legs and entered her with one hard thrust.

Despite the subtle changes in her behavior, he was unprepared for what happened one sultry afternoon in a vacant lot outside Waycross, Georgia. That was where Sheba told him she loved him. And as she spoke, he saw that she meant every word.

"I'm sorry," he said as gently as he could when she was done, "but this isn't going to work."

"Of course it is. It's destiny."

She refused to listen as he said he could never love anyone—he'd had the capacity for loving beaten out of him when he was a kid—and the gleam in her eyes told him she saw his rejection as a game. She rose to the challenge with the same determination she'd used to conquer the triple somersault, and it was only as he stood packing his suitcase to leave after his last performance that she truly comprehended. He meant what he said. He didn't love her. And he wasn't going to marry her.

As the absolute finality of his rejection finally sank in, everything Sheba believed about her entitlement to have whatever she wanted collapsed, and she went berserk. That was when she did the unthinkable, the act for which she would never forgive him. That was when she begged him not to leave her.

He was, perhaps, the only person on earth who could understand the enormity of what she was destroying as she cried and fell on her knees before him. She violated her pride, the very thing that made her who she was.

"Sheba, stop it. You've got to stop." He tried to pull her up, but she clung tightly and cried out with a despair so devastating that he would carry the sound of it to his grave. At that exact moment, he felt her love turn to hatred.

Owen Quest, alerted by the noise, had barged into the trailer and taken it all in. Then he'd looked at Alex and gestured toward the door with his head. "You go on. I'll take over now."

A week later, she'd married Owen, a man nearly twice her age who could not give her children, and Alex was the only one who understood why. His rejection had damaged her very core, and she could only recapture who she was by linking herself with a powerful man who would put her on a pedestal. Since her father was dead, she had turned to Owen.

"Alex!" Heather's frightened voice cut through his disturbing memories. "I saw Daisy! She's over by Sinjun's cage."

Sheba heard what Heather said and left Jack Daily's side to return to Alex. "I'll handle this."

"No, you won't. It's my job."

As their eyes locked in a fierce battle of wills, he silently cursed Owen Quest for putting both of them through this. Only after Owen's death did he realize how the sly old buzzard had manipulated him. He'd counted on Alex and Sheba to patch up their differences, marry, and keep Quest Brothers intact. Owen had never really understood either of their natures. And he certainly hadn't counted on a thieving little brat named Daisy Devreaux to spoil his plans.

Heather fell into step next to him, struggling to keep up as her forehead wrinkled with anxiety. "It wasn't very much money. Only two hundred dollars. That's not much."

He slipped his arms around her shoulders and gave her a squeeze. "I want you to stay out of this, Heather. Do you understand me?"

She gazed up at him, her eyes dark and troubled. "You're not going to whip her, are you Alex? That's what my brother said. He said you were going to whip her."

Voices woke Daisy. She raised her head from her bent knees and realized she had dozed off as she sat on the ground in front of Sinjun's cage. As she stretched, she remembered the pain she had experienced and her eerie sense of identification with the tiger. How bizarre. She must have dreamed it, but everything had seemed so real.

She looked over at the cage. Sinjun's head was raised, his ears turned so that their white marks showed. She followed the direction of his gaze and saw Alex storming toward her, with Sheba and Heather trailing. Slowly she rose to her feet.

"Where is it?" Sheba demanded.

"I'll take care of this," Alex snapped.

Daisy felt a trickle of dread as she saw the cold, set expression on his face. Sinjun began to pace restlessly in his cage. "Take care of what? What's wrong?"

Sheba regarded her with chilling contempt. "Don't bother to play innocent. We know you took the money, so hand it over. Or did you already hide it someplace?"

Sinjun growled.

"I didn't hide anything. What are you talking about?"

Alex transferred the coiled whip from one hand to the other. "Two hundred dollars is missing from the cash drawer, Daisy."

"That's impossible."

"It's true."

"I didn't take it."

"That remains to be seen."

She couldn't believe this was happening. "I wasn't the only one working there. Maybe Pete saw something. He took over while I was trying on costumes."

Sheba moved closer. "You're forgetting that I stopped in to check the money drawer right after you came back on duty. Everything reconciled. The two hundred dollars disappeared after that."

"That's not possible. I was there the whole time. It couldn't have disappeared."

"I'm going to search her, Alex. Maybe she still has it on her."

Alex didn't raise his voice, but the note of command was unmistakable. "You're not going to touch her."

"What's happened to you?" Sheba exclaimed. "Since when did you start keeping your brains in your cock?"

"Not another word." He turned to Heather, who was taking in the exchange. "Go on now, sweetheart. This'll all be sorted out by morning."

Heather moved away reluctantly, but Daisy noticed that others were beginning to gather. Neeco Martin, the elephant trainer, came over with Jack Daily, and Brady approached with one of the showgirls.

Alex also noticed they were attracting a crowd, and he turned back to Daisy. "If you hand the money over now, we can keep this from getting any uglier."

"I don't have it!"

"Then I'll have to look for it, and I'm going to start by searching you."

"No!"

He grabbed her arm, and Sinjun emitted a great, barking roar as Alex began marching her toward their trailer. Sheba walked just off to Alex's left, making it clear that she intended to come along.

Out of the corner of her eye, Daisy saw the stern, unsmiling expressions of the others, the same people who had been gathered around the wedding cake the night before. Jill was there, but this time she refused to meet Daisy's eyes. Madeline turned away, and Brady Pepper glared at her.

As Alex's fingers bit into her flesh, she felt a sense of betrayal that went all the way to the depths of her soul. "Don't let this go any further. You know I'd never steal."

"As a matter of fact, I don't know anything of the sort." They were at the trailer, and he reached around her to open the door with the same hand that held the whip. "Get inside."

"How can you do this?"

"It's my job." With a push, he propelled her up the step.

Sheba followed them into the trailer. "If you're innocent, you don't have anything to worry about, do you?"

"I am innocent!"

He tossed the whip down on a chair. "Then you won't mind letting me search you."

Her gaze flew from one of them to the other, and the cold purpose she saw in both sets of eyes made her feel ill. Regardless of their past history, the two of them were now united against her.

He took a step closer, and she backed against the kitchen counter, the place where only a few hours ago he had kissed her with such passion. "I can't let you do this," she said desperately. "We spoke vows, Alex. Don't turn your back on them." She knew she was making herself look guiltier in his eyes, but marriages were built on trust, and if he destroyed that, they wouldn't have a chance.

"Let's get this over with."

She moved sideways along the counter. "I can't let you touch me. Please take my word for it! I didn't steal the money! I've never stolen anything in my life!"

"Stop it, Daisy. You're only making it worse for yourself."

She saw he wasn't going to give in. With a singleness of purpose that frightened her, he backed her against the storage closet.

She gazed numbly up at him. "Don't do it," she whispered. "Please. I'm begging you."

For a moment he froze. Then his palms cupped her sides. While Sheba watched, he drew them down over her waist and hips, then moved up to feel her stomach, her back, the breasts he had cupped so gently in his hands only hours earlier. She shut her eyes in revulsion as he slipped them between her legs.

"You should have believe me," she whispered when he'd finished.

He took a step away, and his eyes were troubled. "If you didn't have it on you, why did you fight me?"

"Because I wanted you to trust me. I'm not a thief."

Their gazes locked. He looked as if he were about to say something when Sheba stepped forward.

"She had plenty of time to get rid of the money. Why don't you search the trailer, and I'll look in your truck?"

Alex nodded, and Sheba left. Daisy's teeth began to chatter even though the night was warm. It said something about the relationship between Alex and Sheba that in this matter at least, each seemed to trust the other. Neither, however, trusted her.

Daisy collapsed on the couch and clasped her hands around her knees to keep herself from shaking. She didn't watch as Alex went through the storage closets and riffled her belongings. A sense of inevitability had come over her. She could no longer remember what it felt like to have her life under control. Maybe she never had. First she'd done her mother's bidding, then her father's. Now this dangerous new husband had taken over her life.

The rustling noises were replaced by a heavy silence. She stared down at the worn pattern on the rug. "You found the money, didn't you?"

"In the bottom of your suitcase, right where you hid it."

She looked up and saw the bag lying open at his feet. A small pile of folded bills rested in his palm. "Someone put it there. I didn't hide it."

He pushed the money into his pocket. "Stop playing games. You're backed into the corner. At least have the guts to tell the truth and face the consequences."

"I didn't steal the money. Someone wants to frame me." It seemed obvious to Daisy that Sheba was behind this. Surely, Alex saw that. "I didn't do it! You have to believe me."

Her pleas died on her lips as she saw the rigid set of his jaw and realized there was nothing she could do to change his mind. With an awful feeling of resignation, she said, "I'm going to stop defending myself. I've told the truth, and I can't do anything more."

He walked over to the chair across from her and sat down. He looked tired but not as tired as she felt. "Are you going to call the police?"

"We handle our own problems."

"And you're judge and jury."

"That's the way it works."

A circus was supposed to be a magical place, but all she'd found was anger and suspicion. She stared at him, trying to see through the impenetrable facade he presented. "What if you make a mistake?"

"I don't. I can't afford to."

She felt a chill of foreboding at the certainty in his voice. Such perfect arrogance was a sure invitation for disaster. A lump grew in her throat. She'd said she wouldn't defend herself again, but a tumult of emotions dragged at her. Swallowing hard, she stared at the limp, ugly curtains that covered the window behind him. "I didn't steal the two hundred dollars, Alex."

He rose and walked toward the door. "We'll deal with the consequences tomorrow. Don't try to leave the trailer. I promise that I'll find you if you do."

She heard the chill in his voice and wondered what kind of punishment he would impose. It would be harsh, of that she had no doubt.

He opened the door and stepped out into the night. She heard the roar of a tiger and shivered.

Sheba watched Alex walk away from her. As she gazed down at the two hundred dollars he'd given her, she knew she had to get away, and moments later she was speeding down the highway in her Cadillac, not caring where she was going, merely needing privacy to celebrate Alex's humiliation. For all his pride and arrogance, Alex Markov had married a common thief.

Just hours ago when Jill Dempsey had told her Alex was married, Sheba had wanted to die. She'd been able to tolerate the ugly memory of the day she'd lost her pride and degraded herself in front of him because she'd known he would never marry anyone else. How could he find a woman who understood him as well as she did, his twin, his other self? If he wouldn't marry her, he wouldn't marry anyone, and her pride had been salved.

But today all that had come to an end. She couldn't believe he had rejected her for that useless little toy, and the memory of herself, crying and clinging to him, begging him to love her, grew as fresh as if it had just happened.

And now, more swiftly than she could have imagined, Alex was being punished and she could keep her head up. She couldn't imagine a more bitter blow to his pride than this. At least her humiliation had been a private one, but his was revealed for all the world to see.

Sheba hit the button on the radio and flooded the car with the sound of hard rock. Poor Alex. She pitied him, really. He'd passed up the chance to marry the queen of the center ring and ended up with a common thief.

As Sheba Quest flew down the moonlit North Carolina highway, Heather Pepper sat huddled behind her father's Airstream with her thin arms wrapped around her chest and her cheeks wet with tears.

Why had she done such an awful thing? If her mom were alive, she could have talked to her about it, explained how she hadn't planned it, but the cash drawer had been open and she hated Daisy, and the whole thing had just happened. Her mom would have helped her straighten everything out.

But her mom wasn't alive. And Heather knew if her dad ever found out what she'd done, he would hate her forever.

8

"Here's the shovel, Miz," the elephant man said. "And there's the wheelbarrow. Get the truck mucked out."

Digger, who took care of the animals for Neeco Martin, the trainer, pushed the shovel at her and hobbled away. The old man was wizened and arthritic, and his mouth had collapsed from lack of back teeth. Digger was her new boss.

. Daisy stared dully down at her shovel. This was her punishment. Somehow she had expected that Alex would keep her confined in the trailer, using it as a traveling jail cell, but she should have known he wouldn't do anything that simple.

Last night she had cried herself to sleep on the couch. She had no idea when he'd come in, or even if he'd returned. For all she knew, he could have spent the night with one of the showgirls. Misery welled inside her. He had barely spoken during this morning's ride other than to tell her she would be working for Digger and that she wasn't to leave the lot without his permission.

She looked from the shovel in her hand to the interior of the truck. The elephants had already been unloaded from the massive trailer through wide sliding doors in the center that opened out onto a ramp. Her stomach rolled, and a wave of queasiness brought the bile up into her throat. There were piles of it inside. *Piles*. Some of the piles were almost neat, with pieces of straw protruding. Others had been squashed by giant feet.

113

And the smell.

She turned her head away and took a gulp of fresh air. Her husband believed she was a thief and a liar, and as punishment, he'd exiled her to work with the elephants, even though she'd told him she was afraid of animals. She looked back inside the truck.

Sweet Mary McFadden.

Defeat swept over her, and at that exact moment, she knew she'd failed. She simply couldn't do this. Other people seemed to have hidden reservoirs of strength to draw upon in times of crisis, but she didn't. She was soft and useless. Everything her father had ever said about her was true. Everything Alex had said. She wasn't good at anything except making party conversation, and that had no value in this world. As the late morning sun beat down on her head, she looked into her soul and couldn't find even the smallest vestige of courage. *I give up.* Her shovel fell to the ramp with a clatter.

"Have you finally had enough?"

She looked down at Alex standing at the bottom of the ramp, and she slowly nodded.

He gazed up at her, his hands resting on the hips of his faded jeans. "The men have been betting on whether or not you'd even make it inside the truck."

"How did you bet?" Her voice was barely more than a whisper, and it had an awkward little croak to it.

"You weren't raised to shovel shit, angel face. Anybody can see that. But just for the record, I stayed out of it."

Not from any loyalty to her, she was certain, but only to protect his reputation as the boss. She regarded him with a distant curiosity. "You knew all along I wouldn't be able to do this, didn't you?"

He nodded slowly. "I knew."

"Then why did you make me go through it?"

"You had to understand you weren't going to be able to cut it here. But you've been slow to catch on, Daisy. I tried to tell Max that you didn't have a snowball's chance in hell of surviving here, but he wouldn't listen." His voice grew almost gentle, and for some reason, that bothered her more than his contempt. "Go back to the trailer, Daisy, and change your clothes. I'm buying you a plane ticket out of here."

Where would she go? she wondered. She had no place left to run. She heard Sinjun's barking roar, and she looked toward his cage, but the water truck blocked her view.

"I'm giving you some money to hold you over until you get a job."

"When we were in the limo and I asked you for a loan, you wouldn't give it to me. Why are you doing it now?"

"I promised your father I'd let you have a fair chance. I've kept my word."

With that, he turned away and began heading for the trailer, certain she was behind him. It was his perfect assurance that cut through her misery and replaced it with a shot of undiluted rage so foreign to her sunny nature that she barely recognized what it was. He was so sure of her spinelessness that he didn't even question the fact that she would surrender.

And she would, wouldn't she?

She gazed back down at the shovel lying on the ramp. Dried manure clung to the blade and the handle, attracting a swarm of flies. As she stared down at it, she realized this filthy shovel was what all the choices she had made in her life had come down to.

With a great shuddering sob, she snatched it up and plunged into the malodorous interior of the trailer. Holding her breath, she pushed the blade under the nearest pile, struggled to scoop it up, and with shaking arms, carried it to the wheelbarrow. Her lungs burned from the effort. She gasped for fresh air and nearly gagged from the smell. Without giving herself time to think, she struggled with the next pile and the next. Her arms began to ache, but she didn't slow down.

Alex's boots thudded on the ramp. "Stop it, Daisy, and get out here."

She swallowed hard against the constriction in her throat. "Go away."

"You're not going to survive here. Your stubbornness is only postponing the inevitable."

"You're probably right." She lost the battle to hold back her tears. They spilled over onto her cheeks. She sniffed, but she didn't stop working.

"The only thing you're proving to me is how foolish you are."

"I'm not trying to prove anything to *you*, and I really don't want to talk any longer." With a shuddering sob, she lifted another heavy pile and barely found the strength to haul it to the wheelbarrow.

"Are you crying?"

"Go away."

He stepped inside and came around in front of her. "You are. You're crying."

Her voice quivered. "Excuse me, but you're in my way."

He reached for the shovel, but she snatched it away before he could touch it. A burst of anger-fueled adrenaline gave her the strength to shove the blade under another pile, scoop it up, and thrust it out at him. "Go away! I mean it, Alex! If you don't leave me alone, you're going to be wearing this."

"You wouldn't dare."

Her arms trembled and tears dripped from her chin onto her T-shirt, but she met his gaze without flinching. "You shouldn't dare a person who doesn't have anything left to lose."

For a moment he did nothing. Then he slowly shook his head and backed away. "Have it your way, but you're only making this harder on yourself."

It took her two hours to clean the trailer. Maneuvering the heavy wheelbarrow down the ramp was the most difficult. On the first trip, it tipped, and she had to clean up the mess all over again. She'd cried the whole time, but she didn't stop. Occasionally, she looked up and saw Alex pass by, his golden eyes watchful, but she ignored him. The pain in her arms and shoulders grew unbearable, but she gritted her teeth and somehow forced herself to go on.

When she had finished hosing down the interior, she stood in the doorway. The jeans and T-shirt Alex had bought her two days earlier were crusted with filth, as was every other part of her. Hair straggled around her face, and her fingernails were broken. She surveyed her work and tried to feel some sense of pride in her accomplishment, but all she felt was exhaustion.

She sagged against the truck's loading door. From her vantage point at the top of the ramp, she could see the adult elephants chained near the road to advertise the circus to those driving by.

"Come on down here, Miz," Digger said. "Day's not over."

She limped to the bottom of the ramp, keeping a wary eye on the young elephants milling untethered not ten yards away.

He gestured toward them. "The babies got to be watered. Use this bull hook to move 'em over to the trough." He indicated a pole several feet long with a hook at the end, then walked over to the baby elephants, each of whom had to weigh close to a ton. With a combination of voice commands and light raps from the bull hook, he got them moving toward a galvanized tank filled with water. Daisy stayed as far away as possible, her heart pounding with fear.

He looked back at her. "You're not gonna git the job done from way over there."

She moved forward gingerly, telling herself that, despite their size, they were only babies. At least they weren't nasty little dogs.

She watched as some of them used their mouths to sip directly from the trough while others sucked water partially up into their trunks, then carried their trunks to their mouths. Digger noticed the way she continued to hold back. "You ain't afraid of 'em are you, Miz?

"Call me Daisy."

"You cain't never let any animal see you're afraid."

"That's what people keep telling me."

"You got to show 'em who's boss. Show 'em you're in charge."

He slapped one animal, moving him to the side to make way for the others. From her vantage point in the bleachers, she'd found the babies cute with their floppy ears, long, curling lashes, and solemn expressions, but now they scared her to death.

She saw Neeco Martin over by the adult elephants—the bulls, she reminded herself, even though she'd been told they were all females. She winced as he gave one of them a strong whack with the bull hook. She might not be an animal lover, but something inside her twisted with revulsion. These elephants hadn't chosen to be in a circus, and she didn't think they should be brutalized because they didn't follow the rules humans set for them, especially when those rules ran counter to the instincts of their species.

"I got to help Neeco git the elephant ride set up," Digger said. "Take the babies back to the picket line. I'll help you tether them in a few minutes."

"Oh, no! No, I don't think—"

"That one there's Puddin'. That's Tater. The one on the end is Pebbles and that there's Bam Bam. We just call him Bam for short. Git on now, Pebbles. You mind yer manners." He thrust the bull hook at Daisy and walked away.

Daisy gazed with dismay from the bull hook in her hand to the elephants. Bam opened his mouth, either to yawn or eat her, she wasn't sure which, and she jumped back. Two of the elephants dipped their trunks back in the watering trough.

Now she'd give up, she thought. She'd managed to shovel out that truck, but getting any closer to these elephants was beyond her abilities. She had reached the absolute limit of what she could do.

In the distance she saw Alex watching her, waiting like a vulture to pounce on her useless carcass and then throw her away.

She shuddered and took one hesitant step toward the baby

elephants. "Uh—let's go, fellas." She tentatively pointed the bull hook toward the picket line.

Bam, or maybe it was Pebbles, raised his head and sneered at her.

She took an uneasy step closer. "Please don't give me any trouble. It's been a terrible day."

Tater lifted his trunk from the trough and turned his head toward her. The next thing she knew, she received a spray of water right in her face.

"Oh!" With a gasp, she sprang back.

Tater lumbered away, heading not for the picket line but for the trailers.

"Come back!" she cried, wiping the water from her eyes. "Don't do that! Please!"

Neeco rushed over holding a long metal rod with a U-shaped prong at one end. He shoved it at Tater, choosing a point behind his ear. The elephant gave a loud, painful squeal, recoiled, and immediately turned toward the picket line. The others quickly followed.

Daisy stared at the animals, then at Neeco. "What did you do to him?"

He transferred the pole from his right hand to his left and brushed his long, dishwater blond hair back from his face. "This is a hot shot. It's a cattle prod. I don't use it unless I have to, but they know they're going to get zapped if they don't behave."

She stared at the hot shot in revulsion. "You shock them? Isn't that a little brutal?"

"You can't get sentimental about the animals. I love them, but I'm not stupid about them. They have to know who's in charge or people can get hurt."

"I'm not going to be good at this, Neeco. I've told everyone that I'm afraid of animals, but no one seems to be listening."

"You'll get over it. You just need to spend some time with them. They don't like sudden noises or people sneaking up on them, so come at them from the front." He pulled the bull hook from her hand and gave her the hot shot. "If they see you carrying this, they'll give you some respect. The babies are easy to control; a couple of quick zaps, and you've got their attention. When you're using the bull hook, get them behind the ears. They've got big nerve centers there.''

She felt as if she had been forced to take hold of something obscene. She glanced over at the baby elephants and saw Tater gazing back at her. He seemed to be taking in the hot shot, and although it was probably her imagination, she thought he looked disappointed.

As Neeco walked away, she approached the babies, giving a series of coughs so she wouldn't take them by surprise. They lifted their heads and shuffled uneasily as they saw what she carried. Bam opened his mouth and emitted a loud, unhappy bellow.

They must be accustomed to being brought in line with shocks, and she found herself disliking Neeco Martin. The hot shot sickened her instead of increasing her confidence. No matter how frightened she was of the animals, she would never be able to hurt them, and she discarded the hot shot behind a load of hay.

She looked longingly toward Alex's house trailer. Only three days ago, she had thought it ugly, but now it seemed the most welcoming spot in the world. She reminded herself that she had survived mucking out that truck. Certainly she could survive this.

Once again she approached them, this time without the cattle prod. For a moment they watched her. Apparently satisfied that she was no longer a threat, they returned to their happy grubbing in the dirt.

All of them but Tater. Was it her imagination or was he smiling? And did the smile have a faintly diabolical cast to it?

"Nice elephants. N-nice babies," she crooned. "And nice Daisy. Very, very nice Daisy."

Pebbles and Bam Bam lifted their heads to look at each other, and she could have sworn they rolled their eyes in disgust. Tater, in the meantime, lifted a clump of hay and dropped it on his back. The other babies continued to watch her, but Tater no longer seemed to be bothered by her presence, making him the most approachable of the quartet.

He dusted his back with another clump of hay. She sidled closer by a few steps until barely ten feet separated them. He began snuffling in the dirt.

"Nice Tater. Tater's a nice baby elephant." She crept forward another few inches, speaking to him as if he were a human baby. "Pretty boy. Good manners." Her voice had begun to shake. "Tater has such fine manners." She was almost near enough to pat his trunk, and her skin was clammy with perspiration. "Tater likes Daisy. Daisy's Tater's friend." She slowly extended her hand, moving it forward inch by inch, telling herself that elephants didn't eat humans, that everything—

Swat!

The baby elephant's trunk caught her across the chest and sent her flying to the ground. She landed so hard that she saw stars. Pain ricocheted through her left side. Her vision cleared just in time for her to observe a small, contented elephant lift his trunk and emit a youthful, and unmistakably victorious, trumpet.

She sat there, too dispirited to get to her feet. Lavender sandals studded with small silver stars appeared in her vision. She raised her head and saw Bathsheba Quest staring down at her through a pair of dark glasses. Sheba wore a stretchy white top and low-slung white shorts cinched at the waist with a lavender belt. Perched on her hip was a dark-haired toddler, a child Daisy remembered having seen with one of the Tolea brothers and his wife. Sheba stared down at her, then slipped her sunglasses to the top of her head, pulling back her hair far enough to reveal enormous star-shaped purple rhinestone earrings.

Daisy expected to see triumph in Sheba's eyes, but instead she merely saw satisfaction, and she realized she had sunk so low that Sheba no longer even regarded her as a threat.

"Where in the hell did Alex find you?"

Shaking her head, Sheba stepped over Daisy's feet, walked up to Tater, and petted his trunk. "You're a little stinker, aren't you, fella? Isn't he, Theo?'' She tweaked the toddler's foot.

Daisy had been bested on every front, and she couldn't take any more. As far as she was concerned, her work was done for the day, and she'd survived, if only barely. She dragged herself to her feet and began walking to the trailer only to see Alex going inside. Unwilling to face another encounter with him, she turned away and began aimlessly wandering through the circus grounds.

Two of the showgirls noticed her coming and turned away. One of the clowns pretended not to see her. She desperately wanted a cigarette.

She jumped as a terrible shrieking split the air. Her head shot up, and she saw Frankie near one of the trucks holding Jill's hand. He pointed at her and screeched. Jill picked him up and, without so much as a word, walked away.

Daisy felt sick inside. The message was clear. She had been declared an outcast.

She walked aimlessly until she found herself at the menagerie tent. The side flap was raised, and all the animals seemed to be inside with the exception of Sinjun, whose cage still sat in the sun. The animal pricked up its ears as she approached and regarded her with disdain. It had been too dark last night for her to see the condition of his cage, but now she noticed that it was filthy. Digger, she'd learned, was supposed to take care of the menagerie, but it must be low on his priority list.

Once again the tiger locked eyes with her and once again she couldn't look away. Last night the tiger's fur had seemed to gleam in the floodlights, but now it looked dull and unhealthy. She stared into those mysterious gold irises, and as the seconds ticked by, she felt herself growing unbearably hot.

Sweat pooled under her arms and gathered in the hollow of her throat. Her face became flushed, her breasts wet. She had never been so hot. She wanted to tear her clothes off and plunge into a pool of ice-cold water. She was burning up, and somehow she knew the heat wasn't coming from her but from the tiger.

"There you are."

She snapped her head around to see Alex approaching. He took her in from head to toe, and beneath the impact of those cool, impersonal eyes, her body grew chill.

"You have some free time before you need to get ready for spec," he said. "Why don't you clean up, and then we'll see about an early dinner?"

"Spec?"

"I told you it was part of your job."

"But not tonight. I can't possibly do it tonight. Look at me!"

As Alex watched her, he almost relented. Every bit of decency inside him demanded that he leave her alone. She was pale with exhaustion and so filthy she was almost unrecognizable. The only cosmetic still visible on her face was a smear of old mascara below her bottom lashes. Her soft little mouth drooped at the corners, and he didn't think he'd ever seen anyone so clearly at the end of her tether.

At the same time, he felt a reluctant spark of admiration for the mere fact that she was still on her feet. He remembered the way she'd held him off with the shovel and knew what a display of courage that had been for her. She'd surprised him today. Unfortunately, her small rebellion had simply prolonged the inevitable.

Why wouldn't she give up? He didn't know what hidden source of strength she'd found to get her this far, but it wasn't going to last and he refused to torture her. He fought against the softness inside him that urged him to relent, knowing that would be a cruelty instead of a kindness. The harder he pushed her now, the sooner she would face the truth.

He firmed his resolve by reminding himself that she was a thief, and regardless of the circumstances, that wasn't something he could forgive.

"The first show's at six. You're going on with the elephants."

"But—"

He spotted a scratch on the back of her hand and snatched it up to examine it. "How long has it been since you've had a tetanus shot?"

She regarded him blankly.

"A tetanus shot. For infection."

She blinked, and she looked so drained that he had to resist the urge to pick her up and carry her back to the trailer. He didn't want to think about holding that small, soft body in his arms. If she hadn't stolen that money, she'd have spent the night in his bed, but as it was, he'd been so furious, he hadn't trusted himself to touch her. He hadn't wanted to touch her.

"How long since your last tetanus?" he said more sharply.

She gazed down at the scratch on her hand. "Last year. I cut myself when I was sailing on Biffy Brougenhaus's yacht."

Christ. How could he be married to a woman who knew someone named Biffy Brougenhaus? The hell with her.

"Get some antiseptic on that," he snapped. "And be ready on time for spec or you'll be cleaning out the horse trailer, too."

As he stalked off, his scowl grew blacker. He'd always prided himself on his fairness, but she made him feel like a bad-tempered bully. He chalked up another black mark against her.

Daisy survived spec, mainly because exhaustion had numbed her to the embarrassment of appearing in public wearing her skimpy red costume. Although Alex had told her to go on with the elephants, she'd stayed well behind them so that she looked like she was one of the Flying Toleas.

It had taken her forever to get herself clean, and her sore arms had protested every step of the process. She'd shampooed and dried her hair, then put on fresh makeup, following Alex's instructions to apply it heavier than normal. Between shows, she'd fallen asleep in the trailer with a peanut butter sandwich in her hand. If he hadn't shaken her awake, she would have missed her entrance

After the last show, Neeco caught her as she was emerging through the back door, the name the performers gave to their entrance to the big top. "Help Digger get the babies back to the truck."

Digger didn't look as if he needed any help, but this was apparently part of her job, and she didn't want another failure for Alex to throw in her face. "I doubt I'll be much help," she said.

"They just need to get used to you, that's all."

She slipped into Alex's blue terry cloth robe, which she'd taken from a hook in the bathroom. Although she'd turned the sleeves up, it was still enormous on her, but it gave her some modesty.

The babies were just beginning to come out through the back door, and she approached Digger gingerly. "You don't need any help, do you?"

"Why don't you jist walk along with 'em, Miz. They're still skittish around you."

She reluctantly fell into step just behind Digger and several yards away from the elephants. She had no trouble picking out Tater since he was the smallest of the quartet, and remembering the swat he'd given her, she eyed him warily as he trotted forward holding Puddin's tail in the curl of his trunk. When they reached the picket line, Digger began to tether them.

"Come here, Bam. Watch me, Miz, so you can see how it's done."

She was so intent on what he was doing with Bam that she didn't realize Tater had sidled up behind her until she felt something moist tickle the side of her neck, just inside the collar of her robe. She yelped and sprang back from the elephant's outstretched trunk.

The baby elephant regarded her with a stubborn glint in its eye, took a step closer, and once again extended his trunk. Too frozen with fear to move, she stared at the two wiggling nostrils coming closer by the second.

"N-nice Tater. N-nice elephant." She let out a frightened squeak as Tater burrowed into her neck, parting the front of her robe.

"Digger . . ." she croaked.

Digger looked up and took in what was happening. "You got perfume on?"

She gulped and gave a terrified nod. The very tip of Tater's trunk dipped delicately into the small space behind her ear.

"Tater's crazy about ladies' perfume."

"What," she gasped, "am I supposed to do now?"

Digger regarded her blankly. "Do about what?"

"T-Tater?"

"Well, I don't rightly know, Miz. What do you want to do?"

She heard a rusty chuckle. "She probably wants to faint. Isn't that right, Daisy?"

Alex came around from behind her, and she tried to summon up a bit of bravado. "Not—not exactly."

"You must be wearing perfume." He reached out and stroked Puddin'. Tater, in the meantime, emitted a happy snuffling sound and let the tip of his trunk nibble around the inside of the collar of Alex's robe to the base of Daisy's throat.

"N-nobody told me not to." To her dismay, the baby elephant began to nudge lower, toward the red sequined flames that made up the bodice of her costume. She remembered the spritz of perfume she'd directed toward her breasts.

"Alex . . ." She pleaded with her eyes. "He's going to— He's getting ready to touch my—" Tater's trunk reached its goal. "My breasts!" she squealed.

"I do believe you're right." He casually patted the elephant's trunk and pushed it aside. "That's enough, fella. You're getting too close to my property."

She was so startled by his statement she didn't notice Tater backing off.

Digger gave a wheezy chuckle and nodded toward the elephant. "Looks like Tater's fallen in love."

" 'Fraid so," Alex replied.

"With me?" She regarded the men incredulously.

"Do you see him looking at anybody else?" Alex replied.

Sure enough, the elephant was regarding her soulfully. "But he hates me. This afternoon he took a swipe at me and knocked me down."

"You weren't wearing perfume this afternoon."

Digger rose, his knees cracking, and headed toward the elephant. "Come on, boy. Yer girlfriend's not interested."

As Digger led him away, Tater gazed back at her over his shoulder, looking for all the world like a love-struck adolescent. Daisy was torn between fright and a fleeting sense of gratitude that at least someone in this awful circus liked her.

That night, she fell asleep as soon as her head hit the couch. She was dimly aware of Alex coming into the trailer some hours later, and as she drifted back into sleep, she felt him pull the covers up over her shoulders.

9

Daisy stumbled up the ramp at ten the next morning. Her leg muscles screamed in protest with every step, and her arms felt as if they'd been stretched on a torture rack. "I'm sorry, Digger. I fell asleep in the truck."

Despite her exhaustion last night, she'd awakened sometime just before three from a dream in which she and Alex had been floating through an old-fashioned tunnel of love in a pink swan boat. Alex had kissed her, and his face had been so filled with tenderness that she'd felt herself melting into the boat, the water, into his very body. The sensation had awakened her, and she'd lain on the couch until dawn thinking about the painful contrast between her beautiful dream and the reality of her marriage.

When they'd arrived at this new lot in a High Point, North Carolina, strip mall, the trailer hauling the elephants hadn't yet appeared, so she'd stayed in the truck for a short nap. Two hours later, she'd awakened with a stiff neck and a headache.

As she reached the top of the ramp, she saw that Digger had nearly finished mucking out the trailer. Mixed with a sense of relief, she felt a stab of guilt. That was her job. "I'll finish up for you."

"The worst part's done." He spoke like a man who had long ago grown accustomed to getting the short end of life.

"I'm sorry. It won't happen again."

He gave a sniff that told her he'd wait and see.

From her vantage point at the top of the ramp, she had a good view of the new site located between a Pizza Hut and a gas station. Most of the performers, Alex had told her, preferred the smooth, regular surface of a parking lot to grass, but setting up on asphalt also meant that the holes left by the stakes had to be repaired before they left.

As the stake driver thumped rhythmically in the background, she looked toward the backyard and saw Heather sitting in a lawn chair outside the trailer, with Sheba standing behind her putting a French braid in the teenager's hair. Yesterday she'd caught glimpses of Sheba helping Heather with her gymnastics. She'd also seen the circus owner patching up one of the workers and trying to console the Lipscomb's six-year-old after he'd taken a fall. Sheba Quest seemed to be full of contradictions: a wicked witch with Daisy, earth mother with everyone else.

A feisty trumpeting brought her up short, and she looked down to see Tater standing at the bottom of the ramp gazing adoringly up at her through his ridiculously curly lashes.

Digger cackled. "Your boyfriend's come to visit you."

"He's going to be disappointed. I'm not wearing perfume."

" 'Spect he'll have to figger that out for hisself. Take him over with the rest, will ya? They all need to be watered." He jerked his head. "Bull hook's right there."

She gazed at the object leaning against the side of the truck with loathing. At the bottom of the ramp, Tater trumpeted again, then began to turn in a tight circle, performing just as he did in the center ring. When he stopped, he lifted one leg and then the other in his baby's tap dance. Unless she was very much mistaken, he was showing off for her.

"What am I going to do with you, Tater? Don't you realize you scare me to death?"

Gathering her courage, she moved gingerly to the bottom of the ramp where she reached into the pocket of her jeans and gingerly extracted a withered carrot she'd found in the refrigerator and brought along just in case. Hoping he'd follow her if he knew she had food, she held it out with a trembling hand.

He extended his trunk and took a delicate sniff, tickling her palm. She stepped back, using the carrot as bait to draw him toward the others. He snatched it from her hand and carried it to his mouth, where it disappeared.

She watched in apprehension as his now empty trunk came toward her again. "N-no more food."

But it wasn't food he wanted; it was perfume. He burrowed into the neck of her T-shirt searching for the scent he loved. "S-sorry, fella. I—"

Swat! With a dramatic squall of betrayal, Tater swiped her with his trunk and knocked her to the pavement. She let out a yelp. At the same time, Tater lifted his head and announced her treachery to the world. *No perfume!*

"Daisy, are you all right?" Alex materialized out of nowhere and crouched down next to her.

"I'm okay." She winced from the pain in her hip.

"Damn it! You can't allow an animal to keep doing that to you. Sheba told me he knocked you down yesterday."

Naturally Sheba couldn't resist passing on a tidbit like that, Daisy thought, flinching as she shifted her weight.

Out of the corner of her eye, Neeco strode toward them. "I'll take care of this."

She sucked in her breath as he snatched up the bull hook. "No! Don't hit him! It was my fault. I—" Ignoring the pain, she scrambled to her feet and leaped forward to put herself between Neeco and Tater, but she was too late.

Horrified, she watched as Neeco struck the baby on the tender spot behind his ear. Tater squealed and backed away. Neeco advanced on him again, bull hook raised for a second blow.

"That's enough, Neeco."

She didn't hear Alex's soft words of warning because she was already throwing herself at Neeco's back. "Don't hit him again!" With a cry of indignation, she lunged for the bull hook.

Startled, Neeco stumbled and then, regaining his balance,

cursed and spun around. As she lost her grip on his shoulders, she felt herself slipping, but instead of falling to the pavement for the second time that day, Daisy felt Alex catch her under the arms. "Easy, there."

Sheba rushed up. "For God's sake, Alex, we've got newspaper people on the lot."

As he set her back on her feet, Daisy braced herself for a lambasting. To her surprise, Alex turned to Neeco instead. "I think Tater got the point the first time."

Neeco stiffened. "You know as well as I do there's nothing more dangerous than an elephant that's turned on his handlers."

Daisy couldn't hold her tongue. "He's just a baby! And it was my fault. I wasn't wearing perfume, and he got upset."

"Be quiet, Daisy," Alex said softly.

"He's a one-ton baby." Neeco's lips narrowed. "I won't let anybody who's working for me get sentimental about the animals. We don't *ever* take chances with safety. People's lives are at stake, and the animals have to know who's in charge."

All her frustration boiled over. "The animals' lives have value, too! Tater didn't ask to be stuck in this awful circus. He didn't ask to be lugged all over the country in a smelly truck, to be chained and shackled and paraded around in front of a bunch of ignorant people. God didn't create elephants to stand on their heads and do tricks. They were meant to roam free."

Sheba crossed her arms and lifted a sarcastic eyebrow. "Next thing you know, Alex, she'll be throwing red paint at fur coats. Either control your wife or get her the hell out of my circus."

Not a flicker of emotion crossed his face as he met Sheba's gaze. "Daisy's supposed to be taking care of the elephants. From what I saw, she was doing her job."

Her heart skipped a beat. Had he just defended her?

Her pleasure faded as he turned back to her, tilting his head toward the trailer that had hauled the elephants. "It's late, and it doesn't look like you have the inside hosed down yet. Get back to work."

She turned away and, silently wishing all three of them in Hades, set about her job. She understood that if animals were going to travel with the circus, they had to be kept under control, but the very idea that they were being forced to behave in ways that went against their nature bothered her. Maybe she found their condition so disturbing because she felt as if she had something in common with them. Like the circus animals, she was held captive against her will, and, like them, her keeper had all the power.

Sheba had almost reached the red wagon when Brady Pepper came up behind her. As much as Brady irritated Sheba, she couldn't deny that he was good-looking with his olive skin and sharp, even features. Although she knew for a fact he was forty-two, his wiry hair was only lightly threaded with gray and his powerful acrobat's body didn't have an extra ounce of fat.

"You sleepin' with Neeco?" he said in that antagonistic fashion that never failed to set her teeth on edge.

"None of your business."

"I'll bet you are. He's just the type you like best. Good looking and stupid."

"Go to hell." Her irritation was piqued by the fact that she *had* slept with Neeco a few times at the beginning of the season. She'd quickly lost interest, however, and hadn't felt any inclination to repeat the experience. She'd never let anyone suspect that sex was losing its appeal to her.

"With a guy like Neeco, you get to call all the shots, don't you. Whereas with somebody like me . . ."

"Somebody like you could never satisfy me." Giving him a phony smile, she ran the tip of her fingernail over his deltoid, which was clearly outlined by his fitted tank top. "The showgirls say you can't get it up anymore. Is that true?"

Much to her annoyance, he failed to respond to her barb, laughing instead. "You got a viper's tongue on you, Sheba Quest. One day it's gonna get you in big trouble."

"I like trouble."

"I know you do. Especially the male variety."

She set off toward the red wagon, but instead of taking the hint, he fell into step beside her. The length of his stride, the set of his shoulders, everything about him announced that he thought he was God's gift to women. He was also a dedicated male chauvinist, which meant she had to keep reminding him who was the boss. Still, as much as he aggravated her, he was the kind of performer she liked best: proud, hard-working, and honest. Beneath his rough exterior, he also had a generous nature, and unlike Alex Markov, there were no hidden depths to him.

He ran his eyes over her as he always did. Brady never made a secret of the fact that he appreciated women, and despite his dalliances with youthful showgirls, he had a way of looking at her that made her feel as if she were still in her prime. Not that she'd ever let him know that. His sexy swagger couldn't hide the fact that Brady was a Brooklyn butcher's son without a drop of circus blood in his veins.

"You and Heather been spending a lot of time together lately," he said.

"I braided her hair today, if that's what you mean."

He caught her arm, pulling her to a stop. "That's not what I mean, and you know it. I'm talking about all that extra coaching you've been giving her."

"What about it?"

"I don't want you getting her hopes up. You know she doesn't have what it takes to be a decent performer."

"Who says? You haven't given her a fair chance."

"Are you kidding? I've been working with her since she got here, and she still stinks!"

"Is it any wonder?"

"And what's that supposed to mean?"

"It means that you might be a great performer, but you're a lousy teacher."

"Hell I am! I'm a great teacher." He jabbed his thumb at his chest. "I taught my sons everything they know."

"Matt and Rob are as hard-headed as you. It's one thing

to teach two rowdy boys, but it's another to work with a sensitive young girl. How can she learn anything with you snapping her head off all the time?''

"What the hell do you know about sensitive young girls? From what I hear, you used to suck arsenic straight from your mother."

"Very funny."

"Try telling me your old man mollycoddled you when he was teaching you to do the triple."

"He didn't have to mollycoddle me. I knew he loved me."

His mouth thinned into a belligerent line. "Are you saying I don't love my daughter?"

She slammed her hands on her hips. "You stupid jerk. Didn't it ever occur to you that it's more important for you to be Heather's father now than her coach? If you'd stop pushing her so hard, she might be able to perform better."

"All of a sudden I've got fucking Ann Landers here."

"You watch your filthy mouth!"

"Look who's talking. I'm warning you, Sheba, don't screw with Heather. She's having a hard enough time as it is without you trying to turn her against me."

He stalked off, bristling with animosity.

She watched him for a moment, then unlocked the door of the red wagon and stomped inside. She and Brady had rubbed each other wrong from the beginning, but there was also a powerful sexual awareness between them that kept her on guard. Brutal experience had taught her to be careful about the men she chose as lovers, and the day she'd married Owen Quest was also the day she'd committed herself to never again going to bed with a man she couldn't control. She had a self-destructive streak when it came to men, and twice it had nearly destroyed her: first with Carlos Méndez and then, far more brutally, with Alex Markov.

She'd made Carlos Méndez pay for what he'd done to her, and now she reminded herself that Alex had gotten his punishment, too. She went over to the window and saw Daisy Markov struggling with a bale of hay. Sheba almost felt sorry for her—if it had been anyone else, she would have—but

Daisy was the instrument of Alex's punishment. How humiliating this must be to him.

She was almost certainly pregnant; there was no other reason for him to have married such a useless woman. But as much as she hated Alex, the circus meant everything to Sheba, and it seemed obscene that the blood of the Markovs—one of the most famous circus families in history—would be passed on through that pampered little thief. Every time she looked at her, Sheba wondered how she could have held her head up if the truth about Daisy hadn't come out.

Later, Daisy couldn't remember how she endured the next week and a half as the circus meandered through North Carolina and then crossed over into Virginia. During the day, she and Alex were only together in the truck, and when he condescended to speak to her, she felt as if she were being pricked to death with icicles. They didn't even share meals. Alex usually opened a can of something while she was in the bathroom getting ready for spec and then left a plate of food out for her while he dressed. He never asked what she wanted to eat or suggested she cook dinner for them, not that she had any energy left for cooking.

Sometimes she thought she'd dreamed that passionate kiss they'd shared. They no longer even touched except on those occasions when she fell asleep in the truck and woke up snuggled against him. When that happened, she would jerk away, only to feel the sexual energy pulsing between them, as palpable as the breeze that blew through the truck.

Or maybe it was just her imagination. Maybe she didn't appeal to him at all. How could he find anyone attractive who had blistered hands, a sunburned nose, scabby elbows, and lived in filthy work clothes? Sometime in the past week, she'd stopped putting on makeup until she had to get ready for spec. During the day, she snagged her hair in a ponytail, with the uneven wisps that escaped the rubber band trailing down her neck and across her cheeks. In the space of two weeks, the grooming habits of a lifetime had been broken.

She didn't even know who she was when she looked into a mirror.

And she was always exhausted. She fell asleep on the couch before midnight, but once Alex came into the trailer, it was nearly impossible for her to go back to sleep. She'd toss and turn for hours, finally tumbling into a fitful dream-like state only to have him growl her awake long before she was rested. She was drained, confused, and incredibly lonely.

Since everyone believed she was a thief, the members of the company continued to avoid her, and her relationship with the elephants hadn't improved, either. Tater still acted as if she'd betrayed him. Several times Daisy had considered spraying herself with perfume, but she was more afraid of his affection than his dislike. When Neeco and Digger were around, the elephant left her alone, but if they weren't in sight, he looked for opportunities to swat her, and he'd knocked her down so many times that she had bruises everywhere.

The other baby elephants had quickly realized she was an easy mark, and she'd become the target for all their mischief. They sprayed her with water, bellowed at her, and swatted her if she got too close. Even worse was the way they waited until she was standing next to them before they did their personal business. Digger told her that as long as she refused to use the bull hook on them, she deserved what she got, but she wouldn't beat them.

Although she'd stayed away from Sinjun, she'd learned about him from listening to the others talk. He was an old tiger, about eighteen, with a reputation for being cranky. According to Digger, none of the trainers had ever been able to befriend him, and everyone regarded him as both unpredictable and dangerous.

Just like her husband. Alex confused her so much she didn't know what to think. As soon as she made up her mind that he was nothing more than a sadistic monster, he'd appear at the elephant truck with a new pair of work gloves or a baseball cap so she didn't get sunburned. And more than once, he'd happened by just in time to wrestle the loaded wheelbarrow down the ramp for her. Most of the time, however, he simply gave her grief.

It was an unseasonably hot day for mid-May. The temperature had soared well into the nineties, and the thick humidity made it difficult to breathe. They were playing in a parking lot again, this one in a small town south of Richmond, and the black asphalt intensified the heat. She'd been swatted twice already by the elephants, badly scraping her elbow the second time she fell. To make it worse, everybody in the circus seemed to be relaxing except her.

Brady and Perry Lipscomb sat in the shade beneath the awning of the Pepper family's Airstream, enjoying a cool beer and listening to a baseball game on the portable radio. Jill spritzed herself with water and lay back on a lounge chair with the newest issue of *Cosmo*. Even Digger was taking a nap in the shade.

"Daisy, get your ass moving and do something with that hay!"

Neeco shouted out his order from the doorway of the trailer the showgirls used, then draped his arm around Charlene's shoulder. Ever since their confrontation over the bull hook, Neeco had been hostile. He gave her the worst jobs and kept her at them for long, backbreaking hours until Alex appeared and told him she'd worked enough for the day.

As she began to move the hay, every muscle in her body burned. Her sweat-soaked T-shirt had a rip at the shoulder seam; filth covered her jeans; dirt, hay, and manure stuck to every inch of her damp skin. Her hair was matted to her scalp, and her grubby fingernails were as broken as her spirit.

Across the lot, Sheba sipped something cool from an orange plastic tumbler and painted her toenails. Perspiration dripped in Daisy's eyes, making them sting, but her hands were too dirty to wipe them clear.

"Hurry it up, will you, Daisy?" Neeco called out, while Charlene giggled. "We've got another load coming in."

Something inside her snapped. She was tired of being everyone's whipping boy. She was tired of being swatted by baby elephants and treated with contempt by humans.

"Move it yourself!" She threw down the pitch fork and stomped away. She'd had enough. She was going to find Alex and demand that plane ticket. Nothing she could face on her own was as bad as this.

A great roar reverberated through the lot. With it, her skin began to burn from the heat, and her parched throat demanded water. She saw a hose running from the water truck toward the menagerie, and she hurried toward it, feeling vaguely panicked because she had never been so overheated.

Once again, she heard a roar, and she looked up to see Sinjun's cage baking in the sun. Waves of heat bounced off the asphalt and made the tiger's orange-and-black stripes shimmer.

Not all the animals were inside the menagerie tent. Some of them had been left in a small fenced-in area between the menagerie and the big top. Chester, a mangy-looking camel, was tethered not far away along with Lollipop, a cream-colored llama with bedroom eyes. A large piece of mildewed white nylon provided a bit of shade for them, but nothing shielded Sinjun from the low angle of the sun that beat through the iron bars. Like her, Sinjun seemed to have been singled out for abuse.

He stared at her with a sad sort of resignation, not even bothering to pick up his ears. Behind him, the llama made a strange clucking sound, while the camel studiously ignored her. The heat from the asphalt soaked through the soles of her sneakers and burned her feet. Perspiration trickled between her breasts. Sinjun's eyes seared her soul.

Hot. I'm so hot.

She hated this place where animals were kept in cages to be stared at. The llama's strange clucking rattled through her ears. Her head ached, and the smell of mildew from the nylon sun shade made her stomach queasy. She took an involuntary step backward, wanting to distance herself from the sun and these sad animals and the awful heat. One of her sneakers squished in a puddle of water. She looked down and saw a leak in the coupling of the hose that fed the animals' watering trough.

Without even thinking about what she was doing, she ran

along the length of the hose until she found the brass nozzle spilling water into the trough. Picking it up, she turned it to shut off the flow of water. It dripped cold in her hands.

She squinted from the glare bouncing off the dirty white sun shade, then felt Sinjun's eyes burning through her already melting skin.

Hot. I'm so hot.

She looked down at the dripping nozzle so cold in her hands. With a savage twist, she lifted the hose and sent the cool water flying directly into the tiger's cage.

Yes!

Immediately she felt relief seeping into her body.

"Hey!" Digger came running toward her, moving as fast as his arthritic knees would carry him. "You stop that, missy! You stop that right now, you hear?"

The tiger flashed his teeth at him. She whirled around and sent the spray of cold water directly at the old man, soaking the front of his grubby work shirt. "Stay away!"

He reared backward. "What're you doin'? You're gonna kill that cat! Cats don't like to get wet."

She turned the water back on the tiger and felt the cool relief moving deeper into her bones, just as if she were spraying her own body. "This one does."

"Stop it, I said! You cain't do that."

"Sinjun likes it. Look at him, Digger."

Sure enough, instead of retreating from the water, the tiger was reveling in it, turning his body into the cold spray. As she continued to douse him, she wanted to tell Digger that this wouldn't have been necessary if he'd done a better job caring for the animals, but she knew he was overworked, and she held her tongue.

"Give me that!"

Neeco had come up behind her, and he reached out to swipe the hose from her hand. She'd had more than enough of Neeco Martin, and she refused to let it go.

Water flew. She gasped as she took the full force of the spray in her face, but she didn't relax her grip on the hose.

He wrenched her wrist. "Stop it, Daisy! Hand it over."

Sinjun's maddened roar vibrated through the heavy afternoon air, drowning out the bustle of everyday noises. The cage shook as he threw his huge body at the bars, almost as if he were trying to get at Neeco to protect her. Startled, the trainer dropped her wrist and turned toward the chilling noises.

Sinjun flattened his ears against his head and hissed at him. Daisy jerked the hose free.

"Damn crazy tiger," Neeco muttered. "Someone should have put him down years ago."

Daisy sent the spray of water back into the cage. Speaking more from bluster than conviction, she said, "He doesn't like it when you mess with me."

"Look at that, Neeco," Digger said. "That sonovabitch likes the water."

"What's going on here?"

All of them turned as Alex approached. Daisy wiped her eyes with one dirty shirt sleeve while she kept the spray of water directed toward the tiger.

"Daisy decided to give Sinjun a shower," Neeco said.

"Daisy decided?" Alex gazed at her with those inscrutable Russian eyes.

"Sinjun was hot," she explained wearily. "He wanted me to cool him off."

"Did he tell you that?"

She was too drained to respond. Besides, how could she explain that Sinjun *had* told her? She didn't understand herself this mystical communication she seemed to have with the tiger.

She directed the stream of water to the muck that had collected in the bottom of the cage. "These cages are filthy. They need to be cleaned more frequently."

Digger took immediate umbrage. "I cain't do everything. If you think the cages is so bad, maybe you should clean 'em yourself."

"All right. I will."

What was she saying? Only minutes ago, she had decided she was leaving, and now she was volunteering for more work. How could she take on another job when she hadn't been able to finish any of those she'd already been given?

Alex frowned. "You're doing enough. You can barely keep your eyes open as it is, and I'm not having you take on more."

She was getting a little tired of her husband dictating her every move. "I said I'd do it, and I will. Now unless you and Neeco want to get as wet as Digger, you'd better leave me alone."

Surprise flickered in Alex's eyes. Neeco pushed forward. "She's not getting all her work done for me. How's she going to handle the menagerie, too?"

"She's not," Alex said firmly.

"I am."

"Daisy—"

"You have no say over what I do in my spare time."

"You don't have any spare time," he reminded her.

"Then I guess I'll just have to work faster."

He looked down at her for a long moment. Something passed between them that she didn't entirely understand. A spark of recognition? A glimmer of respect? "Do you really want to do this?" he asked.

"Yes."

"Are you sure you know what you're getting yourself into?"

She met his gaze without flinching. "I don't have a clue."

An emotion that almost seemed like tenderness flickered over his face and then disappeared in a brusque nod. "All right, I'll try you out for the next few days. You can work here for a couple of hours first thing in the morning, and then go work for Neeco."

Digger began to sputter. "But I need more help than that! I cain't do everything."

"Neither can Daisy," Alex said quietly.

Surprised, she stared at him.

He cocked an eyebrow at her. "Anything else?"

She belatedly remembered that she was afraid of animals,

but now wasn't the time to remind him of it, and she shook her head.

"Then the menagerie's all yours."

As he walked away, it occurred to her that every time she cast him as the principal villain in her life, he surprised her. She also realized she was no longer afraid of him. Not really. His code was a harsh one, and, in her eyes, unfair, but he always acted within its framework, and she couldn't imagine him ever compromising what he believed in.

For the next few hours, she hosed down the cages and cleaned away the accumulated filth while she tried to stay as far from the animals as possible. When she was finally done, she was even dirtier than when she'd started since she'd added mud to the rest of the grime that covered her.

She coerced one of the workers into moving Sinjun's cage to the shade, then put out fresh hay for Chester and Lollipop. The camel tried to kick her, but the llama remained placid, and as Daisy gazed into Lollipop's bedroom eyes, she decided she'd finally found an animal she liked. "You're a sweet lady, Lollipop. Maybe the two of us are going to get along."

The llama drew back her lips and shot a glob of smelly spit directly at her.

So much for gratitude.

10

Alex decided he had never seen anything more pitiful in his life than his poor little ditz of a wife. He turned away from the pot of chili he was making to watch her stumble into the trailer, her clothes filthier than those of the most ill-kempt workers. Pieces of hay and the residue from several kinds of animal feed clung to what was left of her ponytail. Her arms were streaked with mud. She also stank.

Since he'd been the target of an annoyed llama more than once himself, he recognized the smell. "Got too close to Lollipop, did you?"

She muttered something indecipherable and dragged herself toward the donnicker.

He smiled as he stirred the chili. "I didn't quite catch that. What did you say?"

Her response came to him in the polite, well-bred accent of a young woman accustomed to the finer things in life. "Go to blazes." She shut the door with a thud.

He chuckled. "I take it that was your first encounter with a llama?"

She didn't reply.

He threw in another tablespoon of chili powder, added some hot sauce for good measure, and took a taste. Too bland.

There was still no sound from the donnicker, not even running water. With a frown, he set down the hot sauce. "Daisy?" When she didn't answer, he made his way to the door and knocked. "Daisy? Are you all right?"

Nothing.

He turned the knob and looked inside to see her standing frozen in front of the mirror with tears creeping soundlessly down her cheeks as she stared at her reflection.

Something soft and unfamiliar turned over inside him. "What's the matter, sweetheart?"

She didn't move, and the tears continued to trail down her cheeks. "I was never really pretty, not like my mother, but now I'm ugly."

Instead of irritating him, her badly battered vanity seemed somehow touching. "I think you're beautiful, angel face, even dirty. You'll feel better after you're cleaned up."

She remained motionless, gazing at her reflection while the tears dripped off her chin.

He crouched down beside her, lifted her legs one by one, and pulled off her sneakers and socks.

"Please go away." She spoke with the same quiet dignity he'd observed several times in the past ten days as she'd struggled to complete one difficult task after another. "You're just doing this because I'm crying again, but it's only because I'm tired. I'm sorry. You mustn't mind."

"I didn't even notice you were crying," he lied, unsnapping her jeans and, after a moment's hesitation, pulling them down over her hips. The sweet sweep of those slim legs instantly aroused him, and he had to tear his gaze away from the enticing triangle made by her mint green panties.

How much longer was he going to be able to keep his hands off her? For the past week and a half, she'd been so tired she could barely stand up, but all he could think about was burying himself in her soft, pliant body. It had gotten to the point where he couldn't even look at her without getting hard, and that irritated the hell out of him. He liked to be in control of every aspect of his life, and he clearly wasn't in control of this one.

Even a woman who'd been raised in the circus would have had a hard time keeping up with all the work he'd thrown at Daisy. He kept telling himself it would only be a matter of days—hours even—before she'd throw in the towel and leave. That meant he couldn't touch her, not the way he wanted to. Sex between them at this point would only complicate the situation, and no matter what his body wanted, he had to leave her alone.

But she still hadn't given up, and he didn't know how much longer he could stay away from her. When he fell into bed at night, he was so aware of her curled up on the couch only a few yards away that he had trouble falling asleep. And just the sight of her during the day was making it impossible for him to concentrate on his work.

Why hadn't she left? She was soft. Weak. She cried at the drop of a hat. But even as he tore apart her character, he remembered that she'd found the guts to take on Neeco Martin and champion those poor, sad creatures in the menagerie. Daisy Devreaux Markov wasn't quite the weakling he'd thought.

The fact that she hadn't proved to be as predictable as he'd figured irritated him nearly as much as the painful effect she was having on his body, and he spoke brusquely. "Put your arms up."

The events of the day had worn her out, and she automatically obeyed. He peeled her T-shirt over her head, leaving her in the frail mint green bra and panty set that stuck to her skin. She was so worn out her head dropped, but he couldn't trust himself to finish the job, which further annoyed him. Turning away, he adjusted the water in the shower and directed her inside, underwear and all.

"I'll feed you as soon as you're done. I got sick of eating from cans, so I'm making chili tonight."

"I know how to cook," she mumbled.

"You've got enough to do for now."

She turned into the shower and let the spray splash over her, underwear and all.

When she finally came out of the bathroom, she had combed her wet hair back from her scrubbed face and wrapped herself in his blue terry robe. She didn't look much older than a teenager as she slid behind the kitchen table.

He set a hot bowl of chili in front of her, then returned to the stove to get his own.

"May I be excused from spec tonight?" she asked.

"Are you sick?"

"No."

He put his own bowl on the table, sat down across from her, and hardened his heart against her quiet dignity. "Then you're not excused."

She seemed resigned to his refusal, and that bothered him more than if she'd argued with him. "I've never been spit at before."

"Llamas'll do that. Don't take it personally."

"Frankie hates me, too. He threw a box of animal crackers at me today."

"It had to be an accident. Frankie's as gentle as they come. He likes everybody."

She propped her elbow on the table and rested her head in her hand while she listlessly stirred the chili. "Doing nothing more than walking around an arena in a skimpy outfit is female exploitation in its lowest form."

"It's also great for the box office."

He immediately regretted baiting her, especially since he knew she was too tired to fence with him. The truth was, her costume probably bothered him more than it bothered her. She wasn't as tall as the other showgirls or as busty, but her fresh-faced beauty and sweet smile made her stand out, and he'd had to discourage more than a few randy males in the audience from trying to get to her after the show. To his surprise, she seemed oblivious to the reaction she created.

She crumbled a soda cracker in the chili. "For all your talk about how well the circus takes care of its animals, the menagerie is a disgrace."

"I agree. I've been complaining about it for years, but Owen loved that menagerie and refused to get rid of it."

"What about Sheba?"

"She feels pretty much the way I do. I keep hoping she'll close it, but there's not much of a market for aging circus animals. And they're better off with us than if she sold them to some backwoods tourist trap.''

She lifted a spoonful of chili toward her mouth but then set it back in the bowl as if the effort to eat were enormous.

He couldn't stand it any longer. He didn't care if everyone in the circus criticized him for giving his wife preferential treatment because he couldn't tolerate those purple shadows under her eyes for one more day. ''Go to bed, Daisy. I've changed my mind. You can skip spec tonight.''

''Really? Are you sure?''

Her pleasure made him feel even guiltier. ''I said you could, didn't I?''

''Yes! Yes, you did. Oh, thank you, Alex. I won't forget this.''

Daisy slept through the first show, but to Alex's surprise, she appeared just as spec began for the second. Her two-hour nap had done wonders for her, and she looked more rested than she had in days. As he circled the arena on Misha, he could see her just ahead of him waving and throwing kisses at the children, oblivious to the effect she and her flame red costume were having on the children's fathers. Alex had to resist the urge to take out a few John Deere caps with his bullwhip.

When the show ended, he went to the trailer so he could make a quick change from his costume into work clothes. Usually Daisy would already have changed by now, but this time she wasn't around.

Feeling uneasy, he dressed hurriedly, then made his way back over to the big top. A flash of red sequins near the marquee in the front caught his attention, and he saw his wife surrounded by three good-looking townies. They were all behaving courteously toward her, and she certainly wasn't in any danger, but he still wanted to smash his fist right through their smug, young faces.

One of them said something and she laughed, the sound a bubble of music floating on the night air. He cursed under his breath.

''What are you so pissed off about?''

As Brady came up behind him, Alex forced himself to relax. "What makes you think I'm pissed off?"

Brady popped a toothpick into the corner of his mouth. "The way you're looking at those townies."

"I don't know what you're talking about."

"I can't figure you, Alex. I didn't think you cared anything about her."

"Lay off."

"Matter of fact, I'd just about decided to talk to you about her." He transferred the toothpick from one corner of his mouth to the other. "I figure, even though she's a thief and you seem to hate her guts, you don't have the right to work a pregnant woman so hard."

"Who told you she was pregnant?"

"We all just figured. The night of the surprise party, you didn't exactly look like a happy bridegroom."

Alex clenched his jaw. "She's not pregnant."

The toothpick drooped in Brady's mouth. "Then why the hell did you marry her?"

"None of your damn business." He stalked away.

It was a little before midnight when they were done working. As usual, when he entered the trailer, Daisy was asleep, but instead of being tucked away in a nest of rumpled sheets as she normally was, she lay on the couch in her costume, almost as if she had sat down for a few minutes and dozed off without planning to. He decided it was one thing to toughen her up, but it was another to drive her to the end of her strength, and at that moment he knew he couldn't keep working her so hard. As far as he was concerned, she'd paid her debt to society, and it was time to ease up.

Her dark hair fell onto the couch pillow in silky streamers, and her lips were slightly parted. She slept on her stomach, and his mouth went dry as he saw that sweet little ass sticking up, covered only by the diamond-patterned web of her black fishnet stockings. The narrow ribbon of sequins at the center made the sight that much more alluring. Forcing himself to look away, he stripped off his clothes, stalked into the bathroom, and plunged into an ice-cold shower.

The noise of the running water must have awakened her because, when he came out wrapped in a towel, she stood at the sink with his blue terry cloth robe tossed on over her costume. Although she'd turned up the sleeves, her small hands barely peeked out from beneath the cuffs as she opened a loaf of rye bread.

"Would you like me to fix you a sandwich?" She sounded more chipper than she had in days. "I fell asleep before I could eat, and now I'm hungry."

His robe parted, showing the curves of her breasts beneath the sequin flames on her costume. He dragged his eyes away and instead of thanking her for the offer, snapped at her. "If Sheba catches you lying around in one of her costumes, she'll have your hide."

"Then I'll just have to make sure she doesn't catch me."

The renewed spirit in her voice lifted his own mood. "I guess you can't be expected to learn everything at once."

She turned, but whatever she had been about to say seemed to die on her lips. Her gaze trailed down over his chest to the pale yellow bath towel looped low on his hips.

He wanted to yell at her, to tell her not to look at him like that unless she wanted to find herself on her back. His flagging self-control slipped another notch.

"Would you—uh—like your robe back?" she asked.

He nodded.

She tugged on the sash, slipped out of it, and passed it over to him.

He let it fall to the floor.

She stared at him. "I thought you wanted it."

"I wanted it off you."

She licked her lips, and he watched her struggle for a response. Even as he called himself every kind of fool, he knew he couldn't stay away from her for another night.

"I'm not sure exactly what you mean by that," she said hesitantly.

"I mean that I don't think I'm going to be able to keep my hands off you any longer."

"I was afraid that's what you meant." She took a deep

breath and lifted her chin. "I'm sorry, but I've decided I can't do that with you. It wouldn't be right."

"Why is that?"

"Because it wouldn't be sacred. I place value on making love. It's not something I would do with just anyone."

"I'm glad to hear it." Pulled by a force he couldn't resist, he walked over to her.

She drew back against the counter, even as she continued to meet his eyes. "I couldn't do it casually."

"I hope this means I don't have to worry about catching any of those nasty little sexually transmitted diseases you mentioned to that waitress a couple weeks ago."

"Of course not!"

"Good. You don't have to worry about me, either. I'm clean as a whistle."

"That's very nice for you, but—"

"Has anyone ever mentioned that you talk too much?" He set the heels of his hands on the counter behind her, effectively trapping her.

"We *need* to talk about this. It's important. It's—"

"What we *need* to do is stop talking." He cupped her waist with his hands. "We've played cat and mouse long enough, angel face. Don't you think it's time we get serious?"

Her perfume drifted up to tantalize him. He gazed down at her body, so enticingly revealed by the skimpy flame red sequin costume, and her soft breathing stirred the hair on his chest.

"How—how can you even think about doing something like this with a person you don't respect?"

Her eyes drifted shut as he dipped his head and nuzzled the side of her neck with his lips. "Why don't you let me worry about that?"

"You think I'm a thief."

"Let's just say I've cooled down a little."

She tilted her face up to his, and another pang of guilt struck him as her violet eyes came alive with joy and her soft, silly mouth curled with pleasure. "You believe me! You know I didn't steal the money!"

He hadn't said that. He was simply no longer as angry. Although he couldn't condone what she'd done, he knew she'd been desperate, and he no longer wanted to serve as her hanging judge.

"I believe you're sexy as hell." He brushed his thumb over her bottom lip and found it moist to his touch. "Are you taking care of birth control, or do you want me to do it?"

Her eyes flared. "I'm on the pill, but—"

"That's good."

He dipped his head and caught her mouth beneath his own. It quivered. God, she was sweet. She must have nibbled one of the ripe plums in the bag on the counter because he tasted the fruit on her breath.

Her lips parted a bit, but the movement was hesitant, as if she were still making up her mind. He found something infinitely exciting about her tentative, uncertain welcome. At the same time, he knew he wasn't going to give her any more time to think, and he drew her closer.

Outside the small world of the trailer, the first drops of rain began to fall, hitting the metal shell with gentle taps. The sound was soothing and hypnotic. The patter of the rain somehow isolated them, set them apart from everyone else in the universe and gave them a private place.

Daisy sighed as she felt Alex's kiss, gentle and patient. The icon he wore rubbed against her, and as the tip of his tongue brushed the sensitive inner surface of her bottom lip, warm honey poured through her veins. In that moment all her principles evaporated, and any idea she'd had of denying him disappeared. From the beginning she'd wanted him like this, and she could no longer resist the force that pulled her toward him.

Opening her mouth, she let him in.

He took his time invading her, and when he did, his kiss was deep and full. She responded with fervor, and he let her play as she wished.

She used her tongue on him and her lips, kissed the corners of that hard mouth, delved inside again. She wrapped her arms around his shoulders and, standing on tiptoe, nipped his earlobe. She left little teeth marks at the corner of his jaw before she returned to plunge inside his mouth.

Enter and play.

Withdraw and explore.

Inside again.

Her excitement mounted, fueled by the rasp of his breathing and the feel of his hands clasping her so tightly, one at her waist, one splayed across her back. How could she ever have been afraid of him? The image of the whips stored beneath the bed flicked through her mind, but she pushed them aside. He wouldn't hurt her. He couldn't.

She licked a sweet trail from his neck to his chest and poked the tip of her tongue through the dark hair that dusted his pectorals until she could press her lips to the skin beneath. His breathing came more rapidly now, and when he spoke, his voice sounded hoarse.

"If this is the way you kiss, angel, I can't wait to see how you—" He moaned as she found his nipple.

She wrapped her arms around his neck and one of her fingers caught in the gold chain that held the icon. This game of hot kisses and new touches was so delicious she couldn't get enough of it. His body was hers to explore, and she yearned to see every inch of it.

"I want to take off your towel," she whispered.

His fingers sank into her hair.

She reached for the knot, only to have him press his hand over hers. "Not so fast, sweetheart. First you've got to show me something."

"What do you want to see?"

"I'll let you choose."

"In this costume, I think I've already shown off just about everything I have."

"Maybe I want a closer look."

She'd known sex could be exciting, but she hadn't expected the sensuous teasing note in his voice. It flashed through her mind that perhaps she should confess that she was a virgin, but then he'd think she was a freak. And he'd never know if she didn't tell him. Contrary to romantic fiction, fragile maidenheads didn't survive twenty-six years of physical activity and doctors' exams.

Tilting back her head, she watched his eyes roam over her as she stood before him in her showgirl's costume, and she found the idea of playing the experienced femme fatale infinitely exciting. She'd read lots of books, so maybe she could even pull it off. What could she do that was naughty?

She turned her back to him, trying to give herself a moment to think, and in the process saw that the limp blue curtains hanging on the small window just above the kitchen table weren't closed all the way. She doubted anyone would be passing by in the rain, but just in case, she hurried over. Bracing one hand on the Formica top, she leaned across the table to close them.

She heard a muffled sound behind her, almost like a groan. "Good choice, sweetheart."

She had no idea what he was talking about until she felt him come up behind her and rub against her out-thrust bottom. He massaged the flesh through its diamond-shaped veil of fishnet. Her nipples tightened and her skin grew flushed at the unfamiliar sensation. At the same time, her nervousness escalated. No matter what she wanted him to believe, she had no experience with ordinary lovemaking, let alone anything exotic.

One of his fingertips slipped beneath the strip of sequins and traced the cleft of her bottom. She bit her lips to keep from crying out with pleasure. His touch crept lower.

Unable to take any more, she wiggled upright and turned in his arms. "I—I want to kiss again."

He groaned. "Your kisses are a little more than I can handle right now." He adjusted the knot at his belly, and she saw that the towel no longer lay flat against him. As a matter of fact, it wasn't even close to being flat.

She stared and her mouth felt dry. "I st-still want to kiss."

"We'll negotiate. You open up the hook on the back of that costume, and we'll kiss all you want."

She reluctantly raised her eyes from the towel and lifted her arms to unfasten the hook. As it opened, the bodice began to fall away. She clasped it to her chest.

He ducked his head, brushed her lips, and took one of her wrists in each of his hands. As his tongue slipped into her mouth, the costume fell to her waist. He backed her against the wall on the far side of the table, drew her wrists upward, and pinioned them on each side of her head.

"Not fair," she whispered into his mouth as he held her against the wall. "You're stronger than I am."

"It's my turn to play," he whispered back.

And play he did.

Keeping her wrists gently pinioned, he used only his mouth to excite her. He nibbled at her earlobe and the side of her neck. He nipped at her collarbone and the base of her throat. But then he drew back just far enough to be able to gaze down at her body.

Her position against the wall had tipped up the crests of her breasts. He toyed with first one, then the other, suckling until the pool of heat inside her burned so fiercely she could hardly bear it.

"Stop," she gasped. "Let me go."

He immediately released her wrists. "Am I hurting you?"

"No, but—you're going too fast."

"Too fast?" He regarded her with a crooked smile. "Are you criticizing my technique?"

"Oh, no. Your technique is wonderful." The words came from her in a rush, too earnest, too eager, and he smiled. Embarrassed, she avoided meeting his eyes by staring at his mouth. Then she realized that if she were to make love with this fierce, proud man, she had to meet his strength with her own.

Lifting her head, she met his gaze. "I don't want you to take over yet. Maybe later, but not yet."

"Is this your way of telling me you want to direct the action for a while?"

She nodded. Even though she was nervous, she wouldn't let anything prevent her from investigating the wonderful mysteries hidden beneath that towel.

"One condition, angel." He hooked the edge of her costume where it lay at her waist. "It's just going to be you and those tights. Everything else comes off."

She swallowed. The tights had no panty built into them. They were sheer from waistband to toe, and the diamond-pattern was too loosely woven to hide anything.

He raised one eyebrow in challenge, then released her and sat down on the end of his bed. "I want to watch you undress."

This was getting *very* naughty. She cleared her throat and spoke as casually as she could. "Do you mean right here? With the lights on and everything?"

"You're stalling. Peel it down real slow."

She gathered her courage, determined to keep up with him. "You understand, don't you, that your towel's coming off next?"

"One thing at a time."

She slowly slipped the costume over her hips, leaning forward as she lowered it to hide her nudity from him. The costume dropped to her ankles. She brushed a spec of lint from the top of her foot, inspected the wear in the carpet, listened to the rain tap on the trailer's roof.

"Oh, no, you don't." He chuckled. "Straighten up. And leave that costume right there on the floor."

The smoky undertone in his voice nearly undid her. Her hands trembled as she did as he said.

"Beautiful," he whispered, as she stood before him, naked except for the frail black showgirl's tights that enhanced, rather than concealed, the lower part of her body.

She decided the time had come to test him. "Lie back on the bed," she said softly.

He hesitated for only a moment before he stretched out on his side and propped himself on one elbow. "Like this?"

"Oh, no. That won't do at all. On your back, please."

To her delight, he did as she said. He also propped his

head up on two pillows so he wouldn't miss anything.

She licked her lips, not quite certain she could pull this off, but determined to give it her best. "Now raise your hands until they're touching the wall. And, Alex, I want you to keep them there."

He gave her a lazy smile that turned her bones to water. "Are you sure about this?"

"Very sure."

He did as she said, making her exceptionally proud of herself. She approached him. His eyes burned on her breasts and belly in a way that made her feel more naked in the tights than she would have without them. By the time she reached the bed, every part of her body tingled with excitement and anticipation. For a moment the thought of the whips stored just underneath them intruded, but she pushed it away.

She gazed down at him lying with his arms in mock bondage. Her captive. As long as he stayed as he was, every part of his body was hers to explore, including the imposing mound that destroyed the smooth surface of the towel. She drew her eyes away and sat on the edge of the bed.

"Remember what I said," she whispered. "You have to keep your hands where they are. You can't move them."

"If you open your legs just a little bit, sweetheart, I'll be as cooperative as I know how."

Fair was fair, she decided, and she eased her thighs apart. He gazed at what she had revealed. His right arm twitched, as if he were getting ready to move it, but then he relaxed.

She lowered her head and began tasting him again, nibbling near the bottom curve of his rib cage. His flesh was firm and tightly muscled. She slid her hands over his chest, enjoying the texture of hair and skin gone moist. She couldn't resist those brown nipples and ran her lips across them, making him writhe beneath her. Reaching up, she clasped his biceps and squeezed. Her thumbs discovered the pulsing veins that ran beneath his skin. She traced them downward and found her way to the soft hair in his armpits. As she dallied there, goose bumps broke out over his damp skin, and he made an inarticulate noise deep in his throat. Slowly lifting her head, she met his eyes.

"I'm going to take off your towel."

"Are you now?"

The raw desire in his eyes reminded her she was playing with fire. But she had no intention of turning back, and she moved her hands to the top of the towel. With one smooth motion, she opened it and spread it apart.

"Oh . . ." He was magnificent. She extended her hand and touched him tentatively with the tip of her finger. He nearly leaped off the bed, and she snatched back her hand.

Her gaze flew to his face. It was contorted as if he were in pain. "Did I hurt you?"

"You've got sixty seconds," he croaked, "and then I'm moving my arms."

A thrill of pleasure shot through her as she realized this was all part of the game. "Not till I give you permission," she said sternly.

"Fifty seconds," he replied.

She hurried to touch him again, letting her curious fingertips roam along every inch, caressing here and there. She nudged his thighs open a few inches and found more places to touch.

"Twenty seconds," he groaned.

"Stop counting so fast."

He chuckled and moaned at the same time, making her smile. But then her smile faded. After all of these years, how was her small body supposed to accommodate something like this? As she closed her hand around him, it occurred to her that her own internal parts could very well have atrophied from lack of use. She moved her hand.

"That's it!"

Without warning, she found herself flipped to her back with his weight pressing down on her. "I think it's time you got a little of your own medicine, sweetheart. Assume the position."

"What do you mean?"

"Hands against the wall."

She gulped and thought of the whips. Maybe her plan to play the femme fatale had worked too well. He believed her far more experienced than she was.

"Alex?"

"We're not talking till I see that you know how to follow orders."

She slowly raised her arms to the pillow.

"I told you to touch the wall."

She did as she was ordered, and she'd never felt more defenseless or more aroused. As her knuckles brushed the thin paneling behind her she was overcome by an unsettling combination of uneasiness and a deep sensual hunger. She wanted to beg him to be gentle with her. At the same time, she wanted him to love her with all his might.

She lay like a bound captive beneath his gaze. Somehow the fact that there were no true restraints holding her in place didn't make her position of subjugation any less real. He was so much stronger than she, so much more powerful, that he could do whatever he wished, regardless of whether or not she agreed. A prickle of alarm ruffled the edges of her arousal only to fade as he ran the tip of his finger across her stomach, back and forth over the fishnet until she wanted to scream. He moved lower, touching the patch of curls.

"Open up, sweetheart."

She did as he said, but apparently he wasn't satisfied with her effort because he caught her thighs and separated them farther.

The tights were no barrier, and she suddenly felt too open, too vulnerable. She began to moved her hands away from the wall.

"Don't even think about it," he whispered, his touch gliding over what she had revealed.

She moaned and lay back to feel him parting her with his thumbs through the moist diamond web. He dipped his head. She cried out, and her fists banged against the wall as he touched her with his mouth, caressed her through the net. A low, strangled sound of pleasure caught in her throat. She felt the net stretched taut across her, its webbing pressing deeply into her softness.

His shoulders splayed her knees and he held her breasts beneath the palms of his hands as he loved her. The rain thrummed on the metal womb that encompassed them both, and her own womb quivered in response to what was happening. As her senses swirled, she felt the vibration of thunder passing through the wall into her hands and traveling down into every nerve of her body. Her back arched, and she gave herself up to him in a shattering climax.

He held her through the aftershocks. Only when she recovered did she become aware of a strange tugging between her legs. She didn't understand what he had done until he settled over her and she experienced that long-awaited stretching at the very entrance to her body.

"You've torn a hole in my tights," she murmured foolishly, slipping her arms around his shoulders and reveling in the feel of his weight pressing her into the mattress.

He brushed his lips over her temples. "I'll buy you a new pair. I swear." He gave a gentle push.

And went nowhere.

She stiffened. Her worst fears had been realized. She'd atrophied from so many years of being unused.

He drew back a little and smiled down at her, but she could feel the tension in his body and knew he was on the verge of losing control.

"I thought you were ready, but I guess I haven't been thorough enough." He shifted his weight ever so slightly and began caressing her.

Within moments, his voice seemed to come to her from a great distance. "You're so tight, sweetheart. It's been a while for you, hasn't it?"

She sank her nails into his shoulders. "It's—yes. I might have—" she gasped as new sensations spiraled inside her ""—closed up a bit."

He groaned and repositioned his body. "Then let's open you back up." With that, he pressed home.

She cried out and arched to get away from him or to get

closer, she didn't know which. Her body stung from the sweet, aching stretch. He grabbed her bottom and thrust more deeply. At the same time, his mouth covered hers, devouring her. His possession was fierce and strong, but the awful tension she felt in him told her he was still holding back. She didn't understand why until she heard his barely audible murmur.

"Let go, sweetheart. Let go."

She knew, then, that he was waiting for her, and those tender words sent her flying over the edge again.

When she came back, his skin was slick under her hands, his body taut with need. But he was a strong and generous lover.

"Once more, sweetheart. "Once more."

"No, I—"

"Yes!" He drove again, deep and sure.

Outside, the thunder rolled, and inside she did as she had been bid. This time, however, he went along.

Time trickled over them as they lay motionless, their bodies entwined, his remaining inside her own.

She would never forget this. Despite the horrible things that had led to this moment, she could not have had a more wonderful introduction to lovemaking, and she would always be grateful to him for this.

She pressed her lips to his chest and stroked him with her palms. After all this time, it had finally happened. "I'm not a virgin any longer."

She felt his body go rigid beneath her hands. Only then did she realize she had spoken her secret out loud.

11

"What did you say?" Alex reared up over her.

She wanted to bite her tongue. How could she have spoken the words out loud? She had been so drowsy and content that she'd been lulled into stupidity. "N-nothing," she stammered. "I didn't say anything."

"I heard you."

"Then why are you asking?"

"You said you weren't a virgin anymore."

"Did I?"

"Daisy . . ." His voice held an ominous note of warning. "Am I supposed to take that literally?"

She attempted to adopt a tone of moral superiority. "It's really none of your business."

"Bullshit." He vaulted from the bed, grabbed his jeans, and pulled them on as if it were imperative for him to put some kind of barrier between them. He spun back to confront her. "Just what kind of game are you playing?"

She couldn't help but notice that he hadn't fastened the zipper, and she had to tear her eyes away from that enticing V that revealed his hard, flat belly. "I don't want to discuss it."

"Do you seriously expect me to believe you were a virgin?"

"Of course, I don't. I'm twenty-six years old."

He shoved one hand through his hair and began pacing in the small space at the foot of the bed, speaking as if he hadn't heard her. "You were so tight. I thought maybe it had been a while, but I never figured—how could you have been around all these years and never fucked?"

She shot up high into the pillows. "There isn't any need for you to use that kind of language, and I want you to apologize to me right now!"

He stared down at her as if she'd lost her mind. She stared right back. If he thought she was going to back down about this, he could think again. She'd heard enough foul language during her twenty-six years with Lani to last a lifetime, and she wasn't going to subject herself to any more. "I'm waiting."

"Answer my question."

"After you apologize."

"I'm sorry!" he shouted, losing his famous self-control. "Now you tell me the truth right this minute or I'm going to strangle you to death with those tights, throw your body in a roadside ditch, and dance on top of it!"

As an apology, it didn't count for much, but she decided it was the best he was going to do. "I'm not a virgin," she said carefully.

For a moment he looked relieved, and then he regarded her with suspicion. "You're not a virgin right now, but what about when you walked into this trailer?"

"I might have been then," she muttered.

"Might have been?"

"All right. Was."

"I don't believe it! Nobody who looks like you gets to be twenty-six without ever—"

She shot him a warning glare.

"—without *doing it*, for god's sake! Why?"

She toyed with the edge of the sheet. "All my life, my mother had a revolving door on her bedroom."

"What did that have to do with you?"

"Blatant promiscuity isn't a nice thing to grow up with, and I rebelled."

"Rebelled?"

"I decided to be the opposite of my mother."

He sat down at the foot of the bed. "Daisy, taking a lover here and there wouldn't have made you promiscuous. You're a passionate woman. You deserved to have a sex life."

"I wasn't married."

"So what?"

"Alex, I don't believe in sex outside of marriage."

He regarded her blankly.

"I don't believe in sex outside of marriage," she repeated. "Not for women. And not for men either."

"You're kidding."

"I'm not judgmental about it, but that's the way I feel. If you want to laugh, go ahead."

"How could anyone in this day and age think that way?"

"I'm illegitimate, Alex, and that sort of thing tends to change your perspective. You probably think I'm a prude, but I can't help it."

"After what happened between us tonight, I would hardly call you a prude." For the first time he smiled. "Where did you learn all those tricks?"

"Tricks?"

"Like that 'hands against the wall' stuff, for starters."

"Oh, that." She realized she was blushing. "I've read a few dirty books."

"Good for you."

She frowned, suddenly unsure. "Didn't you like it? I can take constructive criticism. I want to learn, and you can tell me the truth."

"I liked it a lot."

"But maybe it wasn't inventive enough for you." She thought about the whips. "To be honest, I don't think I can get much kinkier. And you should probably know right now that I'm not interested in physical pain."

For a moment he looked confused, and then he smiled. "You've got a real thing about those whips, don't you?"

"It's a little hard not to think about them when they're lying around all the time."

"I guess I'm having a tough time believing someone

who's so interested in kinky lovemaking has such a narrow view of sexual morality.''

''I didn't say I was interested; I was just trying to make certain we understand each other. And as to my narrow views—just before Mother died, she had lovers who were younger than me. I really hated that.''

He rose from the foot of the bed. ''Why didn't you tell me you were a virgin from the beginning?''

''Would it have changed anything?''

''I don't know. Maybe. I sure as hell wouldn't have been so rough.''

Her eyes widened. ''You were being rough?''

The hard lines around his mouth eased. He sat down next to her and ran his thumb across her lips. ''What am I going to do with you?''

''I have an idea, but you might not like it.''

''Tell me.''

''Could we—I don't know exactly how long it'll take you to recover, but, when you have . . .''

''Are you trying to tell me you want to do it again?''

''Yes, please.''

He smiled down at her, but at the same time, he seemed troubled. ''All right, sweetheart, I guess anybody who's waited this long deserves to make up for lost time.''

She parted her lips, eager for his kiss, only to have him pull back the sheet and embarrass her by telling her he wouldn't go any further until he'd made sure she was all right. Ignoring her protests, he stripped off what remained of her tights and did just that. When he was finally satisfied that he hadn't harmed her, he began to love her all over again. The rain *tap-tap-tapped* on the windows, and when they were done, she fell into the first restful sleep she'd known in months.

They had barely gotten under way the next morning before he began to cut her into slivers verbally. And all because she'd let him distract her before she'd had time to explain one small detail.

"I assumed. *Assumed!* God, what an ass I am. I *deserve* to be married to you. Why should I have assumed you'd get this right when you haven't gotten anything else right?"

After the tender magic of last night, his attack was doubly hurtful. When they'd first met, his anger had been cold and quiet, but now a pressure valve seemed to have exploded.

"Couldn't you have finished explaining?" he raved. "No, of course not. That would have been too logical."

She blinked her eyes hard and hated herself with all her might for not being the kind of person who could scream right back at him.

"When you said you were taking birth control pills, you needed to finish the story, Daisy. You needed to tell me you'd just started to take them, that you hadn't been on them for a full month yet, that there's still a chance I could *get you goddamn pregnant!* Couldn't you have finished the story, Daisy?"

She dug her fingernails into her palms to keep from crying. At the same time she cursed herself for letting him get to her like this.

"Answer me right now!"

The lump in her throat had grown so large she had to choke the words out. "I—I was o-overcome by p-passion."

Some of the tension seemed to leave his body. He eased up on the accelerator, looked over at her, and scowled. "Are you crying?"

She lifted her chin and shook her head, even as a tear skidded down her cheek. She'd couldn't stand the idea of crying in front of him again. She'd always hated her easy tears.

He slowed and his voice gentled. "Daisy, I'm sorry." He glanced into his side mirror and began to pull off the road.

"Don't you dare stop this truck!" she said fiercely.

The tires kicked up gravel as he brought the rig to a stop, ignoring her wishes as usual. He reached out for her, but she drew away.

"I'm not a wimp!" She lashed out at him and angrily dashed away her tears with her fingers.

"I didn't say you were."

"You're thinking it! I just cry easily. But it doesn't mean anything, and I'm not trying to manipulate you with tears. I want you to apologize because you're acting like a jerk, not because I'm crying and it's made you feel guilty."

"I'm definitely acting like a jerk."

"Because I can't help crying. I've always been emotional. Newborn babies, long-distance telephone commercials, a good country-western song. I see something or hear something and the next thing I know—"

"Daisy, I'm trying to apologize. You can go ahead and cry if you want, but just don't talk, okay?"

She sniffed and reached into her purse for a tissue. "Okay."

"I had no right to yell at you like that. I was mad at myself, and I took it out on you. I was the one who cut you off last night before you'd had time to explain. It's my fault. I've never been this irresponsible before, and I can't explain it. I guess I just . . ." He hesitated.

She wiped her nose. "Got swept away by passion?"

He smiled. "I suppose that's as good a reason as any. But, Daisy, if you're pregnant because of my stupidity . . ."

The dread she heard in his voice made her want to start crying all over again. Instead, she gave her nose a business-like blow. "I'm sure I won't be. It's not the right time. My period is supposed to start in a couple of days."

She could almost see his relief and that hurt her even more. Not that she wanted to be pregnant, because she didn't. But neither did she like it that the mere idea repelled him.

He plowed his fingers through his hair. "I get a little crazy when this subject comes up, but I can't help it. I don't want to have children, Daisy."

"There isn't any need to worry. Amelia sent me to her own doctor a couple of weeks ago."

"That's good. I can't begin to explain how strongly I feel about this. When I say I don't want to have children, I mean I don't ever want to have them. I'd make a terrible father, and no child deserves that. Promise me that you won't get forgetful with those pills.''

"I wouldn't do that. And, frankly, Alex, I'm getting a little tired of being treated as if I'm incompetent.''

He checked his side mirror and pulled back out onto the highway. "I'll use condoms until next month when you're safe.''

She didn't like the way he took it for granted that she would continue sleeping with him. "I'm not sure there's going to be any need.''

He glanced over at her. "What do you mean?''

"You're acting as if what happened last night is going to happen again.''

"Trust me. It's going to happen again.''

His smugness offended her. "I wouldn't be too certain of that.''

"Don't try to pretend you didn't enjoy yourself. I was there, remember?''

"I'm not pretending anything. It was wonderful. One of the most wonderful things that's ever happened to me. I'm simply telling you that your attitude toward lovemaking leaves a lot to be desired.''

"What's wrong with my attitude?''

"It's irreverent. Take your vocabulary, for example. The words you use. They're definitely irreverent.''

"I don't believe this.''

"Lovemaking is supposed to be sacred.''

"It's supposed to be dirty and sweaty and fun.''

"That, too, I suppose. But holy.''

"Holy?'' He regarded her with disbelief. "How can somebody who grew up around a bunch of social parasites and drugged-out rock stars be such a prude?''

"I knew it! I knew you thought I was a prude, but you weren't honest enough last night to admit it.''

"Now I get it. You're deliberately trying to make me crazy. No matter what I say, you're going to get mad at me, aren't you?'' He gave her a sideways look that further aggravated her.

"Stop trying to be cute. You're too mean to be cute."

He cocked his head and, to her surprise, looked genuinely hurt. "Do you really think I'm mean?"

"Not all the time," she admitted. "But most of the time. You're definitely mean most of the time."

"Anybody in this circus will tell you I'm the most fair-minded manager they've ever worked for."

"You do seem fair-minded." She paused. "With everybody but me."

"I've been fair with you." He hesitated. "Maybe I wasn't fair the night they had the cake party for us, but I was surprised, and—that's no excuse, is it? I'm sorry, Daisy. I shouldn't have embarrassed you like that."

She studied him, then gave a small nod. "I accept your apology."

"And I wasn't mean last night."

"I'd rather not talk about last night. And I want your promise that you won't try to seduce me again tonight. I have some thinking I need to do first, and I'm going to do it on the couch."

"I don't know what there is to think about. You don't believe in sex outside of marriage. You're married. What's the problem?"

"I'm circumstanced," she pointed out gently. "There's a subtle difference."

He muttered a particularly nasty obscenity. Before she could chastise him for it, he jerked the wheel to the right and pulled into the Cozy Corner Truck Stop.

This time their waitress was sullen and well past middle age, so Daisy felt safe leaving him alone at the table to go to the rest room. She should have known better, however, for when she came out, he had struck up a conversation with a flashy blond sitting in the opposite booth.

She knew he'd seen her, even as she watched the woman pick up her coffee and slide over next to him. She even thought she knew why he was doing this. He wanted to make certain she didn't attach any emotional importance to what had happened between them.

She gritted her teeth. Whether Alex Markov wanted to admit it or not, he was a married man, and all the flirting in the world wouldn't change that.

She stalked over to a pay telephone on the wall not far from the booth where the blond was admiring his muscles. As soon as she had her temper under control, she picked up the receiver and kept it pressed to her ear while she counted to twenty-five. Finally, she turned back to her husband and called out, "Alex, darling! Guess what?"

He lifted his head and regarded her warily.

"Good news!" she chirped. "The doctor says this time it's triplets!"

Alex was finally speaking to her again by the time they arrived at the new lot. As he climbed out of the truck and began unhitching the trailer, he told her she wasn't going to be working with the animals anymore. Instead, she would start doing lighter duty, keeping the costumes mended, and, of course, appearing in spec every night.

She frowned at him.

"I thought you'd be happy not to have to work so hard," he said. "What did I do wrong now?"

"Why did you wait until this morning to lighten my duties?"

"No particular reason."

"Are you sure?"

"Stop beating around the bush and tell me what's on your mind."

"I feel a little bit like a hooker who's just gotten paid for duties performed."

"That's ridiculous. I'd made up my mind about this even before we slept together. Besides, who says you're the one who should get paid. I think I performed pretty damn well, too."

She ignored his baiting. "I said I'd take over the menagerie, and I meant it."

"I'm telling you that you don't have to."

"And I'm telling you that I want to." It was true. From

her experience with the elephants, she knew the work would be hard, but it couldn't be worse than what she'd already survived. And she *had* survived. She'd shoveled manure until her hands blistered, hauled heavy wheelbarrows, been swatted by cantankerous baby elephants. She'd looked fear in the face, and she was still on her feet—battered, maybe, and certainly bruised, but still standing.

He regarded her with a mixture of incredulity and something that almost seemed like admiration, although she knew it couldn't be that. "You're going to see this thing through, aren't you? You're not going to run away."

"I'm not making any long-term predictions. One day at a time is the most I can manage right now." She caught her bottom lip between her teeth and frowned. "All I know is that I have to do this."

"Daisy, it's too much work."

"I know." She smiled. "That's why I have to do it."

He gazed at her for a long moment and then, to her astonishment, dipped his head and kissed her. Right there, in the middle of the backyard as the workers bustled around them, as Brady and his sons practiced their acrobatics and Heather juggled, he gave her a deep, long kiss.

When they finally drew apart, she felt warm and breathless. He raised his head and glanced around. She expected him to look embarrassed by their public display, but he didn't. Maybe he was trying to make up for the incident with the cake, or maybe his motivations were more complex than that, but for whatever reason, he'd let everyone in the circus know that she meant something to him.

She had little time to ponder the incident as she set about her duties in the menagerie. A young worker named Trey Skinner appeared and told her Alex had assigned him to help her with the heavier work. She had him position Sinjun's cage in the shade and haul some hay for her, then she let him go.

To her relief, Lollipop didn't try to spit at her again, but she still gave the llama a wide berth. In addition to Lollipop, Sinjun, and Chester, the menagerie contained a leopard named Fred, a vulture who'd had his wings clipped, and a gorilla. There was also a boa constrictor, but to Daisy's relief, the snake had become Jill's pet, and she kept him in her trailer when he wasn't on display.

Following Digger's sketchy instructions, Daisy fed the animals, then began cleaning out the cages, starting with Sinjun's. The tiger regarded her with lofty condescension as she gave him his shower, acting as if he were granting her a privilege by letting her serve him.

"I don't like you," she grumbled as she turned the water on him.

Liar.

She nearly dropped the hose. "Stop it," she hissed. "Stop putting thoughts in my head."

He yawned and ducked into the spray, making her feel unbelievably foolish.

When she was done with Sinjun's shower, she wandered back into the tent and stared at the lowland gorilla named Glenna who was caged in the corner. Her dark chocolate eyes were sad and resigned as she stared out through the iron bars of a battered old cage that seemed much too small for her. Something about the animal's quiet resignation fascinated Daisy, and she found herself approaching the cage.

Glenna sat quietly watching her, assessing this new human being in what must have seemed like an endless parade of humans who passed by her cage each day. Daisy stopped and waited, feeling as if she somehow wanted Glenna's permission before she came closer, as if in this one small event, the gorilla should have a choice.

Glenna moved to the front of the cage and observed her. Slowly she raised her arm and pushed her hand through the bars. Daisy stared at it and realized the gorilla was reaching out to her.

Glenna waited patiently, her hand extended. Daisy's heart thudded. She could barely bring herself to pet a kitten, let alone touch a wild animal, and she wanted to turn away, but the gorilla seemed so human that to ignore the gesture would have been an unforgivable breech of good manners, and she walked hesitantly forward.

Glenna's hand rested palm upward. With the greatest reluctance Daisy extended her own hand and, using the tip of her index finger, gingerly touched the tip of Glenna's finger. It was soft and smooth. Feeling a bit braver, she stroked its supple length. Glenna closed her eyes and gave a soft gorilla sigh.

Daisy stayed with her for some time, stroking her hand and feeling as if her life had somehow found a sense of purpose.

As the morning slipped by, her questions about the proper care of the animals multiplied. Several times she ran over to ask Digger for advice about feed and daily routine, and each time she approached, Tater trumpeted at her like a playground bully.

Digger answered her questions reluctantly, and she knew he was still put out by what had happened between them yesterday. As she turned to leave after her second series of inquiries, he spat, barely missing her sneaker.

"Don't have time for any more of your questions, Miz. Wouldn't want nobody to think I'm *lazy*."

"Digger, I didn't say you were lazy. I was just worried about the conditions in the menagerie." She secretly wondered how much Digger really knew about the proper care of the menagerie animals. He loved the elephants, but he didn't really care about the others. He certainly hadn't known that tigers loved water. She resolved to do some research herself in her free time.

His rheumy eyes were full of resentment. "I been around animals for fifty years. How long you been around?"

"Only two weeks. That's why I need your advice."

"I ain't got time for no talk. Got too much work to do." He looked past her, and his lips parted in a grin that showed yellowed teeth curling in on several gaping holes. Too late, she saw the source of his amusement. Tater had sidled up behind her.

Swat!

She felt as if she'd been hit in the chest with a tightly rolled piece of carpet. With no time to brace herself, she flew across the ground before stumbling against a bale of hay. Her hip hit the dirt, sending shards of pain shooting up into her body. Digger's wheezy laughter echoed in her ears. She lifted her head just in time to see an expression in Tater's eyes that looked very much like a smirk.

Fireworks went off in her brain. She'd had enough!

Ignoring the pain in her leg and hip, she vaulted to her feet and descended on the baby elephant, shaking her fist. "Don't you *ever* do that to me again! *Ever!* Do you hear me?"

The elephant took a lumbering step backward as she went after him. "You're rude, nasty, and *mean*! And the next time you swat me, you're going to be sorry! I won't stand for being abused! *Do you understand me?*"

Tater let out a pitiful little elephant bleat and ducked his head, but she was a woman who had been pushed too far. Forgetting her aversion to touching animals, she poked his trunk with her index finger. "If you want my attention, you earn it by being *nice*! You don't earn it by swatting me every time I come near!"

His trunk drooped, and one of his ears turned inside out as it flopped forward. She reared herself up to her full height. *"Do we have an understanding or not?"*

He lifted his head just far enough to butt it gently against her shoulder. She crossed her arms, rejecting his peace offering. "I can't just pretend none of this happened."

He nudged her again, his brown eyes baleful. She steeled herself against the sweep of those impossibly curly lashes. "I'm sorry, but it's going to take time. You have a lot to make up for. Now if you'll excuse me, I have to get back to the menagerie." She turned to walk away.

He bleated. Pitiful. Heartbroken. Every boy in the world who'd lost it all for love.

Her steps slowed and her heart softened as she saw the woebegone baby elephant with his sagging ears and mournful brown eyes. His defeated little trunk dragged on the ground, the tip curling in the dust.

"You brought this on yourself," she pointed out.

A tiny, plaintive trumpet.

"I tried to be nice."

Another pathetic trumpet. And then, to her astonishment, she saw tears begin to trickle from his eyes. Digger had told her that elephants were one of the most emotional animals in existence and they'd been known to cry, but she hadn't believed him. Now, as she watched the tears running down over Tater's wrinkled skin, her resentment dissolved.

For the second time that day, she forgot her aversion to petting animals. She reached out her hand and stroked Tater's trunk. "That's not fair. You're as big a crybaby as I am."

His head perked up and he took a few tentative steps toward her. When he came close, he stopped as if to ask for permission before he rubbed his head against her shoulder.

Once again he nearly sent her flying, although this time the gesture was one of affection. She rubbed his forehead. "Don't think that just because I forgive you I'm going to be a pushover. You have to mind your manners or it's all over between us."

He snuggled against her as gently as a kitten.

"No more swats. No nasty bathroom tricks."

He let out a soft puff of air, and she surrendered. "You silly baby."

As Daisy lost her heart, Alex stood by the back door of the big top and watched it all happening. He saw the elephant curl his trunk over her arm and smiled to himself. Whether Daisy knew it or not, she'd just made a friend for life. He chuckled and headed toward the red wagon.

Heather had never been so miserable. She sat at the kitchen table of their Airstream and stared down at her day's schoolwork, but the print on the page wouldn't come into focus. Like the other circus kids, she was doing her schoolwork by correspondence through the Calvert School in Baltimore, a place that specialized in teaching children who couldn't go to regular school. Every few weeks a fat envelope arrived full of books, papers, and tests.

Sheba had gotten into the habit of supervising Heather's schoolwork, but Sheba's own formal education hadn't been terrific, and she was pretty lame at anything except monitoring the tests. Heather was having trouble with geometry, and she'd gotten a D on her last English composition.

Now she pushed her book aside and stared down at the piece of notebook paper in front of her that she'd been doodling on. *Mrs. Alex Markov. Heather Markov. Heather Pepper Markov.*

Shit. Why had he let her do it? Why had Alex let Daisy kiss him like that right out there in front of everyone? Heather had wanted to die when she saw that kiss. She hated Daisy's guts, and the best thing about these past few weeks had been seeing her all dirty and nasty from hauling shit. She deserved to haul shit.

Over and over Heather tried to ease her guilt about what she'd done to Daisy by telling herself that Daisy deserved what had happened to her. She didn't belong here. She didn't fit in. And she should never have married Alex. Alex had been Heather's.

She'd fallen in love with him six weeks ago when she'd first set eyes on him. Unlike her father, he always had time to talk to her. He didn't mind having her follow him around, and before Daisy had come along, he'd even taken her with him sometimes when he'd gone to run errands. Once when they were in Jacksonville, they'd gone into this art gallery together and he'd explained stuff to her about the pictures. He also encouraged her to talk about her mother and had said a couple of things about why her dad was so stubborn.

But as much as she loved him, she knew he still thought of her as a kid. Lately she'd been thinking that maybe if he'd realized she was a woman, he'd have looked at her differently and not married Daisy.

Once again, guilt stabbed at her. She hadn't planned to take that money and hide it in Daisy's suitcase, but she'd gone into the red wagon, and Daisy had taken that phone call, and the cash drawer had been open, and it had just happened.

It was wrong, but she kept telling herself it wasn't too wrong. Alex didn't want Daisy—Sheba said the same thing. Daisy was going to make him miserable, and because of what Heather had done, he could find it out right now instead of later on.

But the kiss she'd witnessed this morning told her Daisy wasn't going to let him go that easy. Heather still couldn't believe the way she'd thrown herself at him. Alex didn't need her! He didn't need Daisy when he could have Heather.

But how was he supposed to know the way she felt about him when she'd never told him? She pushed aside her books and jumped up. She couldn't stand it any longer. She had to make him see that she wasn't a kid. She had to make him understand that he didn't need Daisy.

Without giving herself time for second thoughts, she rushed from the trailer and headed toward the red wagon.

Alex looked up from the desk as Heather walked in. She'd tucked her thumbs into the pockets of her plaid shorts, which were almost entirely covered by an oversize white T-shirt. She looked pale and unhappy, like a fairy-sprite with clipped wings. His heart went out to her. She had it rough, but she kept fighting, and he liked that about her.

"What's up, honey?"

She didn't reply at first. Instead, she began to wander aimlessly around the trailer, touching the arm of the couch, the handle on a file cabinet. He saw a faint orange mark on her cheekbone where she'd tried to camouflage a pimple, and he felt a rush of tenderness. Someday soon, she was going to be a real beauty.

"Troubles?"

Her head snapped up. "Not me."

"That's good."

Her throat worked as she swallowed. "I just thought you might want to know . . ." She ducked her head and began to poke at the cuticle around one chewed fingernail.

"Know what?"

"I saw what Daisy did to you today," she said hurridly, "and I just want you to know that I know you couldn't help it and everything."

"What did Daisy do to me?"

"The way she—you know."

"I'm afraid I don't."

"You know." She gazed at a spot on the carpet. "Kissed you like that out where everybody could see and everything. Embarrassed you."

The way he remembered it, he'd been the one who'd instigated the kiss. He hadn't liked knowing that everyone in the circus was staring at her waist and counting months on their fingers. He also didn't like the way people ridiculed her behind her back, especially when he knew he was partially to blame.

"I don't understand what this has to do with you, Heather."

She clutched her hands at her sides and let it all come out in a rush. "Everybody knows how you feel about her and everything. How you don't like her. And when my dad told me she wasn't pregnant or anything, I couldn't figure out why you married her. Then I remembered that guys get kind of crazy if a girl's real pretty and maybe they want to—you know—have relations with her, but she might say she won't unless they get married. And so I figured out that's why you married her. But what I want to tell you is—I mean, if you want to make her leave and everything . . ."

For the first time since her tirade had begun, she looked him directly in the eye, and he saw desperation there. She screwed up her face and let the words tumble out. "I know you think I'm a kid, but I'm not. I'm sixteen. I might not be pretty like Daisy, but I'm still a woman, and I could—I could let you have sex with me and everything, so you wouldn't have to have it with her."

Alex felt as if he'd been poleaxed, and he couldn't think of a thing to say. Her cheeks had turned bright red—probably the same color as his—and she was once again staring a hole through the floor.

He rose slowly to his feet. He'd faced down nasty drunks and knife-wielding truck drivers, but he'd never faced anything like this. She'd mistaken his friendship for something more, and he had to set her straight right away.

"Heather . . ." He cleared his throat and walked around the end of the desk. As he came to a stop, Daisy appeared in the doorway behind Heather, but the teenager was so wrapped up in what she'd done that she didn't notice. Daisy must have sensed that something important was going on because she immediately went still and waited.

"Heather, when a young girl gets a crush . . ."

"It's not a crush!" Heather lifted her head, and her eyes were moist with entreaty. "I fell in love with you at first sight, and I thought maybe you liked me, too, but because I was so young and everything, you might be afraid to say anything about it. That's why I decided I had to tell you."

He wished Daisy would help him out, but she stood quietly, taking it all in. For Heather's own good, he had to make her see the reality of the situation. "You don't love me, Heather."

"I do!"

"You think you do. But you're young, and it's only a silly crush. You'll get over it. Believe me, in a couple of months we'll both laugh about this."

Heather looked as if he'd just slapped her, and he realized he'd said the wrong thing. She drew in her breath, and her eyes filled with tears. Appalled, he tried to think how to repair the damage.

"I like you, Heather, I do. But you're only sixteen. I'm a grown man, and you're still a child." He saw by her face that he was making it worse. He'd never felt so helpless, and he shot Daisy a look of entreaty.

To his annoyance, she rolled her eyes at him, as if he were the stupidest person on earth. Then she came stalking forward advancing on poor Heather with guns blazing.

"I knew I'd find you here, you hussy! You think just

because you're young and incredibly lovely that you can steal my husband, but I'm going to fight you for him!''

Heather's mouth gaped, and she took an automatic step backward. Alex stared at Daisy in disbelief. Of all the lame-brained, idiotic things she'd done, this one took the cake. Even a moron could see through her histrionics.

"I don't care how youthful and beautiful you are!" she exclaimed. "I won't let you ruin my marriage!" With a dramatic sweep of her hand, she pointed her finger toward the door. "Now I suggest you get out of here right now before I do something I regret."

Heather slammed her mouth shut. At the same time, she stumbled toward the door and fled.

Several long seconds ticked by before Alex slumped down on the couch. "I blew it, didn't I?"

Daisy regarded him with something like pity. "For a smart man, you certainly don't have much sense."

12

Alex stared at the door through which Heather had just disappeared, then looked back at his wife. "That was the lousiest performance I've ever seen. Did you really say, 'I'm going to fight you for him'?"

"She believed me, and that's all that counted. After what you said, she needed to have someone treat her like an adult."

"I didn't mean to hurt her, but what was I supposed to do? She's not an adult; she's a kid."

"She gave you her heart, Alex, and you told her it didn't mean anything."

"It wasn't only her heart she was offering. Just before you came in, she let me know that her body was part of the package."

"She's feeling desperate. If you'd taken her up on it, she'd have been scared to death."

He shuddered. "Sixteen-year-olds aren't on my list of favorite perversions."

"What is?" She immediately bit her lip. When was she going to start thinking before she spoke?

He gave her a maddening smile that made goose bumps break out on her skin. "It'll be more fun for you to find that out for yourself."

"Why don't you just tell me?"

"Why don't you just wait and see."

She studied him. "Does it have anything to do with—no, of course not."

"Are you worrying about those whips again?"

"Not really," she lied.

"Good. Because you don't have anything to be concerned about." He paused. "If I do it exactly right, it hardly hurts at all."

Her eyes widened. "Will you stop it!"

"What?"

His innocent expression didn't fool her one bit. "Stop planting all these seeds of suspicion in my mind."

"I haven't done a thing. You've put the suspicions there all by yourself."

"Only because you keep playing games with me. You've baited me about this from the beginning, and I don't like it. Just answer one simple question. Yes or no? Have you ever whipped a woman?"

"Yes or no?"

"That's what I'm asking."

"No qualifiers?"

"None."

"All right, then. Yes, I have definitely whipped a woman."

She swallowed and said weakly, "I take that back about the qualifiers."

"Sorry, sweetheart, but you lost your chance." With a grin, he sat down behind his desk. "I have work to do, so maybe you'd better tell me what you wanted to see me about."

Several seconds passed before she could gather her wits enough to remember what had brought her here in the first place. "It's Glenna."

"What about her?"

"She's a large animal and that cage is too small for her. We need a new one."

"Just like that? You want us to buy a new gorilla cage?"

"It's inhumane keeping her so closely confined. She's really sad, Alex. She has these wonderful soft fingers and she pushes them out through the bars as if she's starved for contact with another living being. And that's not the only problem. All the cages are so old that I'm not even sure they're safe. The lock on the leopard cage is being held together with wire.''

He picked up a pencil and absentmindedly tapped the eraser on the battered desktop. ''I agree with you. I hate that damned menagerie—it's barbaric—but cages are expensive, and Sheba's still thinking about selling off the animals. You'll just have to do your best.'' He spotted something out the window, and his chair creaked as he leaned back to get a better view. ''Well, will you look at that. It seems you have a visitor.''

She looked outside and saw a baby elephant standing untethered in front of the red wagon. ''It's Tater.''

As she watched, he lifted his trunk and bellowed, looking for all the world like a tragic hero calling out for his lost love. ''What's he doing over here?''

''Trying to find you, I imagine.'' He smiled. ''Elephants form strong family ties, and Tater seems to have bonded with you.''

''He's a little large to be a pet.''

''I'm glad you feel that way because he's not sleeping in our bed, Daisy, no matter how much you beg me.''

She laughed. At the same time she refrained from telling him that she wasn't certain she'd be sleeping there, either. Too much still needed to be settled between them.

As Sheba approached Alex, she was having the grandmother of bad days. Just that morning Brady had told her that Daisy wasn't pregnant. The idea of that woman bearing Markov babies was so abhorrent she should have been relieved, but instead, something ugly had pooled in the pit of her stomach. If Alex hadn't married Daisy because she was pregnant, then he must have done it out of choice. He must have done it because he loved her.

Acid burned inside her. How could he love that no-talent little rich girl when he hadn't loved her? Couldn't he see how unworthy Daisy was? Had he lost all his pride?

Now she intended to put into action a plan that had been taking shape in her mind for days. It made business sense—she never did anything that wasn't for the good of the show, regardless of her personal feelings—but this idea also might finally pull the blinders away from Alex's eyes regarding his new bride.

She came up behind him as he worked on the stake driver. His damp T-shirt clung to the strong muscles in his back. She remembered how that taut skin had once felt beneath her hands, but instead of arousing her, the memory filled her with self-hatred. Sheba Quest, the queen of the center ring, had begged for this man's love and been rejected. Her stomach curled with loathing.

"I need to talk to you about your act."

He picked up a greasy rag and wiped his hands with it. He'd always been a first-rate mechanic, and he'd somehow managed to keep the ancient stake driver running, but right now she couldn't summon any gratitude for the money he was saving her.

"Go ahead."

She shaded her eyes, taking her time, making him wait. Finally she spoke. "I think you need a change. You've only made a few variations in your act since the last time you went out with us, and there's too much of the season left for you to get stale."

"What do you have in mind?"

She pulled the sunglasses from the top of her head and folded in the stems. "I want you to put Daisy in it."

"Forget it."

"Afraid she won't be able to do it?"

"You know she won't."

"Well, then, you'll have to make her. Or does she wear the pants in the family?"

"What are you trying to do, Sheba?"

"Daisy's a Markov now. It's time she started acting like one."

"That's my business, not yours."

"Not while I own this circus. Daisy has a way with the crowd, and I intend to take advantage of it." She gave him a long, hard stare. "I want her in the show, Alex, and I'll give you two weeks to get her ready. If she needs persuading, remind her that I can still file a criminal complaint against her any time I want."

"I'm getting real sick of your threats."

"Then think about the good of the show instead."

Alex finished repairing the stake driver, then stalked to the trailer to scrub the grease off his hands. As he took a nail brush and a bar of Lava from a chipped saucer under the kitchen sink, he forced himself to acknowledge the truth of what Sheba had said. Daisy did have a way with the crowd, and although he hadn't admitted it to Sheba, he'd already thought about putting her in his act. He'd hesitated, however, because of the difficulties of training her.

The assistants he'd worked with in the past had all been seasoned circus performers, and the whips hadn't bothered them, but Daisy was full of fears. If she flinched at the wrong time . . .

He pushed away the thought. He could train her not to flinch. His Uncle Sergey had trained him. Even when the show was over and the perverted son of a bitch was beating the shit out of him for some imagined offense, Alex had held himself completely still.

He'd mentally traveled the torturous path of his childhood too many times, and he had no interest in stirring up the muck again, so he pushed the old images away. There was another advantage to using Daisy as his assistant, one that was more important to him at the moment than simply sprucing up his act. This would give him a valid reason to ease her workload, a reason she couldn't argue with.

He still couldn't believe that she'd refused to let him make things easier for her. This morning when he'd started to insist, he'd seen something in her expression that had made him back off. Her work had become important to her, he realized, a survival test.

But regardless of what she thought, he didn't intend to let her drive herself into exhaustion. And whether she knew it or not, performing in the ring with him would be a lot easier than hauling elephant manure and cleaning out animal cages.

As he rinsed his hands and reached for a paper towel, he remembered how fragile she'd felt under his hands last night. Their lovemaking had been so good it scared him. He wasn't quite certain what he'd expected, but he'd never imagined that Daisy would have so many facets to her: sultry and tempting, innocent and unsure, both aggressive and giving. He'd wanted to conquer her and protect her at the same time, and that confused the hell out of him.

On the opposite side of the lot, Daisy stepped out of the red wagon. Alex wouldn't be happy when he saw that she'd been making long-distance calls on his cellular phone, but she was more than satisfied with what she'd learned from the keeper at the San Diego Zoo. He'd suggested some changes she was going to try: adjustments in the animals' diets, additional vitamins, alterations in their feeding schedules.

She walked toward the trailer, where she'd seen her husband heading a few minutes earlier. When she'd finished her work in the menagerie and gone to help Digger out, the old man had growled at her that he didn't need her help, so she'd decided to grab the extra few hours and make a trip to the library. She'd spotted it earlier as they'd driven through town, and she wanted to do some more research on the animals. First, however, she had to get Alex to part with the keys to his truck, which, until now, he'd refused to do.

As she entered the trailer, she saw him standing at the sink drying his hands. A silly sort of giddiness passed through her. He looked too big for such small confines, and she decided those dark, brooding good looks were better suited to roaming a nineteenth-century English moor than managing a twentieth-century traveling circus. He turned and she caught her breath against the impact of his amber eyes.

"I'd like to borrow the keys to the truck," she said when

she found her voice. "I need to do some shopping."

"Are you out of cigarettes already?"

"You must not have noticed. I've stopped smoking."

"I'm proud of you." He tossed the damp paper towel in the trash, and she saw how his T-shirt clung to his sweat-dampened chest. A grease mark cut across the sleeve. "If you wait an hour or so, I'll drive you."

"I'd rather go alone. This morning I noticed a laundromat next to the town library. I thought I could do the laundry and catch up on some reading at the same time. Is that a problem?"

"Not exactly. I just think it might be better if I drive you."

"Are you afraid I'll run off with your truck?"

"No. I just—it's not really my truck. It belongs to the circus, and you're probably not used to driving anything like it."

"I'm an excellent driver. I'm not going to wreck it."

"You don't know that for a fact."

She held out her hand, determined to have her way in this. "Please give me the keys."

"I wouldn't mind a trip to the library myself."

She gave him her steeliest gaze. "The keys, please."

He rubbed his chin with his knuckle as if he were thinking it over. "I'll tell you what. Unbutton your shirt and I'll give you the keys."

"What?"

"It's my best offer. Take it or leave it."

As she saw what passed for mischief glinting in his eyes, she wondered how someone so serious could have such a playful nature when it came to sex. "You actually expect me to . . ."

"Uh-huh." He leaned back against the sink and crossed his arms over his chest waiting for her.

A flare of heat bolted through her as she saw the desire in his eyes. She was by no means certain she was ready for another sexual encounter with him, but on the other hand, what would be the harm in a little naughty foreplay? The dampness of her blouse reminded her she'd been working all morning and wasn't any too clean. On the other hand, neither was he, and after all, they were just playing around, so what did it matter?

She looked down her nose at him in her best imitation of royalty. "I'm certainly not going to use my body as barter. That's offensive."

"I'm sorry you feel that way." He withdrew the keys from his pocket and, with exaggerated innocence, tossed them up and down in his palm.

The soft skin of her breasts prickled beneath her damp shirt, and the nipples pebbled. "How would you like it if I did something like this to you?"

"Sweetheart, I'd *love* it."

Suppressing a smile, she slowly opened the top button. "Maybe just a peek." An inner voice told her she was playing with fire, but she ignored it.

"A peek might get you the key to the tailgate, but not the ignition."

She opened another button. "What do I have to do to get the ignition key?"

"Have you got a bra on?"

"Yes."

"You'll have to take it off."

She should call a halt to this game right now, but instead she opened another button. "You *are* responsible for the truck, so I suppose it's only fair that you dictate the terms."

He looked amused.

She took her time with the last buttons. When they were open, she lightly clasped the front edges of the blouse in her palms and toyed with them, deliberately teasing him even as she recognized that this was a dangerous sort of mischief. "Maybe I should think about this some more."

"Don't make me get rough." His smoky whisper didn't bear the slightest trace of menace, but it still made her shiver.

"Since you put it that way..." She parted the blouse, revealing the floral print bra that stuck to her skin.

"Open that clasp."

She toyed with it but didn't unfasten it.

"Do as I say and nobody'll get hurt."

She couldn't hold back a smile as she opened the clasp. Slowly, she peeled the moist lacy cups away from her breasts and stood before him like a wanton, fully dressed, but with her blouse open and her breasts exposed.

"Beautiful." His whispered compliment made her feel like the most treasured woman on earth.

"Good enough for an ignition key?"

"Good enough for the whole damn truck."

In two long strides, he had her in his arms. His mouth swooped down to cover hers, and the world spun like a crazy carousel. He shoved her blouse down over her shoulders, then clasped her hips and lifted her just enough so he could grind against her. She felt him hard and demanding and knew the time for teasing had come to an end.

Blood rushed hot and needy through her veins. She opened her mouth to his tongue as he swept her from her feet and carried her toward the bed where he dropped her none too gently on the mattress.

"I'm dirty and sweaty."

"I am, too, so we don't have a problem." With one powerful motion he stripped his grimy T-shirt over his head. "You're also overdressed."

She kicked off her grubby shoes and tugged at her jeans, but she wasn't working fast enough to please him.

"You're taking too long." Within moments, he'd stripped her so that she was as naked as he.

Her eyes took in his nude body with its whipcord strength and workingman's tan. Strands of hair on his chest feathered around the icon he wore. She needed to ask him about that. She needed to ask him about so many things.

As he lay down beside her, she smelled the earthy scent of sweat and hard work on both their bodies and wondered why she wasn't repulsed. There was something primitive about coming together like this that aroused her in a way she would never have been able to imagine. Her abandon embarrassed her. "I'm—I need to shower."

"Not till we're done." He pulled a condom from a small

drawer in the chest beside the bed, tore it open, and put it on.

"But I'm so dirty."

He wedged her knees apart. "I want you like this, Daisy."

She moaned and sank her teeth into his shoulder as he thrust into her. She tasted salt and sweat and knew he was tasting the same on her breasts. Her voice caught in her throat. "I really need to wash."

"Later."

"Oh, God, what are you doing?"

"What does it feel like?"

"It feels like you're—"

"I am. Do you want more?"

"Yes. Oh, yes . . ."

The smells and tastes. The touches. The sweat and grit beneath her palms. The thrust and parry.

Her hair stuck to her cheeks, and a piece of straw poked her neck. He pushed his fingers into the cleft of her bottom and turned her on top of him, smearing grease from his arm down her side. He squeezed the backs of her thighs hard in his hands.

"Ride me."

She did as he said. She arched and plunged, moving instinctively, and then wincing as she hurt herself on him.

"Slow down, sweetheart. I'm not going anywhere."

"I can't." She gazed at him through the haze of her pain and passion and saw his sweat-slicked face, lips drawn thin and pale. Flecks of dirt stuck to those harsh Russian cheekbones and a bit of straw clung to his dark crisp hair. Sweat trickled over her breasts. She plunged again and gasped with pain.

"Don't, sweet. Shh . . . take your time."

He slipped his hands up along her back and pulled her down to stretch out over him, breasts to chest where he helped her find a new rhythm.

The insides of her thighs clasped the outsides of his, the icon abraded her skin, and she moved on his body, slowly at first, then writhing, loving the sensation of being in control, of dictating the rhythm and thrust. There was no pain, only sensation.

He gripped her bottom and let her have her way. She knew by the coiled tension she felt in those hard muscles beneath her what it cost him to relinquish control. He sank his teeth into the flesh over her collarbone, not hurting her, merely using another part of her body to fill another part of his.

She gave herself up to skin and sweat and musk. He made incoherent sounds and she answered in the same language. Both were lost to all that was civilized, thrown back to the jungle, the cave, the place of wildness until, for one suspended moment, they gripped creation's source.

She left him as soon as she could and sealed herself in the bathroom. As the shower water rushed over her, she was shaken by this new barbaric part of herself. Was it sacred or profane? How could she have abandoned herself like that with a man she didn't love? The question tormented her.

When she came out, wrapped in a towel with her skin scrubbed cleaner than her troubled soul, he was standing at the sink. Wearing only his dirty jeans, he held a beer bottle in his hand.

When he saw the expression on her face, he scowled. "You're going to make this complicated, aren't you?"

She pulled her clean clothes from the drawer and turned her back on him to dress. "I'm not sure exactly what you mean."

"I can see it in your face. You're having all kinds of second thoughts about what just happened."

"Aren't you?"

"Why would I be? Sex is simple, Daisy. It's fun and it feels good. It doesn't have to be complicated."

She nodded toward the bed. "Did that seem simple to you?"

"It was good. That's all that matters."

She zipped up her shorts and pushed her feet into her sandals. "You've had sex with a lot of women, haven't you?"

"I haven't been indiscriminate, if that's what you mean."

"Is it always like that?"

He hesitated. "No."

For a moment, some of her tension eased. "I'm glad. I want it to mean something."

"All it means is that, while our minds may have trouble communicating, our bodies don't have any problem at all."

"I don't think it's that simple."

"Sure it is."

"The earth moved," she said softly. "That has to be more than bodies communicating."

"Sometimes it works between two people, sometimes it doesn't. It works between us, and that's all there is to it."

"Do you really believe that?"

"Daisy, listen to me. You'll only get hurt if you start imagining things that aren't going to happen."

"I don't know what you mean."

He stared straight into her eyes, and she felt as if he were gazing into her soul. "I'm not going to fall in love with you, sweetheart. It's just not going to happen. I care about you, but I don't love you."

How his words hurt. Was love what she wanted from him? She lusted after him. She respected him. But how could she fall in love with someone who had so little regard for her? She knew to the very depth of her being that she wasn't tough enough to love a man like Alex Markov. He needed someone as stubborn and arrogant as himself, someone just as hardheaded and impossible to intimidate, a woman who could hold her own beneath the force of those dark scowls and give as good as she got. A woman who felt at home in the circus, who wasn't afraid of animals or backbreaking work. He needed—

Sheba Quest.

Jealousy snapped at her. While her mind recognized the logic of Alex and Sheba together, her heart rejected the idea.

Living with him had taught her something about pride, and she lifted her head. "Believe it or not, I haven't been spending all my time worrying about how I'm going to make you fall in love with me.'' She picked up the brimming laundry basket. ''As a matter of fact, I don't want your love. What I do want are the keys to your darned *truck*!''

She snatched them off the counter and stomped toward the door. He moved swiftly to block her way. Taking the laundry basket from her, he said, ''I'm not trying to hurt you, Daisy. I care about you. I didn't want to, but I can't seem to help it. You're sweet and funny, and I like looking at you.''

''You do?''

''Uh-huh.''

She reached up to rub a speck of dirt from his cheekbone with her thumb. ''Well, you're bad-tempered and humorless, but I like looking at you, too.''

''I'm glad.''

She smiled and began to take the laundry basket back, only to have him hold on to it. ''Before you go . . . Sheba and I have been talking, and you're getting a new assignment.''

She regarded him warily. ''I'm already helping with the elephants and working with the menagerie. I don't think there's time for anything more.''

''As of now, you're off elephant duty, and Trey can take over the menagerie.''

''The menagerie's my responsibility.''

''Fine. You can supervise him. The fact is, Daisy, the crowd likes you and Sheba wants to take advantage of that. I'm putting you in my act.''

She stared at him.

''I'll start rehearsing you tomorrow morning.''

She realized he wasn't quite meeting her eyes. ''Rehearse me doing what?''

''Mainly, you'll just stand around and look pretty.''

''What else?''

''You'll need to do some holding for me. No big deal.''

''Holding? What does that mean—holding?''

''Just what I said. We'll talk about it tomorrow.''

''Tell me now.''

''You hold some things, that's all.''

"I hold them?" She gulped. "And you whip them out of my hand, don't you?"

"Out of your hand." He paused. "Your mouth."

She felt the blood drain from her head. "My mouth?"

"It's a standard trick. I've done it hundreds of times, and there's absolutely nothing to worry about." He opened the door for her and set the laundry basket in her arms. "Now if you're going to stop at the library, you'd better get to it. I'll see you later."

With a light push, he propelled her outside. She turned around to tell him there was no way she'd ever go into the ring, but the door shut before she could say a word.

13

"**T**his time could you maybe try it with your eyes open?"

Daisy could tell that Alex was losing patience with her. The two of them stood behind the trailers in a Maryland baseball field, a field very much like the one they'd stood in the day before and the day before that for almost two weeks. Her nerves were strung so tight she felt as if they would snap.

Tater stood off to the side where he alternated between sighing over his lady love and grubbing in the dirt. After her confrontation with the baby elephant a few weeks ago, Tater had started breaking away from the others to try to find her, and eventually Digger had punished him with the bull hook. Daisy hadn't been able to tolerate that, so she'd taken over responsibility for the small elephant during the daytime when he was most likely to roam. Everyone in the circus except Daisy seemed to have grown accustomed to the sight of her walking around with Tater trotting behind like an overgrown lap dog.

"If I open my eyes, I'll flinch," Daisy pointed out to her whip-wielding husband, "and you told me the only way I can get hurt is if I flinch."

"You're holding that target so far from your body that you could dance *Swan Lake* and I wouldn't hit you."

There was a certain truth to what he was saying. The paper tube in her hand was a foot long, and she held it with her

194

arm extended, but every time he cracked the whip, slicing off the end of the tub, she winced. She couldn't help it.

"Maybe I'll open my eyes tomorrow."

"You're going into the ring in three days. You'd better do it before then."

Daisy's eyes snapped open at the sound of Sheba's voice, caustic and accusatory. The circus owner stood off to the side near the place where one of Alex's whips lay coiled on the ground. Her arms were crossed and her unbound hair gleamed hellfire in the sunlight.

"You should be used to this by now." She bent over and snatched up one of the six-inch tubes lying on the ground. Those were the real targets Daisy was supposed to hold in the performance, but so far Alex hadn't been able to bully her into practicing with anything shorter than a foot.

Sheba rolled the small, cigar-shaped tube between her fingers, then walked over to stand next to Daisy. "Move out of the way."

Daisy backed off.

Sheba regarded Alex with the glint of challenge in her eyes. "Let's see what you've got." Turning in profile to him, she brushed her hair behind her shoulders and placed the tube between her lips.

For a moment Alex did nothing, and Daisy felt as if an entire history passed between him and the circus owner, a history of which Daisy knew nothing. Sheba almost seemed to be daring him, but daring him to do what? So suddenly that she barely saw the motion, Alex drew back his arm and flicked his wrist.

Crack! The whip popped just inches from Sheba's face, and the end of the tube flew off.

Sheba didn't move. She stood there as serenely as a guest at a garden party while Alex cracked the whip again and again, each time sending another piece of the tube flying. Inch by inch, he destroyed it until only a stub was left between Sheba's lips.

She removed it, bent down to pick up a fresh one, and held it out to Daisy. "Now let's see you do it."

Daisy knew a challenge when she heard one, but these people had been raised to court danger. Whatever amount of courage she'd been born with, she'd used up when she'd faced down Tater. "Maybe later."

Alex sighed and tossed down his whip. "Sheba, this isn't going to work. I'll keep doing the act by myself."

"Is this what it's come down to, Alex? Five generations of circus in your blood, and you've given the Markov name to someone who doesn't have the guts to go into the ring with you."

Her green eyes darkened with scorn as she regarded Daisy. "No one's asking you to walk the high wire or ride bareback. All you have to do is stand there. But you can't even manage that, can you?"

"It's—I'm sorry, but I'm just not good at this kind of thing."

"What are you good at?"

Alex stepped forward. "That's not fair. Daisy's been taking care of the menagerie, even though she doesn't have to work there anymore, and the animals are in the best condition they've been in in years."

"Bully for her." Daisy felt the impact of Sheba's eyes as sharply as the crack of the whip. "Do you know anything about the Markov family?"

"Alex doesn't say too much about his past." He didn't say much about his present, either. Whenever she tried to ask him about his life away from the circus, he changed the subject. She gathered that he'd been to college and that the icon he wore was a family piece, but little else.

"Leave it alone, Sheba," he warned.

Sheba walked past him, keeping her gaze firmly fixed on Daisy. "The Markovs are one of the most famous circus families in history. Alex's mother was the greatest bareback rider of her time. Alex might have been a champion equestrian, too, if he hadn't grown so tall as a youngster."

"Daisy doesn't care about this," he said.

"Yes, I do. Tell me, Sheba."

"His mother's family goes back five generations to Russia

where the Markovs performed for the czars. The interesting thing about the Markovs is that the family traces most of its history through its women. No matter who they've married, they've kept the Markov name and passed it on to their children. But the Markov men have been great performers, too, masters of the bullwhip and some of the finest horsemen the circus has ever known."

Alex began stuffing the paper tubes in an old canvas bag. "Come on, Daisy. I've had enough for the day."

Sheba's expression grew bitter. "The Markov men have always honored tradition and chosen their wives carefully. At least until Alex came along." She paused, her eyes icy with contempt. "You're not fit to stand in his shadow, Daisy, let alone carry the Markov name."

With that, she turned and walked away, her bearing so dignified she made her shabby surroundings seem regal.

Daisy felt vaguely nauseated. "She's right, Alex. I'm not good at any of this."

"Nonsense." He coiled the whips and looped them over his shoulder. "Sheba regards circus tradition the way some people regard religion. Don't pay any attention."

Daisy stared at the bag of small paper tubes. Numbly, she reached down and picked one of them up.

"What are you doing?"

"Trying to be a Markov woman."

"For God's sake, put that down. I told you to ignore her. She has a distorted view of Markov history, anyway. There were a lot of scoundrels in the family, too. My uncle Sergey was the meanest bastard I've ever known."

"You're just trying to make me feel better, but I can't ignore what she said." She walked over to the place she'd been standing earlier and turned in profile to him. "I'm tired of coming up short all the time."

As she raised the tube to her lips, her knees were shaking so badly she was certain he'd notice. If Alex missed, he would hit her face and, perhaps, scar her for life.

"Stop it, Daisy."

She closed her eyes.

"Daisy . . ."

She removed the tube, but she didn't look at him. "Just do it, Alex. Please. The longer you wait, the harder you're making this for me."

"Are you sure?"

She wasn't sure at all, but she put the tube back in her mouth and closed her eyes, praying she wouldn't flinch.

Crack!

She screamed as the noise exploded in her ears and a fierce current of air lashed her face. Her ears rang from the sound. Tater opened his mouth and bleated.

"Did I hit you? Damn it, I know I didn't hit you!"

"No . . . no . . . it's fine. I just—" She bent over and picked up the tube she had dropped, noting that a small piece had been sliced off the end. "I'm just a little nervous, that's all."

"Daisy, you don't have to . . ."

She put the tube back in her mouth and closed her eyes.

Crack!

She screamed again.

Alex's tone was dry. "Daisy, your screaming is starting to make *me* nervous."

"I'll be quiet! Just don't get nervous, whatever you do." She picked up the tube—much shorter now than it had been earlier. "How many more times?"

"Twice more."

"Twice?" Her voice squeaked.

"Twice."

This time she placed only the barest tip between the very edge of her lips.

"You're cheating."

A trickle of perspiration slid between her breasts as she repositioned it. She took a deep breath . . .

Crack! Another vicious air current whipped a lock of her hair against her cheek. She nearly fainted but somehow managed to swallow her scream. Only one more. One more.

Crack!

Slowly, her eyes eased open.

"You're done, Daisy. It's over. All you have to do now is style for the crowd."

She was alive and unmarked. Stunned, she turned to him and spoke in a hoarse whisper. "I did it."

He smiled and tossed down his whip. "You sure did. I'm proud of you."

With a great whoop, she ran toward him and leaped into his arms. He caught her automatically. As he drew her close against him, a slow sizzle coursed through her body. He must have felt it, too, because he jerked away and set her back on the ground.

She knew he was unhappy over her refusal to make love with him since that afternoon of sweat and sex that had so deeply disturbed her. Her period had given her an excuse for a while, but that had stopped several days ago. She'd asked him to give her a little time to sort her thoughts out, and he'd agreed, but he hadn't been happy about it.

"There's just one more trick," he said, "and then you're done for the day."

"Maybe we should wait till tomorrow."

"It's an easier trick than the one we've just done. Let's get it over with before you lose your nerve. Go stand back where you were."

"Alex . . ."

"Go on. It won't hurt. I promise."

She moved reluctantly back over to the place where she'd been standing earlier.

He picked up the longest of his bullwhips and held the butt loosely in his hand. "You can go ahead and close your eyes."

"I don't think I want to."

"Trust me on this, sweetheart. You definitely want your eyes closed."

She did as he said, but her right eyelid began to twitch.

"Raise your arms above your head."

"My arms?"

"Above your head. And cross your wrists."

Her eyes sprang back open. "I think I forgot to tell Trey about Sinjun's new feed."

"Every Markov wife in history has done this trick."

With a sense of inevitability, she raised her arms, crossed her wrists, and closed her eyes, telling herself all the while that nothing could be as bad as having him cut the tube from her mouth.

Crack!

The snap of the whip had barely registered in her brain before she felt the lash coil tightly around her wrists, securing them together.

This time her scream came all the way from her toes. She dropped her arms so quickly she felt a wrenching in her shoulders. In disbelief, she gaped at her bound wrists. "You hit me! You said you wouldn't hit me, but you did."

"Hold still, Daisy, and stop yelling. It didn't hurt."

"It didn't?"

"No."

She stared down at her wrists and realized he was right. "How—?"

"I cracked the whip before I let it touch you." He flicked his wrist, taking the tension off the lash so that it loosened and she could slip free. "It's an old trick, and the crowd loves it. But after I snare your wrists, you've got to smile at the audience so they know I didn't hurt you. Otherwise, you'll get me arrested."

She rubbed one wrist and then the other. To her amazement, they were perfectly fine. "What if—what if you crack the whip *after* you catch my wrists?"

"I won't."

"You could make a mistake, Alex. You can't always get every trick right."

"Sure I can. I've been doing this for years, and I've never hurt an assistant yet." He began collecting his whips, and she marveled at his perfect arrogance, even as it made her uneasy.

"Things went a little better this morning," she said, "but I don't see how I can go into the ring with you in two days.

Jack said I'm supposed to be an untamed gypsy maiden, but I don't think untamed gypsies scream like I do.''

"We'll think of something." To her surprise, he gave her a swift kiss on the end of her nose, began to walk away, stopped, and turned back. He looked at her for a long moment then returned, dropped his head, and settled his mouth over hers.

Her arms entwined his neck as he pressed against her. While her mind told her that sex should be sacred, her body craved his touch, and she couldn't get enough of him.

When they finally drew apart, he looked down at her for a long, sweet moment and whispered, "You taste like sunshine."

She smiled.

"I'm going to give you a few more days, sweetheart, because I know this is new to you, but that's all."

She didn't have to ask what he meant. "I may need a little longer. We have to get to know each other better. Build mutual respect."

"Sweetheart, when it comes to sex, I've got nothing but respect for you."

"Please don't pretend not to understand what I'm talking about."

"I like sex. You like sex. We like having it together. That's all there is to it."

"That's not all there is! Sex needs to be sac—"

"Don't say it, Daisy. If you say the s-word, I swear I'll flirt with every truck stop waitress between here and Cincinnati."

She narrowed her eyes. "I'd just like to see you try. And *sacred* isn't a dirty word. Come on, Tater, we have work to do."

She flounced off with her elephant trotting behind. If she'd thought to look back, she would have seen something that would have surprised her. She would have seen her tough, humorless husband grinning like a teenager.

Despite Alex's protests, she'd continued to work in the menagerie, although Trey now did many of the routine daily tasks. Sinjun eyed Tater as they approached. Elephants and tigers were natural enemies, but Sinjun seemed more annoyed by Tater's presence than anything else. Alex said he was jealous, but she couldn't imagine attributing such an emotion to the cranky old tiger.

She studied Sinjun with satisfaction. Between adjusting his feed and his daily showers, she thought his coat already looked healthier. She gave him a mock curtsy. "Good morning, your majesty."

He flashed his teeth at her, a gesture she interpreted as his way of reminding her not to get too cute with him.

She hadn't experienced any more of those mystical moments of communication with him, and she'd begun to think they'd been induced by fatigue. Still, just being near him filled her with awe.

She'd left a bag of treats she'd bought with her grocery money near a stack of hay, and she carried it over to Glenna's cage. The gorilla had already caught sight of her, and she pressed her face between the bars, patiently waiting.

Glenna's quiet acceptance of her fate combined with her yearning for human contact broke Daisy's heart. She stroked the petal-soft palm extended through the bars. "Hello, love. I've got something for you." From the produce bag, she drew out a ripe purple plum. The fruit reminded her of the touch of Glenna's fingers. Firm, smooth skin. Softness beneath.

Glenna took the plum and settled back in the cage where she ate it in small, delicate nibbles while she regarded Daisy with sad gratitude.

Daisy handed her another one and continued to talk to her. When the gorilla was done, she once again approached the bars, but this time she reached for Daisy's hair.

The first time she'd done this, Daisy had been frightened, but now she knew what Glenna wanted, and she pulled the rubber band from her ponytail.

For a very long time, she stood patiently in front of the cage and let the gorilla groom her as if she were her baby, picking through her hair for nonexistent gnats and fleas.

When she was finally done, Daisy found that her throat had tightened with emotion. No matter what anyone said, it wasn't right for this humanlike creature to be caged.

Two hours later, Daisy and her pet elephant were heading back toward the trailer when she spotted Heather practicing with her rings near the ball field's home plate. Now that she was no longer so exhausted, Daisy had been able to think more clearly about what had happened the night the ticket money was stolen, and she decided the time had come to talk to Heather.

Heather dropped a ring as she approached, and while she bent to pick it up, she regarded Daisy warily from the corner of her eye.

"I want to talk to you, Heather. Let's sit down on those bleachers."

"I don't have anything to say to you."

"Fine. Then I'll do the talking. Move it."

Heather regarded her sulkily but responded to the authority in her voice. After gathering up her rings, she followed Daisy to the bleachers, dragging her sandals the entire way.

Daisy took a seat in the third row while Heather settled one row lower. Tater found a place near home plate and began picking up dirt and tossing it on his back, part of his instinctive cooling system.

"I suppose you're going to yell at me about Alex."

"Alex is married, Heather, and marriage is a sacred bond between a man and a woman. No one has the right to try to break that apart."

"It's not fair! You didn't do anything to deserve him."

"That's not for you to judge."

"You're a real goody-goody, aren't you?"

"How could I be a goody-goody?" Daisy said quietly. "I'm a thief, remember?"

Heather looked down at her fingers and picked at the cuticle on her thumb. "Everybody hates you for stealing that money."

"I know they do. And that's not fair, is it?"

"Yeah, it's fair."

"But both of us know I didn't do it."

Heather's back stiffened, and she waited a fraction of a second too long before replying. "You did, too."

"You were in the red wagon that night between the time Sheba checked the cash drawer and I closed up."

"So what? I didn't steal the money, and you're not going to pin it on me!"

"A call came in for Alex. I took it, and while I was distracted you got into the cash drawer and removed the two hundred dollars."

"I did not! You can't prove anything!"

"Then you sneaked into the trailer and hid the money in my suitcase so everyone would think it was me."

"You're a liar!"

"I should have figured it out right away, but I was so tired from trying to adjust to everything that I forgot you'd been there."

"You're a liar," Heather repeated, but this time with less vehemence. "And if you go and tell my dad about this, you're gonna be sorry."

"You can't threaten me with anything worse than what you've already done. I don't have any friends, Heather. No one wants to talk to me because they think I'm a thief. Even my own husband believes it."

Heather's face was a picture of guilt, and Daisy knew she'd been right. She regarded the teenager sadly. "What you did was very wrong."

Heather ducked her head, and her fine blond hair fell forward, concealing her expression. "You can't prove anything," she muttered.

"Is this the way you plan to live your life? Acting dishonestly? Being cruel to another person? We all make mistakes, Heather, and part of growing up is learning how to deal with them."

The teenager's shoulders sagged, and Daisy saw the exact moment when she gave up. "Are you going to tell my dad?"

"I don't know. But I have to tell Alex."

"If you tell him, he'll go straight to my dad."

"That's probably true. Alex has a strong sense of justice."

A tear splatted on the top of Heather's thigh, but Daisy hardened her heart against any sympathy.

"My dad said if I got into any trouble, he was sending me back to live with my aunt Terry."

"Maybe you should have thought about that before you framed me."

Heather said nothing, and Daisy didn't rush her. She finally wiped her eyes on the hem of her T-shirt. "When are you going to tell him?"

"I haven't thought about it. Tonight, probably. Maybe tomorrow."

Heather gave a jerky nod. "I just—the money was there, and I didn't plan it or anything."

Daisy tried to swallow her pity by reminding herself that, because of the actions of this child, her husband thought she was a thief and her marriage had been poisoned before it had a chance. "What you did wasn't right. You have to face the consequences."

"Yeah, I guess I know that." She tried to dash her tears away with her fingers. "In a way, I'm almost glad you found out. It's been hard—I know I don't deserve it, but could you maybe tell Sheba first instead of Alex? Let her tell my dad. The two of them, they fight and everything, but they respect each other, and maybe if she tells him, she can keep him from going completely crazy."

Daisy sat up straighter. "Is your father physically violent?"

"Yeah, I guess. I mean he yells and everything."

"Does he hit you?"

"Dad? No, he doesn't ever hit. But he gets so mad that sometimes I wish he would."

"I see."

"And I guess I'd of ended up with my aunt sooner or later. I know she needs me to help out with her kids and everything. I guess I've been pretty selfish wanting to stay here. It's just—the kids are real brats, and sometimes when they do stuff, she sort of takes it out on me.''

Daisy saw more than she wanted to, and she felt as if guilt-nails were being pounded into her.

The teenager rose from the bench, and her eyes shimmered with tears. ''I'm sorry I've been such a jerk and got you into so much trouble.'' A tear slid over her lashes. ''I guess I should know how that feels better than anybody because of Terry's kids and everything. I should never of done it, but I got so jealous because of Alex.'' Her voice was coming out in little gulps. Her chest spasmed. ''It's stupid. He's too old . . . and he wouldn't even want somebody like me. But he's always so nice to me, and I guess . . . I guess I wanted that all the time, even though''—She gasped for air—''even though I know it wouldn't ever work out. I'm sorry, Daisy.''

With a sob, she turned and fled.

Daisy made her way over to Tater and the baby elephant curled his trunk around her. She rested against him, trying to decide what to do. Before she'd confronted Heather, everything had seemed clear to her, but now she was no longer so certain. If she didn't tell Alex the truth about Heather, he would keep on believing she was a thief. But if she did tell him, Heather was going to be badly punished, and she wasn't sure she could live with that.

Over by the road, she saw Alex climb into his truck to head into town. Earlier he'd told her he had to straighten out a problem with the company supplying the donnikers and that he might be gone for several hours. She'd planned to use the time to unearth the secret purchases she'd been making the past few weeks that would transform the ugly green trailer into something resembling a home, but her encounter with Heather had robbed her of some of her enthusiasm. Still, working was better than sitting around brooding.

As she headed back toward the trailer, she felt her spirits lift. Finally she'd be doing something she was really good at. She couldn't wait to see the look on Alex's face.

14

"What in the hell have you done?" Alex froze in place just inside the door.

"Isn't it wonderful!" Daisy gazed with satisfaction at the trailer's transformation into the charming and cozy nest she'd imagined.

Cream-colored bedsheets gaily splattered with pansies in purples, blues, and butterscotch draped the ugly plaid couch, while scatter pillows in the same colors made the old pieces of furniture inviting and comfortable. She'd attached small brass rods above the yellowed blinds that covered the windows and looped them with lengths of unbleached muslin. Using pansy blue and lavender ribbons of various widths and textures, she'd caught up the fabric in soft poofs.

A silky blue-and-violet scarf camouflaged the torn shade on the lamp that sat in the corner, while several wicker baskets held the clutter of magazines and papers. An attractive assortment of mismatched containers ranging from milk-glass vases and pottery bowls to a Wedgwood blue pitcher graced the chipped kitchen countertop, along with a colorful braided cord stretched across them and attached with tacks to the wall at each end to hold them in place when the trailer was moving.

The table was set with matching place mats in a purple-and-violet paisley pattern and mismatched blue willow china featuring the same colors. White stoneware mugs and two crystal goblets, one of which had a hairline crack in its base, sat next to indigo glass salad plates. In the center of the table, a chipped salt-glazed crock held a bouquet of wildflowers she'd picked at the edge of the lot.

"I couldn't do much with the carpet," she explained, still breathless from the last-minute rush to have everything in place, "but I've gotten rid of the worst of the stains, so it's not too bad. When I get the money, I'm going to do the bed, too, with one of those pretty Indian cotton spreads and more scatter pillows. I'm not much of a seamstress, but I think I can . . ."

"Where did you get the money to do this?"

"From my paycheck."

"You used your own money?"

"I found all kinds of thrift stores and second-hand shops in the towns we've visited. Do you know I'd never been in a Wal-Mart until two weeks ago? It's amazing how far you can stretch a dollar if you're careful, and—" The expression on his face finally registered and her smile faded. "You don't like it."

"I didn't say that."

"You don't have to. I can see it in your face."

"It's not that I don't like it; I just don't think it makes sense to waste your money on this place."

"I don't think it's a waste."

"It's a trailer, for god's sake. We're not going to live here that long."

That wasn't the real reason for his objection. As she gazed at him, she realized she had two choices. She could go off and treat herself to a well-deserved sulk, or she could force him to be honest with her. "Tell me exactly what's wrong."

"I already have."

"No, you haven't. Sheba said you'd turned down a nicer trailer for this place."

He shrugged.

"You wanted to make it as hard on me as possible, didn't you?"

"Don't take it personally. I hadn't even met you when I made the decision about the trailer."

"But you'd heard about me from my father."

He walked over to the refrigerator and pulled out a bottle of wine he'd bought the day before, a bottle that she'd considered too expensive for their budget.

She refused to let him shut her out. "Did you want to keep living in this place the way it was?"

"It was all right." He reached in the drawer for the corkscrew.

"I don't believe you. You're a man who enjoys beautiful things. I've seen the way you take in the scenery when we're traveling or point out something pretty in a store window. Yesterday when we stopped at that roadside stand, you said the basket of fruit reminded you of a Cézanne."

"Do you want a glass of wine?"

She shook her head, and as she studied him she began to understand. "I've stepped over the line again, haven't I?"

"I don't know what you mean by that."

"That invisible border you've set up in your mind between a real marriage and a pretend one. I've crossed it again, haven't I?"

"You're not making any sense."

"Sure I am. You've made up a whole list of rules and regulations for our pretend marriage. I'm supposed to follow your orders without question and stay out of your way except when you want me in bed with you. But most of all, I'm not supposed to make any emotional attachments. I'm not allowed to care about you, about our marriage, our life together. I'm not even allowed to care about this dumpy little trailer."

She'd finally gotten to him, and he slapped the flat of his hand down on the counter, shaking the wine bottle. "I don't want you *nesting*, that's all! It's a bad idea."

"I was right," she said quietly.

He shoved his hand back through his hair. "You're such a damned romantic. Sometimes when I see you looking at me, I have the feeling you're not seeing me at all. Instead, you're seeing the way you want me to be. You're doing the same thing with this—this legal tie between us. You're going to try to make it into something it's not.''

"It's a marriage, Alex, not just a legal tie. We made sacred vows.''

"For six months! Don't you understand that I care about you? All I'm trying to do is protect you from getting hurt.''

"Protect me? I see.'' She took a deep breath. "Is that why you've been checking to make certain I'm taking my birth control pills?''

His expression grew stony. "What does that have to do with anything.''

"At first I couldn't figure out why I'd find them on the top shelf of the medicine cabinet when I'd left them on the bottom. Then I realized that you'd been handling them.''

"I was just making sure you weren't forgetting them, that's all.''

"In other words, you've been checking up on me.''

"I'm not going to apologize. I told you how strongly I feel about not having children.''

She gazed at him bleakly. "We don't have anything, do we? No respect, no affection, no trust.''

"We have affection, Daisy. At least I do.'' He hesitated. "And you've earned my respect, too. I never figured you would take your work so seriously. You've got guts, Daisy.''

She refused to feel grateful for his words. "But I don't have your trust.''

"I trust your good intentions.''

"You also believe I'm a thief. That doesn't say much for good intentions.''

"You were desperate when you took that money. You were tired and frightened, or you wouldn't have done it. I know that now.''

"I didn't take the money.''

"It's all right, Daisy. I'm not holding it against you any longer.''

The fact that he still didn't believe her shouldn't be so painful. The only way she could convince him was to implicate Heather, and now she knew she couldn't do that.

What would be the point? She didn't want to be responsible for having Heather banished. And if she had to submit proof to Alex, his belief in her innocence would be meaningless anyway.

"If you trust me, why were you checking to make sure I was taking the pills?"

"I can't take any chances. I don't want a child."

"You've made that clear." She wanted to ask him if it was the thought of having a child that was so repugnant to him, or just the thought of having a child with her, but she was afraid of the answer she'd hear. "I don't want you checking my pills again. I told you I'd take them, and I will. You're going to have to trust me on this."

She saw his struggle. Despite the way her mother had betrayed her with Noel Black, she hadn't lost her faith in the human race. But Alex didn't seem to trust anyone except himself.

To her surprise, she felt her indignation fade and compassion take its place. How terrible it must be to go through life always expecting the worst from those around you.

She brushed her fingertips over the back of his hand. "I would never deliberately hurt you, Alex. I'd like it very much if you'd at least trust me that far."

"It's not that easy."

"I know. But you need to do it anyway."

He gazed at her for a long time before he gave a shaky nod. "Okay. No more checking up."

She somehow knew what this concession had cost him, and she was touched.

"Aaaaaand now, entering the center ring of Quest Brothers Circus for the very first time, is Theodosia, the beautiful bride of Alexi the Cossack!"

Daisy's knees trembled so badly that she stumbled, ruining her first entrance. What had happened to the wild gypsy maiden? she wondered frantically, as she listened to Jack's new spiel for the first time. That morning at the rehearsal, he had begun with the gypsy theme but then walked out in frustration when she'd screamed. She'd known when Sheba had thrust this new costume at her that they were going with another idea, but Sheba had walked away without giving her the courtesy of an explanation.

The music of the balalaika threaded through the big top, which had been set up in a parking lot in the resort town of Seaside Heights, New Jersey. Alexi stood across the ring, the bullwhip dangling from his hand. Shimmering crimson glitter from the balloons he'd just broken clung to the polished tops of his black boots, and the red sequins in his sash sparkled like fresh blood.

"Does she look nervous to you, ladies and gentlemen?" Jack make a sweeping gesture in her direction. "She looks nervous to me. None of us can fully comprehend the courage it's taken for this sheltered young woman to come into the arena with her husband."

Daisy's costume rustled as she moved slowly into the ring. The slimly cut virginal white gown covered her from its high lacy neck to its rhinestone-encrusted hem, and just before he'd gone on, Alex had fastened a tissue-paper pink rose between her breasts. He'd told her it would be part of her costume.

She felt the audience's eyes on her. Jack's voice rose along with the Russian music, and the sides of the tent billowed in the breeze blowing off the ocean. "The child of wealthy French aristocrats, Theodosia was kept secluded from the modern world by the nuns who schooled her."

Nuns? What was Jack up to?

As the ringmaster continued, Alex began the slow whip dance, which had previously served as the climax to his act, while she stood motionlessly in a pool of light across from him. The lighting grew softer, and as the audience listened to Jack's story, they stared with fascination at Alex's graceful movements.

"She met the Cossack when the circus performed in a village near the convent where she was living, and the two of them fell deeply in love. But her parents rebelled at the idea of their gentle daughter marrying a man they considered a barbarian, and they disowned her. Theodosia had to leave everything familiar behind.''

The music became more dramatic, and Alex's whip dance changed from an athletic feat into a bridegroom's dance of seduction. ''Now, ladies and gentlemen, she comes into the ring with her husband, but it's not easy for her. The bullwhip terrifies this gentle young woman, and we ask for you to be as quiet as possible as she faces her fears. Remember that she enters the ring protected only by one thing''—Alex's dance reached its climax—''the love she feels for her fierce Cossack husband.''

The music crescendoed, and without warning, Alex cracked the whip in a dramatic arc over his head. Her breath left her body in a strangled exclamation, and she dropped the tube she had just withdrawn from the special pocket Sheba had finished sewing in her dress only a few hours earlier.

The audience gasped, and she realized that Jack's improbable story had worked. Instead of laughing at her reaction, they'd somehow picked up on her tension.

To her surprise, Alex walked over to her, picked up the tube she'd dropped, and presented it to her as if it were a single rose. Then he dipped his head and brushed his lips across hers.

The gesture was so romantic that she was almost certain she heard a woman in the front row sigh. She would have sighed, too, if she hadn't known he was merely playing to the crowd. Her fingers trembled as she held the tube as far away from her body as she could.

She managed to keep her composure as he cut it away, but when it came time for her to put it in her mouth, her knees once again started to shake. Slipping the tube between her lips, she closed her eyes and presented him with her profile.

The whip cracked and the end dropped off. She balled her hands into fists at her side. If she'd thought having an audience would make this any easier, she was wrong.

He cracked the whip twice more until only the stub stayed

between her lips. Her mouth was so dry she couldn't swallow.

Jack's voice intruded, hushed and dramatic. "Ladies and gentlemen, I ask for your cooperation as Alexi attempts to make the final cut in the small paper tube being held in his young bride's mouth. He needs absolute quiet. Remember that the lash will be passing so close to her face that the slightest miscalculation on his part could scar her for life."

Daisy whimpered. Her fingernails dug so deeply into her palms that she was afraid she had broken the skin.

The noise exploded in her ears as the whip sliced the last of the tube from her mouth.

The crowd erupted in cheers. Daisy squeezed her eyes open and felt so dizzy she was afraid she would faint. Alex gestured toward her with his hand, giving her a cue to style. The most she could manage was a slight dip of her chin.

As she lifted her head, the tip of the bullwhip flew through the air toward her, and the crimson tissue-paper flower tucked between her breasts exploded in a shower of fragile paper petals.

She jumped back with a hiss of alarm, and the audience applauded. He made a sharp upward gesture toward her, the cue to raise her arms and cross her wrists. She numbly followed directions.

The whip cracked and the crowd gasped as the lash curled around her wrists. He waited for a moment before he released the tension. There was an indecipherable murmur coming from the seats. He frowned at her, and she remembered that she was supposed to smile. She managed to pull the ends of her mouth upward and extend her wrists so they could see that she was unhurt. As she was doing that, the whip cracked again.

She winced. Looking down, she saw the lash wrapping her calves. He hadn't done this before, and she shot him a worried look. He released the tension and raised his eyebrow in warning. She gave the crowd another frozen smile. Once again, he gestured for her to raise her arms. With a feeling of inevitability, she did as he commanded.

Crack!

A scream slipped from her throat as the lash coiled about her waist. She waited for him to ease the tension, but this time he didn't. Instead, he tugged on the whip, forcing her to come to him. Only when the skirt of her dress brushed his thighs did he abruptly release the tight coils and draw her into his arms for a dramatic kiss that could have graced the cover of a romance novel.

The audience cheered.

She felt dizzy and angry with him, but somehow deliriously happy all at the same time. He whistled and Misha thundered back into the arena. Releasing her only for a moment, he vaulted onto the horse from the rear as it galloped around the ring. A prickle slithered up her spine. Surely he wouldn't—

Her feet left the ground as he dangled from the side of the horse to scoop her up into his arms. Before she knew what had happened, she was positioned across his lap.

The lights went out, plunging the arena into darkness. The applause was deafening. He loosened one of his arms while she clung frantically to his waist. Moments later, there was an explosion of sound and the great fire whip danced above their heads.

Daisy crossed the narrow asphalt road that separated the parking lot where the circus was set up from the deserted beach. Off to her left the garish lights of the Jersey Shore boardwalk blinked their colorful mayhem in the night: the Ferris wheel and zipper ride, the carousel and concessions.

Her debut had marked the circus's first appearance in the seaside resort, and now she was too keyed up to sleep. The audience at the second show had reacted even more enthusiastically, and a wonderful sense of accomplishment cut through her fatigue. Even Brady Pepper had set aside his customary silence to offer her a frosty nod.

She breathed in the musty sea scent and stepped down into the sand, which had lost its warmth from the day and trickled coolly into her sandals. She loved being near the ocean, and she was glad that this was one of the locations where the circus would spend more than one night.

"Daisy?"

She turned to see Alex standing at the top of the steps, his tall, lean body silhouetted against the faint glow of light reflected in the night sky. The breeze shuffled through his hair and pressed his shirt to his body. "Is this a private walk, or can anybody join?"

"Are you armed?"

"The whips are all packed away for the night."

"Then come along." She smiled and held out her hand.

For a moment he hesitated, and she wondered if the gesture was too personal for him. It spoke volumes about their relationship when holding hands seemed more intimate than having sex. Still, she didn't drop her arm. This was merely one more challenge for her to meet.

The soles of his work boots tapped on the wooden steps as he came down to meet her. He took her hand, and the ridge of calluses in his palm reminded her that he was a man accustomed to hard work. His hand, warm and strong, enfolded hers.

The beach was deserted but still littered with the debris left behind by the day's visitors, anxious to get an early start on the summer season: empty soda cans, a rubber shower thong, the broken lid of a Styrofoam cooler. They wandered toward the water.

"The audience liked the new act."

"I was so scared my knees were knocking. If it hadn't been for the new story line, it would have been a disaster, but when I tried to thank Jack afterward, he said it was your idea." She looked up at him and smiled. "Don't you think you were stretching it a bit with the French nuns?"

"I've heard your lectures on morality, sweetheart. Unless I miss my guess, at least part of that erratic schooling of yours was spent with nuns."

She didn't deny it.

They walked for a while in comfortable silence. The breeze tossed her hair, and the pounding of the surf drove out the distant noises of the boardwalk amusement park, giving her the feeling that the two of them were alone in the world. She waited for him to drop her hand, but he held on.

"You did a good job tonight, Daisy. You're a hard worker."

"You really think so? Do you really think I'm a hard worker?"

"I do."

"Thank you. Nobody's ever said anything like that about me." She gave a soft, self-deprecating laugh. "If they had, I probably wouldn't have believed it."

"But you believe me."

"You're not a man who gives praise lightly."

"Is that a compliment?"

"I'm not sure."

"Not fair."

"What?"

"I said something nice about you. Surely you can come up with at least one good thing about me."

"Of course I can. You make great chili."

To her surprise, he frowned. "Fine. Forget I said anything."

Thunderstruck, she realized she'd hurt his feelings. She thought he'd been teasing, but with Alex, she should have known better. Still, it surprised her that he cared about her opinion. "I was just warming up for the good stuff," she said.

"It's no big deal. It really doesn't matter."

But it did matter, and she was pleased. "Let me think."

"Forget it."

She squeezed his hand. "You do what you believe is right, even if other people disapprove, so I *should* admire your integrity. I *do* admire your integrity, but—" She folded her fingers around his hand. "Do you really want me to be honest?"

"I said so, didn't I?"

She ignored the belligerent thrust of his jaw. "You have a wonderful smile."

He looked faintly befuddled, and his hand relaxed around hers. "You like my smile?"

"I do. Very much."

"Nobody ever said that to me before."

"Not many people get to see it." She hid her own smile as she watched the serious way he pondered what she'd told him. "There's one other thing, but I don't know how you're going to take this."

"Go on."

"You have a really great body."

"A great body? Is that it? That's the second-best thing you can come up with about me?"

"I didn't say it was the second-best thing. All I'm doing is telling you something good about you, and that's something really good."

"My body?"

"It's terrific, Alex. It really is."

"Thank you."

"You're welcome."

The pounding of the surf filled the brief silence that fell between them.

"You, too," he said.

"What?"

"Your body. I like it."

"Mine? But there's not one great thing about it. My shoulders are too narrow for my hips, and my thighs are too fat. My stomach—"

He shook his head. "The next time I hear a woman going on about how neurotic men are, I'm going to remember this. You tell me you like my body, and what do I say? I say, thank you. Then I tell you I like yours and what do I hear? A long list of grievances."

"It's the burden women bear who've grown up playing with Barbie." His grunt of disgust somehow pleased her. "Thank you for the compliment, but—be honest. Don't you think my breasts are a little small?"

"This is a trick question, right?"

"Just tell me the truth."

"Are you sure that's what you want?"

"Yes."

"All right, then." He caught her by the shoulders so that she was facing the ocean, then stepped behind her. His arms slipped around her and he cupped her breasts. Her skin prickled with need as he gently squeezed and molded the flesh. He ran his thumbs down their soft slopes and brushed them over the hardening tips.

Her breath quickened. His lips feathered her earlobe as he whispered to her, "I think they're perfect, Daisy. Just the right size."

She turned, and no force in the world could have kept her from kissing him. Clasping her arms around his neck, she went on tiptoe and pressed her mouth to his, her lips soft and yielding. His tongue teased and hers responded. She lost all concept of time or even of separation. Her body became a part of his and his part of hers.

"Looky there, Dwayne! It's them two from the circus."

Daisy and Alex jumped apart like two teenagers caught necking by the cops.

The owner of the strident voice was a plump, middle-aged woman dressed in a lime green floral outfit and carrying a big black purse. Her husband's blue net gimme cap concealed what was probably a bald head. His slacks were rolled up to his calves and his sport shirt pulled tight over his belly.

The woman beamed at them. "We saw your show. My Dwayne, he didn't believe you two was really in love. He said it was all fake, but I told him you couldn't fake somethin' like 'at." She patted her husband's belly. "Me and Dwayne been married thirty-two years, so we know somethin' about true love."

Next to her, Alex had stiffened like a poker, leaving Daisy to smile at the couple. "I'm sure you do."

"Nothin' like a good marriage to keep your feet on the ground."

Alex gave the couple a curt nod and grabbed Daisy's arm to pull her away. Daisy turned and called out to them. "I hope you have thirty-two more!"

"You, too, hon!"

She let Alex carry her along, knowing it wouldn't do any good to protest. The subject of love made him so skittish that she felt an absurd desire to comfort him. By the time they reached the steps that led back to the boardwalk, she gave into it.

"Alex, it's all right. I'm not going to fall in love with you."

As she spoke the words, she felt a funny little hip-hop someplace around her heart. It scared her because she knew that falling in love with him would be a disaster. They were too different. He was tough, stern, and cynical, while she was exactly the opposite.

Then why was it, she wondered, that he stirred something so elemental within her? And why did she seem to understand him so well when he would tell her nothing about his past and nothing about his life apart from the circus? Despite that, she knew that in some way she couldn't entirely explain, he had helped her create herself anew. Thanks to him, she had a sense of independence she'd never possessed. For the first time in her life, she actually liked herself.

He mounted the stairs. "You're a romantic, Daisy. It's not that I think I'm so irresistible—God knows, I don't—but over the years it's been my observation that the minute any man puts a red flag in front of a woman, she changes it in her mind to a green one."

"Pooh."

They reached the top. He leaned his hips against the rail and studied her. "I've seen it happen too many times. Women want what they can't have, even if what they can't have isn't good for them."

"Is that the way you feel about yourself? That you're not good for the people in your life."

"I just don't want to hurt you. That's why I got upset when I saw what you'd done with the trailer. The place looks great, and it'll be easier to live in, but I don't want us playing at being man and wife. Regardless of the legality, we're having a fling. That's all there is to it."

"A *fling*?"

"An affair. Whatever. All right—a *circumstance*."

"You jerk!"

"You're proving my point."

She fought down her anger. "Why did you marry me? I thought it was because my father paid you, but now I don't believe that."

"What happened to make you change your mind?"

"I got to know you."

"And now you don't think I can be bought?"

"I know you can't."

"Everybody has a price."

"Then what was yours?"

"I owed your father a favor, and I needed to pay him back. That's all there is to it."

"It must have been a big favor."

His expression grew stony, and she was surprised when, after a long silence, he went on. "My parents died in a train wreck in Austria when I was two years old, and I was handed over to my closest relative, my mother's brother Sergey. He was a sadistic sonovabitch who got his kicks from whipping the crap out of me."

"Oh, Alex . . ."

"I'm not telling you this to earn your sympathy. I just want you to understand what you've gotten yourself into." He sat down on the bench, and some of the anger seemed to leave him. Leaning forward, he rubbed the bridge of his nose between his thumb and forefinger. "Sit down, Daisy."

Now that it was too late, she wondered if she should have started this, but she'd gone too far to back away, and she took a seat next to him. He stared directly ahead, looking tired and empty.

"You've read stories about abused kids who are locked away in attics for years." She nodded. "Psychologists say that even after these kids are rescued, they don't develop the same way other kids do. They don't have the same social skills. If they weren't exposed to language by a certain age, they never learn to talk. I guess I think love is like that. I didn't experience it when I was young, and now I can't do it.''

"What do you mean?"

"I'm not one of those cynics who doesn't believe love exists, because I've seen it in other people's relationships. But I can't feel it myself. Not for a woman. Not for anyone. I never have.''

"Oh, Alex . . .''

"It's not as though I haven't tried. I've met some wonderful women in my life, but in the end, all I've done is hurt them. That's why I've been so concerned about your birth control pills. Because I can't ever have a child.''

"You don't believe any relationship you have with a woman will last? Is that it?''

"I know it won't last. But it goes deeper than that.''

"I don't understand. Is there something wrong with you?''

"Haven't you been listening?''

"Yes, but . . .''

"I can't feel the emotions other men feel. Not for anyone. Not even for a child. Every kid deserves to be loved by their father, but I can't do that.''

"I don't believe you.''

"Believe it! I know myself, and this isn't some quirk on my part. A lot of people take the business of having children lightly, but I don't. Kids need love, and if they don't get it, something damaging happens to them inside. I couldn't live with myself knowing I'd done that to a child.''

"Everybody's capable of love, certainly of loving their own child. You're making yourself sound like some kind of . . . of monster.''

"Mutation might be a better word. My upbringing changed me from the norm. I can't tolerate the idea that I could have a child who'd grow up knowing his own father didn't love him. The abuse starts and ends with me.''

The night was still warm, but she shivered as she realized that the ugly legacy of Alex's violent past had never left him. It had also spilled over to hurt her, and she wrapped her arms around herself. She had never consciously imagined them having a child together, but maybe the idea had wormed its way into her subconscious, because now she felt bereft.

She gazed over at him and saw his profile outlined against the spinning carousel in the distance. The juxtaposition filled her with pity. The brightly painted horses with their wooden manes seemed to be everything innocent, carefree, and child-like, while Alex with his brooding eyes and empty heart was one of the damned. All this time she had thought she was the needy one, but he was far more wounded than she had ever been.

They didn't talk while they walked back to the trailer because there was nothing she could say. Tater had gotten loose again and stood in wait for her. He trotted up, giving a trumpety little bleat of welcome.

"I'll take him back," Alex said.

"It's all right. I'll do it. I need to be alone for a while."

He nodded and rubbed his thumb across her cheek, his eyes so bleak she couldn't bear it. She turned away to stroke Tater's trunk. "Come on, sweetheart."

She led him over to the other babies and tethered him, then picked up an old woolen blanket to spread on the ground next to him. As she sat down on it and hugged her knees, Tater shifted his position. For a moment she thought he was going to step on her and she tensed, but instead, he settled his front legs on either side of her and dropped his trunk.

She was in a warm elephant cave. She pressed her cheek to his scratchy, gunnysack body just between his legs and heard the strong thud of his sweet, mischievous heart. She knew she should move, but even though she was resting beneath a ton of baby elephant, she had never felt safer. As she sat there, she thought of Alex and wished he were small enough to fit where she was, right beneath Tater's heart.

15

Alex was asleep by the time Daisy returned to the trailer. She undressed as quietly as she could, then slipped into one of his T-shirts. As she began to make her way to the couch, she heard a husky whisper.

"Not tonight, Daisy. I need you."

She turned and gazed down into half-lidded eyes dark with desire. His hair was tousled, and the golden icon around his neck glittered in a shaft of moonlight that pierced the back window. Her mind still echoed with the memory of Tater's heartbeat thumping out its steady message of unconditional love, and nothing on earth could have made her turn away from him.

This time there were no smiles. No teasing. He possessed her fiercely, almost desperately, and when it was over, he curled his body around hers and didn't let her go. They fell asleep with his palm cupping her breast.

She didn't return to the couch the next night or the one after that. She stayed in her husband's bed and found her heart filling with an emotion she was very much afraid to name.

A week later, they reached central New Jersey, where they set up in another school yard, this one located in the middle of a suburban neighborhood containing comfortable two-story tract homes with swing sets in the backyards and mini-vans parked in the drives. On her way to the menagerie where Tater was tethered, Daisy stopped by the red wagon to make more changes in the feed order, and as she entered, she saw Jack going through several files.

He gave her a brief nod. She nodded back, then went over to the desk to locate the papers she needed. The cellular phone rang, and she answered it. "Quest Brothers Circus."

"I'm looking for Dr. Markov," a man with a slight British accent responded. "Is he available?"

She sagged down on the chair. "Who?"

"Dr. Alex Markov."

Her mind reeled. "He's—uh—not here right now. May I take a message?"

Her hand shook as she wrote down the man's name and number. By the time she hung up, her head was reeling. Alex was a doctor! She'd known he was well educated and that he had another life, but she hadn't imagined anything like this.

The mysteries surrounding her husband deepened, but she had no idea how to discover the truth. So far, he had refused to answer any of her questions, and he continued to act as if he had no existence beyond the boundaries of the circus.

She licked her dry lips and looked over at Jack. "That was a man who wanted to speak with Alex. He called him *Doctor* Markov."

Jack slipped several files back into the open drawer of the file cabinet without looking up. "Leave the message on the desk. He'll see it when he comes in."

He'd shown no reaction, so he obviously knew more about her husband's life than she did. The knowledge hurt. "I know it's just an oversight, but Alex hasn't ever told me exactly which branch of medicine he practices."

Jack picked up another file. "I guess that's the way he wants it, then."

Frustration ate at her. "Tell me what you know about him, Jack."

"Circus people learn not to ask too many questions about anybody's private life. If people want to talk about their past, they will. Otherwise, it's their business."

She realized that all she'd done was embarrass herself. She

made a play of rustling through the papers and escaped as quickly as she could.

She found Alex with Misha, squatting down to examine the horse's fetlock. She stared at him for a long moment. "You're a vet."

"What are you talking about?"

"You're a veterinarian."

"Since when?"

"Aren't you?"

"I don't know where you get your ideas."

"I just got a phone call for you. Someone wanted to speak with Doctor Markov."

"So?"

"If you're not a vet, what kind of doctor are you?"

He straightened and patted Misha's neck. "Did you ever think it might be a nickname?"

"A nickname?"

"From my days in prison. You know how convicts give each other names."

"You weren't in prison!"

"I thought you said I was. For murdering that waitress."

She stomped her foot in frustration. "Alex Markov, you tell me right now what you do when you're not with this circus!"

"Why do you want to know?"

"I'm your wife! I deserve the truth."

"All you need to know is what you see in front of you—a bad-tempered circus bum with a lousy sense of humor. Anything more would just confuse you."

"That is the most patronizing, condescending—"

"I don't mean to be patronizing, sweetheart. I just don't want you fogging up your vision with illusions. This is all there is for us. Quest Brothers. One season. The trailer and hard work." His expression softened. "I'm doing my damnedest not to hurt you. Help me out, will you? Don't ask so many questions."

If he'd been hostile, she would have challenged him, but she couldn't fight that sudden catch in his voice. Pulling back, she looked into the depths of his eyes. They were as golden as Sinjun's and just as mysterious.

"I don't like this, Alex," she said quietly. "I don't like it at all." She headed for the menagerie.

Sometime later, Heather came into the tent, just as Daisy finished hosing down Glenna's cage. "Can I talk to you?"

"All right." As she turned off the hose, she saw pale purple smudges under the teenager's eyes, and she could feel her tension.

"Why haven't you told Sheba about the money?"

She coiled the length of hose and laid it aside. "I decided not to."

"You're not going to tell her?"

Daisy shook her head.

Heather's eyes filled with tears. "I can't believe you haven't told her after everything I've done."

"You can pay me back by promising not to smoke another cigarette."

"Anything! I'll do anything. I'll always remember this, Daisy. Always." Heather snatched up the hose Daisy had just coiled. "Let me help. Whatever you want me to do. I'll do anything."

"Thanks for the offer, but I'm finished." She began coiling the hose again, but this time she carried it outside and set it on the ground against the tent.

Heather came after her. "Would you—I know I'm just a kid and everything, but since you don't have any friends because of me, maybe we could do some stuff together." She seemed to be searching her mind for a common interest that might overcome their troubled history as well as bridge the difference in their ages. "Sometime maybe we could get some pizza or something. Or do each other's hair."

Daisy couldn't help but smile at the tentative note of hope in her voice. "That'd be nice."

"I'm going to make it up to you, I promise."

Some things could never be made up, but Daisy wouldn't tell Heather that. She'd made her decision, and she wasn't going to dangle guilt over the teenager's head.

Brady Pepper interrupted, stalking into their midst like bad news. "What are you doing here, Heather? I've told you not to hang out around her."

Heather flushed. "Daisy's been really nice to me, and I wanted to help her."

"Go find Sheba. She wants to work with you on your headstand."

Heather looked increasingly miserable. "Daisy's real nice, Dad. She'd not like you think. She's good with the animals, and she treats me—"

"Right now, young lady."

"Go on, Heather." Daisy gave her a reassuring nod. "Thanks for offering to help."

Reluctantly, Heather did as she was told.

Brady bristled with animosity—Sylvester Stallone on double testosterone. "You stay away from her, you hear me? Alex might have gone temporarily blind where you're concerned, but the rest of us don't forget so easy."

"I'm not ashamed of anything I've done, Brady."

"Wasn't the crime big enough? If it'd been two thousand dollars you took instead of two hundred, would you be ashamed? Sorry, babe, but to my mind, a thief's a thief."

"Have you led such a blameless life that you've never done anything you regret?"

"I've never stolen anything, that's for sure."

"You're stealing your daughter's sense of security. Doesn't that count?"

His lips thinned. "Don't you dare lecture me on how to raise my daughter. You and Sheba. Neither one of you ever had a kid, so you can both just keep your damned mouths shut."

He stalked away, muscles gleaming, tail feathers rumpled.

Daisy sighed. It was barely one o'clock. She'd argued with Alex and antagonized both Jack and Brady. What else could go wrong today?

The high-pitched chatter of excited voices caught her attention, and she saw another group of schoolchildren coming over from the neighboring elementary school. All morning the classes had been touring the circus lot, and with so many youngsters wandering around, she'd made certain that Tater was firmly tethered, something he didn't like at all. These children were the smallest. They must be the kindergartners.

She wistfully regarded the middle-aged woman who escorted them. Being a kindergarten teacher might not be everyone's idea of bliss, but it was hers.

She watched how skillfully the teacher kept the children from running wild, and for a moment, she imagined herself doing the same. She didn't linger over the fantasy for long. To be a teacher, she needed a college degree, and she was too old for that.

She couldn't resist walking over to them as they approached Sinjun's cage, which was roped off to keep the visitors from getting too close. After smiling at the teacher, she addressed a pudgy little cherub in pink overalls who was regarding the tiger with awe.

"His name is Sinjun, and he's a Siberian tiger. Siberians are the largest of all tigers."

"Does he eat people?" the cherub asked.

"Not people, but he is a carnivore. That means he eats meat."

The little boy next to her perked up. "My gerbil eats gerbil food."

Daisy laughed.

The teacher smiled. "I'll bet you know a lot about tigers. Would you mind telling the children a little bit about Sinjun?"

A ripple of excitement passed through her. "I'd love to!" She quickly sorted through everything she'd learned about the animals in her recent library trips and picked out the details they were most likely to understand. "A hundred years ago, tigers roamed free in lots of parts of the world, but that isn't true anymore. People moved into the tigers' home lands . . ." She kept the explanation about the tiger's gradual extinction simple and was gratified to see the children hanging on to her words.

"Can we pet him?" one of them asked.

"No. He's old and not very friendly, and he wouldn't understand that you don't want to hurt him. He's not like a cat or a dog."

She answered a number of other questions, including several about Sinjun's bathroom habits that elicited a chorus of giggles. She listened to one child's story about a dog who died and another's announcement that he'd just gotten over chicken pox. They were so darling she could have easily spent all day talking with them.

As the class got ready to move on, the teacher thanked her effusively, and the cherub in pink overalls hugged her. Daisy felt as if she were floating on a cloud.

She was still watching them as she made her way to the trailer to pick up a quick bite of lunch when a familiar figure clad in dark brown trousers and a pale yellow polo shirt came out of the red wagon. She stopped walking, hardly able to believe what she saw. At the same time, she was conscious of her dirty work clothes and untidy hair, rumpled from Glenna's latest grooming.

"Hello, Theodosia."

"Dad? What are you doing here?" Her father was such a powerful figure in her mind that she seldom noticed he was rather slight in build, only inches taller than herself. He bore all the accessories of wealth with ease: silver gray hair expertly trimmed by a barber who visited his office once a week, an expensive watch, conservative Italian loafers with a discreet gold snaffle across the vamp. It was hard for her to imagine him ever forgetting his dignity long enough to fall in love with a fashion model and father an illegitimate child, but she was living proof that at one time in his life, her father had been human.

"I drove over to visit Alex."

"Oh." She did her best to hide her hurt that he hadn't come to see her.

"I also wanted to check on you."

"You did?"

"I wanted to make certain you were still with him. That you hadn't done anything foolish."

For a moment she wondered if Alex had told him about the stolen money, but then she knew that he wouldn't. That certainty filled her with warmth.

"As you can see, I'm still here. If you'd like to come to the trailer with me, I can get you something to drink. Or I'll fix you a sandwich if you're hungry."

"A cup of tea would be nice."

She led him toward the trailer. He stopped walking when he saw its battered exterior. "Good God. Don't tell me you actually live in this place."

She felt oddly protective of her little home. "It's not so bad inside. I've fixed it up."

She opened the door and let him in, but despite the changes she'd made, he was no more impressed with the interior than he'd been with the exterior. "Alex could certainly have done better than this."

Strangely enough, his criticism made her defensive. "It's fine for us."

His gaze lingered for a moment on the trailer's only bed. She hoped the sight made him uncomfortable, but she couldn't read his expression.

As she went to the stove to boil water for tea, the gingerly way he sat on the couch made it obvious he was afraid he'd catch some disease. She took the chair next to him while the water heated.

An awkward silence followed, broken finally by her father. "How are you and Alex getting on?"

"We're doing all right."

"He's quite a man. Not everyone could overcome their upbringing as he has. Did he ever tell you how we met?"

"He said you saved his life."

"I don't know about that, but when I found him, his uncle had him on the ground behind one of the trucks. He was holding him down with his foot while he brutalized him with a stock whip."

She winced. Alex had told her he'd been abused, but hearing it from her father's lips made it seem even more horrifying.

"Alex's shirt was ripped. He had red welts across his back, some of them bleeding. His uncle was cursing him for a minor offense while he whipped him with all his strength." She squeezed her eyes shut, willing her father to stop talking, but he went on. "The thing I most remember is that Alex was absolutely silent. He didn't cry. He didn't call out for help. He simply endured. It was the most tragic thing I've ever seen."

Daisy felt sick. No wonder Alex couldn't believe in love.

Her father leaned back on the couch. "Ironically, I had no idea who the child was at first. Sergey Markov was traveling with the old Curzon Circus at the time, and it was only a whim that made me decide to look him up when I learned he was going to be performing near Fort Lee. There'd been some rumors about the family connection. I'd been told it was authentic, but I'm always skeptical about stories like that, and I didn't really believe it."

Although she knew of her father's passion for Russian history, she hadn't known it extended to the circus. As the kettle began to whistle, she walked over to the stove. "The connection is authentic all right. The Markovs are one of the most famous circus families in history."

He looked at her strangely as she began preparing the tea. "The Markovs?"

"For the most part they seem to trace their heritage through the women in the family. Don't you think that's unusual?"

"It's hardly significant. The Markovs were peasants, Theodosia. Circus people." His lips thinned with disdain. "I was only interested in looking up Sergey Markov because of the rumors about his sister Katya's marriage—Alex's mother."

"What are you talking about?"

"It was Alex's *father's* family I was interested in. The family Katya Markov married into. For God's sake, Theodosia, the Markovs are of no importance at all. Don't you know anything about your husband?"

"Not much," she conceded, carrying two earthenware

mugs of tea over to the couch and handing him one. Her hands were tightly clenched around the mug as she took a seat at the other end of the couch.

"I thought he would have spoken about it, but he's so secretive I suppose I should have known he wouldn't tell you."

"Tell me what?" She had been waiting for this, but now that the time had come, she wasn't certain she wanted to know.

A distinct quiver of excitement ran through his voice. "Alex is a Romanov, Theodosia."

"A Romanov?"

"On his father's side."

Her immediate reaction was amusement, but that faded as she realized her father was so obsessed with Russian history that he'd been taken in by circus hype. "Dad, that's not true. Alex isn't a Romanov. He's Markov, through and through. The Romanov story is just part of his act, something he invented to make his performance more dramatic."

"Credit me with some intelligence, Theodosia. I'd hardly be taken in by a show business stunt." He crossed his legs. "You have no idea what I went through to verify Alex's heritage. Once I'd done that, I had to get him away from Sergey Markov for good—the bastard didn't die until ten years ago. Then there was the matter of arranging for Alex's education, which had been abominable up to that point. I took care of his boarding school, but he insisted on putting himself through college, which made it impossible for me to keep him away from the circus. Do you think I would have put myself through all that if I hadn't been absolutely certain who he was?"

A chill slithered along her spine. "Exactly who is he?"

Her father leaned back into the couch. "Alex is the great-grandson of Czar Nicholas II."

16

Daisy stared at her father. "That's impossible. I don't believe you."

"It's true, Daisy. Alex's grandfather was the czar's only son, Alexei Romanov."

Daisy knew all about Alexei Romanov, the young son of Nicholas II. In 1918, at the age of fourteen, Alexei, along with his parents and four sisters, had been herded by the Bolsheviks into the basement of a mansion in Yekaterinburg and executed. She said as much to her father.

"All of them were murdered. Czar Nicholas, his wife Alexandra, the children. They found the remains of the family in a pit in the Ural Mountains in 1993. They did DNA tests."

He picked up his mug. "The DNA tests identified the czar, Alexandra, and three of the four daughters. One daughter was missing—some people think it was Anastasia. And they didn't find Crown Prince Alexei's remains."

Daisy tried to take it in. Throughout the century, there had been a number of people who had claimed to be the czar's murdered children, but most of them had been women presenting themselves as the princess Anastasia. Her father had contemptuously dismissed all of them as impostors. He was a careful man and she couldn't imagine him being taken in by any sort of scam, so why did he now believe the crown prince had escaped? Had his obsession with Russian history grown to the point where he wanted to believe this story so much that he'd lost his judgment?

She spoke carefully. "I can't imagine how the crown prince could have survived such a terrible massacre."

"He was rescued by some monks who hid him with a family in southern Russia for several years until a group loyal to the czar smuggled him out of the country. That was in 1920. He'd seen firsthand how violent the Bolsheviks could be, so it's understandable that he lived quietly after that. Eventually, he married and had one child, who was Alex's father Vasily. Vasily met Katya Markov when she was performing in Munich and, like a fool, he eloped with her. He was only a teenager; his father had just died; he was rebellious and undisciplined. Otherwise, he would never have married so far beneath him. He was only twenty when Alex was born. A little over two years later, he and Katya were killed in a circus train accident."

"I'm sorry, Dad. I don't mean to doubt your word, but I simply can't believe this."

"Believe it, Theodosia. Alex is a Romanov. And not just any Romanov. The man who calls himself Alex Markov is the direct heir to the crown of Russia."

She stared at her father with dismay. "Alex is a circus performer. That's all."

"Amelia warned me you'd react like this." In an uncharacteristic gesture, he patted her knee. "You just need some time to get used to the idea, but I hope you know me well enough to realize that I would never make a claim like this if I weren't absolutely certain it was true."

"But—"

"I've told you many times about my family's history, but you've obviously forgotten. Ever since the nineteenth century, the Petroffs have served the Russian czars, all the way back to Alexander I. We've been linked through duty and custom, but never through marriage. Not until now."

She heard the sound of a jet passing overhead, the roar of a truck's diesel engine. Gradually comprehension seeped through her.

"You planned all this, didn't you? You arranged my marriage to Alex because of this crazy idea you have about who he is.''

''It's not even remotely crazy. Just ask Alex.''

''I'll do that.'' She rose to her feet. ''I finally understand what all this is about. You've made me a pawn in some absurd dynastic dream of yours. You wanted to unite the two families, just like fathers used to do in the Middle Ages. This is so barbaric I can't believe it.''

''I'd hardly call marrying you to a Romanov barbaric.''

She pressed her fingers to her temples. ''Our marriage is only going to last five more months. How can you get any satisfaction out of that? A short-term marriage is hardly the beginning of a dynasty!''

He set down his mug and walked slowly over to her. ''You and Alex don't have to divorce. As a matter of fact, I'm hoping you won't.''

''Oh, Dad . . .''

''You're an attractive woman, Daisy. Perhaps not as beautiful as your mother, but still appealing. If you could learn to be less frivolous, you might be able to hold on to Alex. There are certain secrets to being a good wife, you know. Cater first to your husband's wishes. Be accommodating.'' He frowned at her grubby jeans and T-shirt. ''And you should be more careful about your appearance. I've never seen you look so sloppy. Do you know that you have hay in your hair? Maybe Alex won't be so anxious to get rid of you if you try to be the sort of woman a man looks forward to coming home to.''

She regarded him with disgust. ''Do you want me to meet him at the trailer door with his slippers?''

''That's *exactly* the sort of flippant remark that will drive someone like Alex away. He's a very serious man. If you don't curb that inappropriate sense of humor, you won't stand a chance of holding on to him.''

''Who says I want to?'' Even as she spoke, something painful twisted inside her.

''I can see you're going to be difficult about this, so I'll go now.'' He walked toward the door. ''Just don't cut off your nose to spite your face, Theodosia. Remember that you're not a woman who does well alone. Setting aside the issue of Alex's family lineage, he's steady and reliable, and I can't imagine a better man to take care of you.''

"I don't need a man to take care of me!"

"Then why did you agree to the marriage in the first place?''

Without waiting for her reply, he opened the door of the trailer and stepped out into the sunshine. How could she explain the changes that had taken place inside her? She knew she was no longer the same person who'd left his house over a month ago, but he wouldn't believe her.

Outside, the kindergartners she'd spoken with earlier were grouped around their teacher, prepared to return to the classroom. Over the past month she had grown accustomed to the sights and smells of Quest Brothers Circus, but now she looked at it all with fresh eyes.

Alex and Sheba stood near the big top arguing about something. The clowns were practicing a juggling trick while Heather attempted a handstand and Brady frowned at her form. Frankie played on the ground near Jill, who was working the dogs, little yippy things that made Daisy cringe. She smelled hamburgers sizzling on a charcoal grill the showgirls had lit, heard the ever-present hum of the generator, the snap of the pennants in the June breeze.

And then a child screamed.

The sound was so ear-splitting that everyone noticed. Alex's head shot up. Heather fell out of her handstand, and the clowns dropped the pins they were juggling. Her father came to a sudden stop, just blocking her line of vision. She heard his gasp and pushed past him to see what was causing the commotion. Her heart skipped a beat.

Sinjun had escaped from his cage.

He stood in the short grass between the menagerie and the back door of the big top, while behind him the door of his cage hung open from a broken hinge. The white flags on his ears were up and his pale golden eyes were fixed on an object less than ten yards away.

The chubby little kindergarten cherub in her pink overalls.

The child had somehow become separated from the rest of her class, and it was her piercing scream that had caught Sinjun's attention. The little girl howled in terror as she stood frozen to the spot, her arms jerking at her sides, a stain spreading on her overalls as she wet herself.

Sinjun roared, revealing lethally sharp teeth curved like scimitars, teeth designed to hold his prey in place while he ripped it open with his claws. The little girl screamed again, the sound more piercing. Sinjun's powerful muscles rippled and all the blood left Daisy's head. She sensed him ready to spring. To the tiger, the child with her thrashing arms and shrill shrieks must seem like the most threatening sort of prey.

Neeco appeared from out of nowhere, rushing directly toward Sinjun. Daisy saw the cattle prod in his hand and took an involuntary step forward. She wanted to warn him not to do it. Sinjun wasn't used to the prod. He wouldn't be cowed by it the way the elephants were; it would merely make him more enraged. But Neeco was reacting instinctively, handling the tiger in the only way he understood, as if Sinjun were an unruly bull elephant.

As Sinjun turned away from the child toward Neeco, Alex came running from the opposite side. He dashed toward the little girl and snatched her up into his arms to carry her to safety.

And then everything happened at once. Neeco plunged the end of the cattle prod at the tiger's shoulder. The maddened animal gave a roar of fury and flung his massive body at Neeco, knocking the elephant trainer to the ground. Neeco lost his grip on the prod, and it rolled out of his reach.

Daisy had never felt such terror. Sinjun was going to savage Neeco, and there was nothing any of them could do to stop it.

"Sinjun!" Desperately, she called out his name.

To her astonishment, the tiger lifted his head. Whether he'd heard her or was responding to some unnamed instinct, she didn't know. Her legs were so weak she could barely lift them, but even so, she moved forward. She had no idea what she was going to do. She merely knew she had to act.

The tiger remained crouched over Neeco's motionless body. For a moment she thought the trainer was dead, but then she realized he was holding himself very still, hoping the tiger would forget about him.

"Daisy, don't take another step." She heard her husband's voice, quiet but commanding. And then her father's voice, more shrill.

"What are you doing? Get back here!"

She ignored them both. The tiger turned his body slightly, and they stared at each other. His sharp, curved teeth were bared, his ears flat against his head, his eyes wild. She felt his terror.

"Sinjun," she said softly.

Long seconds ticked by. She saw a flash of auburn between Sinjun and the big top, Sheba Quest's flaming hair as she moved quickly toward Alex, who had just passed the screaming little girl off to her teacher. Sheba handed Alex something, but Daisy's mind seemed to be paralyzed.

The tiger stepped over Neeco's prone body and riveted all his ferocious attention on her. Every one of his muscles was tensed and poised to spring.

"I have a gun." Alex spoke to her in a voice barely more than a whisper. "Don't move."

Her husband was going to kill Sinjun. She understood the logic of what he was about to do—there were people all over the lot; the tiger was wild with terror and clearly a danger— but at the same time, she knew she couldn't let it happen. This magnificent beast shouldn't be put to death merely because he was behaving in accordance with the instincts of his species.

Sinjun had done nothing wrong except act like a tiger. Human beings were the ones who had transgressed. They had taken him from his natural environment, imprisoned him in a tiny cage, and forced him to live his life beneath the stares of his enemies. And now, because she hadn't noticed that his cage was one of those needing repairs, he would be killed.

She moved as quickly as she dared and put herself between her husband and the tiger.

"Get out of the way, Daisy." The quiet timbre of his voice did nothing to soften the force of his command.

"I won't let you kill him," she whispered back. And she began to walk slowly toward the tiger.

His golden eyes blazed at her. Through her. She felt his terror seep into every cell of her body and conjoin with hers. Their souls melded, and she heard him in her heart.

I hate them.

I know.

Stop.

I can't.

She narrowed the distance between them until they were separated by barely six feet. "Alex will kill you," she whispered, gazing into the golden eyes of the beast.

"Daisy, please . . ." She heard the strain in Alex's desperate entreaty, and she was sorry for the distress she was causing him, but she couldn't stop her course of action.

As she closed in on the tiger, she sensed Alex shifting his position so he could get a clear shot from another direction. She knew she had run out of time.

With fear filling her chest until she could barely breathe, she sank to her knees before the tiger. She smelled his feral scent and stared into his eyes.

"I can't let you die," she whispered. "Come with me." Slowly, she reached out for him.

One part of her waited for his powerful jaws to clamp around her arm, while another part—her soul, maybe, since only the voice of the soul could so stubbornly resist logic— the soul part of her no longer cared if she had an arm, not if he was to die. She gingerly touched the top of his head between his ears.

His fur felt both soft and bristly. She let him grow accustomed to her touch, and his heat seeped through her palm. The soft skin of her inner arm brushed against his whiskers, and she felt his breath through the thin cotton of her T-shirt. He shifted his weight and gradually sank down onto the ground with his front paws extended.

Calm seeped through her body, taking the place of the fear. She experienced a blissful sense of homecoming, a peace she had never known, as the tiger became her and she became the tiger. In one fragment of time she understood all the mysteries of creation, that every living being was part of every other living being, that all were part of God, bound by love, put on earth to care for one another. She knew then that there was no fear, no disease, no death. Nothing of any importance existed but love.

And in that fragment of time, she understood that she also loved Alex in the earthly way a woman loves a man.

It seemed natural for her arms to encircle the tiger's neck. Even more natural to press her cheek to him and close her eyes. Time ticked by. She heard the throb of his heart and, overlaying that, a deep, gravelly purring.

I love you.

I love you.

"I have to take you back," she finally whispered, tears seeping through her closed eyelids. "But I won't abandon you. Ever."

The purring and the heartbeat became as one.

She stayed there on the ground for some time, her cheek pressed to his neck. She had never felt so peaceful, not even when she sat between Tater's front legs. There was so much evil in the world, but not here. This place was holy.

Only gradually did the others come into focus. They were frozen like statues. Off to the sides. Before her. Behind her.

Alex still had his gun aimed at Sinjun. Silly man. As if she would let him hurt this animal. Her husband's healthy tan had faded to chalk, and she knew she was causing him terrible fear. With the echo of the tiger's heartbeat beneath her cheek, she understood she had upset Alex's world in a way he would find difficult to forgive. When this was over, there would be terrible consequences to face.

Her father, looking old and gaunt and gray, stood not far

behind Alex, next to Sheba. Heather clutched Brady's arm. The schoolchildren were absolutely silent.

The outside world had invaded, and she could no longer stay where she was. Slowly, she stood. Keeping her hand curved over the back of Sinjun's neck, she let the tips of her fingers sink into his fur.

"Sinjun's going back to his cage now," she announced to everyone. "Please stay away from him."

She began to move and wasn't at all surprised when the tiger came with her since their souls were so intertwined that he had no other choice. The side of her leg brushed against him as she led him toward the cage. With every step, she was aware of Alex's gun trained on him.

The closer they got to their destination, the more she felt the tiger's sadness. She wished she could make him understand it was the only place she could keep him safe. When they reached the cage, he balked.

She knelt and gazed into his eyes. "I'll stay with you for a while."

He gave her his unblinking stare. And then, to her amazement, he rubbed his cheek against the side of her head. His whiskers brushed her neck, and once again she heard his deep, gruff purr.

And then he was gone. With one powerful thrust of his hindquarters, he leaped into the cage.

She heard a rustle of movement behind her and spun around to see Neeco and Alex running toward the cage, ready to grab the broken door and shove it back in place.

"Stop!" She held out her arms, warding them off. "Don't come any closer."

They froze in their tracks.

"Daisy, get out of the way." Alex's voice vibrated with tension, and lines of strain had made his handsome features stark.

"Leave us alone." She moved directly in front of the open cage door and turned her back on them.

Sinjun watched her. Now that he was once again imprisoned, he stood as imperiously as ever: regal, aloof, with everything lost to him except his dignity. She somehow knew what he wanted, and she couldn't bear it. He wanted her to be his jailer. She was the one he had elected to close the broken door of the cage and imprison him.

She hadn't realized she was crying until she felt the tears sliding down her cheeks. Sinjun's golden eyes shimmered, and he regarded her with his customary disdain, making her feel as if she were somehow his inferior.

Do it, weakling! those eyes commanded. *Now.*

Bracing herself, she lifted her arms to grasp the cage door. The broken hinge made it heavy and difficult to maneuver, but with a sob, she managed to close it.

Alex rushed forward and grabbed for the door to secure it, but the moment he touched it, Sinjun bared his teeth and gave a bone-chilling roar.

"Let me do it!" she exclaimed. "You're upsetting him. Please. I'll fasten it."

"Damn it!" He quickly stepped back, sounding angry and frustrated.

Her position was awkward. The platform the cage rested on stood over three feet off the ground, and she had to raise her arms to hold the door shut. Neeco appeared with a wooden stool, which he set next to her. Then he gave her a piece of rope.

For a moment, she couldn't imagine what it was for.

"Loop it through the bars by the hinge," Alex said. "Lean against the door while you work so you can use your weight to keep it in place. And for god's sake get ready to jump back if he decides to attack."

Coming up behind her, he slipped his hands around her hips to brace her. Their support comforted her as she tried to do as he'd said, holding the door closed with her shoulder while she attempted to secure the rope around the broken hinge. Her body began to tremble from the strain of her awkward position. She felt the bulge of the gun he'd tucked into the waistband of his jeans.

His hold on her tightened. "You've almost got it, sweetheart."

The knot was big and clumsy, but it held. She dropped her arms. Alex pulled her off the stool and gathered her against his chest.

She stayed there for several long comforting moments before she looked up into eyes so very much like the tiger's. The new knowledge that she loved this man filled her with a sense of awe. They were so different, yet she felt the call of his soul as clearly as if he'd spoken out loud. "I'm sorry I scared you."

"We'll talk about it later."

He would drag her back to the trailer for a private lambasting. Maybe this was the incident that would finally push him over the edge, and he'd send her away. She pushed aside the thought and stepped back from him. "I can't leave yet. I promised Sinjun I'd stay with him for a while."

The lines of strain deepened near his mouth, but he didn't question her. "All right."

Her father stormed forward. "You don't have the brains of an idiot! It's a wonder you're still alive! Whatever possessed you? Don't you ever do anything like that again. If you even—"

Alex cut in. "Shut up, Max. I'll take care of this."

"But—"

Alex lifted one eyebrow, and Max Petroff immediately fell silent. That was all Alex did—lift one eyebrow—but it was enough. She had never seen her domineering father concede to anyone in that way, and it reminded her of what he'd said. For centuries it had been the duty of the Petroffs to obey the wishes of the Romanovs.

At that moment some part of her accepted what her father had told her as true, but she returned her attention to Sinjun, who looked restless and edgy.

"Amelia will be wondering where I am," her father said from behind her. "I'd better be getting back. Good-bye, Theodosia." He seldom touched her, and she was surprised to feel the soft brush of his hand on her shoulder. Before she could respond, he turned to Alex and said his farewells, then walked away.

The activity of the circus had begun to return to normal. Jack was talking with the teacher as he helped her escort the children to the school. Neeco and the others had gone back to work. Sheba walked forward. "Good job, Daisy."

The words were delivered begrudgingly. Although Daisy thought she saw a glimmer of respect in the circus owner's eyes, she also had the eerie feeling Sheba's dislike of her had intensified. Sheba avoided looking at Alex and walked away, leaving them alone with Sinjun.

The tiger stood, tense and watchful, but still regarding both of them with his customary hauteur. She wrapped her hands around the cage bars. Sinjun moved. She heard Alex's quick, indrawn breath as the tiger began to rub his great head against her fingers.

"I wish you wouldn't let him do that."

She reached farther between the bars to scratch Sinjun behind his ears. "He won't hurt me. He doesn't respect me, but he loves me."

Alex gave a thin chuckle and then, to her surprise, enfolded her in his arms from behind as she stroked the tiger. His jaw moved against the top of her head. "I've never been so scared in my life."

"I'm sorry."

"I'm the one who's sorry. You warned me about the cages, and I should have checked all of them. This is my fault."

"It's mine. I'm responsible for the menagerie."

"Don't you dare blame yourself. I won't allow it."

Sinjun's tongue stroked her wrist. She felt the muscles in Alex's arms tense as the tiger licked her.

"Would you please take your hands out of that cage now?" he asked quietly. "You're giving me heart failure."

"In a minute."

"I've already lost ten years off my life. I can't afford to lose any more."

"I like touching him. Besides, he's a lot like you. He doesn't give his affection easily, and I don't want to offend him by backing away."

"He's an animal, Daisy. He doesn't have human emotions."

She was feeling too peaceful to argue.

"Sweetheart, you have to stop befriending wild animals. First Tater, now Sinjun. I'll tell you what. You obviously need a real pet. First thing tomorrow, we'll get you a dog."

She looked up at him in alarm. "Oh, no, we can't do that."

"Why not."

"Because I'm afraid of dogs."

He looked stunned, and then he began to laugh. At first it was the merest rumble deep in his chest, but it soon turned into a rich, hearty sound that bounced off the walls of the big top and echoed through the lot.

"It figures," she grumbled through her own smile. "Alex Markov finally laughs, and it's at my expense."

He turned his head into the sun, drew her tighter against him, and laughed all the harder.

Sinjun regarded them both with faint annoyance, then stretched out against the bars of the cage to lick Daisy's thumb.

Alex shouldered his way through the group of reporters and photographers that had surrounded Daisy following the final show that evening. "My wife's had enough for today. She needs to get some rest."

Ignoring him, a reporter shoved a small tape recorder toward Daisy. "What went through your mind when you realized the tiger was loose?"

Daisy opened her mouth to respond, but Alex broke in, knowing Daisy was so damned polite she'd answer their questions till she dropped. "Sorry, that's it." Wrapping his arm around her, he began leading her away.

It hadn't taken the media long to get hold of the story of the escaped tiger, and reporters had been showing up ever since the matinee to interview her. At first Sheba had been happy with the publicity. Then she'd heard Daisy comment that the menagerie was cruel and inhumane, and she'd been furious. When Sheba had attempted to interrupt with the interview, Daisy had looked at her with those innocent eyes and said, without a speck of guile, "But, Sheba, the animals hate being in the menagerie. They're all so unhappy there."

As he and Daisy made their way to the trailer, he was so glad she was alive and unhurt that he didn't much mind anything she said. She stumbled, and he realized he was walking too fast. He was always doing that to her. Dragging her along. Pushing her. Making her stumble. What if she'd been hurt today? What if Sinjun had killed her?

He felt a crushing panic as his mind played out gruesome images of Sinjun's claws ripping into her small, slender body. If anything had happened to her, he would never have forgiven himself. She was too important to him. Too necessary.

Her fragrance drifted up at him, sweet and spicy, with a hint of something else, maybe the scent of goodness. How had she managed to work her way under his skin in such a short time? She wasn't his type of woman at all, but she'd made him feel emotions he'd never imagined, even as she turned the rules of logic upside down so that black became white and order became chaos. There was nothing rational about her. She made pets out of tigers and recoiled in fear from a small dog. She'd taught him how to laugh. She'd also done something no one else had been able to accomplish since he was a very young child. She had shattered his rigid self-control, and maybe that was why he was beginning to hurt so much.

An image flickered through his mind, at first elusive, but gradually growing clearer. He remembered frigid winter days when he'd been outside too long and come in to thaw. He remembered the pain in his frozen hands as warmth returned to them. The pain of the thaw. Was that what was happening to him? Was he feeling the pain of thawing emotions?

Daisy looked back at the reporters. "They're going to think I'm rude, Alex. I shouldn't have left so abruptly."

"I don't give a damn what they think."

"That's because you have high self-esteem. I, on the other hand, have low—"

"Don't start."

Tater, tethered near their trailer, bleated as he saw Daisy. "I have to tell him good night."

His arms felt empty as she disengaged herself and went over to Tater where she pressed her cheek to his head. He wrapped her up in his trunk, and Alex had to fight the urge to pull her away before the baby elephant crushed her from an excess of feeling. A cat. Maybe he could buy her some kind of house cat. Declawed so she wouldn't get scratched.

The idea didn't ease his mind. Knowing Daisy, she was probably afraid of house cats, too.

She finally left Tater behind to followed him into the trailer where she began to take off her costume only to sink down on the end of the bed. "Go ahead and yell at me. I know you've been wanting to all day."

Alex had never seen her look so forlorn. Why did she always have to think the worst of him? Even as his heart urged him to go easy, his mind told him he had to rip right into her and give her a lecture she'd never forget. The circus was full of dangers, and he would do anything to keep her safe.

As he gathered his thoughts, she gazed up at him, and all the troubles of the world were reflected in the violet depths of her eyes. "I couldn't let you kill him, Alex. I couldn't."

His good intentions dissolved. "I know." He sat next to her on the bed, picking the hay out of her hair and speaking with difficulty. "What you did today was the bravest thing I've ever seen."

"And the stupidest. Go ahead and say it."

"That, too." He reached out with his index finger and pushed an inky curl back from her cheek. As he gazed into her upturned face, he couldn't remember ever having seen anything that moved him so deeply. "When I first met you, all I could see was a spoiled little rich girl, silly and pampered, too beautiful for her own good."

Predictably, she began to shake her head. "I'm not beautiful. My mother—"

"I know. Your mother was a knockout, and you're paper bag ugly." He smiled. "Sorry to upset all those cherished illusions of yours, but I don't see it your way."

"That's because you didn't know her."

She spoke with such seriousness that he had to suppress another of those urges to laugh that seemed to come over him whenever they were together. "Could your mother have led a tiger back into its cage?"

"Maybe not that, but she was very good with men. They'd do anything for her."

"This man will do anything for you."

Her eyes grew wider, and he wanted to snatch back his words because they revealed too much. He'd vowed to protect her from her own romantic dreams, but he'd just let her see how much he cared. Knowing Daisy, with her old-fashioned views about marriage, she'd imagine his caring to be love and start building pipe dreams in her head about their future, pipe dreams his own twisted emotional makeup wouldn't let him fulfill. The only way he could protect her was to let her see what a mean son of a bitch she'd linked herself up with.

But it was so hard. Of all the cruel tricks fate had played on him, the cruelest of all was joining him to this fragile decent woman with the beautiful eyes and too-generous heart. Caring wasn't enough for her. She needed to be surrounded by real love. She needed children and a good husband—one of those big-hearted guys who marched in Labor Day parades and went to church on Sunday and would love her to distraction.

Something painful twisted inside him as he thought of her married to someone else, but he forced it away. No matter what he had to do, he was going to protect her.

"Do you mean it, Alex? Would you really do anything for me?"

Despite all his good intentions, he nodded like a fool.

"Then sit very still and let me make love to you."

His groin tightened into a hard, throbbing ache, and he wanted her so much he couldn't breathe. At the very last instant, just before his hunger to possess her overpowered him, her mouth curved in a smile so soft and sweet he felt as if he'd been kicked in the gut.

She wasn't holding anything back. Not one thing. She was offering herself to him without reservations: heart, body, and soul. How could anyone be so self-destructive? He pulled himself back together. If she wasn't going to guard herself, he'd do the job for her.

"Sex has to be something more than just bodies," he said harshly. "That's what you told me. You told me it had to be sacred, but it can't be that way with us. There's no love. Don't ever forget that. There's just sex."

To his utter astonishment, she gave him a tender smile that seemed faintly tinged with pity. "You foolish man. Of course there's love. Don't you know? I love you."

He felt as if he'd been sucker-punched.

She had the audacity to laugh. "I do love you, Alex, and there's no need to get all stiff and starchy like that. I know I told you I wouldn't, but I can't help it. I've been hiding from the truth, but today Sinjun showed me how I feel."

Despite all his warnings and threats, all the cautions and caveats he'd thrown at her, she'd decided she was in love with him. And it was his fault. He should have kept more distance between them. Why had he walked on the beach with her? Why had he spilled his guts? And most damning of all, why hadn't he kept her out of his bed? Now he had to convince her that what she regarded as love was simply a reflection of her romantic view of life, and that wasn't going to be easy.

Before he could point out her mistake, she settled her mouth over his. His brain short-circuited. He wanted her. He had to have her.

She ran the tip of her tongue over his lips, then gently probed. He caught her head in his hands and sank his fingers in her soft hair. She became pliable in his arms, offering herself to him and giving everything.

She made a soft, mewing sound. Vulnerable. Needy. The sound threaded into his dulled consciousness and brought him back to reality. He had to remind her how it was between them. For her sake, he had to get tough. Better to deal out a small hurt now than a devastating one later.

He pulled abruptly away from her. With one hand, he pushed her back on the bed, and with the other, he covered the bulge in his jeans. "A good fuck is better than love any day."

He inwardly winced at the expression of shock that swept over her flushed face. He knew his wife, and he braced himself for what would come next. She was going to jump right up off the bed and blister his ears with a lecture on vulgarity.

But she didn't do it. Instead, her shock faded into the same pitying look he'd noted earlier.

"I knew you'd be difficult about this. You're so predictable."

Predictable? Was that how she saw him? Damn it, he was trying to save her, and all she could do was mock him! Well, he'd show her.

He forced his mouth into an ugly sneer. "Get out of that costume. I'm in the mood for some rough stuff, and I don't want to tear it."

"Rough stuff?

"That's what I said, babe. Now take off your clothes."

17

Daisy gulped. "You want me to take off my clothes?"

She knew she sounded like an idiot, but Alex had surprised her. Exactly what did he mean by 'rough stuff'? Her eyes flew across the trailer toward a whip he'd left coiled over the arm of the couch. She'd scared him to death when she'd told him she loved him, but she hadn't quite expected this. Still, he was so skittish on the subject that she should have known he'd overreact.

"Stop stalling." He stripped off his T-shirt. His jeans rode low on his hips, making him look grim and dangerous as he stood before her bare-chested, with that straight line of dark hair bisecting his flat stomach and pointing the way to danger with all the subtlety of a flashing neon arrow.

"When you say, rough stuff . . ."

"I mean that it's time for some variety."

"To be honest, I don't feel as if I've mastered all the basics yet."

"I thought you said you loved me, Daisy. How about proving it?"

He was definitely provoking her, and she mentally counted to ten.

"I'm not a hearts and flowers type of guy. You know that. I like sex. I like it often, and I like it wild."

Good grief! She really *had* scared him. She nibbled on her bottom lip. Despite what she'd said earlier, Alex wasn't all that predictable, so she needed to be careful. On the other hand, Tater and his cronies had taught her one basic rule when dealing with large beasts. If she backed down, she was bound to get swatted.

"Very well," she said. "What do you want me to do?"

"I already told you. Get naked."

"I said I was going to make love to you, not the other way around."

"Maybe I don't want to make love. Maybe I just want to fuck."

That *rat*! He was deliberately goading her, and she had to bite her tongue to keep herself from falling into his clutches. If she lost her temper, she'd be giving him the upper hand, and that was exactly what he wanted. Somehow she had to stand up to him, and she had to do it on her terms. She loved him too much to let him bully her like this.

She considered her options, then rose from the bed to undress. He said nothing; he merely watched her. She kicked off her shoes and slipped out of her costume, but when she got down to her bra and panties, she found herself reluctant to go any further. He was powerfully aroused, a fact the fit of those jeans made evident, and his mood was so dangerous that she wasn't quite sure what to expect. Maybe distraction would be a good option. That way she could buy herself a little time.

So much had happened since her interview with her father that she hadn't had a chance to talk with Alex about his astonishing claims. If she brought the subject up now, she might be able to throw him off guard. A discussion about his family history could also defuse his unpredictable mood.

"Dad told me your father was a Romanov."

"Take off my jeans."

"And not just any Romanov. He said your father was the grandson of Czar Nicholas II."

"Don't make me repeat myself."

He regarded her with such arrogance that it wasn't at all difficult to imagine him sitting on the throne of Catherine the Great and ordering some recalcitrant Petroff female to throw herself into the Volga.

"He says you're the heir to the Russian crown."

"Be quiet and do what I told you."

She repressed a sigh. Lord, he was being difficult. Apparently there was nothing like a declaration of love to make this Russian go on the attack. She found it difficult to meet his gaze with any measure of dignity when she was clad only in her underwear and he looked so alarmingly potent, but she did her best. This clearly wasn't the time to pry loose any of the answers she craved.

He sneered at her. "When you take off my jeans, do it on your knees."

Insufferable *jerk*!

His lips thinned. "Now."

She took three deep breaths. She'd never imagined he'd go this squirrelly on her. It was amazing what fear could do to a man. And now he intended to push her until she threw her declaration of love back in his face. How many tigers did she have to tame in one day?

As she studied the arrogant narrowing of his eyes, the insolent flare of his nostrils, she felt an unexpected rush of tenderness. Her poor darling. He was dealing with his fear in the only way he knew how, and castigating him for it would only make him more defensive. *Oh, Alex, what did your uncle's whip do to you?*

She gazed into his eyes and slowly lowered herself to her knees. Threads of sensation uncoiled inside her as she saw how aroused he was. Even his fear hadn't been able to destroy that.

His fists clenched at his sides. "Damn it! Where's your pride?"

She sat back on her heels and gazed up at his face, harsh and uncompromising, with those Russian cheekbones casting deep shadows and pale lines of strain bracketing his mouth. "Pride? It's in my heart, of course."

"You're letting me demean you!"

She smiled. "You can't do that. I can only demean myself.

And I'm on my knees to undress you because it excites me."

A treacherous silence stretched between them. He looked so tortured that she couldn't bear it. She came up on her knees and pressed her lips to his hard belly, just above the waistband of his jeans. As she nibbled there, she tugged on the snap till it gave way beneath her fingers. Then she struggled to lower the zipper.

His skin broke out in gooseflesh, and his voice sounded ragged. "I don't understand you at all."

"I think you do. It's yourself you don't understand."

He grabbed her by the shoulder and pulled her to her feet. His eyes were so dark and unhappy she couldn't bear it "What am I going to do with you?" he said.

"Maybe love me back?"

His breath left his body in a smothered rush of sound, and his mouth covered hers. She felt his desperation and was powerless to help him. The kiss claimed them both. Like a whirlwind, it swept them into its power.

She didn't know whether they undressed themselves or each other, but they were soon lying naked on the bed. Sensation, warm and thick, spread outward from her belly. His mouth was on her shoulder, her breasts, brushing the crests. He kissed her belly. She opened her legs for him and let him raise her knees.

"I'm going to touch you everywhere," he murmured against the soft skin of her inner thigh.

And he did. Oh, he did.

He couldn't love her with his heart, but he could love her with his body, and he did it with an unbridled generosity that filled her with emotion. She took what he was able to give and, at the same time, she loved him back, using her hands and her breasts, the graze of her skin, the warmth of her mouth.

When he finally buried himself deep within her, she wrapped her legs around his and clung fast.

"Yes," she whispered. "Oh, yes."

The barriers between them disappeared, and as they climbed together, she began to talk.

"Oh, yes. Like that. I love . . . Yes. Deep. Oh, yes. Just that . . ."

She crooned to him from passion and from instinct. If she stopped talking, he'd try to forget who she was and turn her into an anonymous female body. She couldn't bear that. She was Daisy. She was his wife.

And so she talked, held tight, and raced with him into that place of oneness.

Finally, all the darkness gave way to light.

"It was sacred."

"It wasn't sacred, Daisy. It was sex."

"Let's do it again."

"I'm going seventy miles an hour, we didn't have more than three hours of sleep last night, and we're already late getting into Allentown."

"Stuffed shirt."

"Who are you calling a stuffed shirt?"

"You."

He glanced over at her, a devilish spark in his eyes. "I dare you to say that when you're naked."

"I'm not getting naked till you admit it was sacred."

"How about if I admit it was special? Because it was definitely special."

She gave him a smug look and let it go at that. Last night had been more than special, and both of them knew it. She'd felt it in the urgency of their lovemaking and the way they'd held on to each other afterward. When they'd looked into each other's eyes, nothing was hidden, nothing held back.

This morning, she'd expected him to be up to his old tricks again, acting surly and impossible, doing everything he could to distance himself. But to her surprise, he'd been funny and tender instead. It was as if he'd given up the struggle. With every beat of her romantic's heart, she wanted to believe he'd fallen in love with her, but she knew it wouldn't be that easy. For now she'd be grateful that he'd lowered his guard.

Rain began to splatter the truck's dusty windshield with great amoeba-shaped drops. It was a chilly, dreary morning, and according to the forecast, it would only get worse. He looked over at her, and she had the feeling he'd read her mind.

"I can't resist you," he said quietly. "You know that, don't you? And I'm tired of pretending I can." His expression grew more troubled. "But I don't love you, Daisy, and you can't begin to know how sorry I am about that because if I could chose anyone in this world to love, it'd be you."

She made herself speak around the lump in her throat. "The mutation thing?"

"Don't joke about it."

"I'm sorry. It's just so unbelievably—" *Stupid.* It was stupid, but she bit back the word. As long as he believed he couldn't love, she would only set up his defenses by arguing with him about it. Unless it was true. The unhappy thought trailed through her mind. What if he was right and his bleak, violent childhood had scarred him so badly he could never love? Or what if he merely couldn't love her?

The rain began to hammer on the roof of the cab. She looked down at her wedding band. "Tell me what it would be like? If you loved me?"

"If I loved you?"

"Yes."

"It's a waste of time to talk about something I can't make happen."

"You know what I think? I don't think it could be much better than it is right now. Now is very good."

"But it's not going to last. When our six months are over, so is this marriage. I couldn't live with myself if I had to watch you grow bitter because I can't give you what you deserve. I can't give you love. I won't give you children. Those are things you need, Daisy. That's the kind of woman you are, and you'll wither without them."

His words set off small detonations of pain inside her, but she wasn't going to punish him for his honesty by attacking him because of her hurt. She also knew she couldn't take any more at the moment, so she changed the subject. "Do you know what I want?"

"I'd guess a few weeks at a pricey resort and a manicure."

"No. I want to be a kindergarten teacher."

"You do?"

"Silly, isn't it? I'd have to go to college, and I'm too old for that. By the time I graduated, I'd be past thirty."

"How old will you be if you don't go to college?"

"I beg your pardon?"

"The years are still going to pass, whether you go to college or not."

"Are you seriously telling me you think I should do it?"

"I don't know why not."

"Because I've had enough failure in my life, and I really don't want to go through any more. I know I'm intelligent, but my schooling's been slipshod at best, and I'm completely undisciplined. I can't imagine competing in a college classroom with a lot of bright-eyed eighteen-year-olds who've had conventional educations."

"Maybe it's time you stopped selling yourself short. Don't forget that you're a lady who can tame tigers." He gave her a mysterious smile that made her wonder exactly which tiger he was talking about—Sinjun or himself. But, no, Alex was too arrogant ever to think of himself as tamed.

She spotted a series of arrows stapled to a utility pole. "There's a turn ahead."

Finding circus routing arrows was as natural to Alex as breathing, and she suspected he'd already seen them, but he nodded. The rain was coming down harder, and he flipped the windshield wipers to high speed.

"I don't suppose we're lucky enough to be performing on a nice asphalt surface today," she said.

"Afraid not. We're in a field."

"I guess I'm going to learn firsthand why circuses like Quest Brothers are called mud shows. I just hope the rain doesn't upset the animals."

"They'll be fine. It's the workers who'll suffer most."

"And you. You'll be right out there with them. You always are."

"It's my job."

"A strange job for the man who would be czar." She gave him a sideways gaze. If he thought she'd forgotten about this particular subject, he was dead wrong.

"Are we back to that again?"

"Just tell me the truth, and I won't mention it again."

"Is that a promise?"

"I swear."

"All right, then." He took a deep breath. "There's a distinct possibility it's true."

"What!" Her head whipped around so fast, she nearly threw her neck out.

"I definitely have Romanov ancestry, and from what Max has been able to piece together, I'd say there's a good chance that I'm the great-grandson of Nicholas II."

She sagged back into the seat. "I don't believe this."

"Good. Then we don't have to talk about it anymore."

"You really are?"

"Max has some fairly convincing proof. But since I'm not going to do anything about it, there's no point in discussing it."

"You're the heir to the Russian throne?"

"Russia doesn't have a throne. In case you've forgotten, it isn't a monarchy."

"But if it were—"

"If it were, there'd be Romanovs coming out of the woodwork claiming to be the heir."

"And from what my father told me, you'd have a better chance than any of them at making the claim stick, wouldn't you?"

"Probably. But so what? The Russians hate the Romanovs even more than they hate the communists, so it's not as if they're going to put the monarchy back in place."

"What if they did?"

"Then I'd change my name and hide out on a tropical island somewhere."

"My father would hate that."

"Your father is fanatical."

"You know that's why he arranged this marriage, don't

you? I thought he was trying to punish me by finding the most unlikely husband he could come up with, but it wasn't that at all. He wanted the Petroffs and Romanovs united, and he used me to do it." She shuddered. "It's like some Byzantine plot. The whole thing gives me the creeps. Do you know what he wanted to talk to me about yesterday?"

"Probably the same thing he talked to me about. All the reasons we should stay married."

"He told me that if I wanted to hold on to you, I needed to curb the excesses of my personality. I'm also supposed to meet you at the door with your slippers."

Alex smiled. "He told me to overlook your excesses and concentrate on your cute little body."

"He said that?"

"Not in so many words, but that was the general idea."

"I don't understand. Why would he go through all this for a six-month marriage?"

"Isn't it obvious? He's hoping we slip up and I get you pregnant."

She stared at him.

"He wants to insure the future of the monarchy. And he wants the baby to have Romanov and Petroff blood so he can take his place in history. Your father has it all planned. You give birth to this mythical baby, and he doesn't even care if we stay married. In fact, he'd probably just as soon I disappeared so he could browbeat you into letting him take charge of the kid."

"But he knows I'm on birth control. Amelia took me to her own doctor. She even filled the prescription herself because she said she didn't trust me to do it."

"Apparently Amelia's not as anxious to have a little Petroff-Romanov running around the house as your father is. Or maybe she just doesn't want to be a grandmother. My guess is that he doesn't know, and I doubt your stepmother will get around to mentioning it to him."

She stared glumly out the window at the four-lane highway lined with strip malls. A Taco Bell flashed by and then a Subaru dealership. She experienced a sense of unreality at the contrast between these modern signs of civilization and talk of ancient monarchies. And then a terrible thought occurred to her.

"Prince Alexei had hemophilia, and it's hereditary. Alex, you don't have the disease, do you?"

"No. It's passed only through females. Even though Alexei had it, he wasn't a carrier." He moved into the left lane. "Take my advice, Daisy, and put all this out of your mind. We're not going to stay married, and you're not going to get pregnant, so my family connections don't have anything to do with you. I only told you all this so you'd stop nagging."

"I don't nag."

He slid his eyes over her body and gave her a lascivious look. "That's like saying you don't—"

"Stop right there. If you say the f-word, you'll be very sorry."

"What word is that? Whisper it in my ear so I know what you're talking about."

"I'm not whispering it in your ear."

"Spell it."

"I'm not spelling it."

He teased her all the way to the lot, but he still couldn't make her say it.

By early afternoon, the rain had turned into a deluge. Although the slicker Daisy'd borrowed from Alex kept the top part of her dry, by the time she'd finished checking on the menagerie and visited Tater, mud covered her jeans from her knees to her ankles, and her sneakers were so caked they felt like concrete weights.

That evening, before the first performance, all the performers came up to talk to her. Brady apologized for his rudeness the day before, and Jill invited her on a shopping trip later that week. The Toleas and Lipscombs made a point of congratulating her on her bravery, and the clowns gave her a paper flower bouquet.

Despite the foul weather, the publicity surrounding Sinjun's escape had generated a decent audience, and the two o'clock matinee went well. Jack played the story of Daisy's heroism to the hilt, but she spoiled the effect somewhat by yelping when Alex wrapped her wrists with the whip.

When the performance was over, she changed back into her muddy jeans in a makeshift dressing area set up for the performers by the back door so they wouldn't get their costumes wet. Fastening her slicker around her, she ducked her head and plunged out into sheets of driving rain. Although it wasn't even four o'clock, the temperature had dropped rapidly, and her teeth were chattering by the time she reached the trailer. She stripped out of her jeans, turned on a small space heater, and switched on all the lights because it was so dreary.

As the trailer warmed up and the soft light fell on her decorating treasures, the interior had never seemed cozier. She pulled on a fuzzy peach-colored sweat suit and some woolly socks, then set to work in the small kitchen. They usually ate before the last performance, and for the past few weeks she'd taken over most of the cooking, something she enjoyed as long as she didn't have to follow a recipe.

She hummed as she sliced an onion along with several limp pieces of celery and began sautéing them in a small skillet, adding garlic and a touch of rosemary. She found a boxed mixture of wild and white rice but threw away the seasoning packet and added her own herbs. A portable radio sat on the counter, and she turned it to a classical station. Homey cooking smells filled the trailer, along with the lush strains of Rachmaninoff's Prelude in C-Sharp Minor. She made a salad, placed chicken breasts on top of the onion and celery mixture, and splashed in some white wine from a bottle they'd opened several days ago.

The insides of the windows began to steam, and condensation trickled along the panes. The rain drove against the metal shell, while the soft music and cozy cooking smells enclosed her in a warm cocoon. She set the table with her chipped blue willow china, earthenware mugs, mismatched crystal goblets, and an old honey jar containing some red clover she'd picked in the field yesterday before everything had happened. As she gazed around at what she'd done, she found herself thinking that none of the beautiful homes she'd lived in were as perfect as this battered little trailer.

The door swung open and Alex entered. Water streamed from his yellow slicker, and his hair was plastered to his head. She grabbed a towel as he closed the door and handed it to him. A clap of distant thunder rocked the trailer.

"It smells good in here." He gazed around at the warmly lit interior, and she saw something that seemed like yearning in his expression. Had he ever had a home? Not when he was a child, certainly, but as an adult?

"Dinner's nearly ready," she said. "Why don't you get changed."

While he put on dry clothes, she filled each of their wine goblets halfway and tossed the salad. The music on the radio switched to Debussy. By the time he returned to the table in jeans and a gray sweatshirt, she'd ladled out the chicken and rice.

He waited until she was seated before he took his own chair, then he picked up his wine glass and raised it to her in a silent toast.

"I don't know if the meal's any good," she said. "I just used what we had."

He took a bite. "It tastes great."

For a while they ate in companionable silence, lulled by the food, the music, and the snugness of the trailer in the rain. "I'm going to buy you a pepper mill when I get my next paycheck," she said. "That way you'll have something better to use than that awful stuff from a tin."

"I don't want you spending your money on a pepper mill for me."

"But you like pepper."

"That's not the point. The point is—"

"If I was the one who liked pepper, would you buy me a nice pepper mill?"

"If you wanted one."

She smiled.

He seemed puzzled. "Is that what you want me to do? Buy you a pepper mill?"

"Oh, no. I'm not much of a pepper fan."

His mouth curved. "I'm ashamed to admit this, Daisy, but I'm actually starting to follow these convoluted conversations of yours."

"I'm not surprised. You're really quite bright." She gave him a mischievous smile.

"Lady, you are a crackerjack and a half."

"Sexy, too."

"That goes without saying."

"Would you please say it anyway?"

"All right." His expression grew tender. Reaching across the table, he took her hand. "You are, without a doubt, the sexiest woman I've ever known. And the sweetest."

A lump formed in her throat, and she lost herself in the amber depths of his eyes. How could she ever have thought they were cold? She ducked her head before he could see the tears of longing form.

He began talking about the show, and soon they were laughing at a mishap between one of the clowns and a well-endowed young lady in the front row. They shared small details of their day: a problem Alex was having with one of the workers, Tater's impatience at being tethered in a tent. They planned a much-needed trip to a laundromat for the next morning, and Alex talked about changing the oil in the pickup. They might have been any married couple, she thought, going about the business of daily life, and she couldn't suppress a feeling of hope that everything would work out between them after all.

He told her he'd clean up the dishes as long as she stayed where she was to keep him company, then he complained good-naturedly about the number of utensils she'd used. While he teased her, the glimmer of an idea took shape in her mind.

Although Alex had been open about his Romanov heritage, he wouldn't reveal anything about his present life, which was far more important to her. Until he told her what he did when he wasn't traveling with the circus, there would never be any real communication between them. But she couldn't think of any way to get the truth out of him except by using deception. Maybe there wasn't anything wrong with a little deception, she decided, when their happiness was at stake.

"Alex, I think I might be getting an ear infection."

He immediately stopped what he was doing and regarded her with so much concern that her conscience suffered a guilty twinge. "Your ear hurts?"

"A little bit. Not much. Just a little."

"We'll get you to a doctor as soon as the show is over."

"All the offices will be closed by then."

"I'll take you to a hospital emergency room."

"Oh, I don't want to do that. I'm sure it's not serious."

"I'm not going to have you running around with an ear infection."

"I suppose you have a point." She hesitated, knowing this would be the tricky part. "I do have an idea," she said cautiously. "Maybe—would you mind taking a look at it yourself?"

He went very still. "You want me to look at it?"

Guilt seeped through every one of her pores. She ducked her head and toyed with the edge of a crumpled paper napkin. At the same time, she remembered the way he'd grilled her about having a tetanus shot and the number of times she'd seen him give first aid to one of the workers. She had a right to know the truth.

"I assume that, regardless of your speciality, you're qualified to treat a simple ear infection. Unless you really are a veterinarian."

"I'm not a vet."

"Well, then . . ."

He didn't say anything. She held herself tensely while she rearranged the wilting clover and lined up the salt and pepper shakers. She forced herself to remember that this was for his own good. They couldn't make their marriage work as long as he insisted on keeping so many secrets from her.

She heard him move. "All right, Daisy. I'll look at it."

Her head shot up. *She'd done it!* She'd finally trapped him! Using all her cunning, she had gotten to the truth. Her husband was a doctor, and she'd just forced him to admit it.

She knew he'd be angry when he examined her and saw that she didn't really have an ear infection, but she'd deal with that when it happened. Surely she could make him understand she'd only done it for his own good. It wasn't healthy for him to be so secretive.

"Go sit on the bed," he said. "Near the light where I can see."

She did as he asked.

He took his time drying his hands at the sink before he set the towel aside and approached her.

"Don't you need your doctor's kit?"

"It's in the locker in the back of the truck, and I'd rather not get wet right now if I don't have to. Besides, there's more than one way to diagnose an ear infection. Which ear is it?"

She hesitated for a fraction of a second, then pointed to her right. He brushed her hair back and leaned down to examine it.

"The light's bad. Lie back."

She lay down on the pillow. The mattress sagged as he sat next to her and curved his hand around her throat. "Swallow."

She did.

He pressed a bit harder with his fingertips. "Again."

She swallowed a second time.

"Mmm. Now open your mouth and say 'ah.'"

"Ahhh."

He tilted her head toward the light.

"What do you think?" she finally asked.

"You definitely have an infection, but I'm not sure it's coming from your ear."

She had an *infection*?

He slipped his hand just under her waistband and pressed her abdomen. "Does that hurt?"

"No."

"Good." He turned to reach for one of her ankles and moved it slightly apart from the other. "Lie still while I check an alternate pulse."

She lay very still. Her forehead creased with worry. How could she have an infection? She felt fine. Then she remembered she'd had a slight headache the other morning, and sometimes she felt a little dizzy when she stood up too quickly. Maybe she was sick and didn't even know it.

She regarded him with concern. "Is my pulse normal?"

"Shh." He moved the other ankle so that her legs were separated and then gently clasped both her knees through her sweat suit. "Have you had any joint pain recently?"

Had she? "I don't think so."

"Usually, I'd expect joint pain."

"You would?"

He flipped up her sweatshirt and touched her breast. "Any tenderness here?"

"No."

His fingers brushed her nipple, and although his touch seemed impersonal, her eyes narrowed with suspicion. Then she relaxed as she noted the intense concentration on his face. He was being thoroughly professional; there wasn't a hint of lechery in what he was doing.

He touched her other breast. "How about here?" he asked.

"No."

He pulled down her sweatshirt, modestly covering her, and she was ashamed of herself for having doubted him.

He looked thoughtful. "I'm afraid . . ."

"What?"

He covered her hand with his and gave it a comforting pat. "Daisy, I'm not a gynecologist, and normally I wouldn't do this, but I'd like to check you. Do you mind?"

"Mind?" She hesitated. "Well, no, I guess not. I mean, we're married, and you've seen—but what do you think is wrong?"

"I'm fairly certain it's nothing, but glandular problems can be tricky, and I just want to make sure." He slipped his thumbs into the elastic waistband of her sweatpants. She lifted her hips and let him remove the baggy bottoms, along with her panties.

As he tossed her clothing aside, her suspicions once again prickled, only to abate when she realized he wasn't even looking at her. Instead, he seemed distracted, as if he were lost in thought. What if she had some rare disease, and he was trying to figure out how to tell her?

"Would you like me to drape you with the sheet?" he asked.

Her cheeks flamed. "You—uh—don't have to. I mean, under the circumstances . . ."

"All right, then." He pushed gently on her knees. "Tell me if I hurt."

He didn't hurt. Not one bit. As he examined her, her eyelids drifted shut, and she began to float. He had the most amazing touch. Gentle. Exquisite. A brush here. A tender probe there. Delicious. His fingers left a soft, moist trail. His mouth—*mouth!*

Her head shot up off the pillow. *"You pervert!"* she screeched.

He gave a roar of laughter and fell back on the bed, clutching his sides.

"You're not a doctor!"

"I *told* you that! You're so gullible." He laughed harder. She threw herself at him, and he fended her off with one hand while he pulled down his zipper with the other. "You deserved it, you little faker, with your phony ear infection."

Her eyes narrowed as he tugged at his jeans. "What are you doing?"

"There's only one cure for what ails you, sweetheart. And I'm just the man to deliver it."

His eyes sparkled with laughter, and he looked so pleased with himself that her irritation faded and she had to work hard at maintaining her scowl. "I'm going to kill you!"

"Not till I collect my fee." His jeans made a soft whish as they hit the floor along with his briefs. With a wolfish grin, he covered her with his body and entered her in one smooth thrust.

"Deviant! You awful . . . ah . . . you . . . horrible . . . mmm . . ."

His smile stretched from one ear to the other. "You were saying?"

She fought against her rising excitement, determined not to give in to him too easily. "I thought there was something wrong with me, and—and all the time you were—ahh . . . you were copping a cheap feel!"

"Watch your language."

She moaned and grasped his hips in her hands. "Coming from someone who just violated his Hippocratic oath . . ."

He gave a bark of laughter that sent vibrations of pleasure rippling deep within her. As she looked up into his face, she saw that the tense, dangerous stranger she had married had disappeared. In his place was a man she had never seen before—painfully young, joyously carefree. Her heart sang.

His eyes had begun to glaze. He tugged at her bottom lip with his own.

"Oh, Alex . . ."

"Quiet, love. Be quiet and let me love you."

His words made her pulse leap. She matched his rhythm and clung to him while tears filled her eyes. In another few hours she would have to face him in the arena, but for now, there was no danger, only delight. It danced through her body, filled her heart, and exploded in a canopy of stars.

Afterward, as she stood in the bathroom fixing her makeup for the next performance, her feeling of well-being collapsed. No matter what she wanted to believe, there was no real intimacy between them as long as Alex had so many secrets.

"You want some coffee before we go back out in the rain?" he called out.

She set down her lipstick and left the bathroom. He stood at the kitchen counter wearing only his jeans, with one of their yellow bath towels looped around his neck. She tucked her fingers into the pockets of his terry cloth robe. "What I want is for you to sit down and tell me what you do when you're not traveling with the circus.''

''Are we back to that again?''

''I don't think we've ever really left it. I've had enough, Alex. I want to know.''

''If this is about what I did to you . . .''

''That just brought it on. I don't want any more mystery. If you're not a medical doctor or a vet, just what kind of doctor are you?''

''How about a dentist?''

He looked so hopeful that she nearly smiled. ''You're not a dentist. I know for a fact that you don't floss every day.''

''I do, too.''

''Liar. Every other day, max. And you're definitely not a shrink, although you're certainly neurotic enough.''

He picked up his coffee mug from the counter and stared down into its depths. ''I'm a college professor, Daisy.''

''You're what?''

He looked up at her. ''I'm a professor of art history at a small private college in Connecticut. I'm on sabbatical right now.''

She'd prepared herself for a lot of things, but not this, although now that she thought about it, she shouldn't have been so surprised. There had been subtle clues. She remembered Heather saying that Alex once had taken her to a gallery and talked to her about the pictures. There were the art magazines that she thought had been left behind by the trailer's former tenants and a number of references he'd made to famous paintings.

She walked over to stand next to him. ''Why did you make it such a mystery?''

He shrugged and took a sip.

''Let me guess. This is just like what you did with the trailer, isn't it? Choosing this place instead of something nicer? You knew I'd be a lot more comfortable with a college professor than with Alexi the Cossack, and you didn't want me to be comfortable.''

''I couldn't let you lose sight of how different we are. I'm still a circus performer, Daisy. Alexi the Cossack is a big part of who I am.''

"But you're also a college professor.''

"It's a creaky old campus.''

She remembered the threadbare college T-shirt she sometimes slept in. "Did you go to the University of North Carolina?''

"I did my undergraduate work there, and I got my master's and doctorate at NYU.''

"It's hard to take in.''

He brushed his thumb over her chin. "It doesn't change anything. It's still raining like a son of a bitch, we have a show to put on, and you look so beautiful right now that all I want to do is take that robe off you and start playing doctor all over again.''

She forced herself to put aside her worries for the moment and enjoy the present. "You're a brave man.''

"And why's that?''

"Because this time you're going to be the patient.''

That night, halfway through the evening performance, the wind picked up. As the nylon sides of the big top began to swell and deflate like a great bellows, Alex ignored Sheba's assurances that the storm would blow over and ordered Jack to stop the show.

The ringmaster made the announcement in a low-key manner, telling the audience they needed to take down the big top as a safety measure and guaranteeing everyone a full refund. While Sheba fumed and added up the lost revenue, Alex instructed the musicians to play a lively tune to speed the crowd's departure.

Some of the audience members wanted to hang back in the top's marquee to keep dry, and they had to be urged along. As he helped with the evacuation, he kept thinking about getting to Daisy and making sure she'd followed his orders to sit in the truck until the wind abated.

What if she hadn't done as he said? What if she was out there in the wind right now looking for someone's lost child or helping an elderly person get to a car? Damn it, and wouldn't that be just like her! She had more heart than common sense, and she wouldn't think twice about her own safety if she thought someone was in trouble.

A cold sweat broke out on his skin, and it took all his self-control to look reassuring as the crowd filed through. He kept telling himself she'd be all right and even managed a smile as he remembered the dirty trick he'd played on her.

He'd laughed more in the short time they'd been together than he had in his entire life. He never knew what she'd do next; she made him feel like the kid he'd never been. What would he do when she was gone? He refused to think about it. He'd cope, that was all, just as he'd coped with everything else. Life had made him a loner, and that was the way he liked it.

As the last of the crowd left the big top, the wind grew more fierce, and the wet nylon whipped and billowed. Alex was afraid if they didn't get the top down quickly, they'd lose it, and he moved from one group of workers to another, issuing orders and helping loosen the jumper ropes to get the quarter poles down. One of the workers released a rope too soon, and it lashed him across the cheek, but he'd felt the lash before, and he shrugged off the pain.

Cold rain trickled down his neck and blinded his eyes, wind plastered his slicker to his chest, and all the time he worked, he thought about Daisy. *You'd better be in that truck, angel. You'd better be keeping yourself safe. Safe for me.*

Daisy huddled in the center of Sinjun's cage with the tiger curled around her and the rain pommeling them through the bars. Alex hadn't trusted the safety of the trailer in the storm, and he'd told her to go to the truck until the wind abated. She'd been on her way there when she'd heard Sinjun's wild roar and known the storm had terrified him.

He'd been left outside, exposed to the elements, while the workers attended to the big top. At first she'd stood in front of the cage, but the lashing of the wind and rain made it hard to stay upright. He grew frantic when she tried to find some shelter beneath the cage, and that left her with no other choice but to climb inside with him.

Now he curled around her like a big old pussy cat. She felt the vibration of his quiet breathing through her back, and the warmth from his body drove out the chill. As she huddled closer against his fur, she felt nearly as peaceful as she'd been only hours before when she lay in Alex's arms.

Daisy wasn't in his truck.

She wasn't in the trailer.

Alex ran through the lot, frantically searching for her. What had she done this time? Where had she gone? Damn it, this was all his fault! He knew how scatterbrained she could be, and he should have watched her better. The moment the storm broke, he should have carried her to the truck and tied her to the wheel.

He'd always prided himself on having a cool head in a crisis, but now he couldn't think. The storm had eased soon after they'd gotten the top down, and he'd spent a few minutes making a cursory check for damage. Some flying debris had hit the windshield of one of the trucks, and a concession wagon had overturned. They had some ripped nylon, but they didn't seem to have suffered any serious harm, so he set out to find her. When he'd reached his truck, however, she hadn't been there, and that was when his panic had set in.

Why hadn't he watched her better? She was too fragile for this life, too trusting. God, don't let anything happen to her.

On the other side of the lot, he saw a flash of light, but one of the semis blocked his view. As he ran toward it, he heard Daisy's voice and his muscles went weak with relief. He rushed around the front of the semi and thought he'd never seen anything more beautiful in his life than the sight of her holding a flashlight and directing two of the workmen as they loaded Sinjun's cage into the back of the menagerie truck.

He wanted to shake her for frightening him so badly, but he resisted the urge. It wasn't her fault that he'd turned into a lily-livered wimp.

As she caught sight of him, her mouth curled in a smile so full of delight that warmth spread all the way to his toes. "You're safe! I was so worried about you."

He cleared his throat and took a calming breath. "Need some help?"

"I think we've just about got it." She scrambled into the truck.

Although he wanted nothing so much as to carry her back to the trailer and love her until morning, he understood her well enough by now to know that no amount of bullying on his part would get her out of that truck until she'd made certain all the animals under her charge were safely tucked in for the night. If he let her, she'd probably read them a bedtime story.

She finally emerged and, without a moment's hesitation, stretched out her arms and threw herself off the top of the ramp into his arms. As he caught her against his chest, he decided this was what he liked the most about her. The way she didn't hesitate. She'd known he'd catch her, no matter what.

"Did you stay in the truck during the storm?" He planted a rough, desperate kiss in her wet hair.

"Ummm . . . I stayed warm, I'll tell you that."

"Good. Let's get back to the trailer. Both of us could use a hot shower."

"First I need to—"

"Check on Tater. I'll come with you."

"Don't glower at him this time."

"I never glower."

"Last time you glowered. It hurt his feelings."

"He doesn't have—"

"He does, too, have feelings."

"You spoil him."

"He's spirited, not spoiled. There's a big difference."

He gave her a pointed look. "Believe me, I know all about the difference between spirited and spoiled."

"Are you implying—"

"It's a compliment."

"It doesn't sound like one."

He bickered with her all the way to the elephant trailer, but not for one moment did he let go of her hand. And not for one moment could he manage to wipe the smile from his face.

18

During the months of June and July, Quest Brothers Circus reached the heart of its tour, winding its way west through the small towns of Pennsylvania and Ohio. Sometimes they followed the rivers, large and small: the Allegheny and the Monongahela, the Hocking, Scioto, and Maumee. They played the little towns that the big show had forgotten: coal-mining towns with empty mines, steel towns that had been abandoned by the mills, factory towns where the plants had closed. Big industry might have forgotten the everyday people of Pennsylvania and Ohio, but Quest Brothers remembered, and the show traveled on.

By the first week of August, the circus had crossed into Indiana, and Daisy had never been happier. Each day was a new adventure. She felt as if she were a different person: strong, confident, and able to stand up for herself. Since Sinjun's escape, she'd earned the respect of the others and was no longer an outcast. The showgirls traded gossip with her, and the clowns asked her opinion of their newest tricks. Brady searched her out to argue politics and bully her about improving her muscle tone by lifting weights. And Heather spent time with her every day, but only when Alex wasn't nearby.

"Did you ever study psychology?" she asked one afternoon in early August as Daisy treated her to lunch at a McDonald's in the eastern Indiana town where they were performing.

"For a while. I had to change schools before I finished the course." Daisy picked up a french fry, took a nibble, then set it back down. Fried food hadn't been settling too well in her stomach lately. She cupped her hand over her waist and forced herself to concentrate on what Heather was saying.

"I think I might want to be a psychologist or something when I grow up. I mean, after everything I've been through, I think I could help a lot of other kids."

"I'll bet you could."

Heather looked troubled, which wasn't unusual. There was little of the carefree teenager left about her, and Daisy knew that the stolen money still weighed heavily on her conscience, although she never mentioned it.

"Does Alex—I mean, does he ever say like what a dork I was and everything?"

"No, Heather. I'm sure he doesn't even think about it."

"Whenever I remember what I did, I could die."

"Alex is used to women throwing themselves at him. To tell you the truth, I don't think he even notices anymore."

"Really? You're just saying that to make me feel better."

"He likes you a lot, Heather. And he definitely doesn't think you're a dork."

"You sure had a cow when you walked in on us."

Daisy repressed a smile. "It's very threatening to an older woman when a younger woman goes after her man."

Heather nodded wisely. "Yeah. But, Daisy, I don't think Alex would ever screw around on you. Honest. Jill and Madeline and all of them were talking about how he never even notices them anymore, not even if they're lying out in their bikinis. I think it pisses them off."

"Heather. . . ."

"Sorry. It *annoys* them." She absentmindedly shredded the edge of her hamburger bun. "Can I ask you something? It's about . . . well . . . when you have sex and everything. I mean, aren't you embarrassed?"

Daisy noticed that Heather's fingernails were bitten to the quick, and she knew it wasn't worry about sex that had done that to her, but a guilty conscience. "When it's right, it's not embarrassing."

"But how do you know when it's right?"

"You take your time and get to know the person. And, Heather, you wait until after you're married."

Heather rolled her eyes. "Nobody waits until they're married anymore."

"I did."

"Yeah, but you're sort of—"

"A dork?"

"Yeah. But a nice—" Her eyes widened with the first sign of real animation Daisy had seen on her face in weeks. She set down her Coke. "Oh god, don't look!"

"At what?"

"The door. By the door. That boy who hung around to talk to me yesterday just came in. He's—oh god, he is *so* cute."

"Where?"

"At the register. Don't look! He's got on a black tank and shorts. Hurry, but don't let him see you looking."

Daisy perused the area near the registers as casually as possible. She spotted the teenager studying the menu. He was about Heather's age, with shaggy brown hair and an adorably dopey expression on his face. Daisy was delighted that, for once, Heather was acting like a normal teenager instead of someone with the weight of the world on her shoulders.

"What if he sees me?" Heather wailed. "Oh, shit! My hair—"

"Don't swear. And your hair looks fine."

Heather ducked her head, and Daisy knew the boy was approaching.

"Hi."

Heather made a great business out of stirring the ice in her Coke before she looked up. "Hi."

Both of them flushed and Daisy could see each of them searching for something brilliant to say. The boy finally plunged in. "What's up?"

"Nothing."

"You, uh, going to be around today? I mean, like, over at the circus."

"Yeah."

"Okay."

"Yeah, I'll be there."

Another long pause, this one broken by Heather. "This is Daisy. You might remember her from the show and everything. She's like my best friend. Daisy, this is Kevin."

"Hello, Kevin."

"Hi. I, uh, liked you in the show."

"Thank you."

Having exhausted that path of conversation, he turned back to Heather. "Me and this guy Jeff—you don't know him, but he's pretty cool—we were thinking we might hang around there for a while."

"Okay."

"Maybe we'll see you."

"Yeah. That'd be cool."

Silence.

"Okay, see you."

"Yeah, see ya."

As he stumbled off, a dreamy expression came over Heather's face, followed, almost immediately, by uncertainty. "Do you think he likes me?"

"Definitely."

"What am I going to do if he asks me out tonight, like between shows or something? You know Dad won't let me go."

"You'll have to tell Kevin the truth. Your father's very strict, and you're not allowed to date until you're thirty." Once again, Heather rolled her eyes, but Daisy didn't let it put her off.

She considered Heather's dilemma. It would be good for her to have a romance, even a twelve-hour one. She needed to behave like a normal teenager for a while instead of someone doing penance. Still, she knew Heather was right and Brady would object.

"How about if you show Kevin around? He'll like that.

Then if you go sit over by the trucks, your father will be able to keep his eye on you, but you'll have some privacy.''

''I guess that'll work.'' Heather's forehead wrinkled with entreaty. ''Will you talk to Dad and make sure he doesn't embarrass me?''

''I'll talk to him.''

''Don't let him say something stupid in front of Kevin. Please, Daisy.''

''I'll do my best.''

She dipped her head and poked her index finger at her empty french fry container. Once again her shoulders slumped, and Daisy could see the guilt cloud descending.

''When I think about what I did to you, I feel like such a shit—creep! I meant creep.'' She looked up. ''You know I'm sorry, don't you?''

''Yes.'' She didn't know how to help her. Heather had tried to atone for what she'd done in all the ways she knew how. The only thing she hadn't done was go to her father with the truth, and Daisy didn't want her to do that. Heather's relationship with Brady was already difficult enough and that would only make it harder.

''Daisy, I'd never . . . I mean that thing with Alex was just because I was immature. He was so nice to me, but I'd never come on to him now or anything, if you were worrying about that.''

''Thank you for telling me.'' Daisy busied herself collecting their trash so Heather wouldn't see her smile.

The teenager wrinkled her nose. ''No offense, Daisy. He's sexy and everything, but he's really old.''

Daisy nearly choked.

Heather gazed over at the registers where Kevin was finally placing his order. ''He is *so* cute.''

''Alex?''

Heather looked horrified. ''No! Kevin!''

''Ahh. Well, Alex is no Kevin, that's for sure.''

Heather nodded solemnly. ''That's for sure.''

This time Daisy couldn't help it. She began to giggle, and to her delight, Heather joined in.

When they arrived back at the lot, Heather went off to work with Sheba. Daisy unpacked the groceries she'd picked up and collected the produce treats she'd bought for the animals, grateful that Alex had never once protested these expensive additions to their grocery bill. Now that she knew he was only a poor college professor, she'd tried to be even more careful about their expenses, but she would cut back on their own food before she'd short the animals.

As had become her practice, she stopped first by the elephants to collect Tater, and he trailed her to the menagerie. Sinjun generally ignored the baby elephant, but this time he picked up his proud head and regarded his rival with haughty condescension.

She loves me best, you annoying infant, and don't ever forget it.

Lollipop and Chester were tethered outside the tent, and Tater took his customary spot nearby, where a pile of clean hay awaited him. Daisy walked over to Sinjun and reached through the bars to scratch behind his ears. He found animal baby talk demeaning, so she didn't coo to him as she did to the others.

She treasured her time with the animals. Sinjun had thrived under her care, and his burnt orange coat now shone with health. Sometimes, very early in the morning when everything was quiet and they were in a deserted area, Daisy crept from her cozy place curled up next to Alex's side and let Sinjun out of his cage so the great cat could roam in freedom, if only for a little while.

They romped together in the dew-streaked grass, Sinjun keeping his claws carefully sheathed, Daisy maintaining a watchful eye for other early risers. Now, as she caressed him, a feeling of lethargy crept through her.

Sinjun stared deeply into her eyes. *Tell him.*

I will.

Tell him.

Soon. I'll tell him soon.

How long would it be before the new life growing inside her stirred? She couldn't be more than six weeks pregnant, so it would be a while yet. Since she hadn't missed a single dose of her birth control pills, she had attributed her symptoms to stress, but last week after she'd thrown up in a truck stop rest room, she'd finally bought a testing kit and discovered the truth.

She toyed with one of Sinjun's ears. She knew she had to tell Alex soon, but she wasn't quite ready. He'd be upset at first—she wouldn't delude herself about that—but as soon as he adjusted, she was sure he'd be happy about it. He had to be happy, she told herself firmly. He loved her. He just hadn't admitted it yet. And he was going to love their baby.

Even though he still hadn't spoken the words she needed to hear aloud, she knew he had deep feelings for her. How else could she account for the tenderness she saw reflected in his eyes at the most unexpected times or the contentment that seemed to radiate from him when they were together? Sometimes it was hard for her to remember how seldom he had laughed when they'd first met.

She knew he liked being with her. Between the close quarters of the trailer and the long miles they traveled in the truck nearly every morning, they spent more time together than most couples, yet he still sought her out during the day to share a story he knew she would enjoy, grumble about a problem with a local official, or simply give her a quick, proprietary pat on the bottom. Their daily meal between the matinee and evening performances had become an important ritual for both of them. And at night, after the work was done, they made love with a passion and a freedom she hadn't believed possible.

She could no longer imagine life without him, and as one day faded into another and he stopped mentioning their divorce, she knew he couldn't imagine them separated either. That was the real reason she didn't want to tell him about the baby. She wanted to give him just a little more time to get used to loving her.

The next morning all heck broke loose. Alex awakened not long after she'd slipped out of bed and discovered her in the deserted field behind the trailers playing with Sinjun. Two hours later he was still upset about it.

It was her morning to drive. They'd begun sharing driving duties when he'd realized she wasn't going to strip the gears on the truck and that she enjoyed being behind the wheel.

"I should have driven this morning," he said. "It would have kept my hands busy so I didn't have this urge to wrap them around your neck."

"Now, Alex, relax."

"Relax, my ass!"

She glared at him.

He glowered back. "Promise me you won't let Sinjun out of his cage anymore."

"We weren't in a town, and there wasn't a soul around, so will you stop worrying."

"That doesn't sound anything like a promise."

She gazed out at the flat Indiana farmland that stretched on each side of the two-lane highway. "Have you noticed Jack and Jill are spending a lot of time together lately. Wouldn't it be funny if they got married? Because of their names, I mean."

"Stop weaseling around the subject and give me your word that you won't keep putting yourself in danger." He took a sip from the earthenware coffee mug he clutched in his hand.

"Do you really believe Sinjun would hurt me?"

"He's not a house cat, regardless of the way you treat him. Wild animals are unpredictable. You aren't to let him out of his cage again, do you understand me? Not under any circumstances."

"I asked you a question. Do you think he'd hurt me?"

"Not on purpose. He's bonded to you, that's for sure, but the circus is full of stories about supposedly docile animals turning on their handlers. And Sinjun's hardly docile."

"He is with me, and he hates the cage. He really does. I told you earlier that I never let him out if we're close to a residential area. And you'll notice that no one was around this morning. If anyone had been stirring, I wouldn't have opened the door.''

"You're not opening it again, so none of this matters.'' He finished his coffee and set the mug down on the floor of the cab. "What happened to the woman I married? The one who didn't believe civilized people got out of bed before eleven?''

"She married a circus bum.''

She heard his deep chuckle, and returned her attention to the road. She knew the matter of letting Sinjun out of his cage was resolved as far as he was concerned, and she hoped he wouldn't notice that she hadn't made any promises.

Heather closed the door of the Airstream and stepped out into the night. She wore a yellow cotton Garfield nightshirt, and her feet were bare as they sank into the damp grass. The big top had been taken down, but she was too sick inside to pay attention to the familiar sights of the circus disbanding. Instead, her attention was riveted on her father, who sat outside their Airstream in a blue-and-white webbed lawn chair smoking the one cigar he allowed himself each week.

For once there weren't any women hanging around him. No showgirls, and none of the townies who were always after him. The idea of her dad having sex totally grossed her out, even though she knew he probably did. But at least he made sure she didn't find out about it, which was more than she could say for her brothers. Her dad was always getting on them for talking nasty around her.

He still hadn't seen her, and as he took another drag on his cigar, the red tip glowed. Heather hadn't eaten any dinner, but she still felt like she was going to throw up, just from thinking about what she had to do tonight. If only she could stuff her fingers in her ears and drown out the voice of her conscience, but it kept growing louder each day. It had gotten so she couldn't sleep at night and food didn't want to stay in her stomach. Keeping silent had turned into a worse punishment than telling the truth.

"Dad—uh—can I talk to you?'' She had a big frog in her

throat, and the words came out sort of croaky.

"I thought you were asleep."

"I can't sleep."

"Again? What's wrong with you lately?"

"It's—" She twisted her hands. He was going to freak when she told him, but she couldn't keep going on like this, knowing how she'd screwed Daisy over but not doing anything to make it right.

If Daisy had turned out to be a bitch, it might have been different, but she was the nicest person Heather had ever met. Sometimes she wished Daisy had narked on her right at the beginning. Then it would all be over by now.

"What's wrong, Heather? You still worried about missing your cue tonight?"

"No."

"Well, maybe you should worry about it. I don't know why you can't concentrate better. When Matt and Rob were your age—"

"I'm not Matt and Rob!" Her frayed nerves snapped. "It's always Matt and Rob, Matt and Rob! They do everything perfect, and I'm a big screwup!"

"I didn't say that."

"You think it. You're always comparing us. If I'd been able to come live with you right after Mom died instead of having to stay with Terry, I'd be a lot better by now."

He didn't get mad. Instead, he rubbed his arm, and she knew his tendonitis was bothering him. "Heather, I did what I thought was right for you. This is a hard life. I want something better for you."

"I like it here. I like the circus."

"You don't understand."

She sat down in the chair next to him because it was getting too hard to stand up. This had been the worst and the best summer of her life. The best part was being around Daisy and Sheba. Even though they didn't get along with each other, they both cared about her. Although she'd never let Daisy know it, she liked listening to her lectures about swearing and smoking and sex and stuff. Plus, Daisy was funny, and she was a natural petter, always rubbing Heather's arm or back or something.

Sheba fussed over her in a different way. She stuck up for her when her brothers got obnoxious and made sure she ate good stuff instead of junk. She helped her with her acrobatics and didn't ever yell, not even when Heather screwed up. Sheba was kind of a petter, too, always brushing Heather's hair or adjusting her posture or just patting her after she was done performing.

Meeting Kevin last week had also been really good. He'd promised to write, and Heather was going to write him back. He hadn't kissed her that night, but she thought he'd wanted to.

If only everything else this summer hadn't been so terrible. She'd embarrassed herself so bad with Alex that her skin felt crawly whenever she thought about it. Her dad was always mad at her. And worst of all was what she'd done to Daisy, the awful thing she couldn't live with one minute longer.

"Dad, I have something to tell you." She clutched her hands. "Something bad."

He stiffened. "You're not pregnant, are you?"

"No!" Color flooded her cheeks. "You always think the worst about me!"

He slumped back in his chair. "I'm sorry, sweetheart. It's just that you're getting older, and you're so pretty. I worry about you."

It was the nicest thing he'd said to her all summer, but she couldn't even enjoy it because of what she had to tell him. Maybe she should have told Sheba first, but Sheba wasn't the one she feared; it was her father. Tears stung the back of her eyelids, but she blinked them away because men hated tears. Matt and Rob said only pussies cried.

"I—I did something. And I can't keep it a secret anymore."

He didn't say anything. He merely watched her and waited.

"It's just—it's like something ugly inside me that keeps getting bigger and won't stop growing."

"Maybe you'd better tell me."

"I"—she gulped—"That money—when everybody thought Daisy stole that money . . ." The words burst free. "It was me."

For a moment he did nothing, then he shot to his feet. "What!"

She looked up at him, and even in the shadowed darkness she could see the fury in his expression. Her insides churned, but she made herself continue. "It was me. I—I took the money, and then I sneaked in their trailer and hid it in her suitcase so everybody'd think she took it."

"I don't frigging believe this!" He lashed out with his foot, kicking the leg of the chair she was sitting on out from under her. Before she could fall, he grabbed her arm and jerked her upright. "Why did you do something like that? Damn it! Why did you lie?"

Terrified, she tried to pull away from him, but he wouldn't let her go, and she could no longer hold back the tears. "I—I wanted to get Daisy in trouble. It was—"

"You little sneak."

"I told her I was sorry!" she sobbed. "And I am! She's my friend now! I didn't mean—"

He gave her a hard shake. "Does Alex know about this?"

"N-no."

"You let everybody believe Daisy's a thief when all the time it was you. You make me sick."

Without warning, he began dragging her across the lot. Her nose was running, and she was so scared her teeth started chattering. She'd known he'd be mad, but she hadn't thought it would be this bad.

He pulled her around the back of Sheba's trailer toward Alex and Daisy's, which was parked next to it. With one awful motion, he raised his fist and pounded the door. The lights were on inside, and Alex answered right away.

"What's wrong, Brady?"

Daisy's face appeared from behind Alex's shoulder, and when she saw Heather, she looked alarmed. "What's happened?"

"Tell him," her father demanded.

Heather spoke between sobs. "I—I'm the one who—"

"You look at him when you talk!" He clasped her chin and lifted it, not exactly hurting her but forcing her to meet Alex's eyes. She'd rather have died.

"I took the money!" Heather cried. "It wasn't Daisy. It was me! I sneaked into your trailer and hid it in her suitcase."

Alex's whole body went stiff, and his expression was so much like her father's that Heather recoiled.

Daisy made a small sound of alarm. Although she wasn't very big, she somehow managed to push Alex far enough out of the way that she could fly past him down the metal steps. She reached out for Heather, but her father pulled her away.

"Don't you dare give her any sympathy. Heather acted like a coward, and I promise she'll be punished for it."

"But I don't want her punished! It happened months ago. It's not important any longer."

"When I think about all the grief I gave you—"

"It doesn't matter." Daisy got the same stubborn look she had when she lectured Heather about her language. "This is my business, Brady. Mine and Heather's."

"You're wrong. She's my flesh and blood, my responsibility, and I never thought I'd see the day when I'd be so ashamed as I am right now." He looked at Alex. "I know this is circus business, but I'd appreciate it if you'd let me take care of this myself."

Heather recoiled from the chill in Alex's eyes as he nodded.

"No, Alex!" Once again, Daisy reached out, but Alex caught her and pulled her back.

Her father dragged her between the trailers, not saying a word, and Heather'd never been so scared in her life. Her dad hadn't ever hit her, but she hadn't ever done anything this bad either.

He came to a sudden stop as Sheba stepped out of the shadows by her big RV. She wore her green silk robe with

Chinese flowers and birds all over it, and Heather was so glad to see her she was ready to throw herself into Sheba's arms, until the awful look in her eyes made it clear that she had overheard everything.

Heather ducked her head and her tears began to fall anew. Now Sheba hated her, too. She should have expected it. Sheba hated thievery more than anything.

Sheba's voice shook. "I want to talk to you, Brady."

"Later. I have some business to take care of."

"We'll talk now." She made a sharp gesture with her head.

"Go to bed, Heather. Your father and I are both going to deal with you first thing tomorrow morning."

What do you care? Heather wanted to scream. *You hate Daisy.* But she knew that wouldn't mean anything now. Sheba was as tough as her dad when it came to following the rules of the circus.

Her father's grip loosened ever so slightly, and Heather fled. As she ran toward the safety of her bedroom, she knew she had lost her last chance to make him love her.

19

Brady was furious with Sheba. "I don't need you sticking your nose in this."

"I'm giving you some time to cool off. Come in here."

He stomped up the steps and yanked the metal door open. He was too distraught to pay attention to the costly built-ins and expensive furnishings that made Sheba's RV the most luxurious in the circus. "She's a thief! My daughter's a goddamn thief! She deliberately framed Daisy." He pushed aside a set of hand weights to slump down on the couch, where he thrust his fingers through his hair.

Sheba pulled a bottle of Jack Daniels from an overhead kitchen cabinet and splashed a generous amount in two glasses. Neither of them were big drinkers, and he was surprised when she downed the contents of one glass before she brought the other one over to him. As she walked, her robe rippled around her hips, distracting him, if only for a moment, from his distress.

Sheba had a way of turning his brain to mush. It wasn't a feeling he liked, and he'd fought against it from the beginning. She was a man-killer—stuck-up, hardheaded, and spoiled. In any situation, she had to have the upper hand, something he'd never give a woman, no matter how much she attracted him. And there was no doubt in his mind that Sheba Quest attracted him. She was the most exciting woman he'd ever met. And the most infuriating.

She handed him the whiskey in a heavy tumbler and sat

next to him on the couch. Her robe parted, revealing her leg from thigh to calf. It was long-muscled and flexible, and he knew from watching her as she worked with the flyers how strong she was. The RV was scattered with the training equipment she used to keep herself in shape. She'd installed a metal exercise bar about a foot from the top of the arch that led to her bedroom in the back. A mechanical treadmill sat in one corner along with assorted hand weights.

She leaned back into the couch pillows and shut her eyes. Her face contorted, almost as if she were getting ready to cry, which wasn't something he'd ever known her to do. "Sheba?"

Her eyes shot open. "What's your problem?" She crossed her leg like a man, ankle over knee, the position so brazen he couldn't understand how she still managed to look so intensely feminine.

He saw a patch of purple silk between her legs and found a target for his pent-up rage. "Why don't you sit like a lady instead of a slut!"

"I'm not your daughter, Brady. I can sit however I want."

He'd never hit a woman in his life, but at that moment he knew his head was going to explode if he didn't hurt her. With a motion so quick she didn't see it coming, he grabbed the front of her robe in his fist and pulled them both to their feet. "You're asking for it, babe."

"Too bad you're not man enough to give it to me."

He couldn't remember ever feeling such rage, and Sheba became the target for all the emotions that seethed inside him. "Aren't you slumming, Sheba? Can't you do any better than me? I'm a butcher's kid from Brooklyn, remember?"

"You're a crude, loudmouthed bastard."

She was deliberately taunting him. It was as if she wanted him to hurt her, and he was only too happy to comply. With a vicious yank, he pulled open her robe and wrenched it off.

She was naked except for purple silk panties cut high on her thighs. Her breasts were large, with dusky brown nipples the size of half dollars. Her stomach was no longer flat, her hips rounder than they should have been. She was voluptuous, full-blown, past her prime, and he'd never wanted a woman more.

She made no attempt to cover herself. Instead, she looked him in the eye, and with an audacity that robbed him of his breath, she styled. Arching her back, she set her left leg gracefully in front of the right. Then she curved one palm over her buttock. Her breasts lifted, and he was lost.

"Damn you."

She taunted him. "Work for it, Brady. Work for it."

He reached out for her, but he'd forgotten how quick she could be. She darted to the side, her red hair flying, breasts bouncing. He lunged after her, but she darted again. And she laughed, an ugly sound. "Getting too old for this, Brady?"

He was going to tame her. No matter what he had to do, he'd bend this woman to his will. "You don't have a chance," he sneered.

"We'll see about that." She snatched up one of her hand weights and flung it across the floor at him like a bowling ball.

Despite his surprise, he easily sidestepped it. He saw the glitter of challenge in her eyes along with the sheen of perspiration gilding her breasts. The game was on.

He feinted to the left, then made his move to the right. For an instant, he threw her off, but just as his fingers brushed her arm, she leaped straight up in the air and caught the exercise bar set into the archway.

With a cry of triumph, she began to swing her lower body. Back. Forward. She arched her spine and pumped her legs, using them to ward him off. Her breasts swayed in invitation, and her tiny purple panties slid just low enough to disclose a few tendrils of dark auburn hair peeking over the top. He had never seen anything as beautiful in his life as Sheba Cardoza Quest, the queen of the center ring, giving him this very private performance.

It could only lead in one direction. He pulled his T-shirt over his head, then kicked away his sandals. She swung and watched him as he stripped off his shorts. He didn't like wearing too many clothes, and he had nothing on beneath.

Her eyes inspected every part of his body, and he knew she had to appreciate the quality of what she saw.

When he took a step closer, she kicked out, and he caught her ankles. "Well, now, what do we have here."

He slowly spread her legs in an aerial split.

"You're a devil, Brady Pepper."

"You should know." He touched his lips to the back of her knee, then traced his way upward along the long, hard muscle of her inner thigh. When he reached the strip of purple silk, he paused for a moment to gaze into her eyes, then he dropped his head and nibbled at her through the delicate fabric.

She moaned and draped her thighs over his shoulders. He caught her buttocks in his palms and continued his moist caress. Her position shifted as she released the bar. He delved deeper with his mouth while she rode his shoulders and pressed against him.

She ducked her head as he carried her along the passageway to the spacious bed in the back. They fell on it together. She went wild when he whipped off her panties and buried his fingers inside her, then began to feast on her breasts.

She twisted her body so that she was on top and tried to mount him, but he would have none of it. "You're not in charge here."

"You think you are?"

"I know it." He flipped her onto her stomach, then pulled her to her knees so he could enter her from behind, only to discover he couldn't take her that way. He couldn't deny himself the sight of watching that haughty face when he entered her.

Before he had a chance to move away, she made a growling sound deep in her throat. In one powerful motion, she turned her body and kicked her leg over his head so she lay on her back looking up at him. He could feel her sexual arousal as powerfully as his own.

Her chest heaved. "You're not going to break me."

"Maybe I don't want to."

His words surprised both of them, and for a moment, neither spoke.

Sheba licked her lips. "Good. Because you can't do it." Reaching up, she caught his powerful upper arms in her hands and pulled him down on top of her. This put him in the dominant position, but because she had invited it, he didn't feel the mastery he wanted. He punished her with a deep, hard entry.

She countered by lifting her hips to welcome him, and her throaty whisper fell softly on his ear. "Take your time with me, you bastard, or I'll kill you."

He laughed. "You're a pip, Sheba Quest. A real pip."

She balled her hand into a fist and smacked him in the back.

The battle for mastery was on, and by unspoken agreement, the one who shattered first was the loser. An acrobat and an aerialist—the flexibility of their well-trained bodies filled their lovemaking with infinite possibilities. They reveled in their need to conquer, but each erotic punishment they inflicted on the other they also inflicted on themselves. This forced them to bring their rapier-sharp tongues into the battle.

She said, "I'm only letting you do this so you don't hurt Heather."

"Like hell."

"It was the only way I could think of to give you time to cool down."

"You're a liar. You needed a stud. Everybody knows how much little Sheba needs her studs."

"You're not a stud. You're a charity."

"Alex was the only man you wanted for anything more than stud duty, wasn't he? Too bad he didn't want you back."

"I hate you."

On it went, the wounding and punishing until, at some point, the vicious words stopped. They clung together, soared together, and in one shattering moment, lost themselves to everything else.

Afterward, she tried to fling herself from the bed, but he wouldn't let her go. "Stay here, babe. Just for a little while."

For once, her sharp tongue was silent, and she curled into his arms. Strands of auburn hair, like burnished ribbons, trailed across his chest. He felt her tremble as she spoke.

"Daisy's going to be a heroine now."

"She deserves to be."

"I hate her. I hate him."

"They don't have anything to do with you."

"That's not true! You don't know. It was all right when everybody thought she was a thief. But not now. Now he's going to think he won."

"Let it go, babe. Just let it go."

"I'm not afraid of you," she said defiantly.

"I know you're not. I know."

"I'm not afraid of anything."

He kissed her temple and didn't call her on her lie. She was afraid all right. For some reason, the queen of the center ring didn't know who she was any longer, and it scared her to death.

Alex gazed blindly into the darkened window of the Hallmark store. Three doors down, light shone from the doorway of a small pizza parlor, while next to it, the neon sign of a dry cleaner, closed for the night, flickered wearily. He'd long ago stopped holding the theft of the ticket money against Daisy, but he'd never really believed she was innocent. Now he had to face the fact that he was part of the terrible injustice that had been committed against her.

Why hadn't he believed her? He prided himself on being fair-minded, but he'd been so certain that her desperation had pushed her into the theft that he hadn't given her the benefit of the doubt. He should have known that Daisy's strong moral code would never allow her to steal.

She shifted at his side. "Can we go now?"

She hadn't wanted to accompany him on this night walk along the deserted strip mall that sat across the highway from the circus grounds, but he knew he wasn't ready to go back into the cramped confines of the trailer, and he'd insisted. As he turned away from the display of ceramic angels and photo albums, he felt her tension and saw how worried she was.

Inky curls tumbled around her cheeks, and her mouth looked soft and vulnerable. A sense of awe swept through him that this sweet little feather head with the will of iron was his. He brushed his thumb over her cheek. "Why didn't you tell me about Heather?"

"We can talk about it later." Her gaze darted impatiently toward the highway, and once again she turned to get away from him.

"Hold on." He caught her gently by the shoulders, and she stomped her foot like an angry toddler.

"Let me go this minute! You should never have let Brady take her away like that. You saw how angry he was. If he hurts her—"

"I hope he blisters her butt."

"How can you say that? She's only sixteen, and this has been a terrible summer for her."

"It hasn't been too hot for you, either. How can you defend her after what she did?"

"That's not important. The experience toughened me up, and I needed that. Why did you let him take her away when he was so angry? You practically gave him permission to brutalize her. I expect better of you, Alex, I really do. Now, please, I'm *begging* you! Just let me go so I can make certain she's all right."

I'm begging you. Daisy said that all the time. The same words that had poisoned Sheba Quest's spirit two years ago when she'd pleaded for his love rolled off Daisy's tongue without a second thought. In the morning she'd stick her toothbrush in her mouth and call out, "Coffee! Please! I'm begging you!" Last night, she'd tickled his earlobe with a soft, sultry whisper. "Make love to me, Alex. I'm begging you." As if he needed to be begged.

But begging didn't threaten Daisy's pride at all. It was simply her method of communication, and if he were ever foolish enough to suggest that begging might be demeaning, she'd give him that pitying look he'd come to know so well and tell him to stop being so stuffy.

He ran his index finger over her bottom lip. "Do you have any idea how sorry I am?"

She brushed his hand away impatiently. "I forgive you! Now, let's *go*!"

He wanted to kiss her and shake her at the same time. "Don't you understand? Thanks to Heather, everybody in the circus thought you were a thief. Your own husband didn't believe you."

"That's because you have a naturally pessimistic attitude. Now, enough of this, Alex. I understand you're feeling guilty, but you'll simply have to deal with it some other time. If Brady's harmed her in any way—"

"He won't. He's mad as hell, but he won't lay a finger on her."

"You can't be sure of that."

"Brady's a big talker, but physical violence isn't his style, especially against his own daughter."

"There's always a first time."

"I heard Sheba talking to him just before we went inside. She'll guard Heather like a mother lion."

"Trusting Lizzie Borden to protect her doesn't comfort me one bit."

"Sheba's only selectively vicious."

"She certainly hates me."

"She would have hated anybody I married."

"Maybe. But not the way she is with me. When I first came along, it wasn't so bad, but lately . . ."

"It was easier on her when everybody disliked you." He rubbed her shoulder. "I'm sorry you had to get caught up in this war Sheba's fighting with her pride. She was so talented, even as a kid, that people made allowances for her they shouldn't have. Her father worked her hard, but he also inflated her ego, and she grew up believing she was perfect. She can't accept the fact that she has human frailties like everybody else, so she has to blame other people."

"I guess it's never easy to face your own shortcomings."

"Oh, no, you don't. Don't you start feeling sorry for her. You keep your guard up when she's around, do you hear me?"

"But I haven't done anything to her."

"You married me."

She frowned. "What happened between the two of you?"

"She thought she was in love with me. She wasn't—she loved my lineage—but she still hasn't realized that. There was an ugly scene, and she fell apart. Any other woman would shrug it off as an unpleasant memory, but Sheba's not like that. She's too arrogant to blame herself, so she has to blame me for seeing her like that. Our marriage was a huge blow to her pride, but as long as you were in disgrace, I don't think it was too bad for her. Now, I'm not sure how she'll react."

"Badly, I imagine."

"She and I know each other pretty well. She could live with the past when she had something to hold over my head, but now it's going to start all over again. She'll want to punish me for being happy, and I only have one weakness." He gazed at her.

"Me? I'm your weakness?"

"If she hurts you, she hurts me. That's why I want you to stay alert."

"It seems like such a waste of time to expend all that energy trying to convince the world you're better than everyone else. I can't understand it."

"Of course you can't. You like nothing better than to point out all your character flaws to everyone who'll listen."

She must have found his exasperation amusing because she smiled. "They'll discover those flaws for themselves if they're around me long enough. I just save them the effort."

"What they discover is that you're one of the most decent people they're ever likely to know."

An expression that almost looked like guilt flashed over her face, although he couldn't imagine what she had to feel guilty about. It was quickly replaced with worry. "Are you sure Heather will be all right?"

"I didn't say that. Brady's going to punish her for sure."

"Since I was the person wronged, I should decide on the punishment."

"Brady won't see it that way, and neither will Sheba."

"Sheba! That's so hypocritical! She loved believing I was a thief. How can she punish Heather for giving her her dearest wish?"

"As long as Sheba believed it was true, she was satisfied. But she has a strong sense of justice. People in a circus have to live close together, and there's nothing anyone hates more than a thief. When Heather stole and lied, she violated everything Sheba believes in."

"I still think she's a hypocrite, and nothing's going to change my mind. If you don't do something about Brady, I will."

"No, you won't."

She opened her mouth to argue, but before she could say a word, he leaned down and kissed her. She resisted for all of two seconds trying to prove she wasn't a pushover, then she grew pliant.

God, he loved kissing her, feeling the sweep of her tongue, the gentle crush of her breasts. What had he ever done to deserve this woman? She was his own private angel.

An undercurrent of frustration swept through him because she didn't demand the pound of flesh she deserved. Vengeance wasn't part of her nature, and because of that, she was vulnerable.

He drew back just far enough to speak, and he had to force the words past an unaccustomed tightness in his throat. "I'm sorry, sweetheart. I'm so sorry I didn't believe you."

"It's not important," she whispered back.

He knew she meant it, and his heart felt as if it would burst.

20

Sheba stood in the shadows of the marquee fighting back her misery as she watched Alex and Daisy laughing together by the floss stand. He picked a blade of straw from her hair and then touched her face, the caress as intimate as if he'd stroked her breast.

Bitterness spread through her like a parasitic vine, choking everything else. It had been four days since they'd learned the truth about the stolen money, and she couldn't bear watching his happiness. Somehow it had been earned at her expense, and he had no right to it.

"Give it a rest, Sheba."

She spun around to see Brady coming up behind her. Ever since the night they'd spent together, he'd been strutting the circus grounds like a rooster. She half-expected him to tuck his hands under his armpits and crow. In typical Brady Pepper fashion, he'd also decided that having been her lover once entitled him to run her life.

"Leave me alone."

"That's the last thing you want from me."

She hated the look of pity he gave her. "You don't know anything."

"Let him go, Sheba. Alex is part of your past. Just let him go."

"It figures you'd say something like that. You're a champ at letting things go, aren't you?"

"If you're talking about Heather—"

"You know I am."

She glanced toward the elephant truck where Heather was trying to wrestle a wheelbarrow loaded with manure through the doorway. They had given her the worst duty, the one Daisy had been assigned to. Sheba regarded it as a fitting punishment, but Brady wasn't satisfied. He'd made arrangements to send her back to his sister-in-law Terry, just as soon as Terry returned to Wichita from a visit with her mother.

"Heather's my business. Instead of worrying about her, why don't you think about how good we were the other night."

"Good? We almost killed each other!"

"Yeah. Wasn't it great?"

He grinned at the memory, and she felt a traitorous warmth inside her. It *had* been good: the excitement of it, the thrill of coming together with someone as hot-tempered and demanding as herself. She couldn't wait to make love with him again, so she planted one hand on her hip and curled her lip at him. "I'd rather have a root canal."

"And, baby, do I ever have the drill to do the job."

She nearly smiled, and then she saw Alex lean down to kiss the tip of Daisy's nose. How she hated him. She hated them both. He had no right to look at her like that.

"Just stay out of my way, Brady." She pushed past Brady and stalked away.

Three days later, Daisy made her way to the menagerie with a bag of produce treats she had bought when she and Alex had stopped for groceries. Tater trailed behind, and both of them stopped to admire the somersault Petre Tolea's three-year-old son was doing for his mother, Elena. The Rumanian flyer's wife spoke little English, but she and Daisy exchanged greetings in Italian, a language in which they were both fluent.

After speaking with Elena for a few minutes, Daisy went on to the menagerie where she spent a few minutes with Sinjun.

Tell him.

I will.

Now.

Soon. She turned away from the reprimand she was almost certain she saw in Sinjun's eyes. Alex had been so happy lately, like a kid really, and she hadn't been able to spoil it. She knew it would be difficult for him to adjust to the idea of a baby, so it was important for her to pick her time right.

She carried the plums she'd brought for Glenna into the tent only to discover that her cage was missing.

She hurried outside. Tater abandoned his hay and trotted happily behind her as she made her way to the truck that carried the menagerie animals. Trey napped inside, and she leaned through the open window to shake his arm.

"Where's Glenna?"

He hit his battered straw cowboy hat on the rearview mirror as he jerked upright. "Huh?"

"Glenna! Her cage is missing."

He yawned. "Somebody came for her this morning."

"Who?"

"Some guy. Sheba was with him. He loaded Glenna into a van and drove away."

Stunned, she released her hold on him and stepped back. What had Sheba done?

She found Alex inspecting the big top for tears. "Alex! Glenna's gone!"

"What?"

She told him what she'd learned, and Alex regarded her grimly. "Let's go find Sheba."

The circus owner was in the red wagon, sitting at the desk doing some paperwork. She wore her hair down, and the scooped neck of her persimmon cotton-gauze jumpsuit was outlined with Mexican-style embroidery. Daisy pushed past Alex to get to her. "What have you done with Glenna?"

Sheba looked up. "Why do you want to know?"

"Because I'm in charge of the menagerie. She's one of my animals, and I'm responsible for her."

"Excuse me? One of *your* animals? I don't think so."

"Stop it, Sheba," Alex snapped. "Where's the gorilla?"

"I sold her."

"You sold her?" he said.

"You know Quest Brothers is up for sale. None of the potential buyers want to fuss with the menagerie, so I've decided to sell it off."

"Don't you think you should have told me about it?"

"It slipped my mind." She got up from the desk and carried a packet of papers to the file cabinet.

Daisy stepped forward as she slid open one of the drawers. "Who did you sell her to? Where is she?"

"I don't know why you're so upset. Aren't you the one who likes to tell everybody how inhumane our menagerie is?"

"That doesn't mean I wanted Glenna shipped away to just anyone. I want to know where she's gone."

"To a new home." She slid the file drawer closed.

"Where?"

"I really don't feel like being cross-examined."

Alex settled his hand over Daisy's shoulder. "Why don't you go on back to the menagerie and let me take care of this?"

"Because I want to know where she is. And, Alex, there are things I have to tell the new owner about her habits. Glenna hates loud noises, and she's afraid of people in big hats." Her throat began to tighten as she thought about never seeing the gentle gorilla again. She wanted Glenna to have a new home, but she'd also wanted to say good-bye. She remembered the way the gorilla liked to groom her and wondered if any of her new keepers would let her do that. To her dismay, her eyes fill with tears. "She loves plums. I have to tell them about the plums."

Alex cupped her arm. "Give me a list of everything, and I'll make sure the new owner gets it. Go on, now. I need to talk to Sheba."

She wanted to protest, but she realized Alex would have a better chance of getting Sheba to cooperate if they were alone. She made her way to the door, pausing only long enough to look back at the circus owner.

"Don't do anything like this again, do you hear me? The next time you sell an animal, I want to know about it in advance. I also want a chance to talk to the new owner."

Sheba lifted her eyebrows. "I can't believe you have the nerve to give me orders."

"I've got the nerve all right. You just make sure you're paying attention." She turned away and left them alone.

For a moment, neither Sheba nor Alex spoke. He doubted that Daisy's speech had intimidated Sheba, but he was still proud of his wife for standing up to her. He gazed over at the woman who had once been his lover and felt only disgust.

"What's happening to you? You've always been tough, but you weren't cruel."

"I don't know what you're complaining about. You hate the menagerie nearly as much as she does."

"Don't play dumb. You wanted to hurt Daisy and picked this way to do it. You're using her to get to me, and I won't have it."

"Don't flatter yourself into believing you're that important to me."

"I know you, Sheba. I understand how you think. Everything was fine as long as people believed that Daisy was a thief, but now that everyone knows the truth, you can't stand it."

"I do what I want, Alex. I always have, and I always will."

"Where's that gorilla."

"None of your damned business." With a glare, she swept from the trailer.

He refused to go after her, and he wasn't going to give her the satisfaction of asking the question again. Instead, he got on the phone.

It took him a day to locate the private dealer that Sheba had sold the gorilla to. The dealer charged him twice what he'd paid Sheba for the animal, but Alex didn't quibble.

He spent the next few days finding an acceptable home for Glenna, and by Wednesday of the following week, he was able to tell Daisy that her gorilla was on her way to becoming the newest resident in the excellent primate facility at Chicago's Brookfield Zoo, although he didn't tell her his money had made it possible.

Daisy burst into tears and told him he was the most wonderful husband in the world.

Brady stood at the TWA gate at the Indianapolis airport with Heather at his side waiting to board the plane to Wichita. She hadn't spoken a word to him since they'd left the lot that morning, and he didn't like the guilt feelings gnawing away at him. Sheba had already called him every name in the book, and yesterday Daisy had backed him up against one of the concession wagons and read him the riot act. They made him feel like a heel. Neither of them knew what it was like to have a kid you loved so much that you'd do anything for her.

He glared down at his daughter. "You mind your Aunt Terry, you hear me? And I'll call you every week. If you need money, you let me know, and I don't want you dating yet."

She stared straight ahead, her backpack clutched in her hands. She looked so pretty, fine-boned and delicate, that his heart ached. He wanted to protect this baby girl of his from everything bad, to keep her safe and make her happy. He'd give his life for her.

"I'll send you plane tickets for Christmas vacation so you can come down to Florida with us," he said gruffly. "Maybe you and me'll go over to Disney World or something. I'll bet you'd like that."

She turned to him, and her chin trembled. "I don't care if I ever see you again."

Something terrible ripped into his gut. "You don't mean that."

"I wish you weren't my father."

"Heather . . ."

"I don't love you. I didn't ever love you." Dry-eyed and

stony-faced, she gazed straight at him. "I loved Mom, but not you."

"Don't say that, honey."

"You should be happy. It means you don't have to feel bad about not loving me."

"Who said I don't love you? Damn it, did those boys tell you that?"

"You told me."

"I never did. What the hell are you talking about?"

"You told me in a million ways." She shifted the backpack onto one shoulder. "I'm sorry about what happened with the money, but I already told you that. I've got to get on the plane now. Don't bother calling me. I'll be too busy with my schoolwork to talk to you."

Turning away, she flashed her boarding pass at the flight attendant and disappeared down the jetway.

What had he done? What did she mean he'd told her in a million ways that he didn't love her? Jesus, Mary, and Joseph, he'd screwed up bad. All he'd wanted was the best for her. It was a hard world, and you had to be tough raising kids or they'd turn out to be a bunch of bums. But he'd never wanted this.

He knew then that he couldn't let her go. Sheba and Daisy had been right all along.

He pushed past the flight attendant and bellowed down the jetway. "Heather Pepper, you come back here right this minute!"

The alarmed flight attendant stepped in front of him. "Sir, can I help you with something?"

The passengers directly between him and Heather turned to see what the commotion was, but Heather kept walking. "You come back here! You hear me?"

"Sir, I'll have to call security. If there's a problem—"

"You go ahead and call them. That's my daughter, and I want her back."

Heather had nearly reached the door of the plane by the time he got to her. "No daughter of mine is going to talk to me like that! No way!" He pulled her to the side and gave her the piece of his mind she deserved. "If you think you're going off to your Aunt Terry's with that kind of attitude, you're wrong. You're getting your butt back to the circus, young lady, and I hope you liked cleaning up after those bulls because that's what you're going to be doing all the way back to Florida."

She stared up at him, and her eyes were so large they looked like blue mint candies. "I get to stay?"

"You're damn right you're staying, and I don't want to hear another word of disrespect." His voice broke. "I'm your father, and you damn well better love me the same way I love you, or you'll be sorry."

The next thing he knew, he was grabbing her, and she was grabbing him, and all the bozos coming down the jetway trying to get past them were jabbing them with bags and briefcases, but he didn't care. He was holding tight to this daughter he loved so desperately, and he wasn't ever going to let her go.

It was Monday night, the show had a rare evening off, and Alex had asked Daisy out for a date. Soft music filtered through the dimly lit dining room of the expensive downtown Indianapolis restaurant, where they were tucked away in a corner banquette.

Now that she was no longer worried about Glenna, she felt as if a weight had been lifted from her shoulders. Adding to her well-being was the fact that Brady had returned from the airport today with Heather. He'd been prickly as a porcupine when Daisy had asked him what had happened, but she noticed that he'd kept Heather at his side for most of the day. And Heather hadn't looked so happy all summer.

In some ways Daisy thought these past two weeks had been the best in her life. Alex had been so tender and affectionate that he hardly seemed like the same man. She'd made up her mind to tell him about the baby tonight, although she was still working out exactly what she would say.

He smiled at her, and he looked so handsome her heart

did a crazy little flip-flop. Most rugged men didn't wear suits well, but he was a definite exception.

"You look beautiful tonight."

"I was afraid I'd forgotten how to dress up." For once she didn't feel compelled to tell him how much better her mother would have looked, maybe because her appearance was no longer as important to her as it once had been. She'd spent so many days in jeans and a ponytail without a stitch of make-up on her face that tonight she felt quite glamorous.

"I give you my personal guarantee that you haven't forgotten a thing."

She smiled. For their dinner out, she was wearing the only nice outfit she had, a bone silk charmeuse tank with a short, bias cut skirt in the same fabric. She'd made a belt from a long, antique gold scarf, looping it twice around her waist and letting the fringed ends dangle. Her jewelry consisted of her wedding band and a pair of chunky matte-gold earrings. Because she hadn't wanted to waste money on haircuts, her hair was longer than she'd worn it in years, and after so many weeks of keeping it up in a ponytail, it felt incredibly sexy brushing her neck and floating above her shoulders.

Their waiter appeared and set two salads before them, each one a combination of artichoke hearts, pea pods, and cucumber dressed with raspberry vinaigrette and a crumble of feta cheese.

As the waiter disappeared, Daisy whispered, "Maybe we should have ordered the house salad. This is awfully expensive."

Alex seemed amused by her concern. "Even poor folks have to celebrate once in a while."

"I know, but—"

"Don't worry about it, sweetheart. I'll fit it into the budget."

She secretly resolved to plan inexpensive meals for the next few weeks to make up for it. Although Alex didn't talk much about money, she couldn't believe a professor at a small college earned very much.

"Are you sure you don't want any wine?"

"No, this is fine." As she took a sip from her tumbler of club soda, she forced her eyes away from the wine that glistened in his glass. He'd ordered one of the most expensive bottles on the menu and she would have loved a sip, but she wasn't taking any chances with this baby.

They really shouldn't be wasting money like this with the baby coming. As soon as they finished their tour, she'd get a job and work right up until it was time for her to deliver so she could help pay all the additional expenses. Four months ago she would never have been able to imagine such a thing, but now the idea of hard work didn't bother her. She realized she liked the person she had become.

"Eat. I love watching you slip that fork into your mouth." His voice deepened until it grew blatantly seductive. "It reminds me of all those other things you do with your mouth."

Color flooded her cheeks. She turned her attention to the salad, and with every bite she took, felt his eyes on her. Erotic images began flashing through her head.

"Will you stop it!" She plunked down her fork in exasperation.

He caressed the stem of his wineglass with his strong, tapered fingers, then ran his thumb over the rim. "Stop what?"

"Seducing me!"

"I thought you liked being seduced."

"Not when I'm fully dressed sitting in the middle of a restaurant."

"I see your point. I can tell you're wearing a bra under that top. Do you have panties on?"

"Of course I do."

"Anything else?"

"No. I'm wearing sandals, so I didn't put pantyhose on."

"Good. Now here's what I want you to do. Get up and go into the rest room. Slip off every stitch of your underwear and put it in your purse. Then come back to me."

Heat pooled in the most secret recesses of her body. "I most certainly will not!"

"Do you know what happened the last time a Petroff defied a Romanov?"

"I think I'm about to find out."

"She lost her head."

"I see."

"Not without a head. You've got ten seconds."

Although she kept her expression disapproving, her pulse had begun to throb in response to his mischief. "Is this a royal command?"

"You bet your sweet little ass it is."

His words were a sexy caress that nearly undid her, but she managed to tighten her lips and rise from the table with a great show of unwillingness. "You, sir, are a tyrant and a despot."

She exited the dining room to the throaty sound of his chuckle.

When she returned five minutes later, she hurried to their banquette. Even though the lights were dim, she was certain everyone in the room could see that she was naked underneath the thin silk charmeuse fabric. Alex openly perused her as she approached. There was an arrogance in his posture that marked him as a Romanov through and through.

As she settled next to him, he draped his arm across her shoulders and ran his finger along her collarbone. "I was going to make you open your purse and show me your underwear so I could be sure you'd followed orders, but as it turns out, that won't be necessary."

"You can see through, can't you?" Her gaze darted to the side. "Now everybody knows I'm naked under my clothes, and it's all your fault. I should never have let you talk me into this."

He slipped his hand under her hair and clasped the back of her neck. "As I recall, you didn't have any choice. It was a royal command, remember?"

He was pulling her chain three ways from Sunday, and she was enjoying every minute. She glared at him to keep him going. "I don't answer to royal commands."

He leaned closer and brushed her earlobe with his

lips. "With a snap of my fingers, sweetheart, I can have you thrown in the dungeon. Are you sure you don't want to reconsider?"

She was saved a reply by the appearance of the waiter. He had removed the remnants of their salads while she was away, and now he set the main course before them. Alex had blackened salmon, while she'd ordered pasta. Her linguini dish was fragrant with savory herbs and plump, juicy shrimp mingling with an assortment of fresh vegetables. As she sampled the dish, she tried to forget that she was nearly naked, but Alex wouldn't let her.

"Daisy?"

"Hmm?"

"I don't want to make you nervous, but . . ."

He flipped open the napkin that covered a basket of warm rolls and perused the contents. Since each roll was identical, she saw no reason why it should take him so long to make a selection, except to keep her purposely dangling.

"What?" she demanded. "Tell me?"

He split open the roll and slowly spread it with butter. "If you don't completely satisfy me tonight . . ." He gazed over at her, and his eyes filled with mock regret. "I'm afraid I'll have to give you to my men."

"What!" She nearly leaped off the cushions.

"Just a little incentive to inspire you." With a diabolical smile, he sank his strong, white teeth into the roll and ripped it apart.

Who could ever have imagined this stern, complex man would be such an imaginative lover? She decided two could play his naughty game, and she smiled sweetly. "I understand, your majesty. And I'm far too terrified of your royal importance to dream of disappointing you."

One eyebrow lifted diabolically as he speared a shrimp from her plate and lifted it to her lips. "Open for me, sweetheart."

She took her time sucking the shrimp into her mouth and ran her toes up the inside of his calf, grateful that the dim lighting and seclusion of the banquette kept them from making public spectacles of themselves. She had the satisfaction of feeling his calf muscles tighten and knew he wasn't nearly as detached as he was pretending.

"Do you have your legs crossed?" he asked.

"Yes."

"Uncross them."

She nearly choked.

"And keep them that apart for the rest of the evening."

Her food was suddenly tasteless, and all she could think about was leaving the restaurant and falling into bed with him.

She separated her legs a few inches. He touched her knee beneath the tablecloth, and his voice no longer sounded quite as steady as it had earlier. "Very good. You know how to take commands." He slipped his hand beneath her skirt and slid it up along her inner thigh.

His sheer audacity took her breath away, and at that moment she felt very much like a slave girl offered up for dalliance to this man who would be czar. The fantasy made her weak with desire.

Although neither of them gave any overt signs of hurrying, they finished their meals quickly, and both declined either coffee or dessert. They were soon on the road back to the circus.

He didn't speak to her until they were inside the trailer, where he tossed his keys on the counter and turned to her. "Have you had enough games for tonight, sweetheart?"

The caress of silk on bare skin and their flirtation with public discovery had set aside her inhibitions, but she still felt a bit foolish as she lowered her eyes and tried to look submissive.

"Whatever your majesty pleases."

He smiled. "Then undress me."

She removed his suit coat and tie, unbuttoned his shirt, and pressed her lips to his chest. The silky brush of hair tickled her lips, and his skin broke out in gooseflesh. She touched a hard, brown nipple with her tongue. Her fingers felt clumsy as she fumbled with his belt buckle, and when she finally had it open, she began to unfasten his zipper.

"Take off your clothes first," he said. "And give me that scarf."

Her hands trembled as she unwrapped the antique gold scarf from her waist and handed it over to him. She removed her earrings, then kicked off her sandals. With one smooth motion, she drew her tank top over her head and revealed her breasts. The catch on her skirt gave way beneath her fingers, and the fragile silk slid down over her hips. She stepped out of it and stood naked before her husband.

He ran one hand over her body, shoulder to breast, ribs to thigh, as if he were marking his property. The gesture sent liquid heat rushing through her, inflaming her until she could barely stand. Satisfied, he drew the gold scarf through his hand and let the fringe trickle slowly between his fingers.

There was an air of erotic menace in the gesture, and she couldn't take her eyes from the glimmering fabric. What was he going to do with it?

She caught her breath in a hiss as he looped it around her neck so that the sides fell over her breasts. Clasping the fringed ends in his hands, he slowly pulled, first one side, than the other. Back and forth. The metallic gold threads woven through the silk abraded her nipples like the lightest scrape of a fingernail. Sensation, warm and thick, spread through her belly.

His eyes darkened to the color of old brandy. "Who do you belong to?"

"You," she whispered.

He nodded. "Just so you understand."

She finished undressing him. When he was naked, she slid her palms over his thighs, feeling the hard textures of skin and muscle. He was magnificently aroused. Her breasts felt heavy, and she wanted to go further, but she surrendered to the grip of the fantasy.

"What do you want from me now?" she asked.

His jaw was clenched, and he made an inarticulate sound deep in his throat as he pressed down on her shoulders. "This."

Her heart swelled. She followed his silent command and loved him as she wanted to. Time lost meaning. Despite her posture of submission, she had never felt more powerful. His voiceless sounds of pleasure fueled her excitement, while his hands, tangled in her hair, told her without words of his need.

She felt the rigid tension of his muscles beneath her palms and the sheen of sweat that formed on his skin. Without warning, he pulled her to her feet and drew her down on the bed.

He reared back just enough to look into her eyes. "Perform well, and I'll let you service me again."

Oh, my. He must have felt her shiver because his eyes narrowed with satisfaction. She parted her legs.

"Not so fast." He captured her earlobe in his teeth and gave it a gentle nip. "First I need to punish you."

"Punish me?" She stiffened, thinking of the whips stored under the bed, just beneath their hips.

"You excited me but you didn't finish what you started."

"That's because you—"

"Enough." Once again, he reared back and regarded her with all the lofty arrogance of his Romanov heritage.

She felt herself relax. He would never hurt her.

"When I want your opinion, woman, I'll ask for it. Until then, you'd be wise to hold your tongue. My Cossacks have been a long time without a woman."

She gave him a squinty-eyed look that told him he was pushing it.

One corner of his mouth quivered, but he didn't smile. Instead, he dipped his head and brushed his lips across the inside of her thigh. "There's only one fit punishment for a slave who can't stay silent. A vicious tongue-lashing."

The ceiling spun as he delivered on his threat and transported her into a realm of hot delight and ancient ecstasy. His body grew slick with perspiration and the muscles of his shoulders bunched beneath her hands, but still he wouldn't stop. Only when she begged him did he finally force the sweet entry she needed so desperately.

He drove deep and true, and all the mischief faded from

his eyes. "I want to love you now," he whispered.

Her eyes stung with tears as he spoke the words she'd been longing to hear. She clung to his body, and they fell into a rhythm as timeless as the beat of their hearts. They moved as one, and she felt his love filling her, suffusing her, spilling into her very soul.

They swirled together, man and woman, earth and sky, all the elements of creation converging in a perfect melding.

When it was over, she felt a joy she'd never before experienced and a certainty that everything was going to be all right between them. *I want to love you,* he'd said. Not, *I want to make love to you,* but *I want to love you.* And he had. He couldn't have loved her more completely if he'd spoken the words a hundred times.

She gazed across the pillow at him. He lay facing her, his eyes half-lidded, slumberous. Reaching over, she caressed his cheekbone, and he turned his head to press his lips against her palm.

She rubbed her thumb along his jawbone, enjoying the slight abrasion against her skin. "Thank you."

"I'm the one who should thank you."

"I hope that means you're not going to give me to your Cossacks?"

"I wouldn't share you with anybody."

The erotic game they'd been playing had made her forget the promise she'd made to tell him about the baby. Now.

"You haven't said anything about the divorce for a while."

He immediately grew wary and rolled to his back. "It hasn't been on my mind."

She was disheartened by his withdrawal, but she'd known this would be difficult, and she continued to press him as gently as she could. "I'm glad. It's not a good thing to think about."

He gazed over at her, his eyes deeply troubled. "I know what you want me to say, but I can't do it yet. Just give me a little more time, will you?"

With her heart in her throat, she nodded.

He looked as skittish as a wild animal brought too close to civilization. "Let's just take it day by day for now."

She understood that the worst thing she could do was make him feel trapped, and the fact that he wasn't still insisting their marriage would be over in two more months gave her the confidence to wait just a little longer. "Of course we can."

He drew himself up and leaned into the pillows propped against the headboard. "You know you're the best thing that's ever happened to me, don't you?"

"I certainly do."

He chuckled, and the tension seemed to leave him. She rolled onto her stomach, propped herself on her elbows, and stirred his chest hair with her fingertips. "Wasn't Catherine the Great a Romanov?"

"Yes."

"I read that she had a lusty nature."

"She had a long string of lovers."

"And a lot of power." She leaned forward and nipped his pectoral muscle with her teeth. He jumped, so she nipped him again.

"Ouch!" He caught her chin and tilted it. "Exactly what's going on in that devious little brain of yours?"

"I was just imagining all those strong men forced to bow down to Catherine the Great."

"Uh huh."

"Forced to serve her. To submit to her."

"Uh-oh."

She brushed her lips across his. "It's your turn to be the slave, big guy."

For a moment he looked startled, and then he gave a sigh that came all the way from his toes. "I think I just died and went to heaven."

21

Alex had been impossible all week. Ever since they'd gone out to dinner and then returned to play their erotic games, he'd been looking for excuses to pick an argument with her, and now he scowled at her as he wiped the sweat from his forehead with the back of his arm.

"Couldn't you have put some gas in the truck when you went into town for groceries?"

"I'm sorry. I didn't notice it was empty."

"You never notice," he said belligerently. "Do you think it runs on air?"

She gritted her teeth. It was as if she'd gotten too close to him that night and he needed to distance her. So far she'd managed to dodge all the grenades he kept lobbing at her, but it was growing increasingly difficult to keep her temper in check. Now she had to force herself to speak in a reasonable tone of voice. "I didn't know you wanted me to do it. You've always kept the truck gassed."

"Yeah, well in case you haven't noticed, I've been kind of busy lately. We've had sick horses, a fire in the cook tent, and now I've got a blackmailing health inspector threatening to slap us with a batch of safety violations we don't deserve."

"I know you've been under a lot of pressure. If you'd said something, I would have been happy to get gas."

"Yeah, right. How many times have you ever worked a pump?"

She mentally counted to five. "None. But I can learn."

"Don't bother." He stalked away.

She couldn't hold her tongue a moment longer. Splaying one hand on her hip, she called out, "You have a nice day, too!"

He stopped in his tracks, then turned to give her one of his blackest stares. "Don't push me."

She crossed her arms over her chest and tapped the toe of her sneaker in the dirt. Just because he was on the run from a tumult of feelings he didn't know how to cope with didn't mean he could keep taking his frustration out on her. For days now she'd been trying to be patient, but enough was enough.

He set his jaw and stomped toward her.

She dug in her heels, refusing to budge.

He came to a stop directly in front of her, deliberately using his size to intimidate her.

She was forced to admit he did it very well.

"Do you have a problem with something?" he barked out.

This whole argument was ridiculous, and a streak of mischief made her smile. "If anybody ever tells you that you're beautiful when you're angry, they're lying."

His face flushed, and for a moment, she thought he was going to explode. Instead, he lifted her by the elbows and pressed her against the floss wagon. Then he kissed her until she was breathless.

When he finally set her back on her feet, he looked even more foul-tempered than he had before their kiss. "I'm sorry!" he shouted.

As an apology, it wasn't impressive, and as he stomped away, he looked more like a rampaging tiger than a repentant husband. Although she knew he was suffering, she had just about lost patience. Why did he have to make everything so hard for them? Why couldn't he simply accept the fact that he loved her?

She remembered the vulnerability she'd seen in his eyes that night when he'd asked her to give him a little more time, and she suspected he was afraid to give a name to what he felt for her. The conflict between his emotions and what he believed he knew about himself was ripping him apart.

That's what she'd been telling herself, anyway, because the alternative—that he might not love her at all—didn't bear thinking about, especially since she still hadn't told him about the baby.

She had all sorts of excuses for her cowardice. When things had been going well between them, she hadn't wanted to risk spoiling their harmony, and now that everything was falling apart, she'd lost her nerve.

But it was cowardice, nonetheless, and she forced herself to face the truth. Trouble needed to be confronted, but instead, she kept running from it. It had been nearly a month since she'd taken the pregnancy test. She estimated she was about two and a half months pregnant, but she hadn't gone to a doctor because she didn't want to risk Alex finding out about it. The fact that she was taking excellent care of herself was no excuse for not getting started on proper medical care, especially since she needed to make certain the baby hadn't been harmed by the birth control pills she'd been taking before she'd discovered they hadn't done their job and she was pregnant.

She stuck her fingers in the pockets of her jeans and made up her mind. There wouldn't be any more postponements. He was impossible to live with right now, anyway, so what difference did it make? By the time they went to bed tonight, she would have told him. It had taken two people to make this baby, and it was time both of them lived up to their responsibilities.

As soon as the afternoon performance was over, she went to find him, but the truck was gone. She grew increasingly nervous. After putting this off for so long, now all she wanted to do was have it over with.

Her next chance should have been at dinner, but Alex's troubles with the local health inspector kept him away until it was time for the evening performance. Now, as she approached the back door to wait for their act to begin, she saw him standing off to the side with Misha, who was loosely tied to a stake. One of his whips was coiled around his shoulder with the butt hanging free across his chest. The breeze rumpled his dark hair, and the fading evening light cast deep shadows across his profile.

No one approached him. It was as if he'd drawn an invisible circle around himself and the gelding, a circle that shut out everyone in the world, including her. Especially her. The red sequins in his sash glittered as he ran his hand over the horse's flanks, and her frustration with him grew. Why did he have to be so pigheaded?

As the audience inside erupted in laughter over the antics of the clowns, she approached him. Misha snorted and tossed his head. She eyed the horse apprehensively. No matter how many times she did this act, she'd never get used to any part of it, including that terrifying moment when Alex pulled her up on the saddle in front of him.

She stopped well short of the horse. "Do you think you could get someone to cover for you after the show? We need to talk."

He kept his back to her as he adjusted the cinch on the saddle. "It'll have to wait. I have too much to do."

She'd reached the limits of her patience. If they didn't start discussing their problems, they'd never be able to have the kind of marriage both of them needed. "Whatever you have to do can wait."

The full sleeves of his white shirt billowed as he whipped around. "Look, Daisy, if this is about the gas, I said I was sorry. I know I haven't been the easiest person to get along with lately, but it's been a rough week."

"You've had lots of rough weeks, but you haven't taken them out on me."

"How many ways am I supposed to apologize?"

"This isn't about apologizing. It's about the reasons you keep pushing me away."

"Just give it a rest, all right?"

"I can't do that." The clown act was coming to an end, and she knew this wasn't the time to talk, but now that she'd gotten started, she couldn't hold back. "We've been on an emotional marry-go-round, and it's hurting both of us. We have a future together, and we need to talk about it.''

She touched his arm, expecting him to pull away, and when he didn't, she found the confidence to go on. ''These past few months have been the most wonderful time of my life. You've helped me find out who I am, and maybe I've helped you do the same thing.''

She gently pressed her palms to his chest and felt his heart-beat through the silky fabric. The paper flower tucked between her breasts rustled, and the lash of the whip he carried brushed the side of her hand. ''Isn't that what loving is all about? Being better together than we could be apart? We're good for each other.'' Without any planning, the words she'd held back for so long spilled out. ''And we're going to be good for the baby we're having.''

For one small fragment of time everything was fine. And then it all changed. The tendons in his neck bunched, and his eyes darkened with something that looked like fear. Then his features contorted into a mask of rage.

She snatched her hands from his chest. Her instincts warned her to run, but she was a lot tougher now, and she held her ground. ''Alex, I didn't plan this baby; I don't even know how it happened. But I'm not going to lie to you and tell you I'm sorry.''

His pale lips barely moved. ''I trusted you.''

''I didn't do anything wrong.''

The muscles in his throat worked, and his hands clenched at his sides. For a moment she thought he was going to hit her. ''How far along are you?''

''About two and a half months.''

''And how long have you known?''

''Maybe a month.''

''You've known about this for a month, and you just decided to tell me?''

''I was afraid.''

The raucous music of the clowns rose to a crescendo, signaling the end of their act. She and Alex were next. Digger, who was in charge of sending Misha into the arena at the climax, approached to take charge of the horse.

Alex grabbed her arm and pulled her away from the others. "There's not going to be any baby, do you understand what I'm saying?"

"No . . . no, I don't understand."

"Tomorrow morning, you and I are taking off for the day. And when we come back, there won't be any baby."

She stared at him in shock. Her stomach heaved, and she pressed her knuckles to her mouth. The crowd inside the big top fell silent as Jack Daily began his dramatic introduction of Alexi the Cossack.

"*Aaaand now, Quest Brothers Circus is proud to present . . .*"

"You want me to have an abortion?" she whispered.

"Don't look at me like I'm some kind of monster! Don't you dare look at me like that! I told you from the beginning how I felt about this. I spilled my guts trying to make you understand. But, as usual, you decided you knew best. Even though you don't have a trustworthy bone in your goddamn body, you decided you knew best!"

"Don't talk to me like that."

"I trusted you!" His mouth twisted into a snarl as the first strains of the balalaika drifted into the night, the cue for his entrance. "I actually believed you were taking those pills, but all the time you were lying to me."

She shook her head and fought against the bile rising in her throat. "I'm not getting rid of this baby."

"The hell you're not! You'll do what I tell you."

"You don't want this. It's ugly and wicked."

"Not as wicked as what you've done."

"Alex!" one of the clowns hissed. "You're on!"

He snatched the coiled whip from around his shoulder. "I'll never forgive you for this, Daisy. Do you hear me? Never." Thrusting himself away from her, he disappeared into the big top.

She stood there numbly, gripped by despair so thick and bitter she couldn't breathe. Oh, God, she'd been such a fool. She'd thought he loved her, but he'd been right all along.

He didn't know how to love. He'd told her he couldn't do it, but she had refused to believe him. And now she was going to pay the price.

Too late, she remembered what she'd read about the male tiger. *This animal will have nothing to do with family life. Not only does he play no part in raising his own cubs, but he may not even recognize them.*

Alex was going one step further. He wanted this small speck of life that had already grown so precious to her destroyed before it could even draw its first breath.

"Wake up, Daisy! That's your cue." Madeline grabbed her and pushed her through the back door into the big top.

The spotlight hit her. Disoriented, she lifted her arm, trying to shield her eyes.

". . . and none of us can fully appreciate the courage it has taken for this sheltered young woman to enter the arena with her husband."

She stumbled forward, moving automatically to the balalaika music, as Jack wove his story of the convent-reared bride and her mighty Cossack. She barely heard. She saw nothing except Alex, her betrayer, standing in the center of the arena.

Specks of crimson glitter clung to the lash that coiled over the tops of his shining black boots, and blue lights flickered in his dark hair, while his eyes had turned the pale gold of a cornered animal's. She stood in her own small spot of light as he began his whip dance. But tonight the dance didn't speak of seduction. It was frenzied and savage, a declaration of rage.

The audience signaled its approval, but as the act progressed, Daisy's part in it wasn't as well received. The instinctive communication she'd always had with the crowd was gone. She didn't even wince when Alex cut the paper tube from her mouth, but performed automatically, her despair so deep she couldn't summon any feeling at all.

The rhythm of their act gradually fell apart. Alex destroyed one of the tubes in two cuts, another in four. He forgot a new bit he'd added with a ribbon streamer, and when he wrapped her wrists with the whip, the audience stirred uneasily. It was as if the tension between the two of them had somehow communicated itself, and what had formerly been an act of seduction now seemed tinged with violence. Instead of a bridegroom trying to win the affections of his wife, the audience felt as if they were watching a dangerously predatory male attack a small and fragile female.

Alex sensed what was happening, and his pride kicked in. He seemed to realize he couldn't afford to wrap the whip around her again without completely alienating the audience, but he also needed one final gesture to bring this part of the act to a close before he signaled Digger to release Misha.

She saw his eyes settle on the crimson tissue paper flower nestled between her breasts and realized he had forgotten it earlier. He signaled what he was going to do with a subtle nod of his head. She faced him numbly, wanting only to have this done with so she could go off by herself and hide from the world.

The music of the balalaika swelled and she found herself looking across the ring into his eyes. If she had not been frozen herself, she might have seen the suffering there, along with a deep, wrenching grief that matched her own.

He drew back his arms and flicked his wrist. The tip of the lash flew at her as it had dozens of times before, except this time she felt as if she were seeing it in slow motion. With a peculiar sense of detachment, she waited for the paper petals to fly, but instead, she felt a searing pain.

All the air was ripped from her lungs. Her body buckled as liquid fire cut across her from shoulder to thigh. The arena began to spin and she started to fall. Seconds ticked by, and then music erupted, a loud and happy tune that rang out in bizarre counterpoint to a pain so intense she couldn't breathe. Strong arms swept her up as the clowns came racing in.

She was conscious, although she didn't want to be, and she heard a prayer that she hadn't spoken herself. The lively music, the muttering of the crowd, Jack's calming voice, all those things echoed dimly behind the wall of pain that enveloped her.

"Get away! Get back!"

Alex's voice. Alex carrying her out through the back door. Alex the enemy. The betrayer.

She felt the ground, hard and chill against her back, as he laid her down against the side of the big top. Bending over her, he used his body to block her from the view of the others. "Sweetheart, I'm sorry. Oh, God, Daisy, I'm so sorry."

Using what remained of her strength, she turned her head away from him so that she was facing the dusty nylon, only to gasp with pain as his hand brushed the torn fragments of her gown.

Her lips felt dry and so stiff she could barely part them. "Don't . . . touch me."

"I have to help you." His breathing was quick and shallow, his voice reedy. "I'm going to carry you to the trailer."

She moaned as he picked her up, hating him for moving her and making it all worse. She found just enough breath to whisper, "I'll never forgive you."

"Yes . . . yes, I know."

The scorching trail of fire cut from her shoulder across the inside of her breast, then over her belly to her hip. It burned so fiercely she wasn't conscious of his gentleness as he carried her across the lot and into the trailer where he laid her on their bed.

Once again she turned her head away, biting her lip to hold back her screams as he slowly eased the ruined gown from her body.

"Your breast . . ." He drew a ragged breath. "There's a welt. It's—the skin isn't broken, but there'll be bruising."

The mattress moved as he left her, only to come back much too soon. "This'll feel cold. It's a compress."

She winced as he laid a wet towel over the seared skin. She squeezed her eyes shut, willing time to pass.

As the towel warmed from her skin, he removed it and replaced it with a fresh one. Once again, the mattress sagged as he sat next to her. He began to speak, his voice soft and rusty.

"I'm not—I'm not poor like I let you think. I teach, but—I also buy and sell Russian art. And I do consulting work for some of the biggest museums in the country."

Tears leaked through her lids and onto the pillow. As the compresses began to do their work, the pain subsided into a dull, aching throb.

His words were awkward and halting. "I'm considered the leading authority on Russian iconography in the—in the United States. I have money. Prestige. But I didn't want you to know. I wanted you to think of me as an uneducated roughneck living a hand to mouth existence. I wanted to . . . scare you away."

She willed her lips to move. "I don't care."

He spoke rapidly now, as if he had only a short period of time to get everything out. "I have a—a big brick house in the country. In Connecticut, not far from the campus." With a feather-light touch, he replaced the compress with a new one. "It's filled with beautiful art, and there's—I have a barn in the back with a stable for Misha."

"Please leave me alone."

"I don't know why I keep traveling with the circus. Every time I do it, I swear it's the last time, but then a few years go by and I start getting restless. I might be in Russia or Ukraine, maybe in New York—it doesn't seem to matter—I just know I have to go back on the road. I guess I'll always be more Markov than Romanov."

Now that it no longer mattered, he was telling her everything she'd been begging him for months to reveal. "I don't want to hear any more."

His hand cupped her waist in an oddly protective gesture. "It was an accident. You know that, don't you? You know how sorry I am."

"I want to go to sleep now."

"Daisy, I'm a wealthy man. That night we went to dinner, and you were worried about the bill . . . There isn't—you don't ever have to worry about money."

"It doesn't matter."

"I know it hurts. It'll be better tomorrow. You'll be

bruised and sore, but there won't be any permanent damage." He faltered, as if he realized what a terrible lie he'd just told.

"Please," she said tonelessly. "If you care about me at all, leave me alone."

There was a long silence. Then the mattress moved as he bent forward and brushed her damp eyelids with his lips. "If you need anything, just turn that light on. I'll be watching for it, and I'll come right away."

She waited for him to move. Waited for him to leave so she could shatter into a million pieces.

But he had no mercy. He turned back the top corner of the compress and blew softly, sending a soothing ripple of cooling air across her skin. Something warm and damp fell onto her skin, but she was too numb to even wonder what it was.

He finally rose from the bed, and for several moments the trailer was filled with the familiar sounds he always made when he changed from his costume into his work clothes: the thud of his boots hitting the floor, the faint rustle of sequins as he removed his red sash, the rasp of the zipper on his jeans. An eternity passed before she heard the door close behind him.

The growl of a tiger met Alex as he left the trailer. He stood outside and gulped the air. The colored lights shone and the pennants snapped, but he was unable to see anything except the obscene red welt that marred her fragile skin. Tears stung his eyes and his lungs burned. What had he done?

He moved blindly across the grass to the tiger's cage. The performance was still going on inside the top, and the backyard was deserted except for a few of the clowns, who gave him wide berth.

His timing had been off all night. Why hadn't he ended the act right away? He should have signaled Digger to send in Misha and brought the whole thing to a close. But he'd been too caught up in rage. Instead, his pride had demanded he do one more trick to try to redeem the performance. One more trick, as if that would make everything all right again.

He blinked his eyes hard. Her skin was so pale and fragile. The welt marred her breast and passed over the sweet, flat belly that held her child. *Their child.* The child he'd told her they were getting rid of. As if Daisy would ever be able to do anything like that.

As if he would ever have let her do it.

The ugly, hateful words he'd spoken rang in his ears. Words she'd never forget or forgive. Not even Daisy had a heart big enough to forgive him for what he'd said.

As he reached the cage, Sinjun regarded him with unblinking eyes that seemed to peer into the deepest recesses of his soul. What did the tiger see? He stepped over the rope and curled his hands around the bars. The cold, empty place inside him was gone—he knew that now—but what had taken its place?

His gaze locked with the tiger's, and the hair on the back of his neck prickled. For a moment everything stood still, and then he heard a voice—his own voice—telling him exactly what the tiger saw.

Love.

His heart slammed against his ribs. *Love.* That's what this feeling was he hadn't understood, the feeling that had begun with a melting inside him. He'd been learning how to love. Daisy had seen it. She'd known what was happening to him, but he had denied it.

He loved her. Blindly. Absolutely. How could he not have known? She was more precious to him than all the ancient icons and priceless artifacts that had consumed his life for so long. Living with her, he'd learned how to be happy. He'd learned joy, passion, and an awe-inspiring sense of humility. And what had he given her in return?

I don't love you, Daisy. I never will.

He squeezed his eyes shut as he remember how, time and again, he'd rejected the precious gift she'd offered. But with a courage that took his breath away, she'd continued to hold it out to him. No matter how many times he rejected her love, she kept on extending it.

Now that love was embodied in the child growing inside her. The child he didn't want. The child he craved with every beat of his heart.

What had he done? How was he going to win her back? He twisted his head toward the trailer, praying the light calling him back to her would be on, but the window remained dark.

He had to win her back and make her forgive the ugly words he'd spoken. He had been blind and arrogant, so enmeshed in the past that he had turned away from the future. He had betrayed her in a manner no ordinary person would ever forgive.

But Daisy wasn't ordinary. Loving was as natural to her as breathing. She was no more capable of withholding her love than she was of deliberately hurting someone. He'd throw himself on the mercy of her sweetness and generosity. He'd take advantage of her tender, loving heart. There would be no more secrets from her. He'd tell her everything he felt, and if that didn't soften her to him, he'd remind her of those sacred vows they'd spoken. He'd play upon her sympathies, bully her, make love to her until she no longer remembered that he'd betrayed her. He'd remind her that she was a Markov now, and Markov women stuck by their men, even when those men didn't deserve it.

The window of the trailer was still dark. He decided he'd better let her sleep for now and give her time to recover, but when morning came, he'd do whatever was necessary to win her back.

The crowd left the big top, and he set to work. As the top came down, he wanted to prove his love to her, give her some tangible sign that everything would be different between them. He glanced at the darkened trailer window, then raced for his truck. Ten minutes later, he found an all-night convenience store.

The selection was limited, but he filled his arms with everything he could find: a child's box of animal crackers, a blue plastic rattle and fluffy yellow duck, a paperback copy of Dr. Spock, a plastic bib printed with a lop-eared rabbit, fruit juice, and a box of oatmeal because she had to eat well.

He sped back to the circus with his offerings, and the sack tore as he snatched it from the front seat. He held it together in his big hands and ran toward the trailer. When she saw all this she'd understand what she meant to him. What their baby meant. She'd know how much he loved her.

He dropped the rattle as he twisted the knob on the door. The plastic bounced once on the metal step and then rolled into the grass. He rushed inside.

She was gone.

22

Max Petroff glared at Alex. "Why are you wasting your time looking for her here? I told you I'd get in touch with you if she contacted us."

Alex stared blindly out the window that overlooked Central Park and searched for a good answer. He couldn't remember the last time he'd had a decent meal or slept more than a few hours without jolting awake. His stomach was giving him trouble, he'd lost weight, and he knew he looked like hell.

It had been a month since Daisy had run away, and he was no closer to locating her today than he'd been that night she'd fled. As he'd chased one lead after another, he'd missed more performances than he could count, but neither he nor the detective he'd hired had come up with anything.

Max had given him a list of the names of everyone he knew that Daisy might contact, and Alex had spoken with each of them, but it was as if she'd slipped off the edge of the earth. He only prayed her angel's wings were keeping her aloft.

He turned slowly to face Max. "I thought you might have missed something. She didn't have more than a hundred dollars on her when she left."

Amelia spoke from the couch. "Really, Alex. Do you think Max would keep information from you after all the work he did to get the two of you together?"

Amelia's arch manner always set his teeth on edge, and

with his nerves stretched so taut they were ready to snap, he couldn't conceal his dislike. "The fact is, my wife has disappeared, and nobody seems to know a damned thing about it."

"Calm down, Alex. We're just as worried as you are."

"If you ask me," Amelia said, "you should question that worker who saw her last."

Alex had cross-examined Al Porter until he was convinced the old man had nothing more to tell him. While Alex had been making his foolish trip to the convenience store, Al had seen Daisy standing on the side of the highway flagging down an eighteen-wheeler. She'd been wearing jeans and carrying Alex's small valise.

"I can't believe she hitchhiked," Max said. "She could have been murdered."

That terrifying possibility had kept Alex dry-mouthed with fear for three days until Jack had come rushing out of the red wagon one afternoon with the news that he'd just spoken with Daisy on the telephone. She had called to make certain the menagerie animals were all right. When Jack pressed her to tell him where she was, she'd hung up on him. She hadn't asked about Alex.

He'd cursed the circumstances that had kept him from being in the red wagon when she called. Then he'd remembered the half dozen times he'd answered the telephone only to hear a click at the other end. It must have been her. She'd been waiting for someone else to answer so she didn't have to talk to him.

Max had begun to pace. "I can't understand why the police aren't taking this more seriously."

"Because she disappeared voluntarily."

"But anything could have happened to her since then. She's totally incapable of taking care of herself."

"That's not true. Daisy's smart, and she's not afraid of hard work."

Max dismissed his comments. Despite the incident he'd witnessed with Sinjun, he still saw his daughter as incompetent and frivolous. "I have friends in the FBI, and it's high time I contacted a few of them."

"Hundreds of witnesses saw what happened in the ring that night. The police believe she had ample reason for disappearing."

"That was an accident, and for all her faults, Daisy isn't vindictive. She'd never hold it against you. No, Alex. There has to be foul play involved, and I'm not letting you talk me out of this any longer. I'm calling the FBI today."

Alex had never told Max the entire truth, and now he understood why he'd felt compelled to come here today. By holding back the whole story, he was leaving out information that might give either Max or Amelia some additional idea about where Daisy could have gone. He hated the idea of revealing something so ugly about himself, but his pride wasn't nearly as important as Daisy's safety and the well-being of his child.

As he faced the older man, he saw how Max had aged in the past month. Some of the starch had left his diplomat's spine. His movements seemed slower, his voice a bit less firm. In his own way, narrow and judgmental as Alex believed it to be, Max did love Daisy, and he was suffering.

Alex gazed for a moment at the silver samovar he'd located for Max in a Paris gallery. It had been designed by Peter Carl Fabergé for Czar Alexander III and was imprinted with the two-headed Russian imperial eagle. The dealer had told Alex it was made in 1886, but the detail in the work made Alex place it closer to 1890.

Contemplating the genius of Fabergé was easier than thinking about what he needed to tell Max. He shoved his hands in the pockets of his slacks, then drew them out. He cleared his throat. "Daisy had more to be upset about than what I did to her with the whip."

The older man grew instantly alert. "Oh?"

"She's pregnant."

"I told you so," Amelia said from the couch.

Max and Amelia shared a conspiratorial look that made

Alex instantly alert. Max regarded her fondly. "You did tell me, didn't you, my dear."

"And Alex behaved badly when he heard the news."

Amelia was annoying, but she wasn't stupid, and the old pain struck, strong and sharp. "I behaved badly," he agreed.

Amelia regarded her husband smugly.. "I told you *that* would happen, too."

Alex swallowed hard before he forced out the ugly words. "I ordered her to have an abortion."

Max's lips pinched. "You didn't."

"You can't say anything to me I haven't already said to myself."

"Do you still feel that way about it?"

"Of course, he doesn't," Amelia said. "You only have to look at him to see that. Guilt's hanging over him like a bad hairdo." She rose from the couch. "I'm late for my facial. You two will have to sort this out for yourselves. Congratulations, Max."

Alex noted both Amelia's final words and the telling smile she gave Max. He stared at her as she left the room and knew that something important had passed between them.

"Is Amelia right?" Max demanded. "Have you changed your mind?"

"I didn't mean it when I said it. She'd scared the hell out of me, and I was running on adrenaline." He studied Max. "Amelia wasn't surprised to hear about Daisy's pregnancy, yet she knew she was taking birth control pills. Why is that?"

Max walked over to a walnut cabinet where he gazed through the glass doors at his porcelain collection. "We were both hoping, that's all."

"You're lying, damn it! Daisy told me Amelia filled the prescription for her. Tell me the truth."

"It was—we did what we thought was best."

A great stillness fell over Alex. He thought of the small compartmentalized compacts that held Daisy's pills. As if he were seeing them for the first time, he remembered that the pills had been unprotected. In an age when so many medications were in blister packs, these pills hadn't been covered by anything more than the lid of the compact.

The ever-present constriction in his chest tightened. Once again he had failed to trust his wife, and once again he'd been wrong. "You planned this, didn't you; just like you planned everything else. Somehow you substituted pills."

"I don't know what you're talking about."

"The hell you don't. The truth, Max. I want it now."

The older man seemed to collapse. His knees bent, and he slumped down into the chair nearest him. "Don't you see? It was my duty."

"Your duty. Of course that's how you'd see it. I can't believe I was so stupid. I've always known how obsessed you were with family history, but it never occurred to me that you'd do something like this." Bitterness welled in his stomach. From the beginning, he and Daisy had been nothing but puppets serving Max's obsession with the past.

"Something like what? By God, you should be grateful." Max erupted from the chair. His finger shook as he pointed it toward Alex. "For a man who's an historian, you have no sense of your own lineage. You're the great-grandson of the czar!"

"I'm a Markov. That's the only family history that means anything to me."

"A worthless band of vagabonds. Vagabonds, do you hear me? You're a Romanov, and it's your duty to have a child. But you wanted no part of it, did you?"

"It was my decision, not yours!"

"This is bigger than some selfish whim."

"When she told me she was pregnant, I thought she'd done it deliberately. I accused her of lying, you bastard!"

Max winced, and he lost some of his righteous indignation. "Look at it from my viewpoint. I only had six months, and I had to act quickly. As much as I might wish that you'd fall in love with her, I could hardly expect a man with your intellectual gifts to be interested in a scatterbrain like my daughter in any way except sexually."

Alex felt sick. What must it have been like for his gentle,

intelligent wife to have been shackled with a father who had so little respect for her? "That scatterbrain is smarter than both of us."

"There's no need to be polite."

"I'm not. You don't know your daughter at all."

"I know that I couldn't let this marriage end without doing my best to make sure there was a Romanov heir."

"It wasn't your decision."

"That's not exactly true. Throughout history, the Petroffs have always dedicated themselves to the greater good of the Romanovs, even when the Romanovs might disagree."

As Alex looked at Max, he realized Daisy's father wasn't quite sane on the subject. Max might be a reasonable man in all other aspects of his life, but not in this one.

"You were going to let the line die," Max said. "I couldn't allow that."

There was no point in arguing this particular topic any further. To Max, the child Daisy carried was a pawn, but the baby meant something far different to Alex, and he felt a father's instincts to protect it.

"What pills was she taking? What did you give her?"

"Nothing that would harm the baby. A child's fluoride pill, that's all." Max collapsed in the chair. "You have to find her before she does something stupid. What if she's gotten rid of it?"

Alex stared at the old man. Gradually, pity took the place of bitterness as he thought of all the years Max had wasted, all the chances he'd passed by to get to know his remarkable daughter.

"Nothing could make her do that. She has guts, Max. And she'll do whatever it takes to keep that baby safe."

Alex met the circus the next morning just as the first trucks were pulling into a lot in Chattanooga. As the days grew shorter and summer drew to an end, the circus was winding its way back south toward its winter quarters near Tampa, where they would play their last date during the final week of October. His sabbatical from the university wasn't up until

January, and he'd planned to do some research in Ukraine before then. Now he didn't know what he'd do. Without Daisy, he didn't much care.

He automatically scanned the new lot and saw that it was hilly, with barely enough level space to put up the top. He was bleary-eyed from fatigue, but he welcomed the challenge of a bad lot. He knew it wouldn't take his mind off her—nothing could—but at least it would help the time pass.

Trey was driving his trailer on the morning jump, but he hadn't arrived yet, so Alex headed over to the cook tent for some of the bitterly potent coffee that would eat a hole in his already burning stomach. Before he could fill his cup, he heard a shrill, demanding trumpet. He cursed softly under his breath and headed for the elephants.

When he got there, he wasn't surprised to see that Neeco looked peeved. "Give me the hot shot back, Alex. Just one jab, and we can put an end to this bullshit."

Despite Neeco's bluster, Alex knew the elephant trainer had lost his taste for the prod after his encounter with Sinjun. He liked to think that Daisy's ways with the animals had opened Neeco's eyes, because he was gentler with the elephants than he had been, and they were working better for him. Still, he needed to make sure Neeco understood that he couldn't go back to his old ways.

"As long as I'm boss, you're not using the prod again."

"Then get that little prick out of here."

Alex walked over to Tater and suffered the baby's embrace. The tip of the elephant's trunk poked beneath his shirt collar to sniff his neck, just as he'd done with Daisy. Alex untethered him and headed toward the spool truck, with Tater trotting behind.

When Daisy had disappeared, Tater had stopped eating, but Alex had been too entangled in his own private hell to notice. It was only as the small elephant's condition deteriorated that Neeco forced him to pay attention.

It didn't take him long to discover that the elephant found comfort in his presence, not because of anything Alex did, but because the baby associated him with Daisy. He started to eat again, and before long, he was following Alex around the lot as he'd once followed her.

The two of them made their way toward the spool truck, where the nylon was ready to be unrolled as soon as the location for the top was decided on. Brady had arrived there ahead of him, but he stepped aside as Alex approached. Alex didn't know what he'd have done without Brady. Along with Jack, Brady had helped take up the slack from his frequent absences and kept things running.

For the next few hours, Alex labored alongside the workers as they erected the top on the difficult terrain. He was still in the clothes he'd worn on the plane, but he didn't stop to change when Trey arrived with his trailer. Sweat soaked his blue oxford-cloth shirt, and he managed to rip his gray dress slacks, but he didn't care. The mind-numbing labor kept him from thinking.

When he could avoid it no longer, he headed to the trailer, with Tater close behind. He tethered the animal near the hay Digger had left, then hesitated as he approached the door. The trailer was filled with her scent, her touch, everything but her presence, and he hated going inside.

He did it anyway, and as he changed clothes, he was tortured with images of the way she'd looked as she'd rushed through the door with dirt-smeared cheeks, grubby clothes, straw clinging to her hair, and the gleam of accomplishment in her eyes. He wandered over to the refrigerator, but all he could find was a can of beer and a carton of yogurt Daisy had bought for herself. It had expired two weeks ago, but he couldn't bring himself to throw it away.

He grabbed the beer and carried it outside, popping the top as he walked over to Tater. The baby was keeping himself cool by sprinkling hay on his back. He picked up a fresh batch and, as a gesture of friendship, dusted Alex with it instead. It hadn't taken Alex long to figure out why Daisy'd always had hay stuck in her hair.

"I'll bet she misses you, fella," he said softly as he rubbed the elephant's trunk.

She would be missing Sinjun even more. There had been

a strange bond between Daisy and the tiger, one he'd never understood. She'd loved working with the animals no one else had the patience to pay attention to: the troublesome baby elephant, the shy gorilla, the old, regal tiger. It must be hard for her not being around any of the animals she loved.

At that moment everything inside him went still. His skin crawled with gooseflesh, and he forgot to breathe. What made him think she wasn't with one of those animals?

Twenty-four hours later he stood by the railing in the Tropical World compound at Chicago's Brookfield Zoo and stared at Glenna, who was sitting on the rocky mountain in the center, munching on a stalk of celery. He'd been wandering the sloped walkways that surrounded the spacious indoor habitat for hours. His eyes were gritty from lack of sleep, his head ached, and acid burned a hole in his stomach.

What if he was wrong? What if she didn't come here at all? He'd been to the zoo's employment office, and he already knew she didn't work here. But he was sure she would want to be close to Glenna. Besides, there wasn't anyplace left for him to look.

Fool. The word pounded through his head like the noise of a stake driver. *Fool. Fool. Fool. Fool.*

His grief was too private to be put on exhibition, and as he heard the babble of another group of school children, he moved up the curving pathway, which was bordered by tropical vegetation and a railing of iron pipe painted green like bamboo and lashed together with rope. At the top, he found a more deserted location. Glenna tugged on one of the heavy ropes hanging in the man-made tree trunks that stood at the summit of the gorilla mountain and came around to his side. She looked healthy and contented in her new home. She settled back down, this time with a carrot.

Suddenly her head came up and she began making smacking sounds with her lips. He followed the direction of her eyes and saw Daisy approaching the rail below and gazing at the gorilla.

His heart slammed against his ribs, and joy flooded him,

followed almost instantly by distress. Even from fifteen yards away he could see that she wore no makeup, and lines of fatigue were etched in her face. Her hair was restrained with a clip at the nape of her neck, and for the first time since he'd known her she looked almost plain. Where was the Daisy who loved to primp and fuss with her perfumes and powder? The Daisy who took such joy in dabbing herself with apricot-scented lotion and raspberry red lipstick? Where was the Daisy who used up all the hot water taking her showers and left a sticky film of hair spray on the bathroom door? Dry-mouthed, he drank in the sight of her, and something broke apart inside him. This was Daisy as he'd made her.

This was Daisy with her love light extinguished.

As he moved closer, he spotted new hollows under her cheekbones and realized that she'd lost weight. His gaze flew to her waist, but the loose jacket she wore over a pair of dark slacks kept him from seeing if there were any changes in her body. Fear shot through him. What if she'd lost their baby? Was that going to be his punishment?

She was intent on her silent communion with the gorilla and didn't see him as he moved around the children and came up behind her. He spoke softly. "Daisy."

She stiffened and then turned. Her face grew even paler, and her hands twitched in an involuntary spasm. She looked as if she were getting ready to flee, and he took a quick step forward to stop her, but the coldness in her expression halted him in his tracks. The only other time he could remember seeing eyes so empty was when he'd looked into a mirror.

"We have to talk." His words unconsciously echoed the ones she'd spoken to him so many times, and her stony expression as she gazed back at him must be a reflection of the way he'd frequently regarded her.

Who was this woman? Her face bore none of the animation he was used to. Those violet eyes were so lifeless they didn't look as if they ever cried. It was as if something inside her had died, and he began to sweat. Had she lost their baby? Was that responsible for the change in her? Not their baby. Please.

"There's nothing to talk about." She turned and walked away, heading back through the rope curtain that served as the entrance to the habitat. He followed her outside and without thinking, grabbed her arm.

"Let me go."

How many times had she said that to him as he'd dragged her across a lot or pulled her out of bed at dawn? But this time she spoke the words without any of her former passion. He gazed down into her pale, closed face. *What have I done to you, my love?*

"I just want to talk," he said brusquely, steering her off to the side and away from the crowd.

She glanced at his hand, still encircling her arm. "If you're planning to carry me off to have an abortion, it's too late."

He wanted to throw back his head and howl. She'd lost the baby, and it was his fault.

He dropped his hand, and he could barely force out the words. "You'll never know how sorry I am about that."

"Oh, I know," she said with an eerie calm. "You made that very clear."

"I didn't make anything clear. I never told you I loved you. I said hateful things to you, things I didn't mean." His arms ached to gather her close, but she had erected an invisible barrier around herself. "All that's behind us now, sweetheart. We're going to start over. I promise I'll make everything up to you."

"I have to go. I have to be at work soon."

It was as if he hadn't spoken. He'd told her he loved her, but it hadn't made any difference. She intended to walk away and never see him again.

His resolve hardened. He couldn't let that happen. He would deal with his grief later. For now, he would do whatever he needed to to get his wife back.

"You're coming with me."

"No, I'm not. I have a job."

"You also have a marriage."

"It's not a real marriage. It never was."

"It is now. We took vows, Daisy. Sacred vows. That's as real as it gets."

Her bottom lip trembled. "Why are you doing this? I told you it's too late for me to have an abortion."

He ached for her. As deep as his sorrow was, he knew it couldn't match hers. "There'll be other babies, sweetheart. We'll try again. As soon as the doctor says it's all right."

"What are you talking about?"

"I wanted the baby as much as you did, but I didn't realize it until the night you ran away. I know it's my fault you lost the baby. If I'd taken better care of you this never would have happened."

Her brow furrowed. "I haven't lost the baby."

He stared at her.

"I'm still pregnant."

"But you said—when I told you I wanted to talk, you said it was too late for you to have an abortion."

"I'm four-and-a-half months pregnant. An abortion isn't legal."

Even as joy flooded through him, her mouth twisted with a cynicism that he'd never imagined he'd see. "That changes things, doesn't it, Alex? Now that you know the cake's still baking in the oven and it's going to stay right there, I'll bet you aren't so anxious to have me back."

Emotions were traveling through him so quickly he couldn't deal with them. She still carried their baby. She hated him. She didn't want to come back. He couldn't handle that much emotional chaos, so he settled on the practical. "What are you doing about medical care?"

"There's a clinic not far from here."

"A clinic?" He had a fortune in the bank, and his wife was going to a clinic. He had to get her away from here where he could kiss that look of implacable resolve from her face, but the only way he could do that was by playing the tough guy.

"If this is your idea of taking care of yourself, I'm not impressed. You're thin and pale. You're strung so damned tight, you look like you're going to fall apart."

"What do you care? You don't want this baby."

"Oh, I want the baby very much. Just because I acted like a bastard when you told me the news doesn't mean I didn't come to my senses. I know you don't want to go with me, but for now, you don't have any other choice. You're endangering yourself and the baby, Daisy, and I can't let you do that."

He could see that he'd found her weakest spot, but she still fought him. "You don't have any say in this."

"I have a say, all right. And I'm going to make sure you and the baby are safe."

Her eyes grew wary.

"I'll play dirty," he said quietly. "It won't take me long to find out where you're working, and I guarantee I'll make your job disappear."

"You'd do that to me?"

"I won't even hesitate."

Her shoulders slumped, and he knew he'd won, but he felt no satisfaction.

"I don't love you anymore," she whispered. "I don't love you at all."

His throat closed. "It's all right, sweetheart. I love you enough for both of us."

23

Alex drove Daisy to the small house on a narrow street in a working-class neighborhood not far from the zoo. The house had a plaster statue of the Blessed Mother in the tiny front yard, along with a sunflower pinwheel guarding a bed of pink petunias. She rented a bedroom in the back with a view of a chain-link fence, and while she packed her meager possessions, he slipped away to settle up with her landlady, only to discover that Daisy had already paid her rent for the month.

From the chatty woman, he learned that Daisy worked as a receptionist at a beauty shop during the day and waited tables at a neighborhood tavern at night. No wonder she seemed so tired. She had no car, so she either walked or took a bus everywhere, and she was saving all her money to get ready for the baby. The fact that his wife had been living in penury while he had two luxury cars and a house filled with priceless art pounded another nail into his coffin of guilt.

As they set out on the road, he briefly considered taking her to his home in Connecticut, only to reject the idea. She needed more than physical healing; she needed emotional healing, and maybe the animals she loved would help him give that to her.

It was all so familiar that Daisy experienced a moment of well-being as the truck swayed to a stop. She and Alex were on the road, making a jump to the next lot. She was in love and pregnant and—she jolted awake as reality crashed in on her.

He pulled the keys from the ignition and opened the door. "I have to get some sleep before I run us into a bridge abutment. Wait here while I check in." He climbed out of the truck and closed the door behind him.

She leaned back against the seat, and as she shut her eyes against the gathering dusk, she also closed her heart to the gentleness she had heard in his voice. He was filled with guilt, anyone could see that, but she wouldn't be manipulated. The lies he'd spoken earlier had undoubtedly made him feel better, but believing them would only trap her. She had a child to protect, and she could no longer afford the luxury of such foolish optimism.

He'd told her that her father and Amelia had tampered with her birth control pills and apologized for not trusting her. More guilt. She shut him out.

Why couldn't he have left her alone? Why had he forced her to come back with him? For the first time in weeks, the tide of emotions she'd worked so hard to repress rose inside her. She pressed her knuckles to her lips and fought the feelings back until she once again slipped behind the comforting barrier that had kept her functioning this past month.

For as long as she could remember, she had been a woman who had run on emotions, but she hadn't been able to continue to do that and survive. Pride is everything, Alex had told her, and now she knew he was right. Pride had kept her going. It had enabled her to answer the phone and shampoo heads all day, then spend her nights carrying heavy trays loaded with greasy food that made her stomach heave. Pride had kept a roof over her head and let her lay money aside for her future. Pride had kept her running when love had betrayed her.

And now what? For the first time in weeks, she experienced a fear that had nothing to do with making her rent. She was afraid of Alex. What did he want with her?

The biggest threat to a young tiger is an older male tiger. Tigers don't have strong family bonds like lions and ele-

phants. It isn't unusual for a father tiger to kill his own cub.

She fumbled for the door handle only to see her husband stalking toward her.

Alex pulled a chair back from the table where the room-service waiter had set out the meal he had ordered. "Sit down and eat, Daisy."

He hadn't chosen a sleazy highway motel. Instead, he'd booked them into a luxury suite in a shiny new Marriott located along the Ohio River at the Indiana-Kentucky border. She thought of the way she used to count pennies when she grocery shopped and gave him lectures on extravagance when he bought a bottle of good wine. How he must have been laughing at her.

"I told you I wasn't hungry."

"Keep me company, then."

It was less work to take the chair he held out for her than argue. He tightened the knot on the sash of the white terry robe he'd put on after his shower and sat across from her. His hair was still damp, and it curled a bit at the temples. He needed a haircut.

She looked down at the huge quantity of food he'd ordered for her: a dinner-plate-size salad, chicken breasts smothered in mushroom sauce, a baked potato, a side order of pasta, two rolls, a large glass of milk, and a slab of cheesecake.

"I can't eat this."

"I'm starved. I'll eat some of it for you."

Although he enjoyed food, he wasn't a big enough eater to put a dent in all this. She felt her stomach pitch. She'd had more trouble holding food down since she'd left him than she'd had during her entire first trimester.

"Try this." He lifted a bite of lasagna from his own plate and held it to her lips. When she opened her mouth to refuse, he shoved it inside, forcing her to chew.

"I told you I didn't want to eat."

"Just a sample. Good, isn't it?"

To her surprise, once the initial shock had passed, the lasagna did taste good, although she wasn't going to tell him that. She took a sip of water. "I really don't want anything else."

"I'm not surprised." He pointed toward her chicken. "That looks dry."

"It's covered in sauce. It doesn't look dry at all."

"Trust me, Daisy. That chicken is dry as shoe leather."

"You don't know what you're talking about."

"Give me a taste."

She jabbed her fork into the chicken, and as she cut a piece, the juices spurted out. "Look at this." She poked her fork at him.

He obediently pulled the chicken off with his teeth, chewed, and grimaced. "Dry."

She snatched up her knife, cut a piece for herself, and ate it. As she had predicted, it was just as delicious as it looked. She ate another. "There is *nothing* wrong with this chicken."

"I guess the lasagna affected my taste buds. Let me try some of your pasta."

Irritated, she watched him twirl his fork in her pasta and slip it into his mouth. A moment later, he delivered his verdict. "Too spicy for you."

"I happen to like spicy food."

"Don't say I didn't warn you."

She jabbed at the pasta and dribbled some sauce on the tablecloth as she carried it to her mouth. The sauce was mild and flavorful. "It's not spicy at all."

She began to reach for another forkful only to check the motion in midair. Her eyes flew to his as she realized she'd let him trick her, and she set down her fork. "Another power play."

His long, lean fingers curled around her wrist, and he looked at her with a concern she didn't believe for a moment. "Please, Daisy. You're so thin you're scaring me. You have to eat for the baby."

"You have no right!" Pain rushed through her. She choked back the rest of what she had been about to say and retreated behind the icy barrier that kept her safe. Emotion was her enemy. She would think only about what was best for her child.

Without a word, she returned to her meal, eating until she couldn't eat any more. She ignored his attempts at conversation and took no interest in the fact that he ate hardly anything himself. In her mind, she escaped to a beautiful meadow where she and her baby could roam free, both of them guarded by a powerful tiger named Sinjun who loved them and no longer needed a cage.

"You're exhausted," he said when she finally set down her fork. "Both of us need sleep. Let's make an early night of it."

She rose from the table, gathered her things, and went into the bathroom, where she treated herself to a long shower. When she finally came out, the suite was dark, lit only by a faint light seeping through a crack in the draperies. Alex lay on his back on the far side of the king size bed.

She was so tired she could barely stand, but the sight of his bare chest kept her from moving closer.

"It's all right," he whispered through the darkness. "I won't touch you, sweetheart."

She stayed where she was until she realized that it made no difference whether he touched her or not. No matter what he did, she would feel nothing.

Alex shoved his hands into the pocket of his windbreaker and leaned against the hurricane fence that marked the far edge of the lot where they'd be spending the next two days. They were in Monroe County, Georgia, and the October air of midmorning carried the crisp hint of autumn.

Brady approached him. "You look like hell."

"Yeah, well you don't look so good yourself."

"Women," he snorted. "Can't live with them. Can't murder 'em in their sleep."

Alex couldn't even summon a smile. Brady might be having trouble with Sheba, but at least his relationship with Heather was going well. The two of them spent a lot of time together, and Brady was a more patient trainer than he'd been in the past. It was paying off, too, because Heather's performances were improving.

He and Daisy had been back for ten days, and the entire circus knew that something was drastically wrong with her. She didn't laugh anymore or flounce around the lot with her ponytail bouncing. She was polite to everyone—she was even helping Heather with her schoolwork—but all the special qualities that had made her who she was seemed to have been extinguished. And everybody expected him to fix her.

Brady pulled a toothpick from his shirt pocket and slipped it into his mouth. "Daisy's been a lot different since she got back."

"She's adjusting to being pregnant, that's all."

Brady wasn't fooled. "I miss the way she used to be. She was always nibbing in my business—I guess I don't miss that—but I sure miss the way she cared about everybody. Now it doesn't seem like she cares about anything other than Sinjun and the elephants."

"She'll get over it."

"Yeah, I guess."

They watched in silence as a truck dumped a load of hay. Alex saw Daisy pick up one of the long-handled brushes and begin scrubbing Puddin'. He'd told her he didn't want her working, but she said she'd gotten used to work. Then he'd tried to order her to stay away from all of the elephants except Tater, fearing that one of them would swat her. She'd looked right through him and done exactly what she wanted.

Brady crossed his arms over his chest. "I thought you should know—I saw her curled up in Sinjun's cage again last night."

"Damn it! I swear to God I'm going to handcuff her if she doesn't stay out of that tiger cage!"

"It scares the shit out of me, I'll tell you that. I hate seeing her like this."

"Yeah, well you're not the only one."

"Why don't you do something?"

"Just what do you suggest? I had one of my cars brought down from Connecticut so she wouldn't have to ride in the truck, but she said she liked the truck. I've bought her flowers, and she ignores them. I tried to order a new RV, but she had a fit when she found out about it, so I had to cancel. I don't know what else I can do." He shoved his hand through his hair. "Why am I telling you this? If you knew anything about women, you wouldn't be hanging around Sheba."

"You're not getting any argument out of me."

"Daisy's going to be fine. It's just a matter of time."

"Sure. You're probably right."

"Damn right I am."

If he repeated it enough times, maybe he could make it come true. How he missed the way she had been. She never cried anymore. Her easy tears had been as much a part of her as the air she breathed, but now she seemed to have anesthetized herself to emotion. He remembered the way she used to throw herself into his arms from the top of the truck ramp, the sound of her laughter, the brush of her hand in his hair. He ached for her in a way he had never ached for anyone, and last night, it had pushed him over the edge.

He winced at the memory.

He'd dreamed she was smiling at him in that way she used to, her whole face lit up, offering herself to him. He'd awakened to find himself pressed against her. It had been so long, and he wanted her too much to let her go.

He slid his hand along her hip and over the sweet thickening at her waist. She'd awakened immediately, and he'd felt her stiffen as he caressed her, but she didn't pull away. She didn't even resist when he spread her thighs and moved on top of her. Instead, she lay passively while he added one more sin to the list of those he'd already committed against her. He'd felt like a rapist, and this morning he hadn't been able to look himself in the eye when he'd shaved.

"She still talks to Heather," Brady said. "But not the way she used to. Heather's as worried as the rest of us."

Heather finished the tacos Sheba had made for her and wiped her fingers on her paper napkin. "Do you want to hear what Dad said to me last night?"

Sheba looked over from the sink. "Sure."

Heather grinned, then puffed out her chest. "He said, 'Damn it, Heather, get your crap off the couch. Just because I love you doesn't mean I want your makeup plastered all over my ass.'"

Sheba laughed. "Your old man sure knows how to sweet-talk."

"That day at the airport . . ." She blinked. "He had tears in his eyes, Sheba."

"He loves you a lot."

"I guess I know that now." Her smile faded. "I feel sort of guilty being so happy and everything when Daisy's all screwed up. Yesterday I said *shit* right in front of her, and she didn't even notice."

Sheba swiped at the counter with a dishcloth. "Daisy's all anyone talks about anymore. I'm getting sick of it."

"That's because you don't like her, and I can't understand why. I mean I know you and Alex used to be together and everything, but you don't care about him anymore, and she's so sad, so what's the big deal?"

"The big deal is that Sheba can't stand it when anybody gets the best of her." Brady stood just inside the door, although neither of them had heard him come in.

Sheba got her hackles up right away. "Don't you ever knock?"

Heather sighed. "Are you two going to start arguing again?"

"I don't argue," Brady said. "She's the one."

"Ha! He thinks he can tell me what to do, and I won't let him."

"That's what he says about you," Heather pointed out patiently. And then, even though she was beginning to think she was wasting her breath, she said, "If the two of you would just get married, you'd be so busy bossing each other around that you'd leave everybody else alone."

"I wouldn't marry him for anything!"

"I wouldn't marry her if she was the last woman on earth!"

"Then you shouldn't be sleeping together." Heather adopted her best Daisy Markov voice. "And I know you sneak over here to be with her just about every night, Dad, even though sex without a deep commitment to the other person is immoral."

Sheba turned red. Her dad opened and closed his mouth a couple of times like a goldfish, then began to bluster. "You don't know what you're talking about, young lady. Sheba and I are just friends, that's all. She's been having trouble with her water tank, and I—"

Heather rolled her eyes. "I'm not a moron."

"Now listen here—"

"What kind of example do the two of you think you're setting for me? Just yesterday I was reading about adolescent psychology for my homework assignment, and I already have a couple of big strikes against me."

"What strikes?"

"I lost my mother, and I'm the product of a broken home. That, plus what I see going on right now with the two most influential adults in my life, makes me more likely to have a teenage pregnancy."

Her dad's eyebrows shot up practically to his hairline, and she seriously thought he was going to pee his pants. Even though she wasn't afraid of him like she used to be, she wasn't stupid, either. "Got to go. See you guys later."

She slammed out of the trailer.

"Son of a bitch!"

"Settle down," Sheba said. "She's just trying to make a point."

"What point?"

"That the two of us should get married." Sheba plopped a dab of taco meat in her mouth. "Which just goes to show how much she knows about the real world."

"You got that right."

"She still hasn't figured out how incompatible we are."

"Except in there." He jerked his head toward the bedroom in the rear.

"Yeah, well . . ." A foxy smile came over her face. "You peasant boys do have your uses."

"Damn right we do." He drew her into his arms, and she snuggled against him. He started kissing her, but then he drew back because both of them had things to do, and once they got started with each other, they had a hard time stopping.

He saw that her eyes looked troubled. "The season's almost over," she said. "A couple of weeks and we'll be in Tampa."

"We'll still see each other this winter."

"Who says I want to see you?"

She was lying, and both of them knew it. They'd become important to each other, and now he had the feeling she wanted something from him that he couldn't give.

He buried his lips in her hair. "Sheba, I care about you. I guess I even love you. But I can't marry you. I got my pride, and you're always stomping over it."

She stiffened and drew away, shooting sparks at him and acting like he was some kind of cockroach. "I don't think anybody asked you to get married."

He wasn't good with words, but there was something he'd been trying to say to her for a long time, something important. "I'd like to marry you. But it'd just be too hard being married to someone who's putting me down all the time."

"What are you talking about? You put me down, too."

"Yeah, but I don't mean it, and you do. There's a big difference. You really think you're better than everybody else. You think you're perfect."

"I never said that."

"Then name something that's wrong with you."

"I can't fly like I used to."

"That's not what I'm talking about. I'm talking about something inside you that's not as good as it should be. Everybody has things like that."

"There's nothing wrong with me, and I don't know what you're talking about."

He shook his head sadly. "I know you don't, babe. And

until you figure it out, there's not much hope for us."

He let her go, but before he made it all the way to the door, she started yelling. "You don't know anything! Just because I'm tough doesn't mean I'm not a good person. I am, damn it! I'm a good person!"

"You're also a snob," he said, turning back. "Most of the time you don't think about anybody's feelings but your own. You hurt other people. You're obsessed with the past, and you're the most stuck-up person I ever knew."

For a moment she stood there stunned, but then she started to scream. "Liar! I'm a good person! I am!"

"Keep saying it, babe, and maybe one day you'll believe it."

Her cry of fury sent a chill down his spine. He knew she'd fight back, and he managed to make it out the door before the plate of tacos came crashing into it.

As Daisy roamed the lot that night, she found herself wishing she were still performing with Alex. At least it would have kept her busy. When he'd announced that she wasn't going back into the ring with him, she'd felt neither relief nor disappointment. It simply made no difference. In the past six weeks she'd discovered a pain far more hurtful than any that could be inflicted by the whip.

She watched the crowd file out of the top. Weary children clung to their mother's sides and fathers carried tired toddlers with candy-apple stains around their mouths. Not so long ago, the sight of those fathers had made her eyes fill with sentimental tears as she'd imagined Alex carrying their child. Now her eyes were dry. Along with everything else, she had lost the ability to cry.

Since the circus wasn't moving on that night, the workers were free for the evening, and they set off for town in search of food and liquor. The lot fell quiet. While Alex tended Misha, she slipped into one of his old sweatshirts, then made her way through the sleeping elephants until she reached Tater. Kneeling down, she tucked herself between his front legs and let the baby elephant plop the end of his trunk on her knee.

She buried herself deeper in Alex's sweatshirt. The soft fleece carried his scent, that particular combination of soap, sun, and leather that she would have recognized anywhere. Was everything she loved going to be taken from her?

She heard the sound of quiet footsteps. Tater shifted his rear quarters and a pair of denim-clad legs appeared that she had no difficulty recognizing.

Alex crouched down next to her and propped his elbows on his splayed knees, hands dangling between. He looked so tired that, for a fraction of a second, she wanted to comfort him. "Please come out of there," he whispered. "I need you so badly."

She rested her cheek against Tater's wrinkly gunnysack leg. "I think I'll stay here a while longer."

His shoulders sagged, and he poked his finger in the dirt. "My house . . . it's big. There's a guest room on the south side that looks out on an old orchard."

She released her breath in a soft sigh. "It's chilly tonight. Fall's coming."

"I thought we could maybe make it into a nursery. It's a nice room. Sunny, with a big window. Maybe we could put a rocking chair there."

"I've always liked the fall."

The animals shifted, and one of them snorted quietly in its sleep. Tater lifted his trunk from her knee and draped it on her husband's shoulder. The softness in Alex's voice didn't hide its bitterness. "You're not ever going to forgive me, are you?"

She said nothing.

"I love you, Daisy. I love you so much I hurt."

She heard his suffering, saw the vulnerability in his face, and even though she knew it came from guilt, she had endured too much pain herself to find any pleasure in inflicting it on another, especially one who still meant so much to her. She spoke as gently as she could. "You don't know how to love, Alex."

"That might have been true once, but not anymore."

Maybe it was the comfort she received from sitting beneath Tater's heart or maybe it was Alex's pain, but she could feel the icy barrier inside her beginning to crack. Despite everything, she still loved him. She'd lied to him and to herself when she'd said she didn't. He was the mate of her soul, and he would own her heart forever. With that realization came a deeper and more bitter knowledge. If she ever again let herself fall victim to the love she had for him, it might very well destroy her, and for the baby's sake, she couldn't let that happen.

"Don't you see? What you're feeling is guilt, not love."

"That's not true."

"You're a proud man. You violated your sense of honor, and now you're trying to make amends. I understand that, but I'm not going to let my life be dictated by words you don't really mean. This baby is too important to me."

"The baby's important to me, too."

She winced. "Don't say that. Please."

"I'd prove my love if I could, but I don't know how to do that."

"You're going to have to let me go. I know it'll hurt your pride, and I'm sorry about that, but being together like this is too difficult."

He didn't say anything. She shut her eyes and tried to slip behind the icy barrier that had been keeping her safe, but he'd put too many cracks in it. "Please, Alex," she whispered brokenly. "Please let me go."

His voice was barely audible. "Is that what you really want?"

She nodded.

She had never thought she'd see him look defeated, but at that moment some internal spark seemed to be extinguished. "All right," he said hoarsely. "I'll do what you want."

A spasm of anguish ripped through her as she realized it was finally over, and she stifled a sob as he rose to his feet.

If this was what she wanted, why was it so painful?

Off to the side a shadow moved, but both Daisy and Alex were too absorbed in their own misery to notice that their most private conversation had been overheard.

24

"**A**lex!"

His head shot up from the stake driver's engine as he heard Daisy's voice calling out to him and sounding exactly the way it used to. Hope surged through him. Maybe time hadn't run out for him after all. Maybe she hadn't meant what she'd said two nights ago, and he'd no longer have to put her on a plane for New York that very afternoon.

He threw down the wrench he'd been using and turned to face her, only to have his hope fade as he saw the expression on her face.

"Sinjun's gone! They've unloaded all the animals, and he isn't there. Trey's missing, too."

Brady came around from behind the stake driver where he'd been trying to help Alex. "Sheba's behind this. I'd bet anything."

Daisy's face paled with anxiety. "Did she say something to you?"

"No, but she's been a bitch on wheels these last couple of days."

Daisy looked at Alex, and for the first time since he'd found her at the zoo, he felt as if she were really seeing him. "Did you know about this?"

"No. She didn't tell me anything."

"She knows how you feel about that tiger," Brady said. "My guess is that she's sold him behind your back."

"But she can't do that. He's mine!" She bit her lip, as if she realized that what she'd said wasn't true.

"I tried to find Sheba earlier," Brady said, "but she hasn't shown up yet. Shorty drove her RV, but her car's missing."

Daisy clenched her fists. "She's done something terrible with him. I know it."

Alex wanted to reassure her, but he suspected she was right. "I'll make some calls and see what I can find out. Why don't the two of you go talk to the workers and see if any of them know anything?"

But no one did. For the next two hours, they spoke with everyone in the circus, only to discover that Sheba hadn't been seen since the previous evening.

Daisy grew increasingly frantic. Where was Sinjun? What had Sheba done with him? She'd learned enough about the market for aging circus animals to realize that the chances of a reputable zoo taking him were slim. What was going to happen to her tiger?

The time came and passed for her to leave for the airport. Alex had insisted she go to her father's until she decided what she wanted to do, but now there was no question of her leaving. She ignored the pearl gray Lexus with its Connecticut license plates—another of Alex's guilt offerings—and sat on the tailgate of the old black pickup that had carried her on her summer's journey of the soul to this bleak October night. From there, she watched the lot.

The first performance ended and then the second. The last of the crowd filed out. This was the circus's final two-night stay before they reached Tampa. Once again the workers had set off for town, taking along some of the showgirls and leaving the lot with a deserted feeling. She was cold, but she waited until Alex had changed out of his costume and gone to check on Misha before she returned to the trailer.

Her suitcase lay abandoned on the bed. She walked past it and removed his old gray sweatshirt from a wall hook. After slipping into it, she began to go back outside only to hesitate in front of the shabby, built-in chest where Alex kept his clothes. Squatting down, she opened the bottom drawer and moved his jeans out of the way so she could see what she knew was hidden behind them: a cheap blue plastic rattle, a yellow duck, a child's box of animal crackers, a bib stamped with a picture of a rabbit, a paperback copy of Dr. Spock.

She'd discovered these things a few days ago when she was putting away some clothes, but Alex had never mentioned them. Now she touched the rattle with the tip of her finger and tried to understand why he had them. If only she could believe—

No. She couldn't let herself think that way. She had too much at stake.

She shoved the door closed and was on her way back to the truck when she saw Sheba's Cadillac parked near her RV and heard angry voices coming from inside the big top. Alex had also heard them, and they began running in the same direction. They met up at the back door.

"Maybe you'd better stay here," he said.

She ignored him and rushed inside.

The big top was dimly lit by a single work light that threw shadows from the rigging over the arena while it left the periphery in darkness. She was enveloped by the familiar scents of sawdust, animals, and old popcorn. How she was going to miss this, she thought.

Brady and Sheba stood just outside the ring. Brady had her by the arm, and he was clearly furious. "Daisy's never done one damned thing to you, but you still had to go after her, didn't you?"

Sheba jerked away from him. "I do what I want, and no butcher's son's going to boss me around."

"Don't you ever get tired of being a bitch?"

Whatever response Sheba had been about to make died on her lips. "Well, well, look who's joined the party."

Daisy rushed forward to confront her. "What have you done with Sinjun?"

She took her time answering—playing her mind games, dangling her power over them. "Sinjun's getting ready to leave for his new home. Siberian tigers are very valuable animals, did you know that? Even old ones." She sat down on the front row of seats and crossed her legs in a posture that was almost too casual. "Even I didn't realize how much certain people would pay for them."

"What people?" Alex demanded, coming to a stop next to Daisy. "Who has him?"

"Nobody yet. The gentleman won't be picking him up until tomorrow morning."

"Then where are you keeping him?"

"He's safe. Trey's with him."

Alex lost patience. "Cut the crap! Who did you sell him to?"

"There were several people interested, but Rex Webley offered me the best price."

"Jesus." The expression on Alex's face sent chills down Daisy's spine.

"Who's Rex Webley?" she asked.

Before Sheba could reply, Alex interrupted. "Don't say a word, Sheba. This is just between you and me."

Sheba gave him a condescending look before turning back to Daisy. "Webley runs a hunting park in Texas."

Daisy didn't understand. "A hunting park?"

"Men pay Webley to hunt the animals he buys," Brady said with disgust.

Daisy looked from Sheba to Brady. "Hunt them? But nobody can hunt tigers. They're an endangered species."

Sheba rose and wandered into the center of the arena. "Which makes them all the more valuable to rich men who've gotten bored hunting ordinary game and aren't worried about legalities."

As what she was saying sank in, Daisy's voice caught on a bubble of fear. "You sold Sinjun to be stalked and killed?"

Her mind reeled with terrible images. Sinjun didn't have a normal tiger's fear of people. He wouldn't realize the men coming at him with guns wanted to hurt him. She saw his body jerking as the bullets hit him. She saw him lying on the ground, his orange-and-brown striped coat streaked with blood, and she whirled on Sheba.

"I won't let you do this! I'll go to the authorities. They'll put a stop to it."

"No, they won't," Sheba replied. "There's nothing illegal about selling a tiger. Webley told me he's going to exhibit Sinjun at his hunting ranch. That's not against the law."

"Except he's not going to exhibit him, is he? He's going to let him be killed." Daisy felt as if she were choking. "I'll go to the authorities. I will. They'll put a stop to this."

"I doubt it," Sheba said. "Webley's been getting around the law for years. Someone would have to testify that they actually saw the kill, and that's not likely to happen. Besides, it would be too late by then, wouldn't it?"

Daisy had never felt such hatred for another human being. "How can you do something like this? If you hate me so much, why didn't you just come after me? Why did you have to go after Sinjun?"

Alex moved into the center of the ring with her. "I'll pay you twice what Webley offered."

"This time your money's worthless, Alex. You're not buying Sinjun like you did Glenna. I made it a condition of the sale."

Daisy's head shot up. Alex hadn't told her he'd bought Glenna. She'd known he was the one who'd arranged for her to go to the Brookfield Zoo, but she hadn't realized his money had made it possible. The gorilla had ended up in her spacious new home because of him.

"You've thought of everything, haven't you?" he said.

"Webley's people won't be picking Sinjun up until dawn." Her expression grew sly. "I don't sign the final papers till then, and I could always change my mind."

Alex's quiet whisper was barely audible. "Now we get to the heart of it, don't we, Sheba?"

Sheba gazed over at Daisy, who was still standing outside the ring with Brady. "You'd like that wouldn't you, Daisy? If I stopped all this. I can do it, you know. With one phone call."

"Of course, you can," Alex murmured. "And what do I have to do to get you to make that phone call?"

Sheba turned to face him, and it was as if Brady and Daisy had disappeared, leaving only the two of them to confront each other in the center ring they had both been born to. She closed the small distance that remained between them, moving sinuously, almost like a lover, except there was no love between them. "You know what you have to do."

"Spell it out."

Sheba turned toward Daisy and Brady. "The two of you have to leave us alone. This is between Alex and me."

Brady exploded. "This is bullshit, is what it is! If I knew this was what you were up to, I swear to God, I'd of beat the crap out of you!"

His bluster left her unmoved. "If you and Daisy don't get out of here, that'll be the end of the tiger."

"Go on," Alex said. "Do what she wants."

Brady looked as if he'd lost everything he'd believed in, and his voice grew bitter as he turned to Alex. "Don't you let her cut your balls off. She'll try, but don't you dare let her do that."

"I don't intend to," he said quietly.

Daisy threw an imploring look at him, but he was concentrating on Sheba, and he didn't notice.

"Come on, Daisy. Let's get out of here." Brady wrapped his arm around her shoulders and led her toward the back door. These past few months had taught her how to fight and she started to resist, but then she realized that Alex was Sinjun's only hope.

Once outside, she took a deep gulp of the chilly night air, and her teeth began to chatter. Brady hugged her and whispered, "I'm sorry, Daisy. I didn't think she'd go this far."

From inside, they heard Alex's scornful voice, only slightly muffled by the nylon sides of the big top. "You're a businesswoman, Sheba. If you sell Sinjun to me I'll make it worth your while. All you have to do is name your price."

Both she and Brady stood rooted to the spot, knowing they should leave but unable to. Then Brady grasped her hand and pulled her into the shadows by the back door, where they couldn't be seen but had a partial view of the center ring.

She saw Sheba stroke Alex's arm. "It's not your money I want. You should know that. It's your pride."

He pulled himself away, as if he couldn't bear her touch. "What the hell does that mean?"

"If you want that tiger back, you're going to have to beg me for him."

"You go to hell."

"The great Alex Markov is going to have to get on his knees and beg."

"I'd die first."

"You won't do it?"

"Not in a million years." He splayed his hands on his hips. "You can do whatever you want with that damned tiger, but I'm not getting on my knees for you or anybody."

"I'm surprised. I guess I thought you'd do anything for that little simp. I should have known that you don't really love her." For a moment she looked up into the shadows of the rigging, then she returned her attention to him. "I suspected it all along, and I guess I should have followed my instincts. How could you love her? You're too damned cold-hearted to love anybody."

"You don't know the first thing about the feelings I have for Daisy."

"I know that you don't love her enough to get on your knees and beg for her." She regarded him smugly. "So I win. I guess I win either way."

"You're crazy."

"And you're smart to refuse. I got on my knees once for love, and I don't recommend it."

"Jesus, Sheba. Don't do this."

Her voice lost its taunting quality. "I have to. Nobody humiliates Sheba Quest and gets away with it. And either way, you're going to be the loser today. Are you sure you don't want to reconsider?"

"I'm sure."

At that moment Daisy knew she'd lost Sinjun. Alex wasn't

put together like other men. He was held together by steel and grit and pride. If he demeaned himself, it would destroy the man he was. Bowing her head, she tried to turn away, but Brady blocked her path.

Alex spoke in tight, hard tones. "You know what the irony in all this is. Daisy'd do it. She wouldn't even think twice about it." He gave a rough bark of laughter that bore no trace of humor. "She'd be on her knees in a second because she's got a heart beating inside her that's strong enough to take on the world. She doesn't care about honor or pride or anything else when the well-being of the creatures she loves is at stake."

"So what?" Sheba sneered. "This isn't about Daisy. It's about you. What's it going to be, Alex? Your pride or the tiger? Are you going to lay it all out for love, or are you going to hold on to everything that's important to you?"

There was a long silence. Tears had begun to stream down Daisy's face, and she knew she had to get away. She pulled back from Brady, then froze as she heard his angry sputter.

"That son of a bitch."

She whirled back and saw Alex still standing in front of Sheba with his head high. But his knees were beginning to bend. Those mighty Romanov knees. Those proud Markov knees. Slowly, he sank down into the sawdust, but at the same time, she knew she had never seen him look more arrogant, more unyielding.

"Beg me," Sheba whispered.

"No!" The word was ripped from Daisy's chest. She wouldn't let Sheba do this to him, not even for Sinjun! What good would it do to save one magnificent tiger if she destroyed the other? She ran through the back door and into the arena, kicking up sawdust as she flew toward Alex. When she got there, she caught him by the arm and tried to drag him to his feet.

"Get up, Alex! Don't do this! Don't let her do this to you."

He didn't take his eyes off Sheba Quest. They burned.

"It's like you once said, Daisy. Nobody else can demean me. I can only demean myself."

He turned his face upward, and his mouth tightened with scorn. Although he was on his knees, he had never looked more glorious. He was every inch the czar. The king of the center ring. "I'm begging you, Sheba," he said flatly. "Don't let anything happen to that tiger."

Daisy's hand convulsed around his arm, and she dropped to her knees beside him.

Brady made a sharp exclamation.

And Sheba Quest's mouth curled in a crooked smile. The expression that came over her face was a queer combination of wonder and satisfaction. "Son of a bitch. You really do love her after all."

She looked down at Daisy, kneeling next to him in the sawdust. "In case you still haven't figured it out, he loves you. Your tiger will be back in the morning, and you can thank me anytime. Now, do I have to paint another picture for you, or do you think you can take it from here by yourself without screwing up?"

Daisy stared at her, swallowed, and nodded.

"Good. Because I'm getting sick and tired of everyone in this circus moping around worrying about you."

Brady started cussing.

Alex's eyes narrowed.

And Sheba Quest, the queen of the center ring, swept past all three of them, head high, bright auburn hair flying like a circus banner.

Brady caught up with her just before she got to the back door, but before he could speak, she turned on him and jabbed him in the chest as hard as she could with her index finger.

"Don't you *ever again* say that I'm not a good person!"

Slowly a smile replaced the look of shock on his face. Without a word, he bent down, drove his shoulder into her belly, and carried her out of the top.

Daisy shook her head in bewilderment and gazed at Alex as they knelt together in the sawdust. "Sheba set all this up.

She knew Brady and I wouldn't be able to resist eavesdropping. She understood how I felt, and she set this up so I'd believe you really loved me.''

His eyes flicked over her, and they were as hard as amber and coldly furious. ''Not another word.''

She opened her mouth.

''Not a word!''

His pride had been badly battered, and he wasn't taking this at all well. She knew she had to act quickly. After everything they'd been through, she wasn't going to lose him now.

With all her might, she shoved against his chest. She caught him by surprise, and he sprawled backward into the sawdust. Before he could right himself, she threw her body on top of his.

''Don't get stupid, Alex. I mean it.'' She grabbed handfuls of his crisp, dark hair in her fists. ''I'm *begging* you. We've come too far for you to get stupid on me now; I've done enough of that for both of us. But a lot of it was your fault; you know it was. All that talk about how you couldn't love. And then when you really did love me, I thought it was guilt. I should have known. I should have—''

''Let me up, Daisy.''

He could easily throw her off, but she knew he wouldn't do it because of the baby. And because he loved her.

She plastered herself flat on top of him, wrapping her arms in a stranglehold around his neck, pressing her cheek to the side of his head. She flattened her torso and legs against his and let her toes curl on top of his ankles. ''I don't think so. You're in a temper right now, but you'll be all right in a couple of minutes, as soon as you have a chance to think everything over, and until then, I'm not letting you do anything you're going to regret.''

She thought she could feel his body beginning to relax, but she didn't shift her weight because he was tricky and this could be a ploy to catch her off guard.

''Get up now, Daisy.''

''No.''

''You're going to be sorry.''

"You wouldn't hurt me for anything."

"Who said anything about hurting?"

"You're mad."

"I've been happier."

"You're really mad about what she made you do."

"She didn't make me do anything."

"She sure did." Daisy drew her head back far enough so she could grin down into his scowling face. "She got you good, Alex. She really did. If we have a girl, we may name her Sheba."

"Over my dead body."

She curled into his neck again and just waited like that, lying peacefully on top of him as if he were the world's best orthopedic mattress.

His lips brushed her ear.

She snuggled closer and whispered, "I want to get married before the baby's born."

She felt his hand in her hair. "We are married."

"I want to do it again."

"Let's just do it."

"You're going to be vulgar, aren't you?"

"Will that get you off me?"

"Do you love me?"

"I love you."

"You don't sound loving. You sound like you're gritting your teeth."

"I *am* gritting my teeth, but that doesn't mean I don't love you with all my heart."

"Really?" She drew back her head and beamed at him. "Then why are you so anxious to get me off you."

His grin was sly. "So I can prove my love."

"Now you're making me nervous."

"Are you afraid you're not woman enough for me?"

"Oh, no. I'm definitely not afraid of that." She dipped her head and nibbled at his bottom lip. That lasted for about half a second before he turned it into a deep, sensuous kiss. And then she started to cry because it was all so wonderful.

He began kissing her tears away, and she rubbed her fingers over his cheek. "You really love me, don't you?"

"I really do," he said huskily, "and this time I want you to believe me. I'm begging you, sweetheart."

She smiled through her tears. "All right, then. Let's go home."

EPILOGUE

Daisy and Alex were married for the second time ten days later in a field north of Tampa. The ceremony took place at dawn because of the bride's insistence on the presence of one guest the others would just as soon she'd forgotten.

Sinjun lay at Daisy's feet, and the two of them were joined by a length of silver ribbon. At one end, it encircled his neck, while, at the other, it looped her wrist. As a result of his presence, the number of people attending the six o'clock ceremony that October morning was quite small. And understandably nervous.

"I don't know why she couldn't keep him in his cage," Sheba snapped to her husband, the man she had married several days earlier in a center ring ceremony complete with a performance by the Flying Toleas.

"Don't talk to me about stubborn women," he replied. "I'm married to one."

She regarded him with knowing eyes. "Lucky for you."

"Yeah," he smiled back. "Lucky for me."

Heather stood off to the left and stroked Tater's trunk while she gazed critically at Daisy. If this was her wedding, Heather decided, she'd wear something nicer than an old pair of jeans, especially since Heather knew very well Daisy couldn't even get them snapped at the waist anymore. Just as bad, she had on one of Alex's blue dress shirts to hide the evidence.

370

Still, she looked pretty cute. Her cheeks were rosy and her eyes all shiny, and she had this bridal wreath made up of daisies in her hair. Alex had given it to her as a surprise, along with a diamond ring so big it was a good thing the sun hadn't come up the rest of the way or they'd all be blinded.

So many changes had happened in Heather's life this summer that she still couldn't quite take them in. Sheba wasn't selling Quest Brothers, and Heather was pretty sure she and her dad were trying to make a baby. Sheba was the coolest stepmom. She'd said Heather could start dating this year even though her dad said over his dead body. And Sheba'd turned into as big a hugger as Daisy.

Daisy had told Heather she'd be taking classes at Alex's college just as soon as the baby was born so she could learn how to be a kindergarten teacher, and the two of them were going to Russia in December on some kind of buying trip for this big museum Alex represented. Best of all, they were traveling for a month next summer with Quest Brothers, and Daisy even said she was going back into the ring with Alex. She'd told Heather that she wasn't scared anymore because she'd already lived through the worst thing that could happen.

Alex started speaking his vows in a deep, mushy voice, and as he looked down at Daisy, his face was all soft so that everybody there could see how much he loved her. Daisy, naturally, started to cry, and Jill had to hand her a tissue.

Daisy sniffed and blew, then started in on her vows. "I, Daisy Devreaux Markov, take thee . . ." She paused.

Alex looked down at her and lifted his eyebrow. "Don't tell me. You forgot my name again." He looked exasperated, but Heather could tell that he wanted to laugh.

"Of course not. You didn't say your middle name, and I just realized I don't know what it is."

"Ah." He leaned down and whispered it into her ear.

"Perfect." She smiled through her tears, and once again gazed up into his eyes. "I Daisy Devreaux Markov take thee Alexander Romanov Markov . . ."

As she went on, Alex squeezed her hand real tight, and Heather would have sworn to God she saw tears in his eyes, too.

Sinjun rose and stretched until he was about thirty feet long. Sheba got all nervous-looking and started clinging to Heather's dad's arm, which had to be a first. Heather wasn't too crazy about the tiger herself, but she wasn't a wimp about him like Sheba.

Sheba'd surprised everybody by giving Sinjun to Daisy as a wedding present, and Alex already had somebody building this really cool tiger compound behind his house in Connecticut. It sure must be nice to be so rich. Although nobody'd said anything definite about it, Heather had the feeling Tater might end up spending the winter in Alex's barn in Connecticut, too, instead of staying with the other elephants in Tampa.

"I now pronounce you husband and wife."

Daisy and Alex looked at each other, and for a minute it was like they'd forgotten anybody else was around. Finally Alex remembered it was time for the kiss part, and he really laid one on her. Heather couldn't tell for sure if he was frenching her, but she wouldn't have been surprised. While they kissed, Tater dusted both of them with hay, just as if he thought the stuff was rice.

Everybody started to laugh, except for Sheba, who was still watching Sinjun.

Daisy let Sinjun's ribbon leash drop from her wrist. Then she made this funny whooping sound and threw her arms around Alex's neck. Alex picked her up and twirled her, but he held her real careful so he didn't hurt the baby or anything.

When he was done spinning her, he kissed her again. "I've got the best Markov woman of them all."

Daisy got this real saucy look on her face that even Heather thought was pretty cute. "And I've got the best Markov man."

They were acting so silly that Heather started being embarrassed for both of them, except that she was kind of crying, too, because she liked happy endings.

Then she realized it wasn't an ending at all. As she gazed around at all these people she loved, she knew that everybody here was just getting started.